# LIKE CHAFF IN THE WIND

# ANNA BELFRAGE

Previously published titles in **The Graham Saga**:

*A Rip in the Veil*

# LIKE CHAFF IN THE WIND

## ANNA BELFRAGE

Matador
9 Priory Business Park,
Wistow Road, Kibworth Beauchamp,
Leicestershire. LE8 0RX
Tel: (+44) 116 279 2299
Fax: (+44) 116 279 2277
Email: books@troubador.co.uk
Web: www.troubador.co.uk/matador

ISBN 978 1780884 707

British Library Cataloguing in Publication Data.
A catalogue record for this book is available from the British Library.

Typeset in 11pt Bell MT by Troubador Publishing Ltd, Leicester, UK

**Matador** is an imprint of Troubador Publishing Ltd

*To Johan, for always being there when I need you.*

# CHAPTER 1

Matthew Graham congratulated himself yet again on not having brought his wife Alex or wee Mark along to Edinburgh. Not a welcoming city at its best, Edinburgh was cold and dreary in the icy January winds, the tall tenement buildings hunching under clouds the colour of pewter.

The city swarmed with people; in every window, in every narrow close, spectators crowded together, and for all that Matthew was both tall and broad he had to constantly use elbows and feet to avoid being trodden on. He shivered and pressed his hat down harder on his head in a feeble attempt to keep his ears from falling off with cold. His brother-in-law, Simon Melville, laughed and mock punched him.

"It sticks in your craw, no? To be obliged to witness the proud occasion of the laying to rest of the Marquis of Montrose."

Matthew didn't reply. He had nothing against James Graham, a noble man and a warrior of great talent and bravery, and he had not liked it that he was hanged several years ago, victim to the double dealing of Charles the Second. He did, however, resent being forced to pay his dues at this mockery of a burial where the Marquis, ten years after his death, was brought to lie in state at Holyrood Palace at the say so of the king who had so cruelly betrayed him.

He shifted on his feet in a vain attempt to escape the pressure of the sharp stone ledge digging into his back. Slowly the sumptuous coffin made its way down from the direction of St. Giles, preceded by banners and blaring trumpets as if it were indeed a whole man lying there instead of all the bits and pieces that had been brought back to be interred together. The bleached skull had been lifted off its spike on the Tolbooth only this morning, and Matthew doubted if anybody knew whether the body parts now lumped together did in fact belong to the same man.

"Do you think he cares?" Simon asked him.

"Who?" he said.

"Montrose. Do you think it matters to him, all this?"

Matthew pursed his lips. "He might be laughing some. But nay, I don't think it much matters to him how he's buried." He indicated the procession with his head. "It may matter to his wife, though. And his son."

Matthew smiled at the thought of his own son, safe at Hillview – a lad who with every day grew more and more like his sire, from his hazel eyes to the dark hair that fell in soft wisps to frame his face. He stretched as well as he could in his cramped space and closed his eyes, seeing first Mark as he had seen him last, fast asleep in his trundle bed, then his wife.

His wife; just thinking of Alex sent spurts of heat rippling through him. He had woken her in the dark pre-dawn the day he set out, and she had been a sinuous warmth under him. When he got out of bed, she had propped herself up on one elbow to look at him, hair escaping in curls from her thick night braid. His woman, his heart…

"Look!" Simon hissed.

Matthew opened his eyes only to meet those of his brother. Wearing a splendid fur-lined cloak, Luke Graham sat astride a fiery chestnut mare. The rings on his hands, the golden collar round his neck and the royal badge decorating his hat screamed to the world that this was a man high in the king's favour, an impression further underlined by the fact that he was riding side by side with the Governor. Where Matthew had expected to see a disfigured nose, he saw instead an elegant silver covering that elicited surprised murmurs from the crowd.

Luke set a finger to the gleaming metal, letting Matthew know that he well remembered who it was that had so damaged him and had not forgiven, nor ever would. He narrowed his eyes, made a slitting motion over his throat and spurred his horse on, all the while turning to stare at Matthew who stood unmoving until horse and rider disappeared.

"The sooner we leave the better," Simon muttered as they hurried away from the crowds. They took a sharp left, having to lean backwards so as not to topple down the slippery, steep close that led into Cowgate. Matthew agreed, still shaken by the naked hatred that shone out of Luke's eyes.

"I want you to do something for me."

Simon looked at him with a certain caution but nodded.

"I want you to draw up a document, today, that makes you the guardian of Mark should anything happen to me."

"Nothing will happen to you."

"Mayhap not," Matthew shrugged. "But unless I draw up such a deed then both Mark and Alex may find themselves in the not so tender care of my brother. After all, Luke's my closest male relative – unfortunately." Matthew's gut twisted at the thought and it was apparent wee Simon agreed, an uncharacteristic scowl settling on his round face.

"I'll do it when we get back to our room, and you can sign it and have it witnessed by the landlord."

When Matthew prepared to leave for the evening, Simon frowned.

"Should you go abroad alone? What with Luke being here ..."

"I'm invited to dine with Minister Crombie and his brother," Matthew said. "I don't think I'll be in any danger there."

Simon grunted. "Not there, no. But in the going and the coming you might be."

Matthew strapped on his sword. "I'll be careful." And damn if his brother was going to stop him from partaking of the company of men he respected and liked.

It was a long evening, an evening of discussion and far too much wine, and Matthew felt comfortably mellow when he made his way back to the inn. Tomorrow he'd be on his way home, rid of this damp, dark and teeming city, and soon he'd be at Hillview, with wife and bairn around him.

Something clattered against the cobbles and he threw a look over his shoulder, squinting through the dark. He frowned and blinded his lantern, standing very still as he listened. Soft, rustling noises and a cat ran across the narrow close.

Matthew wanted to laugh out loud with relief. Still, he chose to not unblind his lantern and increased his pace. His skin prickled, his pulse thudded loudly. You're being fanciful, he berated himself, it was just a cat, aye? There was a sound behind him and he wheeled, a hand on his sword. He never managed to pull it free. Out of the corner of his eye he saw something and then his head exploded with pain.

Alex woke with a gasp, convinced that something had happened to Mark. From his trundle bed came snuffling noises and she sank back against the pillows, trying to bring her heart rate under control. For some reason she was still agitated, and after an hour of turning in bed she gave up on sleep. It was just some silly dream, she told herself, running a hand over Matthew's pillow before rising to pace up and down the room. She stood by the window and stared out into the dark, arms coming up to cross her chest. Something was very wrong and she had no idea what it was, but her whole body was clanging with alarms.

"Bad night?" Joan, her sister-in-law, asked next morning.

Alex yawned and handed over Mark into Joan's waiting arms.

"I couldn't sleep." She nodded a good morning to their housekeeper, Mrs Gordon, but shook her head at the bowl of porridge. Her insides were clenched tight around a pebble of nagging concern and just the thought of food made her queasy.

With each passing day Alex grew more nervous, making both Joan and Mrs Gordon jumpy as well. He should be back by now, and Alex spent far too many hours with her eyes glued to the lane. When she finally heard the sound of horses, she dropped the basket she was carrying, bunched up her skirts and flew up the lane to meet him.

She saw Samson riderless and turned, bewildered, to Simon. Her heart came to a screeching halt before it started up again and she moved towards the horse, her hands stretched out to touch the man who wasn't there.

"Matthew?" Her eyes nailed themselves to Simon's and the expression she saw in them turned the air in her lungs to lead, a dragging weight that threatened to suffocate her. He was dead, her Matthew was dead, and oh my God, how was she to go on without him? "Matthew?" she repeated, hoping that there was another explanation for the haunted look on Simon's face.

"Ah, Alex," Simon said in a choked voice. "I'm so sorry, lass."

She shook her head; she didn't want him to be sorry, please don't let him be sorry. The household congregated around them; Joan and Mrs Gordon, Rosie with Mark in arms as well as Sam, Gavin and Robbie. She didn't see them, she saw only the empty saddle where Matthew should have been and all she wanted was to die.

"What?" She cleared her thickening throat. "What has happened to him, where is he?" Simon dismounted and Alex flew at him.

"Answer me! Where's my husband? Why isn't he here, with you?"

"He's gone," Simon said, grabbing at her flailing arms. "Dearest Lord, he's gone." He began to cry and Alex was taken over by a slow seeping cold, a thickening of her blood that began at her feet and worked itself upwards.

"No!" She tore herself free from Simon's hands. "No! No!" She wheeled and fled, because maybe if she ran fast enough and far enough none of this would be true.

It was dark when she came back. Without a word she swept a fretting Mark into her arms and shushed him to sleep. She sat in silence for a long time before meeting Simon's eyes.

"Tell me. What happened? And why have you not brought him back? He would want to lie here, you know that." She closed her eyes and opened them slowly again. She'd been doing that all afternoon, hoping that next time she opened her eyes it would be to a reality where Matthew still existed. Belatedly she noticed that Simon hadn't replied to her question, instead he was regarding her with so much pity she wanted to punch him.

"He isn't dead," he said.

Alex did yet another exaggerated blink; apparently it did help.

"But mayhap it would be better if he were."

"He's alive?" Alex said, latching on to the single relevant piece of information. "He's not dead?"

Simon shook his head. No, he told her, as far as he knew Matthew wasn't dead.

"He was assaulted on the street returning to the inn." Simon went on to describe how the innkeeper had come to wake him, gabbling on about how Mr Graham had been struck down just at the corner and dragged away.

Simon had rushed out half-dressed, and in the company of the innkeeper's lad he had walked up and down the darkened closes, searching for Matthew, but not finding as much as a hair. Finally, at the coming of dawn he had stumbled across a baker's lad who'd told him how he'd seen two men load a protesting third into a cart.

"They clobbered him to shut him up," Simon said. "Then they drove off in the direction of the port."

Simon had never run so fast in all his life, he told her, his legs like lark wings as he rushed to fetch his horse and ride hell for leather to Leith. Too late he had stormed out onto the quays, only to see the high stern of a ship disappear into the fog, and he knew, beyond any doubt, that his friend was aboard. He'd gone to the harbourmaster and found out the ship was bound for Plymouth, there to wait for some weeks before setting off across the sea.

"But then Matthew can just get off in Plymouth, right?" Alex said, feeling her shoulders relax. Alive; he was alive!

Simon shook his head. "He's been indentured."

Alex was confused. Indentured people were criminals, convicted of crimes. Simon sighed and rubbed his hands hard across his face.

"He's been set up. The harbourmaster admitted that he had thought it strange that a lone man should be loaded so late, but the captain of the *Henriette Marie* insisted that he was waiting for one more."

"But he can tell them" Alex said. "He just has to talk to someone in authority and they can verify that he's an innocent man."

"They won't let him off the boat. He'll be kept under lock and key until there is no chance of him escaping."

"How do you know?"

"I found the go-between," Simon said, caressing his bruised knuckles. "And I beat it out of him. He's been sold into slavery by that misbegotten cur, his brother, and according to the go-between the amount that changed hands was substantial enough to ensure Matthew didn't set foot on land this side of the Atlantic." Simon crouched down and stroked Mark over his head. "Poor wee lad, no father."

"He has a father," Alex said, slapping his hand away. "And now you're going to explain exactly what all this means so that I can decide what to do." She handed Mark to Joan and glared at Simon. "If nothing else, once he gets to where he's going he can tell them."

"They won't care," Joan said. "They will have no reason to believe him."

Alex looked from one to the other, hating them both for already having given up.

"And what will happen to him?" she asked.

"They'll sell him off upon arrival and then he'll be set to work, a slave that is owned by the man who holds his indenture. They will work him to the bone, and if he dies, well, then so be it." Simon sounded very bleak and Alex felt the ice cold numbness of before return. She twisted her hands around each other, trying hard to think.

"I'm going after him," she declared a few minutes later. "I'll find him and somehow get him home."

"You can't do that!" Simon said.

"Watch me." Alex gnawed at her lip and threw a discreet look in the direction of the kitchen hearth. Not that they were in any way rich, but if she sold everything they had hidden it should be enough to finance both the passage and whatever she might need to buy him free. And they wouldn't charge her for Mark, he could sleep in her berth, not taking up any room of his own.

"And Mark?" Joan asked.

Alex raised her brows. "I'll take him with me."

"A wee lad? Nay, I think not. He might sicken and die." Simon sounded very disapproving.

"He's my son, so if I'm going so is he."

"Nay, he's not. I can't let you take him and risk his life," Simon said.

"You can't stop me!" She was on her feet, nose only inches from his.

"Aye I can. Matthew has appointed me guardian of the lad."

"I'm his guardian! I'm his mother, for God's sake!"

"You're a woman. You can't be responsible for a child's welfare." Simon blocked the enraged slap and took a firm hold of Alex' hands. "I can stop you from going as well, but that I won't do. The lad, however, stays here. He's the new master of Hillview should Matthew not return. If Mark dies Hillview comes to Luke. Do you think Matthew would want that?"

Alex slumped into her seat. Simon was right; Matthew would never want his son to be put at unnecessary risk. Matthew… where was he now? Had they put him in chains, beaten him? Alex encircled her wrist and squeezed down hard. He would panic at finding himself once again in manacles. Without a further word she retrieved her son and stumbled up the stairs to the haven of her bed.

She didn't sleep. She tossed and turned, she hung for hours over Mark's bed drinking in his presence, every detail of his solid little body that slept, froglike, on his front. Her baby... Her hand came down over her wedding ring and she turned it hard round her finger. Her man... Oh God! Her man, her son, her Matthew, Mark – through the dark hours they stalked her head. Alex emitted a strangled sound and fell back against the pillows, her face hidden in her hands.

Daybreak found Alex in the kitchen, her lap filled with their few pieces of jewellery and what seemed to her a very insignificant pile of coins. Mrs Gordon gave her a quick look and busied herself with breakfast, nodding a good morning to a yawning Joan who appeared in the doorway.

"What am I to do?" Alex said to no one in particular. "How can I leave Mark to go to Matthew, but how can I not go after Matthew?"

Mrs Gordon patted her on the shoulder. "You know what you must do, no?"

Alex nodded; there was no choice but it was tearing her apart.

"I lost a child once," she said, ignoring the surprised look on Joan's face. "My little Isaac... but I found Matthew instead and it was enough. Now I have to leave a second child behind."

She stared vacantly into the hearth. Very rarely did she allow herself to think about the stranger aspects of her life and as a consequence she generally kept her vague memories of Isaac well at bay. He would be almost six by now, and she hoped he was safe and well cared for, living a normal life in 2005. Oh God; her gut tightened. She shouldn't be here, she was an impossibility, a freak, and should anyone find out she came from a future time they'd lash her to a stake and set her on fire as some sort of witch. It wasn't as if she'd actively done anything, it had just sort of happened. The fine hairs on her nape bristled upright at the memories of that awful, spinning drop through time. Two years and counting since a freak lightning storm tore the weave of time apart and sent her flying to land here, in Matthew's time, now the year of our Lord 1661.Matthew... She bit back on a sob and manhandled it down her throat.

Mrs Gordon placed a mug of heated cider in front of her. "Your son will be well cared for here, you know that."

Alex sipped her cider in silence. Joan and Simon doted on Mark, and they'd love him as if he were their own. And Mark would forget her, not recognise her when she returned, shrinking back to hide behind Joan's skirts. It cut her just to think it. Mrs Gordon levelled her black eyes at her.

"Your son has others, lass. Your man has only you."

"Mrs Gordon…" Joan protested.

"I know." Alex picked at the valuables in her lap and swept them back into their pouch. "I'm going after him. I have to."

Mrs Gordon nodded her agreement. "I'll go with you. You can't be travelling on your own."

Alex gave her a grateful smile and got to her feet. "We'd better start packing, right?"

# CHAPTER 2

It was a glorious spring day, the day Alex rode out of Hillview in search of her abducted husband. The trees stood in bright new leaf, robins and blackbirds chirped loudly in the shrubs, and high against the pale blue sky hung a single lark. The tilled fields filled the air with the scent of warm, moist earth, and in the kitchen garden pale shoots stood timid and fresh in their well-tended beds.

Not that Alex noticed; all her attention was on her son. Fourteen months old, Mark sat in the arms of his aunt. He cooed and laughed, a high bubbling sound, when his mother first kissed him, then blew in his ear, and he jumped up and down in the restraining arms, hands extended towards Alex.

"Love him for me as well," Alex said, leaning forward to kiss Mark's brow. "Love him for me and for Matthew."

Joan just nodded, eyes grey streaks in a red and bloated face. Alex gave her a wobbly smile and then she just had to hug her son one last time, bury her nose in his hair and draw in the scent of him, so uniquely his own she could find him in the dark. Mark chortled, but protested when Joan took him back, small starfish hands waving in the direction of his mother. He stretched himself towards Alex when she sat up on the horse. When she turned the horse and clucked it into a walk, Mark began to cry.

By the time Alex, Mrs Gordon and Simon crested the hill, the air rang with Mark's high voice. Alex could barely see through her tears.

"What am I doing? How can I leave my son behind?"

"You have to," Mrs Gordon said from where she sat pillion behind Alex. "You know that, no?"

Simon held his silence. He was still not convinced that letting Alex loose on the world in a desperate attempt to find

Matthew was the right thing to do. Mayhap he should have insisted that she stay at home, safe. Ever since the day he rode back heavyhearted from Edinburgh to tell Alex that Matthew was gone, he'd tried to make her see reason; there was nothing she could do, and Matthew wouldn't expect it of her.

"Well I expect it of myself," she'd said, dark blue eyes narrowing. "What do you suggest I do? Sit here and ignore the fact that somewhere someone is harming the man I love, starving him and using him like a beast? Will I be able to live with myself, knowing he's dying a slow death, if I don't try?"

Simon had not known what to say and had promised that he would help her as well as he could.

He twisted in his saddle to study Alex. She rode Samson far more competently that he'd thought she would, remembering a day not quite three years ago when he'd seen her eye the huge roan with apprehension, all of her indicating that she'd never been this close to a horse before.

He pursed his lips. The story of how Matthew had found her wandering the moors after a freak thunderstorm still sniffed of subterfuge, and he recalled the first time he saw her, hair a short cap of bright brown curls around her head, barefoot and with an air of strangeness around her. Mayhap because she was Swedish, aye, but he wasn't entirely sure.

A year ago he'd come upon her in the woods, and she'd been dancing, swinging a burbling Mark around her while she sang a most peculiar song about heaven being on fire. No, there was more to Alex than met the eye… And what was this about a lost child? Joan had attempted to raise the subject of this unknown Isaac, but had been so rudely rebuffed she had confided to Simon that she would never, ever ask again.

"Six weeks," Alex said, breaking almost an hour of silence. "We've lost six weeks!"

Now that they were firmly on their way towards Edinburgh, she had managed to banish the thought of a distraught Mark from her mind, focusing instead on the task at hand – to find Matthew.

"Nay we haven't," Mrs Gordon replied. "You know there are no crossings during winter. And the boat with the master will still be in Plymouth, no?"

Alex gave Simon a dark look. She'd repeatedly argued that they should ride down to Plymouth and there get Matthew freed, but Simon had told her that he didn't think it possible, that the captain would make it difficult for anyone to come on board, and that anyway he could wave a very formal document of indenture in their faces.

"But it's false!" she'd said.

"Aye, but it's up to us to prove it is. Besides," he'd added darkly, "what's to stop yon captain from heaving Matthew overboard should he feel threatened?"

"Do you think he's still alive?" she said. For weeks she'd had a recurring nightmare of Matthew dying due to the wounds he'd received when he was abducted, courtesy of his evil, nose-less brother.

Mrs Gordon slapped her hard on her thigh. "Silent, lass! Do you not feel him still?"

Every night she felt him, rolling in the direction of where he should be lying only to discover his half of the bed empty and cold. And now, when she turned inward she was sure; a flutter in the pit of her stomach told her that yes, he was still alive.

"They'll keep them alive on the crossing," Simon put in. "There's no value to a dead man, is there?"

Alex threw yet another black look in his direction. To be kept alive to be sold off as a slave, what would that do to him?

"Bend," she whispered to the wind. "Don't let them break you." Not like they had done in prison, where he'd not known how to submit, fighting in rage at the injustice of it all.

"He'll live lass," Mrs Gordon said. "He'll do what he must to stay alive. He owes it to you and your wee lad."

Four days later they rode into Edinburgh. The wind blew from the firth, carrying the unappetizing stench of the Nor

Loch before it. Actually, even without that open cesspit perfuming the air, Edinburgh was a palette of nasty smells, far too many people, stray dogs and the occasional gaggle of fowl. It took them ages to thread their way up past Greyfriar's to the small inn off Cowgate, and for all that it was neither particularly clean nor particularly light, the room they were to share seemed a haven of peace after the ruckus of the city outside.

Alex opened the window to let in some air, called for the maid to come and change the sheets – no way was she sleeping in linen grey with use – and after a quick wash she took Samson's reins in a firm grip and led him off to Grassmarket to sell him. What was she to do? She needed every penny she could get and Samson was a magnificent horse, eliciting interested looks from a number of men. Still; she felt as if she was selling off a family member. Alex sniffed and blew her nose before giving Samson one last parting pat.

"You're not ugly," she told the broad-backed stallion. "And you're a very nice horse. I hope you'll find a good home and someone who'll love you as much as Matthew has."

"It's just a horse," Mrs Gordon said, sounding somewhere between amused and worried. "No point in weeping over a beast, is there?"

"I'll cry if I want to, okay? I didn't cry when I kissed Mark good bye, I didn't cry when I saw Hillview disappear behind me – well, not much – and as God is my witness I haven't cried for Matthew except for that first day. So if I feel like crying my eyes out over Samson, I'll do it and you can just stuff it." Alex felt somewhat ashamed at venting all this on Mrs Gordon, but she seemed quite unperturbed.

"Stuff it," Mrs Gordon repeated with a faint smile. "Stuff it. I like that, aye?" She slipped her hand in under Alex' arm and squeezed. "You do cry for the master, every night, no?"

"Yes, but never when I'm awake."

"Why not?"

Alex hitched her shoulders and pushed a strand of hair

off her face. "I've promised myself I won't. Not until I find him." She kept on glancing at the men that surrounded them. It was market day and Grassmarket was heaving with people come in to town from the outlying farms.

"Who are you looking for?" Mrs Gordon asked. She raised her stout frame on tiptoe and scanned the crowds.

"Luke." Should she see him… Her hands fisted when in the distance she saw a tall man. Was that him? She half ran in the direction of the man, Mrs Gordon puffing in her wake. The man turned, Alex came to a halt. Not her damned brother-in-law.

"And what would you do if you found him?" Mrs Gordon panted, holding a hand to her side.

Alex let her eyes travel the crowd, looking for Luke's distinctive red hair. "Brain him, or even better tear his balls off and have him eat them."

"Sounds like a very good idea," Mrs Gordon nodded. "I can sit on him, aye?" Her eyes shone jet black as she took Alex' hand. "First things first, lass; you need to find your husband and bring him home. But then you and I can do some ball-cutting. With a very blunt knife…"

Despite her misery, Alex burst out laughing and hugged Mrs Gordon hard.

On their last night in Edinburgh there was a discreet knock on the door of their room and Simon strode over to open it, dirk in hand. He fell back in surprise.

"Margaret! What are you doing here?"

A hooded shape glided into the room, and with one person more the cramped space became positively crowded, what with Simon's pallet bed, the four-poster Alex shared with Mrs Graham, the table and the few stools.

"Come to gloat?" Alex very much wanted to throw something in the face of this woman, once Matthew's wife, but first and foremost Luke's lover and now spouse. "Happy now that your bastard husband has succeeded in his attempt to have Matthew disappear from Scotland?"

"I swear I didn't know," Margaret said. "I swear…" Her voice shook, eyes huge in the pale oval of her face.

Yeah; right. "Just like you didn't know when Luke falsely accused Matthew of treason, huh?" To Alex' satisfaction, Margaret looked very ashamed – but then she should, shouldn't she? Alex cleared her throat of a wad of rage. "This is all your fault, if you hadn't told Luke all those terrible lies about Matthew, then none of this would have happened."

"Lies? What lies?"

"Come off it! We both know, don't we? How you let Luke believe Matthew had forced you into marriage, while it was you – yes, you, goddamn it – who seduced him."

"Well, he didn't say no, did he?" Margaret flashed back, straightening up to glare at Alex. "In fact," she added with a smirk, "he was most eager, he was."

If Simon hadn't stepped between them, Alex would have hit her. Instead she retreated and drew in a couple of breaths, eyes never leaving Margaret. Bloody woman! Alex hated it that they were so alike, and even more did she hate the fact that the drop-dead gorgeous one was Margaret, not her.

In deep red silk that shimmered in the candle light, a daring neckline edged with lace and linen of the highest quality, Margaret looked every inch the courtier's wife, all the way from the peeping toes of her silk slippers to the fashionable black ringlets that adorned her head. Alex twitched at her simple green bodice and fiddled with her lace cap; all home made by yours truly, well sewn and neat, but with none of the flair of Margaret's clothes.

"I did not come to discuss the past," Margaret said with some dignity, placing a velvet pouch on the table. "Here."

Simon nudged it with a finger, making the contents clink. "What's this?"

"Thirty silver pieces," Margaret replied with a wry smile. "It should be enough to buy him free if you find him."

"Not if, when," Alex corrected sharply.

Margaret looked at her and ducked her head. "I hope

you do. He didn't deserve this." She pulled the hood of her cloak back up, her features swallowed into shadow. "You have to make haste. Luke says the indentures die like flies."

"All part of his nasty little plan," Alex said.

Margaret shrugged, gloved hands fidgeting with the decorated clasps of her cloak.

"Aye, it most likely is."

"If he dies, I'll ..." Alex choked on a bitter combination of fear and rage.

Margaret just nodded and left.

Alex waited until the door had closed before moving over to pick up the pouch. It weighed heavily in her hand and she opened it to see that not only did it contain several coins but also a collection of small valuables; earrings, a ring set with a dark red stone, one huge baroque pearl in a silver pendant...

"Generous," Simon said. "Margaret's raided her own little chest, hasn't she?"

Mrs Gordon picked up a golden bracelet and weighed it in her hand.

"This is a right fortune, it is. Yon Luke will be enraged when he hears what she's done."

"He won't," Alex said, "she isn't about to tell him, is she?"

"You think not?" Mrs Gordon touched the large pearl. "And when he asks her to put this on, what will she say?"

"I'm sure she'll lie convincingly," Alex said. "After all, we all know Margaret is good at lying." Well she was, wasn't she? To her great irritation Alex felt herself blushing under their reproving looks.

"Alex," Simon admonished, "that was unkind. And no matter that Luke loves her, she'll pay dearly when he finds out, you know that."

Alex squirmed; it went against the grain of her to concede any good qualities to Margaret, but reluctantly she agreed it must have taken courage to do this.

After a last restless night on land they made their way down to Leith and the wharves early next morning. Alex took in the wooden, insubstantial vessel with scepticism. Cross the Atlantic in that? She laughed at her disappointment. What had she been expecting, a twentieth century cruise ship? Actually; yes. She paced up and down, calculating that at most it was fifty metres from stern to bow. One major storm and the whole thing would probably capsize, she swallowed, knotting her hands into the woollen material of her skirts.

"She's crossed several times," Simon said in a reassuring tone. "The captain's an experienced man." Alex nodded and went back to studying the line of people making their way up the gangway, small bundles pressed to their chest.

"They're all women," Alex said.

"Aye, wives for the colonists. They go in the hold, I reckon."

"Wives? They have husbands waiting for them?"

"Well ..." Simon looked uncomfortable. "Not as such. They'll meet them there, and their future husband will reimburse the captain for the passage."

"Ah," Alex nodded.

Mrs Gordon held Alex' arm in a tight grip all the way up the gangway and once on board they tread with caution over the wooden deck, having to negotiate coils of ropes, several barrels, and a small pen with goats. Alex followed Simon into the little cabin below quarterdeck that would be her home for the coming months and allowed him to make a thorough inspection of the closet size space, grunting when he found things to be as promised.

Together they took a turn around the deck and then it was time for Simon to leave. She didn't want him to; she wanted to grab hold of his coat and beg him to come with her. But she didn't, of course. Instead she cleared her throat and tried to smile.

"My son is in your keeping," she said, "my son and my home."

"They'll be there when you come for them. I swear to you I'll keep them safe."

"I know," Alex said, "otherwise how could I have left?"

Simon swept her into an embrace. "Find him, lass. Find our Matthew and bring him back. You can do it. You will do it."

"Of course I will," she said, injecting her voice with as much conviction as she could muster. She kissed him, watched him make his way back down to land, and went to stand by the railings, waving for as long as she could see the shrinking point of brown that she knew to be Simon.

Simon stood rooted until the ship disappeared from sight. He rubbed a hand through his sparse hair, produced a handkerchief from his sleeve, blew his nose and wiped his face. Such a little thing on all that water, totally in the hands of our Lord, blown hither and thither like chaff in the wind. He sighed and pressed his hat down on his head.

"Dear Lord, hold Your hand over them and keep them safe," he prayed. "Turn the light of Your countenance unto them and guide them back home."

# CHAPTER 3

Matthew woke to hammering pain and the unwelcome realisation that the floor below him was moving, rolling from side to side. He tried to sit up and knew himself to be in irons, fettered like a beast. He groaned as he levered himself upright.

"So you're awake then?" a voice said by his ear. Matthew jerked and the voice laughed. "I don't mean you any harm, lad, none of us do."

"Where am I?" Matthew asked, trying to make out his surroundings.

"On the *Henriette Marie* – we sailed at daybreak, bound for the colonies"

"The colonies!" Matthew attempted to stand, only to fall at the next rolling of the ship. "I have to get off! I have a family to get back to."

"We all do," the voice beside him said. "But unless you're planning on swimming, chains and all, you won't be getting off this ship until we arrive at Jamestown."

Matthew struggled back to sit. In the light that filtered down from the barred hatches he saw several men, grey shapes that sat or lay in silence all around. The air stank of vomit and excrement and from himself came the distinct smell of dried piss. He studied his soiled breeches with disgust. Alex wouldn't be glad to see the state of them. Alex!

Matthew slumped back against the planking and closed his eyes. This couldn't be happening to him, no, it was just a dream, and if he allowed himself to drift off to sleep, he'd wake to the dark dawn of a winter morning at Hillview, Alex snoring softly by his side. The screeching noise of the hatches recalled him brutally to this new reality and he crossed his arms in a self-hug, trying to stop himself from trembling.

"Don't fret, lad," the unknown voice said. "It is just them coming down with food and water."

Matthew nodded and sat immobile until the hatches were back in place.

"Here." A piece of bread was placed in his hand and a strong hand on his nape supported him while he drank. "You have a nasty bump to your head."

Matthew raised a shaking hand to his head and winced.

"They clobbered me! I was walking back to the inn and..." He frowned with the effort to remember; low voices arguing over his head as they dragged him along, another painful clap to his head, a creaking cart, someone holding him down while his wrists were fitted with chains, and then nothing.

"I've been abducted," he said and a surge of anger rippled through him. Luke! This was the work of his hell spawn of a brother and now, oh Dearest Lord, now there was no one there to protect his wife and son!

He twisted his head to the side and threw up the half masticated bread. The man beside him patted his shoulder and to his embarrassment Matthew felt his eyes fill up with tears.

"It's no shame," the man said, "we all weep."

"I have to get back," Matthew said. "If not he'll destroy them."

"Who?"

"My brother, God curse his soul," Matthew said.

He must have talked for nigh on an hour as he told this stranger of the hatred and rivalry that existed between him and his brother. He described finding his first wife, Margaret, in bed with Luke and how his brother had connived to have him accused of treason. Several years later, when Matthew finally returned home with his new wife, Luke had in a fit of rage beaten Alex so badly she lost the bairn she was carrying. His newfound acquaintance made a disgusted sound at this.

"A year later he threatened her again, and I should have

killed him then as I should have killed him so many times before. Instead I sliced off his nose." And now…Matthew studied his surroundings and the chains around his hands. "What has he done to me?"

The man sat back on his heels. "He's sold you into indenture, I reckon. All of us are going as indentured to Virginia, being the beneficiaries of the good king's mercy." He spat as he said that. "I'm James McLean – condemned to hang for preaching that all men are equal. I dare say they begrudged me the length of rope required, and so I'm here instead." He sighed and shuffled his feet. "I won't be preaching much where we're going, I fear I won't be preaching much at all for the rest of my days." A flicker of despair flew through his brown eyes and Matthew pressed his hand.

"Of course you will."

James shook his head. "Seven years, aye? And I am three and fifty…"

Over the coming days Matthew listened to the stories of the men around him, in many cases heartbreakingly similar, tales of hunger and of being driven from their homes for not keeping up with rents and taxes. Tales of how they were forced to steal to feed their families, and of how they'd been arrested and condemned to hang for their theft, only to have the sentences commuted to years of servitude somewhere far across the sea.

He could see it in their eyes; the resignation, the lack of hope. None of these men expected to ever make it home again, supposing they would either be worked to death or find themselves too poor to ever pay the passage back to wife and bairns. Not me, he promised himself, I won't die far from home, I'll somehow make it home to Alex and to Mark.

One night as he lay unable to sleep, drowning in worry for his son and wife, Matthew recalled that he had in fact left them some protection. Simon would take care of them, and Matthew thanked the Lord for having signed a deed of guardianship, stating clearly that in the event of his demise it was Simon, not Luke, who was to stand as father to Mark.

It almost made him laugh to think of Alex' reaction at not being considered an adequate guardian. His peculiar, God given wife would argue that she was fully capable of defending her son, and he could see her eyes slitting into flashing sapphires as she remonstrated with Simon. He shifted on the hard boards, attempting to shut out the sound of the chains. His wife... he ran his hand up and down his forearm, pretending it was her caress he felt. It made him weaken with longing for her.

"Alex." He smiled when he said her name, struck by the certainty of what she would do; she'd come after him, find him, and in his gut a flower of hope grew. If anyone could do such, it would be her, but it would cost her, because Simon would never let her take Mark with her – nor should he. He rolled over on his side. Poor Alex; to be torn from another son, just as she'd lost Isaac to the vagaries of time. But deep inside he was dizzyingly happy as the conviction in him grew that no matter the cost to her she would come for him.

It was difficult to hold on to that ray of hope over the weeks that followed. For a month they lay at anchor in Plymouth, and while the other in the hold were allowed out on deck to take air, Matthew was kept sitting in the dark, the captain making a point of informing him that he would be given no chance to escape. Matthew raged in his chains and on one occasion lost his temper completely which resulted in him crawling in pain as the cudgels rained over his shoulders and back.

"You mustn't provoke them," James chided him. "You must keep your head down." But it was too late, and the guards found one reason after the other to taunt and manhandle Matthew. Bend, he told himself, bend Matthew Graham or they will break you. Mostly he did, but sometimes the injustice of it all was too much, and that was how he came to be chained to the main mast in nothing but his shirt, unable to escape the biting iciness of the March wind as the *Henriette Marie* began her long journey across the open sea.

To distract himself from his helpless shivering and the way his fingers and toes ached with cold he thought about the day he'd found Alex, a strangely dressed lass lying sprawled face down on a hillside. He stretched his chapped lips in a weak smile as he recalled those odd breeches – djeens, she'd called them – and her short hair. And he'd known, already then, that this lass was somehow meant for him, a gift from God no less, for how else to explain the propitious coincidence that had him on the moor just when she came tumbling through time? He laughed; Alex was somewhat more sceptical to this whole divine intervention, voicing that it was all due to the fluke lightning storm, a freak misalignment in time.

When he was brought back down into the hold he was unconscious with fever, small bubbles of lucidity popping through his brain. At times he recognised the man who sat by his side and he'd make an effort to smile at this familiar person before being dragged under yet again.

James' face was the first thing Matthew saw when the fever finally broke, and he slumped into a deep dejection. In his delirious dreams he'd been home, wandering green fields and wide woods, laughing as he chased Alex up the slope, holding his wee son in his arms. Now he woke to chains and creaking boards, to men who coughed and farted in their sleep, and the despairing insight that mayhap he wouldn't make it, maybe he would die without ever seeing her again.

They all thought they would die some weeks later when the *Henriette Marie* was tossed from wave to wave, all of her protesting when the sea slammed into her creaking sides. For days the storm raged, sweeping anything not securely lashed to the deck overboard. In the hold they sat in ice cold water as huge waves broke above them, sea water cascading through the hatches. It was a relief to see a pale spring sun filter through and James led them in grateful prayer that this at least they had survived.

All of them were allowed out on deck to dry themselves and the hold was mopped up as well as could be done. The captain even accorded them a tot of brandy, muttering something about them being worth nothing to him dead, before ordering them back down into their dark, damp quarters.

Three men died; one of what James said was the ague, shivering to death, two of consumption, coughing their lungs apart. Where the other men drew back, afraid of catching these deadly diseases, James sat with them, talking to them and soothing them as best he could.

"Are you not afraid then?" Matthew said.

James just shrugged. "If I die, I die."

"But… don't you want to live, to return to your family?"

James sighed and picked a weevil or two out of the bread. "I'll not be going back, Matthew. I feel it in my bones."

"Of course you will, we'll help each other."

James didn't reply, his eyes misting over.

"We'll help each other," he said after a while. "And mayhap one of us will make it home."

"Both of us," Matthew insisted, making James give him an exasperated look.

"You don't know, do you? Most of us will die before our years of service are up, treated like beasts of burden on endless fields."

"Not me."

James gave him a sad little smile. "Nay, lad, not you."

Matthew shivered at his tone and threw a look down his own tall frame. It would be just like it had been in gaol, with him singled out for the heaviest work on account of his size and strength. And he'd spend never ending days in back breaking labour – yet again – and a frightened voice in the pit of his stomach wondered how long it would take before he began to wear down. Matthew shook himself. He was here wrongfully and once they'd landed he'd find someone he could complain to. But even as he thought it, he knew it wouldn't help. Who would listen? Who would care? He leaned back against the planking and sighed.

"She'll come, my Alex will come." His woman; she'd come for him.

"Of course she will," James said. Matthew closed his eyes; he could hear it in James' voice, that he didn't believe she would.

The day the ship anchored in the James River the hold sighed in relief. Land, soon there would be land beneath their feet, and nothing could possibly be as bad as the sea crossing, could it? A low buzz of excitement spread, the younger men surreptitiously inspecting their wasted bodies. Did they look healthy enough? Only James sat in silence.

To Matthew the heat came as a shock. It was May and the humidity hung like a drenched blanket around him, making it an effort even to breathe. He stared at the buildings huddled together on the swampy island, and up his spine snaked a tendril of fear. What kind of land was this? Everything was green, a heavy, smothering green, and just moving made him perspire, sticking his worn and grimy linen shirt to his skin. He couldn't breathe, his throat closing up in protest at this hot, wet air. How could anyone work in this?

He was manhandled into a boat and rowed across, and the following minutes he spent in a daze. Only vaguely did he understand he was being sold and when he tried to object that he was not an indenture, that he was a kidnapped man, he was laughed in the face. Had he not been in chains he would have struck the huge man in front of him, but now he just gritted his teeth and swore that someday that bastard would choke on his contemptuous laughter.

He saw James disappear from him, tried to call his name and assure him they would meet again, but a hard hand wrenched him off in another direction, shoving him and six others from his ship in the direction of a waiting cart. Chains were struck off to be replaced by ropes, they were tied to the tailgate like dumb animals and the huge overseer, Jones, gave Matthew a taunting smile, all the while fingering the strop he carried. Matthew broke eye contact and stared down at his feet.

Much later they were finally allowed to stop. Chests were heaving with the unfamiliar humidity and their clothing hung damp and uncomfortable. None of them had said a word, concentrating on keeping up with the cart. Jones ignored them, leaving them to stand, still tied, and said something in a low voice to the two drovers. They all laughed, eyes slinking in the direction of the new men.

"Three years," Matthew heard one of them say. "No more than that." With a sinking feeling he understood they were betting on their survival. It made his stomach turn itself inside out.

# CHAPTER 4

Mrs Gordon quickly decided travelling by sea had its advantages, and spent most of her days chatting up the cook or one of the sailors, coming back to share nuggets of information with Alex who to her surprise discovered she was prone to seasickness and therefore remained in bed.

"Did you know the captain's crossed the Atlantic thirty times?" Mrs Gordon asked, sitting down on the single stool.

"Great; I suppose that means he knows what he's doing, right?"

Mrs Gordon nodded and went on to tell Alex one more blood curdling story after the other, stories of shipwrecks and pirates and ships sitting becalmed for weeks in the middle of the ocean, the whole crew convinced that soon they would die, maddened by thirst.

"Are you doing this on purpose?"

Mrs Gordon laughed and said that as distraction it served, did it not?

After a couple of claustrophobic days in the dark cabin, Alex made her way out on deck, sniffing the fresh air with appreciation. For the first time since they set off she had woken hungry and she'd consumed a hearty breakfast consisting of salted fried pork, beer and somewhat stale bread.

"We'll be anchoring off Plymouth tomorrow," Captain Miles told her, coming to join her by the railing. "We have one new passenger coming aboard." He smiled at Alex and went back to studying the sea. "Your companion tells me you're on your way to join your husband."

"Yes, in Virginia." She wasn't about to tell him more than that. "How long will it take?"

"Seven to ten weeks, depending on the weather and the winds."

Late June then, she sighed, wondering how she would

stand it. The last few nights he'd been so close, and she had arched herself to meet his touch only to bang her head against the wall of the berth and jerk awake. She missed him; there was a jagged hole inside of her that grew larger with every day. Their son sat aching in her heart, but Matthew, well him she missed with everything. With her hands, where she wanted nothing more than to let her fingers rest against his skin, with her mouth, with her breasts… Every part of her was left diminished, damaged, now that he wasn't here to blend seamlessly into her.

"You'll find him." Mrs Gordon appeared like a giant, overweight magpie by her side.

"You think?"

Mrs Gordon tut-tutted with irritation. "Of course you will. " She cocked her head to one side and gave Alex a swift pat. "He's not dead, lass, and as long as he's alive you'll find him. He calls to you, doesn't he? Just like my Robbie…" She broke off. Alex regarded her narrowly, studying her in a way she'd never done before. Always black, never anything but black, except for her old-fashioned caps and collars that stood starched and white. And not once had Alex thought to ask.

"How long were you married?"

"Twenty years." Mrs Gordon's short fingers caressed the ring she wore on her pinkie. "Twenty years and four lasses, and then all five died within a year." She shrugged off Alex' hand. "I was very blessed, aye? I loved and was loved." She tightened the shawl around her and patted Alex on the arm. "So do you, no? You love him so much you'd die for him."

Alex nodded.

"That's why you had to go after him. You'd never have forgiven yourself if you didn't."

It was not the most elegant of entrances. Despite several attempts the new passenger was unable to clamber aboard using the rope ladder, and Alex hung over the railings watching while a rope was tied round his waist to hoist him aboard instead. The man landed in a heap, but quickly regained his feet, brushing at his cloak, his breeches – well, his everything – before turning to face the captain. With a flourish he bowed, sweeping his flashy hat off his head. Alex took one look at his face and was sure she would die. There, on the spot.

"At your service; Ángel Benito Muñoz de Hojeda – from Spain."

Alex gawked at him. It couldn't be! Ángel was dead! Well, to be precise, he wasn't even born yet, but he'd died in 1999, she saw him die with her own eyes. And now he was here, in 1661, or at least someone looking eerily like him and using the same name was here, and it made her throat clog. She retreated behind the captain, but managed to curtsey and mumble an adequate greeting, all the time fearing her guts would drop out and land with a sickening plop on the deck.

Unbidden and definitely unwelcome, the image of her mother wrapping herself round a frozen Ángel and self-combusting them both into nonexistence sprung to the front of Alex' mind. Oh God, oh God! Just thinking of it made her hyperventilate; her mother some sort of witch, and Ángel, God curse him, Ángel was a lowlife, a living contradiction of his given name. She stared down at the oak boarding and counted back from a hundred in an attempt to calm down.

She peeked at the stranger; Holy Matilda! This could be Ángel's twin!

"A mouthful, all those names," Mrs Gordon remarked.

"My friends call me Benito," the stranger smiled. "Don Benito."

Alex softened. Not the same then; besides, this man had nice, warm eyes and a tentative but genuine smile – not at all like the future Ángel Muñoz. She smiled back and dropped her eyes to his extravagant petticoat breeches, decorated with yard upon yard of pink ribbon at waist and knee. My, my; a budding fashionista – down to the polished buckles of his shoes.

"And what may a Spanish gentleman be doing so far from home?" Captain Miles said, sounding as if Spanish gentlemen were a dangerous species best thrown overboard.

"I'm an envoy of the Tabacalera." There was a slight hesitation in Don Benito's reply, dark eyes sliding to the side. Hmm, thought Alex, grinning internally at Mrs Gordon's sharp look in the Spaniard's direction.

"The Tabacalera?" the captain said.

"It's a tobacco company, the oldest in the world." Don Benito puffed up with pride.

"*En Sevilla*," Alex nodded, "*ya lo sé.*"

Don Benito beamed at her, his whole face alight with pleasure.

"*Habla usted Castellano?*"

"Obviously," Alex muttered.

"Are you perhaps familiar with my home city?" He sounded pathetically eager. Alex nearly told him that of course she was – she was born in Seville, in 1976 – but stopped herself from blurting that. He'd tear her apart with questions about her family and she would have no answers.

"Not really, a short visit many years ago, that's all. My mother was from there," she said, which meant she was anyhow drowned in a flood of questions that she handled by referring to the fact that her mother had died many years ago and she didn't know.

"What was her name?"

"Mercedes. Mercedes Gutierrez. She was a famous painter." She was a weird painter, a woman who painted miniature time portals and littered the world with them. Alex studied Don Benito carefully, but there was no reaction. She relaxed; it was all a coincidence, this man must be somewhere up the future Ángel's family tree that's all.

"A tobacco spy?" Captain Miles interjected, eyeing his new passenger with a slight frown.

"Captain!" Don Benito said. "Of course not. I have

business to conduct with the Virginia Governor, Sir William Berkeley."

The captain looked impressed.

"Really?" Alex said. This might be a most opportune meeting, for it would help to know the Governor, even at a once removed.

"Do you know him?" Don Benito asked.

"Never heard of him," Alex said, making him smile.

"I don't know him either – except by repute. I am but a glorified messenger boy." A very well dressed messenger boy, Alex concluded, even if she had serious doubts as to the state of his undergarments, given how the man kept on scratching himself.

Don Benito proved most pleasing company, regaling Alex and Mrs Gordon with stories of his life. It seemed that he had become loosely attached to the English Court in exile some years ago, and when the king was invited to return to England in May of 1660, Don Benito had been requested to come along.

"Why?" Mrs Gordon asked. "Is the king perchance interested in tobacco?" Don Benito laughed and explained that his present mission was a new development, and in his personal opinion the king was more prone to wine than tobacco. He then changed the subject, asking Alex what she remembered of his hometown, before launching himself into a dreamy description of his beloved Seville. With a little wave Mrs Gordon escaped, winking at Alex over Don Benito's head.

Sometimes Alex suspected Don Benito suffered from verbal diarrhoea, because God, how that man could talk! But when he ruefully admitted to being overjoyed at meeting someone with whom he could speak his mother tongue she was somewhat ashamed of her uncharitable thoughts. Besides, she found their conversations invigorating, even if they did tend to drift off into yet another discussion about the Bible. This man must know the whole thing by heart, she reflected, ears shut as he yet again quoted something from Romans – his obvious favourite.

Time and time again, Don Benito returned to his favourite subject, Seville, describing the scent of orange blossom, the procession of the virgins and the silence of a midday siesta in summer, when the air was so hot it almost hurt to breathe it.

"It's not quite as nice in spring, the Guadalquivir tends to flood on a regular basis, leaving the whole city covered in water and mud. "

"Doesn't happen now, with the new redirected river channel," Alex mumbled, frowning down at her recalcitrant knitting.

"Channel? What channel?"

Shit; that particular little channel wasn't even on the drawing board yet. Alex gave him a bland smile. "Mmm? Oh, don't mind me, I was thinking of Stockholm." Don Benito looked unconvinced, but didn't push.

One evening Captain Miles requested the presence of his passengers on deck, a foreboding wrinkle on his brow.

"I have reason to suspect I have a woman on board who has been…err… free with herself and requested payment."

"A whore," Mrs Gordon clarified. Behind her, Don Benito converted what sounded like a laugh into an extended coughing fit.

"Aye," Captain Miles said stiffly, preceding them onto the deck.

The women from the hold – around sixty or so – stood ranged on one side, while the crew, a motley collection of two dozen men, stood on the other. Between them sat a young woman, flaxen hair escaping the tight braid that hung down her back. At the captain's command she stood, chin held high while the captain outlined her sins.

"I did no such thing," the woman said once he'd finished.

The captain eyed her with irritation. "So if I were to search your belongings I wouldn't find…" He stopped and pulled a written list towards him, squinting down at the words. "… three pewter buttons, one small silver ring, five silk ribbons in green, one half crown, one pink silk stocking…" He gave an amused snort. "… are you holding out for the other one, Smith?" Smith pulled out a pink silk stocking from his pocket and waved it at the captain, making the crew collapse in laughter.

"Well?" the captain demanded, glaring at the woman in front of him. She hung her head, muttering that she wasn't really doing anything wrong was she? They wanted to, so…

"On my ship I won't condone immoral behaviour, you hear? You'll be punished for whoring." He studied the assembled women and turned to look at Alex, standing to one side with Mrs Gordon. "We have ladies on board, and if you can't behave you must suffer the consequences."

"We're not all like Nell," one tall redhead protested, with supporting murmurs from her friends.

"I'm glad to hear that, and I expect to see you back tomorrow for the punishment." The captain nodded to one of his men and the unfortunate woman was led off to spend her night under lock and key.

"What will you do to her?" Alex asked over supper.

"She will be whipped. Twelve lashes, I think; enough to humiliate, not enough to cause serious damage."

"And to the men?"

Captain Miles choked. "The men?"

"You said you were going to punish immoral behaviour," Alex said, "and as far as I can make out it isn't only the girl who's been fornicating. After all she's been doing it with someone, right?"

Don Benito had yet another long coughing fit, making the captain glare at him.

"So," Alex sat back. "Will they also get twelve lashes? You know, enough to humiliate but not enough to damage?"

Clearly it had never struck the captain that men should be punished for following their baser instincts, and over the following half hour the debate rang louder and louder, the captain insisting that this was his ship and he would dispense justice as he saw fit.

"She profiteered, she tempted them," he snapped, glowering at Alex who glowered back and stood up.

"You'll do as you want, Captain Miles." She leaned across the table and sank her eyes into him. "But don't you dare say that you'll not allow immorality on your ship when you choose to only punish one party." And with that she swept out.

# CHAPTER 5

Alex was impressively good at cold shouldering when she felt like it, and for the coming days Captain Miles tagged after her like a little dog in his pathetic attempts to repair their relationship.

"The lass is perfectly fine," he informed Alex one morning, with a look on his face that begged her to smile at him.

"Oh, good, and her morals are now fully repaired, right?"

The captain beamed at her and nodded. If only you knew, Alex thought, but decided that there was no point in telling him of what went on under cover of the dark. Captain Miles shifted closer to her.

"The women in the hold, don't they pay for their passage?" she asked. Simon's somewhat garbled explanation had left her confused as to what these women were; voluntary emigrants? Bond servants?

"No, some of them are bonded to me and I will sell their term of service once we arrive at our destination. Some I ship over and they're auctioned off as wives. There are very few women out there."

"How awful," Alex said. "Like a cattle auction."

Captain Miles gave her a worried look. "It's them that have chosen it, aye? And if there's an auction it is mostly the other way; the lasses will pick, and the poor sod they choose will burst himself to buy her."

"So all the women down there are here because they want to."

Captain Miles sighed. "Or because they have to. Some come from the Highlands, there's not much there for a woman alone in the world."

"But none of them have been forced? Carried aboard against their will?"

He looked mightily offended. "Mrs Graham! What do you take me for?"

"Just asking, and it does happen, right?"

"Aye," he agreed. "It does."

He stood looking at the water below them for some time before giving her a perceptive look.

"Is that was happened to your man, then?"

Alex was so unprepared for the question that she didn't need to reply.

"Ah, lass. I'm sorry for you."

"I'm sorry for him."

"So how? If you don't mind telling me." He sounded genuinely interested and Alex gave him a brief summary. "And the ship was the *Henriette Marie*, you say?"

Alex nodded, not at all liking how the captain's face had pulled together.

The captain braced himself against the railings. "The *Henriette Marie* is owned by a certain Mr Fairfax, owner not only of that ship but several. And he also has a plantation somewhere in Virginia, but I don't know its name. Every time one of his ships lie at port in Scotland or in England, men disappear. They never return, probably carried over the sea to work themselves to death there, at his place. He doesn't want them to survive, I'd assume."

"What?" she gasped.

Captain Miles gave her shoulder a reassuring pat. "Most of them don't have a wife who comes looking. So mayhap you'll find him safe and sound." He didn't sound as if he believed what he was saying, the impression further reinforced by the strained smile he sent Alex' way.

"Oh, I will, I most definitely will." She scowled down at the water. "Why hasn't someone stopped him? If you know, then so do others, right?"

Captain Miles shrugged and tapped his nose. "Powerful friends, Mrs Graham. I wouldn't advise you to threaten him with exposure. A cornered rat is a nasty piece of works."

Alex didn't reply; she was busy stopping herself from crying.

"Why are you weeping, lass?" Mrs Gordon's concerned

voice made her jump and Alex wiped at her wet eyes.

"I'm not."

"Och aye, you are. Why?"

Alex summarised what Captain Miles had said.

"No major change, no? You already knew that he'd be sold and mayhap badly treated."

"It's easy for you to say, it isn't your husband, is it?"

"Nay, but I care for him as well." She gave Alex a little shake. "It doesn't help him, child, for you to weep. Nor does it help you."

"No," Alex squared her shoulders. "You're right; it doesn't."

"That's my lass," Mrs Gordon said and smiled at her. "I told you already years ago that you're his Ruth, no? He won't die without you."

"What a comfort," Alex muttered. *"Wither thou goest, I will go,"* she breathed. Yes, of course she would and if that Fairfax character had any sense of what was good for him he'd better have a very live Matthew Graham on his hands when she found him.

A week later Mrs Gordon rushed into their cabin, bug-eyed, and threw the door closed behind her, leaning against it as if she expected the four riders of the Apocalypse to force their way through.

"You won't believe this!" Mrs Gordon said, her ample bosom heaving.

"Believe what?" Alex gave her an irritated look; such a nice dream, involving her and Matthew.

"The Spaniard, I knew it!"

"Knew what?"

"Have you not seen then?"

Seen what? The incredible amount of ribbons? The way his hair was always neatly curled and perfumed?

"You have no eyes in your head, lass. Have you not seen how he scratches himself, all the time like?"

Alex wrinkled her brow; of course she had. "So he has

lice?" Alex' eyes dashed across the cabin in search of a potential infestation.

"Nay. Or mayhap he does, but nay, that's not it." Mrs Gordon sat down on the stool and flapped her hands. "That I should live to see the day…"

Alex was by now very curious, but waited until Mrs Gordon's high colour faded into her more normal piggy pink.

"A priest," Mrs Gordon said, eyes wide. Alex total lack of reaction was obviously a huge disappointment. "He's a papist priest!"

"He is?" Alex said, mainly because something was expected of her. She wanted to laugh, but from the look on Mrs Gordon's face being a papist priest was to hover somewhere close to the inner circle of Hell. "And how do you know?"

"It was the hair shirt, aye?"

"Hair shirt?"

Mrs Gordon spoke so fast Alex could barely make out what she was saying, but finally she grasped that Mrs Gordon had caught Don Benito in some state of undress – she refused to explain how that had happened, although Alex had her own ideas – and seen that the man was wearing a hair shirt.

"You should see his skin. All chafed, and with huge blotches of rash. He must have been wearing it for a long time."

"So he wears a hair shirt. That doesn't automatically make him a priest, does it?" Alex felt uncomfortable; a zealot on board.

Mrs Gordon agreed that it didn't, but as per chance she had happened upon his cabin unlocked.

"Per chance?" Alex frowned.

Mrs Gordon shrugged and went on with her story. How she'd found cassock and Bible and rosary beads, and a golden crucifix and you know, those long bits of cloths they hang round their neck. Alex interrupted her mid-steam by standing up and clapping her hands.

"Enough! You'll not go around talking to anyone about this. You've been spying on him and that's wrong. I'm sure there's a rational explanation to all this."

"Aye? And how do you mean to find out?"

"I'll ask him of course."

"You will?" Mrs Gordon beamed. "And then you'll tell me."

"We'll see about that; if I think you can take it." She escaped from the cabin, laughing at the dull thud of Mrs Gordon's hairbrush hitting the door.

Alex found Don Benito standing on the quarter deck, staring off in the direction of Europe.

"*Pax vobiscum,*" Alex murmured, smiling at the responding start.

"*Y contigo, hija.*"

"So, you want to tell me?" She turned to lean her back against the railing.

"Tell you what?"

"About the hair shirt, all the paraphernalia of a catholic priest that apparently litters your cabin."

He looked at her with disappointment. "Have you been through my things?"

"No, I wouldn't do something like that, nor have I attempted to ogle you in states of undress. But someone else has."

"Ah," Don Benito said resignedly. "Mrs Gordon."

"Yes, I'm sorry. She won't say anything. So are you? A priest, I mean."

"*Sí.*" He threw her a look. "I would ask you not to tell, it might make things difficult for me where I'm going."

Alex smiled. "Clandestine conversions? Secret baptisms?"

"Perhaps; there are those in Virginia that would be glad of a Catholic priest, but it's something that is best done discreetly. Especially with a Governor so firmly committed to the Anglican Church." Don Benito sighed and shifted on his feet. "My going to Virginia has nothing to do with my calling as a priest. The timing was opportune for other reasons." He sounded very casual, his dark eyes wide when they met hers. Good try; he was lying through his teeth.

"But your position with the English Royals does have something to do with it, no?" Alex said, recalling that the present king's mother was a Catholic.

"Maybe, but those are questions to tread very carefully around."

Alex hitched her shoulders, not caring one way or the other. "And the hair shirt?"

Don Benito's face froze into impenetrability. "That's none of your business, *hija.*"

"Probably not." She let the subject drop, leaned her elbows against the railings and locked her eyes on the frothing wake.

"My turn," Don Benito said.

"Your turn?"

"To ask you some questions."

Alex shrugged and nodded go ahead.

"Your mother was Spanish, no?"

"Yes."

"So you've been baptised into the Holy Church."

"No… I, well, my father…" She had been baptised by Matthew at the advanced age of twenty-six in a ceremony she still considered somewhat doubtful, but that wasn't something she intended to share. "My father insisted that I be brought up in his faith."

"Ah," the priest nodded. "And was he of strong faith?"

Alex suppressed an urge to giggle. Magnus had never expressed any interest in God. To him, the world was ruled by the natural laws of science and common sense.

"Sometimes."

"And you? Are you of strong faith?" His dark eyes bored into her.

"I don't know, I…" She broke off. To Matthew it was self-evident, to all the people that now inhabited her world it was a fact that God existed. "I would like to be." She laughed at herself; every night she prayed to God that he may keep her Matthew safe, and still she wasn't sure. Talk about hedging your bets.

"Do you think I was wrong?" Alex asked to change the subject.

Don Benito looked bewildered.

"You know, the other night, when I argued with the captain about the hypocrisy of punishing just the girl."

Don Benito's mouth curved into a smile. "It hasn't helped, has it?" He threw his head in the direction of the forecastle.

"No, if anything the reverse." She returned to her original question, and he sighed.

"No, I think you were right. But so, to a point, was the captain. Men are weak willed when it comes to female temptation."

"Even a priest?"

Don Benito looked away. "Yes, sometimes even a priest."

Alex covered his hand with hers. "I hope it was worth it, you seem to be paying a very heavy price."

Don Benito kept his eyes on the horizon. "I loved her, I still love her and that, I fear, is my greatest sin; I can't truly repent, because every night I see her in my dreams."

"To love isn't a sin," Alex said. "You know that, and so does God."

"*Ojalá*," he whispered. "I hope so."

John Orrock stopped at the garden gate, watching Magnus Lind with some concern. Over the last few months Magnus had sunk into a deep depression, and as he moved round the garden, working his way from one rose bush to the other, there was none of the normal vibrancy in his movements. His blond hair, heavily streaked with grey, was messy and too long, his tall body moved slowly, almost hesitantly, and an air of constant, brooding sorrow hung over him. According to Diane he was becoming obsessive, unable to let Alex go.

"It's easy for you to say," John had remonstrated with his wife. "Keep in mind that not only Alex, but also Mercedes just vanished. Here one day, gone the next. Difficult to deal with, to never know where his wife and daughter ended up."

"Hmm." Diane said, making a face. "I'm still not sure whether I believe all that crap about Mercedes and Alex and rifts in the fabric of time."

John had grinned at her. "There are days when I don't believe it either – but don't tell Magnus that."

John opened the creaking gate, smiling in the direction of Magnus.

"Hi, I thought I'd find you out here – beautiful day that it is."

Magnus just nodded and stood back to eye a gigantic, rambling rose.

"I always forget how much work it is," John said. "In summer when the whole garden's alive with colour I tend to think it just happens by itself."

Magnus snorted, his blue eyes on his almost son-in-law. "It definitely doesn't." He looked down at his swollen joints and clenched and unclenched his fingers a couple of times. "I have to stop for today, so if you want I'll make us both a coffee."

"Where's Isaac?" John asked once they were settled in the kitchen.

Magnus jerked his head upwards. "Where he always is; in the studio, painting." He bit into a huge slice of carrot cake. "He's quite good."

"He is, isn't he? His teachers are quite impressed." So was John, amazed at the drawings that flowed from Isaac's hands. "Genes, I suppose." He shared a quick look with Magnus; as long as those were the only genes Isaac had inherited from Mercedes, things were alright in the world. Just thinking of Mercedes' magic pictures had something cramping in John's belly, sending cake and frosting back up the way they'd come. John coughed and swallowed a couple of times.

"How are the twins?" Magnus said, stretching himself for another slice of cake. John beamed. In his opinion Olivia and Alice were the most perfect beings in the world, with their mother a potential runner up. He felt a flash of guilt at how easily Diane had superseded Alex in his heart, but comforted himself with that it was only natural; Alex was gone, she was never coming back and he, John, had a life to lead.

"Both of them can sit by now, and I think Olivia tried to say Daddy the other day."

"Really?" Magnus sounded incredulous, but smiled all the same.

"Well, according to Diane, they can both say Mummy – ask her when she comes over."

"Oh, I will," Magnus laughed and extracted a gigantic chicken from the fridge. "We're having Coq au vin, with a lot of au vin." He handed John a chopping board and a substantial amount of carrots and shallots.

It had become a family tradition; Sunday dinners at Magnus' complete with white linen on the table, lit candles, wine and a succession of increasingly more complicated desserts.

"We worry about you," Diane said once the dishes were cleared away.

Magnus gave her a guarded look. "Why would you do that?"

Diane made an exasperated sound and handed Magnus one of the twins to feed.

"You can't let her go, can you?"

Magnus pulled his brows together; this was not a subject he wanted to discuss, but Diane ploughed on.

"It's almost three years, you know she isn't coming back."

He ignored her, concentrating on the child in his arms and the contented little murmurs she made as she emptied her bottle.

"She's dead, Magnus," Diane said, reaching across to place her hand on his arm.

"No she isn't, she's just somewhere else, in another time."

"But she's still dead," Diane said. "Even if she's fallen through to another time – and we don't really know that for sure, do we? – even then, she's dead by now."

Magnus wanted to deny this, but nodded in agreement.

"It makes my head ache, I spend nights trying to unravel this circular reference. How my daughter has gone back in time and died before I was born…"

John came over and relieved him of Olivia, punching him on the shoulder.

"Of course it makes your head ache. It's not exactly an everyday occurrence, is it?"

"Tell me about it." Magnus poured them all some more wine and carried his glass over to the window to stare unseeing at the darkening garden outside.

April, month of unfulfilled promise, of budding shrubs and exploding greens, month of blue twilights and of dusks that fell like gentle fogs over the ground, month when it was so difficult to be alone and wish desperately for what once had been. His wife and his daughter – both gone, none found. The loss of them lay like a crown of thorns around his heart, and with every day the ache just grew worse.

"It would have been easier if she'd been dead," he said,

feeling horrible for voicing it. "Now she's just … gone, and even if I know in my head that I'll never see her again, in my heart I can't stop hoping."

Diane hurried over to give him a warm hug. "You have to let her go, Magnus, you have us, your living family, and we want you to be happy, not always pining for someone you've lost."

"Family?"

Diane hugged him even harder. "Family. Not by blood perhaps, but definitely of the heart."

His hand floated up to caress her well-coiffed chestnut hair. Yes, in Diane he had a daughter, a girl he'd seen grow at almost as close range as Alex.

"So," Diane said, craning back to see his face. "Let her go, say goodbye."

Magnus lifted his shoulders in a helpless gesture. "I want to find her."

John sat up in the sofa and blinked. "Find her?"

"Yes, find some proof that what we believe happened to her actually did."

"Oh for God's sake!" Diane shook her head at him. "You have no idea when or where…You don't even know her name!"

"Of course I do!" Magnus snapped. "She's Alex Lind, isn't she?"

"I think Diane means that she might have married," John said. "And she does have a point; where would you start?"

"Here, somewhere here in Scotland, and not that far back. She's not a woad dyed Pict – or an aluminium wrapped space traveller."

"Well, thank heavens for that," Diane muttered. "Although she would probably look great in blue skin and nothing else." She covered Magnus' hand and shook it.

"The probability of you ever finding anything is microscopic. One very small needle in a gigantic haystack of history."

"I know," Magnus replied with a deep sigh.

Later that night Magnus refilled his whisky glass and moved out to stand in the long hallway that ran from the front door to the back of the house. The Alex gallery, Diane called it, sixty-seven pictures of Alex from the day she was born to that last photo of her and Isaac, two weeks before she went up in thin air. He tapped a forefinger at this last one. A complicated relationship; an unwanted child and a mother that had taken a long time to overcome that initial dislike. But in this picture she smiled down at Isaac, and her short hair shimmered in the sun.

Just by the kitchen door hung the only picture he had of Mercedes, and he blew her a kiss. His magic wife; witch, some would say. He missed her every day, dreamed often of her. Sometimes the dreams were erotic, dreams of him and her in a long gone southern night. Mostly they were dreams of a young Mercedes who danced across a poppy studded meadow. She had achieved her goal ; she was at peace – he could see it in her eyes.

# CHAPTER 7

By the time they staggered into the yard of the farm that was going to be Matthew's new home, the seven indentures were dizzy with exhaustion. None of them had the energy to do more than throw a disinterested glance at the surrounding structures, and when they were led into the shed that was theirs to share they lay down and rolled over to sleep.

Matthew couldn't sleep. The space was cramped, so small that seven men on the floor per definition meant involuntary body contact, and Elijah, the man beside him, was snoring him loudly in the ear. Through the minimal aperture high up in the wall Matthew could see new unfamiliar skies, and inside of him a small voice expressed that mayhap these would be the skies beneath which he'd die – far away from home, without the comfort of a loving hand. He twisted at the thought and closed his eyes in an attempt to find something to hold on to in all this dark.

She smiled at him, she lifted her hands to her hair and drew out the pins to shake it loose and he wondered where she was, because this was not their bedchamber, this was somewhere else. Alex wrapped a shawl around her – the one he had given her last autumn with the wee embroidered roses on it – and stepped out into a night where the stars hung within touching distance of her hand. He saw her move over to a railing and something warm and light fluttered through his belly. A ship, she's on a ship... aye, she was coming for him, her eyes promised, and with that small comfort he shoved his hands under his head and drifted off to sleep.

In the grey light of dawn they were dragged outside. Matthew's eyes widened as he took in the size of the farm. Plantation, he corrected himself, this was a plantation. Huge wooden buildings stood to one side, and even from where they stood he could make out the smell of tobacco. Jones led them round and explained that these were the curing barns, indicating how the tobacco was hung on poles to dry.

"Heavy work," Jones informed them, pointing at a man who was precariously balancing a loaded pole on his shoulders. Finally, he led them down to the fields. To Matthew's eyes they seemed endless, line after undulating line of dark green tobacco plants, with here and there a pale yellow flower showing through.

As they were walking towards the cook house Matthew took the opportunity to fall in step with the overseer.

"There's been a miscarriage of justice, I'm here unjustly."

Jones gave him a disinterested look.

"I was abducted by force in Edinburgh," Matthew went on. "And now I must return to my family and home. I have a farm to run as well," he smiled, trying to find some point of contact with the silent mountain beside him. "Not at all on this scale, but mine."

Jones regarded him for a moment. "We paid twenty pounds for you."

"Then I'll see you reimbursed."

"Really?" Jones said. "How?"

"Once I get back home," Matthew began but was interrupted by Jones' loud braying laugh.

"Get back home? And you aim to swim? Fly like a bird?"

"Nay, of course not. I'll go by ship."

"And how will you pay the passage?" Jones' eyes glinted maliciously. Matthew fell silent and trudged beside him for some paces.

"I shouldn't be here, I must get home, aye?"

Jones came to a halt. "But you are, and we've paid good money for you. Unless you can reimburse us, you'll just have to work your years off."

Matthew shook his head angrily. "Nay, that isn't right. You know it isn't!"

Jones gave him a bored look and yawned. He pointed his hand in the direction of the cook house.

"Get some breakfast. You'll need it." He nodded and despite his bulk swivelled elegantly on his toes, hurrying up towards the main house.

Behind him Matthew stood clenching and unclenching his fists. How was he to find twenty pounds in this place, here where he couldn't even find the few coins needed to send a letter back home?

After a tasteless breakfast of watery gruel and bread, Jones lined them up in the yard and took his time inspecting them. Matthew stared straight ahead and pretended he was elsewhere as the overseer hemmed and hawed over his physique. Jones fingered Matthew's coat, his breeches, and stood back, eyeing Matthew with a small quirk to his mouth.

"Take them off," he said. "You won't need clothes such as those here."

"Nay," Matthew said, "they're mine."

"Are they? Well, I'm telling you to strip."

"No," Matthew replied, squaring himself. "Why should I?" Too late he became aware of the sudden light in Jones' eyes, and the whip caught him straight across his face, splitting his lip.

"Now," Jones repeated, "strip."

Matthew dabbed at his lip with his sleeve and considered his options. Either he undressed himself or he would be undressed, here, in front of all the people that were slowly assembling. He stiffened; if they wanted his clothes they'd have to tear them off him.

Ten minutes later Matthew lay curled around himself, as naked as the day he'd been born. All of him was covered with welts and he was bleeding from nose and mouth. His clothes lay in torn tatters on the ground beside him and even in his semi-conscious state he felt a vague satisfaction that no one would have the use of them. A bucket of ice cold water was poured over him and hands pulled him to his feet. A grey, worn shirt landed at his feet, followed by equally worn breeches in an undefined colour that may once have been brown.

"Get dressed."

He complied and followed Jones and his shipmates to the barns.

"You'll be packing all day," Jones informed them and waved his hand at the full interior. "All of this has to be baled today."

"This is your fault, Graham," Elijah muttered much later. They could scarcely move their arms, and in the dark above them pole after pole of unpacked tobacco still hung.

"You reckon?" Matthew slurred.

"Aye, this is for you not doing as he said."

Matthew attempted a snort through his swollen nose. "Nay, Elijah. We would have been doing this no matter. This is him breaking in his new men."

For the first few months of his life at the plantation this was all Matthew did. He baled and baled, lifted heavy loads of dried tobacco leaves until he was certain his arms had lengthened permanently. Often he couldn't sleep, the air in the little shed smothering him, and he crawled out of his makeshift bed to stand for hours in hot summer nights trying to find some oxygen to draw into his overworked lungs.

He hated it here; the heat and the humidity, the far too vivid greenery, the strange bugs and unfamiliar birds. He longed for cool winds and the rustling shade of oaks and alders, he yearned for robins and blackbirds and the endless twilights of the northern summer skies. He was a servant, and he had never been one before, never had to adapt himself completely to the will of another man. His days began when someone else decided and they ended when that someone chose them to. And sometimes the days were very long, with a disinterested Jones insisting that the barn had to be emptied, however late the night.

Initially, Matthew entertained ideas of running away, somehow evading the dogs and making it unscathed to Jamestown. Whatever notions he had of escaping were wiped clean out of his mind a couple of days after his arrival when one of the veteran indentured workers jerked his head in the direction of six desiccated objects nailed to one of the barns.

"Hands," he said, "they tried to run."

"Ah," Matthew said. All that day his wrists itched.

Matthew attempted repeatedly to convince Jones that he was here erroneously, ignoring the big man's warning scowl as he once again explained what had happened to him.

"Please listen," he pleaded one Saturday, lengthening his stride to match Jones'. "Will you not try and help? I have a family, a wee lad who needs his father." He could hear the begging note to his voice, but he had to try. Jones ignored him, his eyes on the barn for which they were heading. Once inside the barn, Jones wheeled, bringing his open hand down in disdainful slap across Matthew's face. Jones hit him again, this time with full force. Matthew stumbled back, raising his arms in defence.

"I don't care," Jones said, advancing on him. "I've already told you; Twenty pounds and you are free to go. Until then you will hold your tongue and do as you are told."

Matthew stood his ground. "I have a right to speak out, and I'm here unlawfully. Mayhap I should walk into town and talk to the magistrates there." The moment he said it, Matthew understood it had been a mistake. At the look in Jones' eyes, the way the small mouth was sucked in to all but disappear into the heavy jowls, Matthew retreated a couple of paces.

"Threatening to abscond?" Jones asked, crowding Matthew. He moved his head slowly from side to side. "We can't have that, can we?" He lunged with surprising speed and felled Matthew to the ground with one well directed kick. The next kick hit Matthew squarely in the stomach, and he couldn't breathe, mouth wide open as he tried to draw some air into his lungs. A fist in his face, and Matthew groaned. Yet another blow, and Matthew bit through his tongue.

"I will not tolerate more complaints," Jones said only

inches from his ear. Matthew remained where he was until he heard the barn door creak closed.

"You bring it on yourself," Elijah berated Matthew, supporting him to stand. "You must learn, no? To hold your tongue." Matthew tried to speak, but his jaw hurt, his mouth hurt, his whole face hurt.

"Aye," Duncan put in, slinging Matthew's arm around his shoulders. "You rile him. And now he won't leave you alone."

Elijah nodded in solemn agreement and together his two shipmates half carried, half dragged Matthew back to the shed. As they lowered Matthew down onto his blanket Matthew closed his hand around Elijah's wrist.

"I shouldn't be here," he managed to say.

"But you are."

Aye, Matthew sighed, unfortunately he was.

Duncan was right. Matthew's life deteriorated further after this incident. Jones consistently singled him out for the chores he considered most demeaning. Not a day without small jibes, a sardonic bow in the direction of the abducted gentleman, sudden requests that he do this or that, often coinciding with the dinner bell.

Matthew held his tongue as well as he could, reminding himself that he must stay alive, must survive because otherwise all that would be left of him would be a sad little cross in the makeshift graveyard – in earth so definitely not his own. But every now and then his temper flared, and he would raise his chin in silent defiance, reminding Jones that he was not a slave, not him, not Matthew Graham. Jones smirked, swatting his boot with his whip.

All through that sweltering summer men died; of the ague, of strange, swift fevers, of measles, racking consumption and of general neglect – full grown men whose bodies weighed no more than a half grown lad's, their bones standing in stark outline against dirty, grey skin.

Graves were dug hastily, and sometimes the man who died no longer had anyone there who knew who he was or from where he came. Mostly these men died silently, expiring in the bleakest hours of the night, but every now and then their deaths were loud, agonising affairs, the sound echoing through the heavy summer night. And then there was Samuel, the tailor's lad from Lincoln who strung himself up to hang in the furthermost barn.

"Could you do that?" Elijah asked Matthew in a shaky whisper, his eyes glued to the limp, still shape. Matthew shook his head.

"Nay, 'tis a sin, no?"

"I could, and then it would be me deciding."

Matthew gripped Elijah hard around the wrist. "You don't mean that, Elijah. To do that..." He indicated the body now lying on a board. "... to do that you must have lost all hope."

"Aye," Elijah replied in a colourless voice.

Their days began at dawn with a silent breakfast of ubiquitous gruel. Once a week there was salted pork, and sometimes even beans. Matthew found wild raspberry canes and ate the tart, unripe berries and the small leaves, recalling how Alex had insisted he always eat something green to keep his health and teeth. Alex; during the days he'd banished her to the furthest reaches of his mind, because the memory of her was too painful, but at unexpected moments he'd confuse a distant female figure with her, and he would be so blindingly happy until he remembered where he was; on a plantation with Alex nowhere in sight.

In the evenings Matthew and his companions were so tired they collapsed into silent heaps on the floor, all of them longing for the short release of dreams of somewhere else – anywhere but here.

The first few days Matthew had gone in search of water and kept at least his face and hands clean, but now he didn't care, all he wanted to do was lie down and rest his aching muscles. But every night he cleaned his teeth as his wife had taught him, running a careful tongue over them to ensure they still sat as they should. Alex... he couldn't keep her at bay when he hovered on the brink of sleep, and her name was often his last conscious thought.

Matthew moved silently through his days, keeping his head down as much as possible, and as July shifted into August he began to take his blanket and retreat to a small copse he had found by chance well behind the cook house. There was a small spring, a soft gurgling that widened into a small pond and then trickled away between the trees. The sound of water reminded him of home, and he rediscovered the simple pleasure of keeping somewhat clean, taking the time to wash before he wrapped himself in his blanket and sat back to watch the stars that flew so tantalisingly close above his head. It was a relief to be alone; only him and the skies spread out above him. It was anguish to be alone; only him here in the dark with his wife and son perhaps lost to him forever.

One evening he caught sight of himself in the still surface of the water and for an instant he had no idea who this heavily bearded man might be. The sight frightened him so that he stood and undressed, examining himself to ensure that he was still there, that it was still him. Muscled and strong, but very thin, the knobs on both ankles and wrists far too protruding under his skin. He ran a hand down his ribs – he could count them all – and studied his member, sluggish in the dark hair of his groin. He prodded it with a finger and his cock rose half-heartedly before it shrank back into inertia. All there, more or less, but for how much longer?

# CHAPTER 8

It all started to go wrong in the first week of June. Alex woke to creaking boards, to straining ropes and to the disorienting sensation of being on a roller coaster, with waves of nausea washing through her.

"Oh my God," she groaned after having thrown up for the third time. "What's the matter with the stupid boat?" Mrs Gordon shrugged and told her they were in the midst of a storm.

"Unseasonal, the captain says, very unusual."

"You have the most fantastic ability of saying the wrong things at the wrong time." Alex fumbled again for the basin.

The captain ordered all passengers indoors, tied down his ship as well as he could and grimly sat it out, refusing to consider sleep for the four days the storm raged. Everything heaved, a goat was lifted straight out of its pen and disappeared bleating into the sea, and in the galley the cook struggled to secure his foodstuffs, narrowly avoiding being crushed by a rolling keg of beer. Worst of all was the woman. For some reason, yon Nell had not been in the hold when the storm broke, but appeared halfway through the second day from the direction of the cramped forward space just beyond the forecastle.

"Nell?" The captain wiped at his face. "Is that Nell?" Smith shouted back that aye it was, and what was the daft lass thinking off, she should have stayed where she was.

"Why was she ..." the captain broke off. He was no fool, after all, and from the look on Smith's face he reckoned wee Nell was now the owner of two pink stockings. Besides, at present Nell's morals were not his prime concern, her safety was.

Inch by inch Nell progressed towards the hold, moving crabwise over the heaving deck. The captain hollered at her to go back, to not brave the open deck, but the wind snatched the words out of his mouth, and to his dismay she pressed on, so drenched her garments glued themselves like a second skin to her body. Captain Miles prayed; loudly he begged the good Lord to see her safe, no matter that she was an unrepentant whore. The lass was halfway to the hold when the wave came crashing down, sweeping her into the raging sea.

There was another storm; and another. The goats were all swept away, two of the crew were washed overboard, and in the hold a couple of women sickened and died without there being any possibility of sinking them with ceremony into the sea.

"I've never seen anything like this," Captain Miles said to a very green Alex. "Three storms in a row, aye?" He shook his head and glared in the general direction of the stubbornly overcast sky. He needed to take a mark to establish their position, because at present he had no idea where they were. Never during his thirty years at sea had he felt so totally lost.

On St. John's Eve the weather changed, and for some weeks they made good progress, even if the captain concluded that they'd been blown severely off course.

"Backwards," he sighed. At the captain's insistence the crew fished, and for several days all they ate was fish, Captain Miles keeping a concerned eye on his food supplies. The cook agreed, and together the two men began rationing, both of them worried that this was not yet the end.

"I feel it," Davies the cook told the captain. "I can smell it. There be other storms coming."

Captain Miles agreed; he felt it too, in every bone of his body he felt it.

It began as a squall, developed with horrifying speed into a thunderstorm that sent the *Regina Anne* bucking hither and thither over waves the size of houses. Lightning tore through the night, and Alex lay in her berth and shrieked in panic, because she didn't want to disappear, please don't throw me into another age, don't take me away from him.

She was so distraught that Mrs Gordon went to find Don Benito, who knelt on the damp floor beside Alex' berth telling her that all would be well, for surely she couldn't think their Heavenly Father intended them to die like this?

She grabbed at him; her fingers sank into his forearms. Here was what she needed, an anchor to hold on to, and if she hurt him he didn't say, allowing her to hide against his chest. At every clap of thunder she opened her mouth and screamed, deaf to Mrs Gordon's soothing sounds and Don Benito's assurances. What did they know? Had they ever been sent flying through time?

"Matthew!" she screamed. "I want my Matthew!"

Don Benito prayed; a low, constant mumble in Latin that Alex found enervating rather than comforting. But she didn't have the energy to tell him to shut up, and there was Mrs Gordon, kneeling down beside the priest. Her alto joined his baritone, English mingled with Latin in a heartfelt plea for mercy and deliverance from an untimely death. God seemed to be busy with other things; the ship continued to toss like a walnut shell across the seas.

Alex held on tight to Don Benito, she closed her eyes and prayed as well, a long stream of please and damn you mixed together. And then, just as suddenly as it had come, the storm waned, leaving a limping, damaged *Regina Anne* to roll in long, soothing swells. In her berth Alex slumped into a deep sleep, her pillow pressed to her sweaty chest.

All through the day Alex slept, waking that night to the stifling heat of the confined cabin. After several hours of tossing on the lumpy mattress she gave up. To sleep in this cramped space with Mrs Gordon snoring was impossible, so she wrapped a shawl around her shoulders and slipped outside.

It was a tropical night, warm and soft it enveloped Alex in a cloak of darkness, and she drifted over to lean her elbows against the railings. She stretched and wondered as she always did what Matthew might be doing and if he was alive and well. She looked deep inside of her and yes, there it was, the certainty that he was still here on this earth and it filled her with peace.

She gazed down into the dark waters. Strange that in the middle of the night the sea should be so alight with colours, swirling greens and bright blues and wasn't there a quickly growing point of light? She stared at the sluggish maelstrom of flaring colours that was forming in the sea, her heart rate peaking in a matter of seconds. A time funnel – just like the one she'd been sucked into three years ago. Alex emitted a whimper, half closing her eyes against the pull of the whirling waters and the accompanying nausea. She heard singing, and from the sea rose veils of fog, shimmering in purples and greens, shot through with bolts of dazzling light.

She clutched at the railing. No way was she going to allow herself to be dragged down into another time. The music faded, her stomach settled, and she couldn't keep herself from peeking, and there in the water was Magnus, standing on a boat as well. He looked happy, his arm around a woman he kissed and murmured something to. He turned, and for an instant they could both see each other, and on Magnus' face Alex saw an expression of absolute joy that she supposed must be mirrored in her own.

"*Pappa?*" she croaked.

"*Lilla hjärtat?*" he replied, using his own special endearment for her.

She so wanted to let go off the railing and extend her hand towards him, but she didn't dare to, if anything tightening her hold on the worn wood. The sea heaved and murmured, her father's face was so very close, but Alex hung on, fingers aching. Magnus began to fade.

"What year?" he called.

"1661, Alex Graham." She saw him nod and raise his hand in one last wave and then he was gone, swallowed into the receding point of light. "Bloody hell," she muttered as she unclenched her hands from the railing. She rubbed at her face, drew in several steadying breaths and slid down to sit before her knees gave way.

She started at the sight of the priest, standing a few metres downwind from her.

"What was that?" Don Benito squeaked.

"What?"

"The man in the water, who was he?" Don Benito peered down into the water and crossed himself.

"He's my father." She threw him a sidelong glance. Maybe this undercover priest could make sense of her story, because she sure couldn't. "Or rather, he will be my father, when I'm born in 1976."

Don Benito looked as if his jaw had permanently dislocated itself from the rest of his face.

"1976? *Ay, Madre de Dios!*"

Alex leaned back against the railings, her face towards the stars. "May I tell you? Under the seal of confession?"

"Yes, you may." He sat down beside her. "That's why you know they'll dig a new channel for the Guadalquivir! And you know my city well, but as it will be three centuries from now."

"It won't really change that much, not in the parts that exist today. It will still be a city that sleeps through the heat of the summer to wake at dusk, and the Madonnas will still be carried from their churches to the cathedral for their annual blessings." He liked that, she could see, his face acquiring that dreamy look it always wore when he spoke of his beloved city. Alex pulled up her knees and tightened her arms round them.

"It all began with a lightning storm," she said. "Suddenly I was thrown out of my time and landed here." Don Benito opened and closed his mouth several times, looking like a landed goldfish.

"Lightning?" he managed to say.

"I don't know if it's the lightning, not really. I think it's

60

crossroads – perfect intersections that occasionally open up a gap in time, funnels of bright colour and blinding light. Lightning or heat seems to help."

"Crossroads?" The priest looked at the sea and then back at her.

"I know." Alex made a face. "But this was different. More of a peep hole than a chasm."

"That's why the storm frightened you so much."

"I can't go back, I can't leave Matthew behind, it would tear me to pieces." She twisted at her wedding ring, counting the turns like she always did; one for every month she'd known Matthew.

"But you must have left people when you came," Don Benito's voice was very gentle.

"Yes, I did; but this is my place. I belong here – with him."

Over the coming hour she told him everything; of how she'd met Matthew, of Luke and his cruel, vindictive streak and how this journey was a quest to find her man before it was too late. At his insistence she told him of that earlier life, now so hazy she sometimes imagined it was all a dream. She told him of Magnus, of John and of Isaac. Isaac... She paused and looked at him.

"Some years before all of this happened I had a pretty bad experience," she said, "and all at the hands of a man called Ángel Muñoz de Hojeda." She shivered at the name; a man who had started out as a wonderful and conscientious lover had morphed into quite the creative jailer.

"What?" Don Benito breathed.

"The day you came on board I actually thought it was him, here, however impossible." She bit at her lip. "You look just like him, or rather he looks just like you. The same eyes, the same facial structure, even the same mouth. Thank heavens you don't use your first name." She sneaked her audience of one a look. In the weak light of from the stars and the waning moon his eyes were black ink stains in a very pale face.

"What did he do to you, this future relative of mine?"

What didn't he do? Alex trembled, her brain taken over by images she generally kept well at bay. And all because Ángel intended to use Alex to trap her witch mother, destroy Mercedes once and for all.

"A lot," she abbreviated, "and I ended up pregnant." She omitted to tell him that the future Ángel had ended up immolated, courtesy of her weird mother. "So somewhere in the future lives a boy, Isaac, and he's my son and the son of your descendant." She laughed and took his hand. "Except of course that he'll not be your direct descendant – given your profession, I mean."

Don Benito averted his eyes.

"Can it happen to anyone?" he said after some moments of silence.

"I guess so. And…" she hesitated but then decided there was no reason not to tell. "I saw a painting in a shop front two years ago, a small, very bright painting that made my head spin." A square of swirling blues and greens, of miniature whirlwinds that drew your eye to the white, throbbing point of light at its centre. And if you looked for too long, or leaned in too far, she'd been told you'd be sucked in as well – but she didn't know, she added, suppressing a tremor, she'd never actually seen it work. Don Benito's mouth hung open, yawning so wide he could easily have swallowed a suckling pig. Okay, okay, that was an exaggeration, but not that far off.

"The strangest thing is that I knew immediately who had painted the picture," Alex said, eyeing him nervously. "My mother."

"*Ay, Dios mío!*" He crossed himself – twice. She totally agreed.

Don Benito's head rang with snippets of prayers and hymns, short incoherent sequences of holy words that he hoped would protect him. He snuck Alex a look, crossed himself yet again. A painting, she said, a painting filled with evil,

evil witchcraft, and he, God help him, he had one just like it in his cabin.

"*Proteja me, Señor,*" he mumbled, clasping his hands hard. The small oblong package, wrapped in oilcloth, was destined for the private collection of Sir William, courtesy of Charles the Second. The one time he'd seen it, he'd broken into a cold sweat, all of him overtaken by nausea. Why, oh why hadn't he refused to take it? But then, how could he have refused, him being nothing more than a servant to his royal master? An urge grew in him to retrieve the package and throw it overboard, but even as he thought it he knew he wouldn't do it – he couldn't do it, not when the king had personally addressed the parcel to the unknown Sir William.

"And where do these pictures lead?" He made an effort to sound casual.

"I don't know. I think they can lead you back. I burnt it, it seemed the right thing to do."

He nodded his silent agreement but chose not to tell her about the vivid blues that rested at the bottom of his bag.

"And your mother?"

"She's dead," Alex said shortly. "Very dead."

To distract himself from thinking about the painting and its creator – the woman who'd painted it had to be a witch, a most powerful witch – he asked Alex to tell him more about this future life. He gaped at her descriptions of this future world, every now and then bursting into incredulous, nervous laughter.

"And God?" Don Benito asked once Alex fell silent.

"Poor old God doesn't stand a fighting chance. I come from an age where proof is king, and how can you prove God exists?"

"But that's why it's called faith!" He shook his head at the idiocy of these future generations.

"Yes, but in my time man will prefer to believe in his own capacity to change his destiny rather than to leave it up to God."

Don Benito laughed. "Even now God expects you to

63

work for your happiness, child. He doesn't just drop things in your lap."

"He did to me," Alex said, "He gave me my husband. Will He take him from me, do you think?" She leaned against him, in an intimate but platonic gesture.

"*No hija.* He has given you to each other, no?"

She nodded and yawned, looking exhausted. He levered them both to stand. As they reached her cabin door he stopped her and drew his fingers in the sign of a cross on her forehead.

"You have faith; deep inside you know you do." He bent forward and kissed her on her cheek. "Go with God, child. *Que duermas con los ángeles, hija mía.*"

All that night Matthew sat beside her, and in his hands Alex could see the ruby that was her heart thudding steadily. Just before dawn she felt his lips brush her cheek and then he left her, his eyes a glinting green in his dark, tanned face.

# CHAPTER 9 – 2005

Magnus barely made it back to his cabin. Alex! Here, in the middle of the sea, framed by a wreath of twisting blues and greens. Just like in Mercedes' disturbing paintings, twists of colour that pulled you towards a pulsing centre. And the look in her eyes when she'd seen him… it made his heart sing with joy. Alex Graham, 1661. What was she doing here, halfway across the Atlantic? Taking a cruise perhaps, he suggested, bursting out in loud, nervous laughter. No; the one taking a cruise was him, courtesy of Diane and John who'd bundled him onto a plane and told him they expected him to come back exhausted.

"Do something about that frustrated libido of yours," Diane had said. "Let your cock see some action okay?" John had gone beetroot red, but Magnus had laughed and promised her he would. Just the thought of seeing some action had his cock stirring, and he had grinned when he opened his suitcase to find that Diane had added an emergency pack consisting of an assortment of condoms.

Now in his third week he spent more and more time with Eva, a woman a couple of years his junior who could drink like a horse and dance like a willow. One fantastic dancer, was Eva, and as Magnus wasn't exactly left footed they owned the dance floor, to the irritation of some of the younger cruise participants. Younger in this case being relative, he admitted, not having seen anyone that looked below forty.

A soft knock on the door interrupted any further musing, and Magnus opened to let in Eva and the bottle of champagne she was brandishing.

"Room service?"

"I can't recall ordering any."

"Age," Eva sighed. "Alzheimer's light."

Magnus pretended to be offended, but opened the door wide.

"He needed to."

"Absolutely, but did it never strike you that even men occasionally have a tendency to link sex with love?"

"No," she said, "it didn't."

John chuckled and gave her an amused I-told-you-so look.

It was not until they were seated that the conversation turned to the cruise, initially a rambling description of food and entertainment, but after a couple of minutes Magnus cleared his throat and after a quick look at Eva began to talk. Diane just stared at him. What on earth was he saying?

"You can't seriously expect us to believe this!" she said. "That's impossible."

"I'm just telling you what I saw," Magnus said. "On the third anniversary of her disappearance I saw Alex – in the sea"

"The projection of a sick, obsessed mind," Diane muttered.

"Maybe. Except that Eva saw it too."

Diane gave Eva a dark look. To agree to having seen an obvious delusion smelled of quite the opportunist, and God knew what this strange woman might be after. She lowered her eyes to the table and concentrated on chasing peas across her plate.

"So what exactly did you see?" John asked.

"She was on board an old wooden ship – like the replica of the Golden Hind down in London – and she was standing by the railings, looking at me."

"In a polka dot bandana and with an eye patch, no doubt," Diane broke in.

"No," Magnus said with an icy edge. "She wasn't dressed like a Halloween pirate."

"But why would she be on a ship?" John's voice coloured with concern, and Diane swallowed back on a wave of jealousy.

"No idea," Magnus said. He dragged his hand through his thick hair, scrubbing at it until it stood untidily around his head.

"Early form of charter tourism?" Eva put in.

"Yeah," Diane snorted, very irritated with this woman. "Down to the fleshpots on the Canary Islands."

"At least I know the year," Magnus said. "1661. And I have a name, Alex Graham."

"You were wrong, though," John said to Magnus. "You said you thought she was somewhere close to here. But you saw her on a ship, so obviously she isn't here, she's somewhere else."

Diane rolled her eyes; seen her on a ship? Why was John encouraging him, for all the world sounding as if he believed this preposterous tale?

"She could come back," Magnus replied. "Maybe she just went on a trip."

"In 1661?" Eva sounded very doubtful. "People didn't do much globetrotting then, definitely not women." She grimaced. "Women stayed at home and had babies."

Many babies, Diane thought, and then they died around fifty, looking like seventy-five. She felt a flash of pity for Alex, a flash mirrored in Eva's eyes. Neither Magnus nor John had caught on, busy discussing why Alex would have been at sea.

"Maybe she *is* a pirate," John suggested, jumping up to adopt a ferocious pose, his coffee spoon an imaginary cutlass.

"Don't be an idiot," Diane snapped, "it's not even funny."

John held up his hands in a conciliatory gesture, mumbled something about checking on the girls, and left the room.

"Well it isn't," Diane said defensively. "Actually there's nothing funny about this at all, is there?"

"No," Magnus sighed, "you're right. If Alex is – or was – living in the seventeenth century then she's had to cope with a life for which she was totally unprepared. And that's not even mildly amusing, it's just bloody frightening." He shrank together, his tall frame stooping under an invisible burden.

Diane leaned forward to clasp his hand. "She'll manage."

"You think?" Magnus' voice wobbled.

"Of course she will; she's just like you, stubborn to a fault."

"Oh dear," Eva murmured. "Is that a compliment?"

Diane tilted her head to the side. "In Alex' case yes, in Magnus' case I'm not so sure. He can be quite difficult, you know."

"Difficult?" Magnus' voice fluted into a squeak. "Me?"

Diane laughed and took the opportunity to steer the conversation away from Alex.

# CHAPTER 10

As summer came to an end, Matthew detoured as often as he could to look down the narrow road. Shouldn't she be here by now? He tried to count backwards from his own arrival to now, and deep inside he began to worry that perhaps she wouldn't come, hoping he would somehow make it home himself. He would never get back on his own; he'd done four months of eighty- four, and so far he hadn't spoken to any one of the field hands that had seen anyone survive more than four, perhaps five years.

He was shrinking at a worrying pace, the combination of an insufficient diet and long, gruelling days under a relentless sun. He scratched; bug bites all over but as yet no lice, something he feared was shortly due to change given to the way Elijah's long, unkempt hair crawled with them. Matthew exhaled, shaking his head. A few lice were not his major problem. Why hadn't she come? He stood staring down the lane, willing her to appear until there was no daylight left.

"Mayhap she's forgotten you," Elijah said one evening.

Matthew scowled; he could see it in their faces, how amused they were by his conviction that one day Alex would come to buy him free.

"And anyway, who's ever heard of a woman setting off alone across the world?"

Matthew lunged, spitting with anger and suppressed fear, and he had to be pulled off Elijah before he beat his face to pulp.

"You mustn't say such," Matthew said between heaving breaths, glaring at Elijah. "My Alex will come, aye? She will, because she knows I need her."

"Aye, man, of course she will," Davy said, "it's just that Elijah is jealous."

"I'm not," Elijah said, "I have my own woman at home. And two lasses. She was with child the last time I saw her, and I never knew if it was a lad or yet another lass."

"You will, some day," Davy tried.

"You think?" Elijah shook his head. "Nay, Davy, I think not. This is where I die. This is where all of us die, including you Matthew." He scooted backwards, away from Matthew.

"I won't die here," Matthew said. "I won't die like an overworked nag."

Davy coughed heavily. "But you are," he said to Matthew. "An overworked, underfed nag. And how will you, or any of us, survive seven years of this?" They all fell silent, contemplating the truth in that.

"We should run away, now," Elijah said, "we'd be well gone by daybreak."

"And go where?" Matthew said. "To Jamestown? The constables would drag you back here before noon." The constables, the magistrates… to hear it, Fairfax had them all in his pocket.

"Aye," Davy said, "and Jones would …" His voice tailed off. Matthew crossed his arms and stuck his hands into his armpits.

Elijah looked from one to the other. "We could go the other way – sneak off into the wilderness," he muttered.

Into the thick, unknown forest with venomous snakes littering the ground. Matthew suspected Jones and Sykes exaggerated the threat of snakes, and so far he hadn't seen any himself, but he'd seen one man carried in from the furthest fields, mouth open in silent agony. Jones had placed him in one of the sheds, sat a stone jar of cane liquor at his mouth and left the man to die, informing them there was nothing to be done for a rattlesnake bite.

"Nay, Elijah," Duncan said with a note of shame in his voice. "I fear that thick, green growth." Davy nodded in agreement, leaning against his twin. He coughed, a rattling sound that was echoed by his brother.

"And you?" Elijah asked Matthew.

Matthew shook his head. "She would never find me there. And I don't like snakes."

"Me neither," Elijah said, "but there are human snakes as well, no?"

Matthew nodded; aye, there were definitely human serpents, and chief among them was his own brother. With a little sigh he stood, grabbed at his blanket and with a muttered good night made for the door.

"May I come?"

Matthew stopped mid step, wanting very much to say no, but the sight of Elijah's battered face shamed him into saying yes, and so there were two that slipped out into the night to sleep by the little spring. Elijah dipped his hand in the spring, laughing at the feel of cool, clean water on his skin. Matthew smiled, and half stripped to wash.

"You wash all that?" Elijah sounded amazed, even worried.

"I try," Matthew said, patting himself dry with his dirty shirt. He sat down against the tree he had come to consider as his own. The sky was overcast tonight, the air oppressive with concentrated humidity.

"Are you that sure then?" Elijah asked, breaking a long stretch of silence. "That she will come for you?"

"Aye," Matthew said, slapping at a midget. Yes, of course she would come; something had delayed her, but soon she'd be here and... he halted himself mid thought. Something had delayed her! She might have found herself with child, and then how could she cross the sea to find him? He counted rapidly on his fingers. Now it was August and any child would have been conceived at the latest in early January, so then it wasn't even born yet. And before it was weaned and she could leave the wean it would be another year and by then he would be dead. No; he shook his head. He wouldn't be dead. Somehow he had to live.

Matthew's nights at the spring came to an end one evening when Jones stumbled upon him sitting in the dark.

"What are you doing here?" Jones demanded in a menacing voice.

Matthew was already on his feet, his back hard against the trunk behind him.

"It gets so hot in the shed," he said, angered at the defensiveness in his voice.

"Oh dear, and that of course is insufferable for a man here due to a 'miscarriage of justice'," Jones chuckled at his own jibe. "Mayhap you'd like a bed as well, and perhaps a window." Matthew didn't reply. Jones swatted Matthew lightly over his arm. "Get back, and in the future you stay where I put you or I'll have you under lock and key."

Matthew had no doubt he meant it and hurried off in the direction of the shed.

Jones lined up all the men the day they began the harvest. Field after field in which the tobacco plants were to be cut, long wooden sleds on which to load them and then the hard, never ending trudge dragging the sled behind until it was all unloaded in the yard. He smiled to himself. This was when quite a few of the new men would balk; no man was comfortable being harnessed like a mule to a sled. He needed strong men, and his eyes rested for a while on Matthew. Since the incident in the barn there'd only been one time where he'd had to beat him properly, the day the stupid man protested that they were not being adequately fed, otherwise Graham had kept his head to the ground, avoiding any kind of conflict. But now and then Jones caught a vivid green stare from those hidden eyes, and he nodded to himself: definitely on one of the sleds – Matthew Graham needed to be broken once and for all.

To Jones' mild disappointment Matthew didn't protest at being strapped into the leather harness, nor did he say anything when Jones indicated the sled. He just nodded and adjusted the straps to minimise the chafing. One of the other new men – Elijah? Jones couldn't remember – did protest, but a vicious cut across his shoulders made him shut up. Out of the corner of his eye Jones saw Graham tense at the treatment of his friend, but the wide shoulders slumped when Jones turned to look him in the face, the riding crop raised.

All that day Matthew pulled. His shoulders throbbed with pain, his legs were shaking with exertion after each load, and still Jones sent him back for more, flicking his crop in the air to indicate Matthew had to hurry, he was falling behind the harvesters.

"Water," Matthew panted at midday. "I must have some water." He leaned forward, bracing himself against his knees. Jones signalled to one of the women busy sorting tobacco leaves and she came towards him with a ladle. "Thank you," Matthew said hoarsely. The woman smiled, a very nice smile, and Matthew smiled back, noting the golden hair and deep brown eyes.

"Kate," she replied to his unspoken question. "I'm Kate."

"I'm Matthew — Matthew Graham."

"I know," she said, "of course I know." Her mouth softened into yet another little smile.

Jones cut any further conversation short, and Matthew went back to his work. But every time Matthew came in with a load, Kate contrived to be there, ladle in her hand, and each time Matthew drank he met her eyes, smiling his thanks.

Five unbearable days, and on the afternoon of the sixth day he was so tired that he accidentally upended the whole sled, tipping the load of tobacco plants into the dirt. Jones flew at him.

"Fool! Look at what you've done!"

Matthew got to his feet, an effort involving far too many protesting muscles. His shoulders were permanently on fire, the harness had left broad, bleeding sores on his skin, and no matter how he tried to use his worn shirt as padding the sores deepened and widened, a constant, flaming pain.

"I'll just load them back." He bent to pick up an armful. His arms were clumsy with weariness, and it took far too long to reload the sled, with Jones an irate, vociferous spectator. Matthew leaned forward into the straps, bunching his thighs. Dear Lord! He couldn't budge the load, the leather cutting even deeper into his lacerated skin. He tried again, and still the sled wouldn't move. Matthew looked back across his shoulder to find Jones sitting on the sled.

"Go on," Jones sneered, "get a move on."

"You're too heavy," Matthew said, "you can walk, no?"

Jones raised a brow. "Of course I can. But now I want you to pull."

Matthew felt his pulse begin to thud. Wafting curtains of red clouded his vision.

"I'm a man, aye? I'll work as you tell me to, but you can move of your own accord, fat though you may be. I won't be your yoked beast, I'm a man." There was absolute silence around him, his companions staring at him with a mixture of admiration and exasperation.

Jones stood up and moved towards him. "That's where you're wrong, Graham. You're no man, not here, not now. You're a slave, a beast to be worked until you're no use." He looked at Matthew expectantly, his hand tightening on the handle of his crop.

Matthew knew he should back down, grovel and mumble but inside of him the fire grew, red hot rage at the man in front of him, at his traitorous brother and the injustice of it all.

"I told you, I've never done anything wrong. I'm a free man."

Jones laughed. "Free? Then why are you still here? Why aren't you on a ship back home?"

"You know why! I have no money."

"And we own you, until you can pay yourself free, we own you."

"Nay, no one owns me. I'm a free man."

"And I tell you you're but a slave," Jones hissed.

Matthew punched him straight into the face, having the distinct pleasure of hearing the cartilage in Jones' nose crack. That was really the last thing he observed clearly, then it was all hands and feet, and the stinging of the leather crop, and he heard Jones call men to him and Matthew had the shirt torn from his back, he was thrown face down onto the ground and then there was the snap of leather that came down time and time again on his bared skin. One of his arms was twisted up behind his back, and in his ear he heard Jones' heavy breathing.

"So, what are you?"

"A free man," Matthew gasped. The pressure on his arm was tearing at his tendons.

"What are you?"

Bend! Alex shrieked in his head, for God's sake Matthew, bend. But he didn't want to, he had to salvage some pride, and the pain in his shoulder increased to the point where he knew it would soon be dislocated.

"What are you?" Jones hissed again, throwing his considerable weight against Matthew's trapped arm. Matthew groaned. Please! Alex cried, please, Matthew, for me. Don't let him maim you for life, my love, please! In his fuddled state Matthew wasn't sure if she was here for real or if it was a hallucination, but the despair in her voice rang through his head.

"I'm a slave," Matthew mumbled, closing his eyes so that he might still see Alex, not the dirty red earth an inch from his nose.

"What? I didn't hear you."

"I'm a slave," Matthew mumbled again.

"Say it out loud." Jones heaved Matthew to his feet. "Look at all the men before you and say it." To his everlasting shame Matthew did as he was told.

"I am a slave," he said, repeating it time and time again until Jones let him go to tumble to the ground.

He lay where he had fallen, and around him he heard the sound of people moving off, leaving him to lie unaided. No one dared to touch him, lest Jones should vent his anger on them as well, and Matthew found himself staring at his hand, so close to his face. He didn't want to move. He no longer wanted to live.

77

"Please let me die, Sweetest Lord, just let me die." He closed his eyes and in his mind he saw Hillview, he saw a wee lad running up the lane to meet him and there she was, laughing and crying at the same time, her skirts bunched high as she flew towards him and he knew that of course he couldn't die. He owed it to Alex to stay alive; he owed it to himself.

# CHAPTER 11

Coleridge had it down pat, Alex thought, hanging over the railing. A hell of a lot of water, miles and miles of empty, shimmering sea and not a bloody drop to drink ... She licked her lips, wincing as the cracks broke open again. She did another turn back and forth across the poop deck and fanned herself. It wasn't funny actually; she could see in Captain Miles face that he was more than worried, and the crew was getting restless, the men scanning the sky with hopeful eyes that glazed at the sight of the perfect, unclouded blue. Yesterday a fight had broken out by the water barrel, and the captain and his mate had used cudgels to break it up, removing the barrel to stand under the beady eye of the cook.

Four weeks of strange winds and long stretches of lying becalmed; Captain Miles had never experienced anything like it, he told Alex, all the while straining his eyes in all directions for any sign that this weather would break. He looked exhausted, a greyish tinge to his skin that made Alex worry he might be developing a heart condition.

"So, do you know where we are?" Alex said.

"Aye, ma'am, I do. Much too far to the south."

Well, that didn't impress her; she could have told him that, given the heat.

He studied the sky to the north, shielded his eyes with his hand and looked for a long time at something he saw on the horizon.

"But we won't stay becalmed for long, it'll rain before the evening."

Alex gave him an incredulous look and made a great show of scanning the bright blue skies.

Captain Miles smiled and bowed, muttering something about needing to talk to the cook.

In the event Captain Miles was right, too right, and yet

again the *Regina Anne* bucked in a transformed sea, sails trimmed as much as they could. Alex spent three miserable days in her berth and when she made it out on deck it was to a speeding ship as the captain attempted to make up for lost time. Very many weeks of lost time as Alex pointed out, acerbically dropping a comment that tomorrow, the twenty-fourth of August, was her birthday, and she had hoped to spend the day reunited with her husband, not stuck in the middle of the sea.

"*Dios manda, querida,*" Don Benito said, patting Alex' hand. "At least now we won't thirst to death." No, but perhaps starve; Alex spent more time picking weevils out of the dry biscuits than actually eating anything. Not that she wanted to, shivering all over at the thought of swallowing one of those disgusting little bugs by mistake.

"There are definite advantages to modern life at time," Alex said. "Like now, a plane wouldn't come amiss." Don Benito listened with interest as Alex described a plane, insisting that she draw one for him as well.

"Seven hours to cross the ocean?" Don Benito stared down at the birdlike shape she had drawn on the deck .

"They're pretty fast." She studied the priest and laughed. "Should you really be believing everything I tell you?"

Don Benito gave her a confused look. "Are you lying?"

"No, but I would have thought the normal reaction to my story would be to make the sign against evil and then tie me to a stake." She glanced at him nervously. Maybe that's what he intended to do once they made landfall; have her dragged off to stand in front of a tribunal as a witch.

"Are you a witch?" Don Benito asked, his lips twitching.

"Of course not!"

"Well then," Don Benito shrugged. He frowned down at the water. "Why shouldn't I believe you? Do you think your tale is that extraordinary?"

Alex made a derisive noise. "Why would I think that? I keep on falling over time travellers all the time."

"There are probably more than you think, no? And to a

man that accepts the miracle of God's creation, of immaculate conception and the birth of God's son as a mere human, your story is just another example of God's amazing... His amazing..."

"...sense of humour?" Alex suggested.

Don Benito laughed. "God most certainly has a sense of humour, but I was looking for another word... complexity! Yes, that's it."

"Hmm," Alex replied.

"I've decided to make for Barbados," Captain Miles informed them over supper.

"Barbados?" Alex said. "But that's miles from Virginia!"

"I have to get the ship repaired, and we lack victuals to make it all the way to Virginia."

"And how long will that take?" Two weeks? A month? Surely not more than that, right?

"I make it that we will be in Barbados in four weeks at best, and then some months for repairs...I am sorry Mrs Graham, but you won't make it to Virginia this year. The seas are restless in the final months of the year – only a fool would attempt a crossing." He threw out his hands in a helpless gesture. "What am I to do? I have a damaged ship, a crew to pay and a hold of starving lasses."

"And from Barbados to Virginia? How long does that take?" Alex tried to sound matter-of-fact when all she really wanted to do was retreat to her cabin and cry. But she couldn't, could she? After all, she'd made herself a promise.

Captain Miles pursed his mouth. "Anything from three weeks to six."

Alex frowned while she calculated how much this would cost her. So far, she had plenty of money left in one form or another, she and Mrs Gordon carried important quantities sown into their waistbands. But a month, or even several months in Barbados...

"And will you be reimbursing me for the passage? I bought a passage to Virginia, not to Barbados."

Captain Miles dragged a hand over his face. "I'll tell you what I'll do. Once the ship is repaired I'll sail you up to Jamestown myself. But it will not be this year. I'm sorry for that, but it is out of my hands."

Alex pressed her hands against her churning stomach and Captain Miles wilted under her eyes.

"He'll be alright, your man will be waiting for you."

"How do you know?" She stood up so abruptly the chair fell over backwards. "How the hell do you know?"

Don Benito rose and placed a hand on her arm. "I think the captain means that it would take a very brave man to die away from you."

She shrugged him off and left the cabin at half run.

She woke when she hit the floor and rolled over onto her hands and knees. What a terrible dream! Her whole back hurt, as if the flogging she'd been dreaming of had been for real. Something was missing; she stood on all fours and searched for his beat, the sound of his heart, but inside her it was silent – very silent. Oh God, she gulped, he's dead! She sat down with a thud, and closed her eyes, listening inwardly with such concentration her head began to throb. Don't you dare Matthew Graham, don't you dare give up!

"Move," she whispered to the supine shape she saw in her head. "Move and go on living!" Fingers twitched, and inside of her the sonar echo of his heart began to thud. Slow and steady, deep and strong. She sank her face into her hands.

Next morning Don Benito came over to stand beside her.

"What is the matter?"

She lifted her shoulders and let them drop.

"I dreamt," she said, eyes fixed on the swift, dark shapes that escorted the ship underwater. "Do you think it's possible? That I can somehow dream of things that are happening to him? Because I do, and last night I dreamt that he almost died, that he no longer wanted to live." She wrinkled her brow in concentration. "But I told him; I told him that he had to live, and I saw him move." Alex fisted her hand and studied her wedding ring. What had they done to her Matthew, to her beautiful man, to leave him lifeless on the ground?

"I dream too," Don Benito sighed. "Night after night I dream, and I see her as she must be, not as she was, so yes, I believe it is possible to dream of what happens to someone you love." He turned to lean back against the railings, watching the mother who sat nursing her baby by the main mast. "I have a son." He filled his lungs and looked at Alex. "I've never seen him and never will, but his mother walks my waking mind, she sits burning in my heart and when I close my eyes to sleep I see her, and in her arms she holds a child."

"Is she pretty?"

Don Benito made a dismissive gesture. "I don't think so, she's no Helen, not even a Juliet. But to me she is beautiful, she has a smile that can melt a heart of stone, and when she laughs it sounds like rain falling in a pewter bucket. And I was wrong to ever touch her." He scratched at his chest for some time. The heavy hair shirt must be a torment in this heat, but when Alex had suggested he might stop using it he'd gone rigid, telling her that he was honour bound to wear it, a just penance for breaking his priestly vows.

"She's married since several months back, to a much older man. I hope he treats her kindly." He looked away. "I never intended to, I have been a priest for over fifteen years, and I have never had a problem with that particular vow. Until I met her, a woman I could laugh with."

"How did you meet?" Alex said, imagining all sorts of sordid scenes in the confessional booth.

"She was a maid in waiting to the princess Henriette," Don Benito said, "probably chosen for her somewhat plain face and her lovely voice. I was the chaplain, the up and coming man of God, delighted to find himself chosen by the Queen Mother to be a member of the exiled royal household." He grimaced. "It was wrong; I was entrusted with her spiritual wellbeing, and she came to talk to me so often about what she perceived as her vocation to serve Christ, her eyes glittering with longing. And then one evening as she was leaving she placed her hand on my sleeve and just... she just kissed me." The tip of his tongue darted out to wet his lips as if he were recapturing a sensation once experienced and since then lost.

In a low voice he detailed months of clandestine meetings, long afternoons spent in secret designations that were put to a brutal end the day the Queen Mother came upon them.

"She threatened me with public exposure, and berated poor Louise for having had the temerity to seduce a man of the Church. I tried to tell her that wasn't how it was, but my lady Queen ordered me to be quiet."

The next day he had been removed to a nearby Benedictine abbey, charged with doing heavy penance to expiate his sin. A month later a messenger came from the Queen, and he was informed that he had to find a home for the expected child.

"I turned to my brother, and he showed me great kindness by promising to raise the child as his own." At a price, he added, looking towards the east. Raúl had made it very clear that Benito was no longer welcome in Seville, disgraced priest that he was. And so it was all decided; Louise was to have the child and give it up and then she would be hurriedly wed – to a man chosen by the Queen Mother.

"I was never allowed to see her again, not even to write to her. Instead I was sent to accompany his Majesty when he returned to his kingdom last year."

Alex raised her brows, thinking he couldn't have loved this unknown Louise all that much, given how quickly he had given up. He frowned , shifting from foot to foot as he studied her face.

"You have not been much about the royals, have you? There is very little an ordinary man can do."

"Elope? Ride off into the night?"

He made a disparaging sound. Louise was used to a high level of comfort; how was he to keep her in such style? Well, he had her there. Alex had no idea what a former priest could do for a living, suspecting that whatever options available would lead to penury.

"Are you still a priest?" Alex asked.

"Yes, I will remain always a priest. The ordination is a sacrament that cannot be reversed, but somehow I feel God has turned his face away from me. I have been charged with a mission, and that's why I'm going to Virginia. Not as a representative of the Tabacalera." He turned towards her. "I'm carrying certain things from the King to his Governor, that much is true, but my main task has been given me by his mother. I am to spread the word of God – among the heathen Indian tribes." He looked at her bleakly. "Do you think they will be willing to listen? Or do you think they will put me to death?"

"I don't know." She gnawed at her lip. "I don't think you should do this, to me it smells of petty revenge, not of any genuine wish to bring the word of God to the Indians."

Don Benito blinked. "Not do as I've been ordered to?"

"Who would ever know?" She scrunched up her brows, thinking hard. "You could go south; to Cartagena de las Indias, or Lima. They would never ask where you came from or what you were fleeing from. No one would ever know."

"I would," he said severely. "And so would God."

"Was it worth it?" Alex asked after a few minutes.

"No, it wasn't. Had I fully understood the consequences, I think I would have held firmer to my vow, for her sake and mine." He exhaled loudly. "But I will love her, I think, until the day I die. Her and my son, the boy I'll never see."

Mrs Gordon was very impressed when Alex told her Don Benito was off to christen the heathen, voicing that even being a papist was better than living like an unknowing savage in the woods.

"Not that he will last long, narrow like a lass across the shoulders and not much flesh on him at all."

"Yes, you would know," Alex murmured. "Seeing as you've been spying on him."

Mrs Gordon chuckled and adjusted her collar to lie closer to her skin.

"He's right good looking, yon wee priest, well, he would be, if he weren't all red with rash." She bent down to rummage through her capacious canvas bag. After a while she gave a satisfied grunt and came up with a small stone jar, extending it to Alex. "You give it to him, it might help, no?"

Alex shook her head. "He wants it to hurt, that's why he's wearing that thing."

The last few weeks on the *Regina Anne* were miserable. Alex was torn in two with longing; she yearned for her son during the day and dreamed of her man at night, and the dreams were of a man that stared at her in supplication, hazel eyes dulled with months of toil. She woke to pillows that were soaked with her tears and a certainty that she had to hurry to his side, and she twisted in frustration because there was nothing she could do, no way she could hasten her voyage towards him. She avoided them all, sitting in solitude by the bow, her eyes locked on the west as she pleaded with him in her head to not give up.

Sometimes she pretended she could fly and saw herself beat her way swiftly to the as yet unseen shore. And she found him, a small speck that grew recognisable as she dove towards the ground, and she swished by like a daring swift, turning to dart by him time and time again, until he lifted his face from his work to follow the bird's spectacular flight. She hoped he knew it was her, that the bird he saw was her longing reaching across the world to softly graze his cheek.

# CHAPTER 12

Alex was very relieved when they anchored in the deep bay just off Bridgetown. She'd been to Barbados once before, and she looked with surprise at the unexploited coastline. No calypso beats in the air, no enthusiastic American tourists in flower print shirts and very few black people. Instead, a lot of scruffy looking white people, fair skin either deeply tanned or an unbecoming flaking pink, that stood and studied the limping *Regina Anne*.

"Journeymen," Captain Miles explained. "Carpenters, coopers, sail makers… And they can see I'll be needing their services." Alex nodded, looking round. The main mast had been expertly repaired at sea, but the mizzen mast needed to be replaced – even she could see that – and there were holes in the planking on the port side. The captain squinted up at his sails.

"I'll need a new lanteen," he muttered, which was more or less Greek to Alex. "But otherwise they just need to be mended."

"Couldn't the women help you repair them?"

Captain Miles gave her a condescending look. "A sail requires special skills, it's not just a matter of pushing a wee needle through some fabric."

"Well, excuse me," Alex muttered, and went back to studying the harbour.

"Are there no slaves?" she asked a bit later, gesturing in the direction of the assembled men.

"Aye there are. Very many. But they are inland on the plantations. All sugar now, a harsh crop as I hear it." He sighed and looked at Alex. "There are many kind of slaves, Mrs Graham. And here you find a number of white slaves. Irish, aye? And a number of our countrymen as well, barbadosed here by the Protector that was."

"Barbadosed?"

"Another word for what happened to your husband, but in this case with the support of the powers that be." He described the events briefly; thousands of Irish men lifted off the street and transported over to work in the heat, many with no limit to their term of service. "As for black slaves, aye, they are brought over in very large numbers." He compressed his mouth, muttering something about not stomaching the way some of the planters treated their property.

If the *Regina Anne* looked battered, so did her crew and passengers. Alex' skirt slid down her hips with every step she took, and even if she had tightened the stays as hard as they went, they filled very little function, moulding more air than flesh. Her hands were a startling brown as were her feet, her hair had the general appearance of a crow's nest – brittle and dry it screamed for egg yolks – and all of her was coated with a salty glaze. At least all her teeth were there, thanks not only to regular cleaning but to the dried apricots she had been munching throughout.

Don Benito was equally thin, the crew members looked starved, Captain Miles had tightened his belt into a third new notch, and Mrs Gordon looked entirely unchanged. Still the same ample bosom, and Alex knew first hand that those stays still hugged tight around a round, strong body. Probably the beer, Alex concluded, and gave Davies a narrow look. No doubt he'd been slipping Mrs Gordon more than her ration at times. Come to think of it, the cook wasn't looking all that ravaged either.

Alex was handed down into a longboat and held on tight for the short but choppy ride to the harbour proper. Mrs Gordon struck up a conversation with one of the rowers, and after only a couple of words discovered this to be a Scotsman, a carrot headed man with, in Alex' opinion, awful teeth. Mrs Gordon frowned as he rowed back out for his next load.

"Papist – one of them Highland folk."

"Oh," Alex nodded, not really that interested.

She regarded her surroundings with curiosity. What looked like a transplanted English seaside town rose round her; a picturesque cluster of buildings along the wharves that lined what Captain Miles called the careenage, tree lined streets – or maybe tree lined dirt roads was more correct – and a little church in the distance. There were some very English houses, somewhat incongruous in the heat, but adapted by additions of balconies and verandas to the needs of tropical living. A strong breeze tugged at her hat, and Alex clapped down one hand on her head to keep it in place.

Not only were there very few black people versus what she remembered, but there were also very few women. To be quite correct, at present there were only two women on the wharf, namely Mrs Gordon and herself. She was aware of hungry eyes travelling down her body, and moved closer to Mrs Gordon who stared back at the men with a warning look in her dark eyes.

"You knee them," she said. "If they get too fresh you knee them. Hard."

"Thank you," Alex murmured back. "I'll be sure to remember." She bit back a smile; let them come too close and she'd do more than knee them – she'd send them flying, courtesy of the martial arts skills she still, at some level, retained. She rose up and down on her toes a couple of times, tensed the muscles of her right forearm, her hand. She might not be able to smash a board anymore, but she could definitely fight should she need to.

"What about the women?" Alex asked the Captain once he came ashore. He studied the surrounding men and shook his head.

"It will be best to take them ashore this evening."

"Or…" Alex prompted.

"Or I might find myself without any women to deliver to Virginia."

"Do you think they would mind? Staying here instead?"

"Some no. But some have family already in Virginia, and they will want to reach Jamestown safely. Besides," he added,

" the rich planters here find their own wives, and the poor white settlers don't have the money required to buy a wife."

"Ah," Alex nodded, pursing her mouth. He flushed and looked away.

Alex looked at the bed with pleasure. No more nights sleeping like a curled eel, here she would be able to stretch out, even if sharing a bed with Mrs Gordon was somewhat daunting. The room was bright with sunlight, shutters thrown wide to the afternoon breeze, and Mrs Gordon fingered the thin gauze hung over the bed with a disdainful face.

"Not much of a bed hanging, aye?"

"It's to keep you from being eaten alive by the midgets." Alex returned her attention to the basin, already filled to the brim with delicious cool freshwater, a relief to her skin after all these months using only saltwater. "Tomorrow I'm going to wash every single piece of clothing I own," Alex said, sniffing at her least dirty shift.

"Mmm," Mrs Gordon agreed.

Across the landing Alex could hear Don Benito installing himself in the room he was to share with Captain Miles. Clean and reputable as their lodgings were, the captain showed a strong streak of parsimony, arguing that none of them really needed more than half a bed anyway, and surely Don Benito wouldn't mind sharing, would he? He would; very much, but as he couldn't explain why without letting the whole company know he was living in a stinking hair shirt, he'd agreed.

"*Que hago?*" he asked Alex with desperation. "What do I do?"

"You could take it off," Alex suggested receiving an uncompromising look in return. "Well, in that case you'll just have to sleep with it under your shirt – as you've been doing all the time."

Don Benito looked very depressed. "I scratch, all night I scratch."

"In which case the captain will conclude you have fleas

and leave the room to you." Alex narrowed her eyes at him. "Do you have fleas? Have you even washed properly since you started using that... thing?"

"Of course I have," Don Benito said with dignity. "And I do not think I have fleas. Perhaps lice, but not fleas."

"In my book not a major improvement," Alex said, stepping away from him.

"Nor in mine," Don Benito sighed, scratching himself over the chest. He offered her his arm and led them off in the direction of the dining room and the waiting food.

Mr Coulter beamed at his guests, which if anything only accentuated his face's general resemblance to a foot.

"I am honoured," he said, bowing in their direction, "two ladies, no less, to grace my table." Alex had to bite her lip to stop herself from laughing at his appearance. Heavy, silvered locks hung to his shoulders, topped by a shiny bald dome that began at ear height.

"It looks like an egg with a grass skirt," she said to Mrs Gordon. "He should shave it all off."

"Aye well," Mrs Gordon muttered back, "it's very nice hair, no?" She smiled at their host, revealing bright white teeth, her dark eyes crinkling together so that they glittered in the sun that streamed in through the windows.

Mr Coulter couldn't stop staring at Mrs Gordon. Repeatedly his eyes returned to travel over her dark bodice, the pristine white collar and cuffs. Alex was totally ignored, a cursory glance in her direction no more, before Mr Coulter went back to his fascinated inspection of Mrs Gordon. Alex almost felt insulted.

"Have you lived here long?" Alex asked, sipping at the soup. Soup! Boiling hot as well, and she already damp with perspiration between her breasts, on the back of her thighs and under her arms.

"Ten years, I came here to help the reverend, and have stayed on..." Mr Coulter's eyes moistened. "It's my wife, you see, she died six years ago, and I can't leave her, can I? Not to lie untended here."

"No, of course not," Mrs Gordon said. "And you must show me tomorrow where she lies, aye?"

Alex looked at her in surprise. She was flirting with him! From across the table Captain Miles glared at nothing in particular and Alex turned to look at Mrs Gordon again. Primly she sipped at her soup, her back straight, one hand folded in her lap. And when she put the spoon down she stretched even straighter, breathing deeply. Mr Coulter's eyes were glued to her generous bosom, as were Captain Miles', both men hypnotised by the rise and fall of that swell.

"*A cada uno lo suyo*," Don Benito said, catching Alex' eye. Absolutely, and in this case both men apparently found Mrs Gordon to be their cup of tea. This was going to be a most interesting winter.

The first few days on land, Alex spent trying to find a ship going to Virginia, but what few vessels were presently moored in the Barbados harbour were all destined to cross the Atlantic towards Europe, their holds filling up with hogshead after hogshead of sugar.

"I told you," Captain Miles said.

"And that doesn't help one whit," Alex snapped.

The captain's brow furrowed, the corners of his mouth drooped, giving him the overall look of a basset hound.

"I know," he sighed. "And I'm right sorry. But what was I to do, when all the elements conspired against me?"

Alex had no idea; she pinched herself hard to stop the tears from welling and walked off to kick stones into the water until she had herself under control. Behind her, she heard the captain shuffling, but she waited until he moved away before turning to hurry back to the boarding house.

"So, has he complained?" Alex asked a week or so later, jerking her head in the direction of the captain strolling a few yards before them. "About you scratching yourself."

"No," Don Benito yawned. "But then how would he

notice? He sleeps like the dead, on his back, and he snores. And farts."

"We all do. It might have to do with all the beans we're getting."

Don Benito grinned. "I love beans, they remind me of my father. He was very fond of beans."

"Well I'm not," Alex sulked, "at least not on a daily basis. How about some fish? Or a nice roasted chicken?" She curtsied to an elderly man who bowed to her, and continued their desultory walk along the crooked little streets of Bridgetown. A very industrious little town, it teemed with men who all gave her the eye, looking her over as if assessing her potential as a breeding wife – it made her itch.

"I don't think the cook knows how to, or maybe he just doesn't want to." Don Benito bowed to yet another man who eyed him with some misgiving, muttering something about garish foreigners. Alex suppressed a smile. Don Benito was very flamboyant in these new surroundings where men opted for dark, broad brimmed hats, narrow breeches, shirts and open coats.

"*Cabrón.*"

"*Pero Padre!*" Alex pretended disapproval. "For a man of God to utter such invectives!"

"Hmph!" Don Benito snorted and went on to point out yet another detail the English colonists had stolen from the architecture of his homeland.

Very discreetly, Alex raised the subject of the monotone diet at supper. Their host pulled a face and nodded.

"He's really my yardman, not at all a cook, but when the old one died he just took over." Mr Coulter sighed and prodded at the overcooked meat. "I haven't had the opportunity to buy a new one."

Alex was taken aback. "So the cook, is he a slave?"

"What? John? Oh, no. He's a paid servant now that he's worked off his bond."

"Another unwilling émigré," Alex muttered, using spoon and knife to separate the gristle from the meat.

93

Mr Coulter shook his head. "I can assure you that he is not. John came here very much on purpose. We even travelled over on the same ship, although that is not something we were aware of at the time." He sat back from the table, wiping his fingers free of fat. "But he is a most awful cook."

"I can cook," Mrs Gordon suggested. "I can bake you pies and make you a roast of lamb or even a nice fish stew." By the time she had finished listing all the things she could do, Mr Coulter had a dreamy expression on his face. She eyed their landlord speculatively. "Not for free, but mayhap we can agree on a lower rent."

To Alex the days rolled by in terrible slow motion. One long day after the other, interminable hours spent thinking about Mark and Matthew with her eyes fixed on the ceiling. Every day she made her way to the harbour to stand staring at *Regina Anne*, willing her to repair herself overnight. She worried about money; even with Mrs Gordon's contribution in kind, the weekly accommodation was an unexpected drain on her resources, and she sometimes woke up sweating with fear after yet another realistic dream where she just couldn't pay Matthew free and had to watch him die before her eyes.

"You're being fanciful," Mrs Gordon soothed. "There's still plenty of money left, no? And you haven't sold the pearl yet, have you?"

No, Alex agreed, but where would she possibly find a buyer?

"Talk to the captain," Mrs Gordon said. "Or if you like, I can do it."

The only distraction from her constant worrying about Matthew was the unfolding soap opera starring Mrs Gordon. Alex hadn't noticed before how attractive she was, dismissing her as being quite old, but now that two men's eyes hung off Mrs Gordon, Alex began to see her in a different light. She had a strong face, thick, grey hair that was always carefully brushed and braided – a few softening tendrils allowed to float free from under her cap – a plump mouth and then those bright eyes. Yes, her skin was lined, and when she laughed her eyes almost disappeared inside a pouch of wrinkles, but her complexion was rosy, she had all her teeth, and then of course she had her chest.

"You've done something," Alex said, tilting her head to one side. Mrs Gordon flushed and muttered something along the lines that she most certainly had not. "The neckline," Alex grinned, "my, my, Mrs Gordon, you're showing quite an expanse of skin." Expanse was an exaggeration, but there was definitely more white skin visible, so much more that even Don Benito noticed, half stopping on the way to the dinner table to look at Mrs Gordon.

If there hadn't been three feet of table between them, Mr Coulter would have fallen face first into that bosom, so eagerly did he lean towards it, and Captain Miles had to get up from the table on several occasions, always detouring round Mrs Gordon's chair. The object of all this interest merely smiled and inquired if anyone wanted more pie.

During daytime, Mrs Gordon distributed her attentions fairly between the two men. She mended Captain Miles' shirts, took a daily walk to the little cemetery with Mr Coulter, listening to his rambling accounts of his wife.

"He found her dead in the yard one afternoon. Her heart just gave out. And the poor man blames himself, because she wanted so badly to return home," Mrs Gordon shared with Alex, patting the little headstone. She sighed and let her eyes sweep the little graveyard. "All these souls, buried so far from their homes." Alex nodded, a pitching sensation inside of her. Matthew, she groaned, and she knew that he was tottering on the razor's edge, hanging somewhere between life and death. She fell to her knees and prayed, to God that he might keep him safe, to Matthew that he must stay alive; for her as well as for himself.

"Ah, lass," Mrs Gordon sank down to kneel beside her. "He's in God's hands, and there he lies safe."

Captain Miles spent most of his mornings overseeing the

repairs on his ship, and after an extended dinner break he'd slip out, mumbling something very vague as to where he was going. One afternoon Alex followed him as he hurried off in the opposite direction of the port, making for a small building behind a stout wooden fence. He knocked on the gate and was let in by a man Alex recognised as Smith. From the fenced yard Alex could hear voices, high voices, and she understood that this was where Miles was lodging the women from his hold, safe from the roving eyes and hands of the local males.

She was still standing there when she saw him come out again, this time with two of the younger girls in tow. The three of them walked back in the direction of the town, with Alex tagging after them. By the church a cart was waiting, and the two girls were helped up to sit in the back. One of them was crying, her hands clutched around her bundle. There was a low voiced discussion between Captain Miles and the man holding the reins, a pouch flew through the air and the mules were clucked into walk.

"Bond servants or wives?" Alex asked Captain Miles, startling him so much he nearly dropped the pouch.

"Bond servants." He frowned at the criticism in her voice. "They chose themselves, no?"

"To go to Virginia, not to bloody Barbados."

"Not all that different." And he had asked the girls, he told her, selecting only the ones who said they would gladly stay here instead of risking yet another leg at sea.

"It must cost you a fortune to keep them in food over the winter."

"Aye." The women were bringing in some money themselves, he explained, doing laundry and the odd bit of sewing, but that barely covered the cost of food.

"And why do you keep them locked up?"

"I'm not keeping them locked up, I'm keeping them locked in. I won't have them stolen away at night." He threw Alex a look. "You should be careful, Mrs Graham. You're being unnecessarily bold in following me like you did today."

"Right; so someone would try and rob me away."

"As I said; there are different kind of slaves, no? And some of them are women who are kept locked out of sight." If his intent was to scare her he succeeded; Alex stopped walking out alone.

# CHAPTER 13

After the incident with the sled, Matthew retreated even further into himself. He rarely spoke, kept his eyes to the ground, and concentrated on keeping the gasping flame of life inside of him alive.

It had been Kate who had snuck back to help him once dark had fallen, Kate who had steadied him all the way to the shed after first having washed his lacerated back. He had scarcely noticed, all of his concentration required to set one foot before the other, but he had managed to whisper a weak 'thank you' when she left.

For the days immediately after his beating he had not been able to move, but once he was back on his feet he was singled out for the hardest labour, drenching him in sweat during the day and making him shake with chills in the early evenings. Not once did he complain, he just plodded, a witless beast that did as he was told, when he was told.

September passed into October, and with a heavy heart Matthew closed the door of hope on Alex coming this year, because with winter just around the corner there were no ships.

"You still think your wife will come for you?" Elijah asked Matthew in an undertone as they hoed their way down the harvested fields.

"Aye, she'll come." And I must keep myself alive till then, he told himself. He ate everything that was set before him and still his stomach yawned open with hunger. Occasionally he stole; a raw turnip, some carrots from the kitchen garden, the odd egg and once a fragrant pie left to cool outside the kitchen window. He gulped it, and was immediately sick, his stomach repelling such richness after months on meagre, insufficient rations.

Halfway through October he fell sick. Not even Jones

considered him fit for work, studying him with impassiveness.

"Take him over to the cook house," he instructed Elijah. "Put him in the backroom there. I'll have one of the women come and tend to him."

It was blissful to lie in a room where one wall was constantly warm, and Matthew huddled as close as possible to the warm stone, wrapping his long, thin arms tight around himself. He might have the ague, but he didn't really know. His head felt about to burst, horrible twisting headaches that bloomed behind his frontal lobes and crept down to paralyse his neck and spine. Any movement made black spots dance before his eyes, and he was so weak he couldn't stand to piss, someone had to help him even with that.

Glimmers of consciousness dropped through his head, and he saw that he was naked and that someone had covered him with an extra blanket. Another glimmer and there were soft hands on him, a supporting grip around his shoulders as someone helped him to drink.

He floated; high above himself he soared, and he flew all the way back home, hanging unseen over woods that flared with autumn colours, over his meadows and his house. He saw Joan kiss the boy in her lap, and he floated down to place his own soft kiss on curling hair, wishing that he be allowed to hold his son at least once more before he died.

He drifted even further, drawn to her, his heart, his wife. She was crying in her bed and he knew it was for him, and he tried to whisper words of comfort in her pretty, tight and slightly pointed ears. All this drifting wearied him, and with relief he dropped back into himself and there was yet another glimmer, and now he recognised the eyes and the hair.

"Kate," he said, and the angel smiled and nodded.

He shook with fever and there was another body close to him, as naked as he was, and he heard someone tell him she was here, and that she'd hold him tight throughout the night. Matthew Graham smiled and thought that maybe he would live after all.

He didn't know how it all came about. He woke to a moment of lucidness and found her beside him on his pallet, and he was filled with the urge to prove that he still could, that deep inside there lived a man. She turned towards him and he was safe in her arms. He moved slowly inside her, one part of him here, the other part on a Scottish hillside with a strange lass named Alex smiling up at him. He drifted away, and for the first time in a week he slept, a heavy dreamless sleep.

"What happened?" Matthew asked Kate a day or so later. He was sitting up in bed, feeding himself.

"What happened when?" She smiled and smoothed a long strand of hair away from his face. He recoiled, forcing her to drop her hand.

"Did we…" Matthew frowned. He was sure they had, but he couldn't recall when or how.

"Several times," Kate said.

Matthew felt sick with shame.

"It's alright, I know you're a married man. You've called her name so often these last few days." She sighed and heaved herself back on her heels before standing up. "You still think she's coming?"

Matthew nodded.

Kate gave him a sad little smile. "I thought my sweetheart would come as well. But it's been three years now…" She gave Matthew a frank look from nutmeg brown eyes, and shook her hair free of its faded linen cap before she deftly re-braided it and covered herself. "What if they don't? What if you and I spend what little time we have left to us hoping they will come and then they never do?"

The thought chilled Matthew to the bone. "She will, I know it here, aye?" He clapped himself on his chest.

"And if she does, will she mind? Will she resent that you took what comfort you could?"

He smiled faintly; knowing Alex she'd claw his eyes out

– or perhaps not, given the circumstances.

"I don't know." He closed his eyes and let himself fall back into sleep.

In the middle of the night she came to him, and he was half asleep and disorientated, but not enough not to know that this was Kate, not Alex. And he didn't care, he held her to him, silencing the humming voice of conscience by saying he was ill, and he needed this. Urgent hands on his skin, a warm and welcoming place to burrow himself into, a short escape from an existence he didn't want, a life he needed so desperately to forget. Kate was there, and Alex wasn't, and he was angry with her for that; she should have come by now, somehow she should have found him and saved him. But Kate was here ... so gentle, with hair that smelled of sun and a dark, surprised laugh when he took her yet again. He fell asleep on top of her, barely noticing when she slipped out from underneath him. But he woke when she kissed his nape, murmuring a goodnight before she tiptoed out into the dark.

Next time Matthew woke Jones was standing beside him, scrutinising him.

"On the mend?" He used a foot to nudge Matthew into sitting and then standing. Matthew fell as the blood rushed from his head, landing on hands and knees.

"Two more days," Jones said, "then I expect you out in the yard."

Matthew gritted his teeth to keep the bile washing through his mouth from splattering all over the well-polished boots in front of his nose.

Kate found him shivering all over and crawled down to him in an attempt to warm him.

"What happened?" she asked, her voice loaded with tenderness.

"Jones, he expects me back at work in two days." He had no words to describe the fear that flowed through him as he contemplated staggering out to work. Jones would not spare him, nor make allowances for his weakened state, and

Matthew doubted he would make it to Christmas if he was put to work in the same way again.

"I don't want to die, I want to live." He twisted to see Kate's face. "I have to, I have to be alive when she comes."

Kate just nodded, dark eyes growing even darker. Something flitted over her face, and Matthew was uncertain as to why she looked so disgruntled. And then he understood, and however mean spirited it made him, he was flattered by her jealousy.

"I'll keep you alive." She hugged him close, he let her. Her hands danced over him, they touched and held and guided him, and he drowned himself in her, in this welcoming woman with dark, dark eyes and hair the colour of ripening rye.

Two days later, Matthew stood as unsteadily as a new-born foal and listened as Jones distributed the tasks. To his great relief he was not sent out to the fields, but down to the stables, and he almost fell to his knees to thank Jones. It was hard work anyway for a man who should still have been in his bed, and by noon he was uncomfortably cold as the wind that whistled through the open doors cooled his sweating skin. Jones stood and watched through hooded eyes, making sure Matthew knew that every shovelful of horse manure, every barrow load was counted.

"Where are you going?" he asked Matthew once the day was done. Matthew stopped mid step to the cook house.

"To bed," he replied, very confused.

"Not there." Jones used his riding crop to indicate Matthew's old living quarters. "You go back there." Matthew turned and walked in the direction he was pointed. He couldn't help it; his head swivelled back to where Kate was standing and for an instant their eyes met.

For three days Matthew managed to remain on his feet before collapsing in a new bout of fever and Jones reluctantly agreed to have him moved back to the cook house.

Once again there were nights when Matthew swam in

and out of consciousness, nights with Kate pressing herself very, very close as she warmed him and held him. And Matthew responded to her, using hands and all of himself to give her something back. She was lithe and soft, a welcoming embrace that rocked him and soothed him, that roused him until he clenched his buttocks with need. Her long, fair hair, so soft against his skin, her hands, her thighs – her every part he explored, and she was willing and eager under him.

Occasionally he wondered if perhaps somewhere Alex was doing the same, drowning her sorrows with someone else, but just thinking that made him set his teeth. She was his, goddamn it, and she wasn't allowed... He, after all, was a man, with stronger urges and hotter needs.

The hypocrisy didn't escape him, and one morning Matthew turned to face Kate. There were some things he hadn't done with her; he had never spooned himself around her like he used to do with Alex, and he had never held her hand, fingers braided together like he always did with Alex.

"I can't do this anymore."

Kate's eyes darkened with hurt. "Why not?"

"I can't. I expect Alex to remain faithful to me, so how can I not do the same?"

"But it's different, you're a man. You need this, all men do." Her hand strayed down his belly but he arrested it and shook his head.

"Nay, Kate. This has to stop. I'm a married man, and I have vows to keep." He let his hand rest on her cheek. "You saved my life. You nursed me and gave me back myself when I was sure I would die. I owe you for that, and will always be grateful. But I don't love you, lass. In my heart Alex sits alone, and I can't do this anymore; not to you or to her." He stood with his back to her and dressed, aware all the while of her eyes on him, on his legs, his bare buttocks. He tightened the piece of rope he used instead of a belt and crouched down beside her.

"Will you still be my friend?" he asked, stroking her hair. She nodded, her eyes shiny with tears. "That makes me glad, and I couldn't ask for a better one." He tweaked her cheek and stood up. "I have to go."

Kate smiled unsteadily and gave him a slight wave.

"Will I be seeing you tonight?" he asked as he stood at the door.

"Of course," she said. "I'll be here; where else?"

It was strange how one single point of human contact could make such a difference, Matthew mused some days later. Every night there were some moments of conversation with Kate, a quick sharing of the events of the day, and suddenly he was no longer an invisible slave, he was a man again. And there were evenings when he couldn't help himself, pulling her close, once almost tumbling her behind the cook house, but at the last moment he'd regain his sanity and back off, leaving both of them panting with stoked desire.

It was a slow burning fuse to a keg of gunpowder, and inevitably one night it exploded and afterwards he drowned in shame, apologising repeatedly and promising it would never happen again. Kate just smiled.

Kate glowed and bloomed, she raised her hand as if by chance to her hair, she smoothed aprons and skirts to lie close to the shape of her body, and all the while her eyes would dart to where Matthew was sitting. He wasn't sure what he felt for her; gratitude, aye, lust, undoubtedly, but at times there were more complex emotions involved as well, and Matthew felt his face heat with shame. Here he was professing that his beloved wife, his Alex, would come for him, and on the sly he was swiving another. It didn't help when he realised Jones was an amused spectator, intelligent eyes flying from Matthew to Kate – eyes that sharpened with interest when they studied Kate.

After one hasty coupling behind one of the curing barns, Matthew decided that this had to end – he was behaving despicably. However, matters were taken out of his hands, and one day Kate was no longer at the cook house, replaced by a surly woman who slammed the plates down before the men. When he asked, he received blank stares and shrugs; no one seemed to know where she had gone, and it worried him that something might have happened to her. Whenever he could, he gravitated towards the big house, but all through the last weeks of the year he saw her not once.

"She may have been sold," Elijah said.

Matthew hadn't even considered that option and looked at him, aghast.

"Sold to where?"

Elijah had no idea.

The day before Christmas he saw her again and he wished he never had. He'd been called for, Jones needed a scribe, and Matthew was crossing in the direction of the plantation offices when he saw the door to Jones' lodgings swing open. He increased his pace, not wanting to incense the overseer by being late, and just as he passed the open door he saw Kate, half dressed in the arms of Jones. Over her disarrayed hair the overseer met Matthew's eyes, and Jones' big hand slid down to rest on Kate's buttocks and squeeze. Jones smiled. Matthew looked away.

Christmas that year was the bleakest Matthew had ever lived through. Utterly alone, stranded amongst people he had no ties to or even cared for, he crept out to stand under the dark night skies and stare up at the stars. Like Alex did on Hogmanay, he smiled wryly. She'd go out and face the sky, silently toasting her father. May she be alright, he prayed, wherever she is may she be safe and may she always know I love her. And in the night he heard her voice, he heard her laugh and tell him that she already knew, but it was nice of him to say so – even if it was only once a year.

"If she was on a ship in August of 1661 then she must have embarked sometime late spring," Eva said.

Magnus made a concurring sound. The information he had so far gleaned was pitiful to say the least; the name of some ships known to have crossed the seas several times - the *Regina Anne* an impressive thirty times -but there were no other records, no neatly printed passenger lists, no splashy route description along the lines of modern day cruisers.

"We'll never find anything here," he sighed, sending the papers on his desk flying.

"No, especially if you're going to be this silly about it. Concentrate instead. Where could she have gone? South America? One of the new Colonies?"

Magnus had a vague idea that many Scottish immigrants had ended up in Barbados and other such places rather than in the new Colonies, but he really had no idea. They spent a further two days perusing barely legible documents without finding any trace of someone called Graham, and Magnus got increasingly more frustrated.

"Diane tried to warn you," Eva said, "she did try and explain how difficult this would be."

"But now I have a year! It's just that there's nothing there from that bloody year!"

"There's tons of information, but the problem is it isn't systemised. And also, if we're going to be quite honest, the only proof we have that she lived in the seventeenth century is that you heard her say so – when you saw her in the sea."

"I did see her," Magnus said through gritted teeth.

"I know you did, I saw her too, remember? But what we don't know is if we saw someone who really did live then, in 1661, or if it was just some kind of... I don't know, holographic imprint?"

Magnus gave a short laugh. "Holographic imprint? What the hell would that be?"

"I have no idea, but it has a far better ring to it than ghost."

He rang her three days later, buzzing with excitement.

"I found her!"

"You did?" Eva sounded very impressed.

"Well, no, not as such, but I found a court document regarding the guardianship of a boy called Mark Magnus Graham." He waited for her exclamation of congratulations, but found himself listening to a very silent line.

"And this has to do with her because..." Eva asked after a while.

"Magnus of course! Like me!"

"It's not an uncommon name in Scotland."

"In the Shetlands or the Orkneys, no," Magnus said, "but here, in southern Scotland... and it's dated early 1661." He sighed at her continued silence. "You think I'm building a mountain out of a molehill."

"Yes, I do. And I don't like it that you do, because you'll never know – not really."

"You promised you'd help me," Matthew said.

"And I will. But I won't stand by and cheer if I think you're barking up the wrong tree. So, yes, this little boy might be her child, but in that case, was he there on the boat with her? Or do you think she would have left him to go to wherever she was going?"

"I don't know," Magnus said, gripping the phone very hard. "I have no fucking idea."

"Exactly, and you never will, honey. You might find the odd piece of information here and there, but it will be like holding six pieces of a thousand piece jigsaw puzzle." He heard her sigh. "It's a choice you have to make, Magnus, to try and find something but know you'll never find it all, or to let it go before you drown."

He hung up.

He called her again a few hours later.

"I'm sorry…" they both said and then laughed.

"I'm sorry for being so blunt before," Eva said. "And I know I've promised you I'll help you, but I'm worried this will be more distressing than healing."

"You're right, and I know that at best I'll only find the odd trace of her. It's not as if she's the journal type of girl, leaving behind thick notebooks for us to find. But…" He exhaled, wishing Eva had been here within touching distance instead of in London. "… all I want is something, one sign that she lived and lived well."

"That's two things honey, and while you may find the odd mention of her, you'll never know what her life was like. You'll just have to hope that she had the guts and the brains to carve herself a new existence, wherever she ended up."

He fell silent, mulling this over. "Alex has guts," Magnus finally said, "and brains. And in general she's had good taste in men, so I'll just have to hope this Graham fellow does right by her. Anyway, you have to get back to your meeting, right? And I have to write an article about the healing properties of the foxglove."

"Sounds absolutely riveting," Eva murmured, making Magnus laugh.

# CHAPTER 15

As weeks rolled into months, Alex became increasingly more depressed, spending far too much time on her own in their little room, and after a hushed little conference Don Benito and Mrs Gordon sat her down and insisted this nonsense had to stop – it wasn't doing her any good. She shrugged, not caring one way or the other.

Yet another little conference, this time anything but hushed, and Alex was browbeaten into accompanying Don Benito on long, exploratory walks. The enforced exercise helped – a bit. Now, two days after the most depressing Christmas Alex has ever celebrated, they were standing in a cove on the western side of the island, some miles north of the swampy area where Bridgetown was situated. Alex snapped open her fan and stood looking down at the inviting waves that washed over the sandy bottom.

"I'll wait," Don Benito said, surprising her. "If you want to go into the water, and I know you do, then go ahead." She gave a doubtful laugh and looked at the blue, glittering sea. The sun was still low in the eastern sky, Don Benito preferring to start just before daybreak, but it was already hot, a humid heat that was made bearable only by the constant wind.

"Don't you want to?"

"God bless you, *hija*," he laughed. "I don't know how to swim."

"I do," Alex said, giving the water a longing look. She took a quick decision and leapt down onto the sand, already undoing her skirts and bodice. There was a muffled exclamation behind her and when she turned Don Benito had covered his eyes with his hand.

"I'll keep my shift on."

"That won't help; you know as well as I do what happens when you soak a sheet."

"You don't have to sit like that," Alex said. "It's not as if you haven't seen naked women before, is it?"

"I'll sit as I choose, and will you please hurry up?"

Half an hour later she sat down beside him, damp but happy for the first time in weeks, and shoved at him.

"Done. All dressed – well, except for my feet."

"I'm sure I can survive the sight of them," Don Benito smiled, uncovering his eyes. "Is that something you do a lot? In your time?"

Alex nodded. "This whole coast is one long stretch of holiday resorts. People come from all over the world to spend a week here, swimming in the sea, lying in the sun." Don Benito grimaced at the thought of voluntarily sitting out in the baking heat and Alex laughed.

"In this I totally agree." She indicated her heavy skirts and long sleeved bodice.

They were well on their way back when they saw the man, or rather they heard him. A high, yelping sound, a gibbered pleading followed by a dull thwack, yet another yelp, and at the next gap in the surrounding shrubs they stopped, struck dumb by the spectacle played out at the further end of the field.

Cane, Alex thought in an attempt to distract herself, this is sugar cane and it must be some sort of grass, right? Yet another whistling stroke and the bound man jerked, pulling at the ropes that held him upright against a tree. He was naked, except for a tattered pair of breeches, and even at this distance Alex could see the skin breaking open in pink streaks, blood running down the dark back. The man administering the whipping said something to his companion, they laughed and traded places. Alex was considering just what to do to stop this when apparently the beating was over, the ropes sliced to release the slave to fall to the ground.

"Come away," Don Benito whispered, tugging at Alex. By the tree the slave was hauled to stand, a rope was tied round his neck and his two tormentors mounted their horses, nudging them first into a walk, then a slow canter, forcing the poor man to run full speed unless he wanted to be dragged over the ground. Inevitably he fell, and the horses cantered on, raising a cloud of dust behind them.

"We just stood there," Alex said, still disgusted with herself. "We should have told them to stop or something, right? He must have been terribly hurt when he fell like that behind the horses."

Mr Coulter looked at her in surprise. "Why would you interfere, my dear?" he asked, smiling sweetly in the direction of Mrs Gordon.

"They were hurting him!" Alex turned to Don Benito for support. "They were, no?"

"But..." Mr Coulter's face was a study of incomprehension. "... he was black, wasn't he?"

"So?" Alex said, standing up. Captain Miles put a hand on her sleeve, coaxing her back into her chair.

"Mr Coulter is just making the point that the man is a slave."

"Thank you CNN, for that update," Alex muttered through her teeth. "Yes," she went on slightly louder. "Even I gathered that. But you can't just do anything to a man, just because he's a slave, right? And anyway, how can good Christian men even hold with the concept of slavery as such?"

"He's black," Mr Coulter repeated as if this explained everything. "Black men aren't like us, they are simple and wild. You cannot consider them the equal of civilised man."

"Oh really?" Alex said with deceptive mildness. "Why not?"

"I just said, did I not? They are barbaric creatures, given to cannibalism and other heathen practises. Africa is a dark and savage place, Mrs Graham."

"Ah, so we're doing them a favour, are we?"

Mr Coulter beamed at his star pupil, nodding eagerly.

"Somehow I don't think they'd agree. Being abducted, torn from your family and friends, carried overseas never, ever to return home doesn't sound like the most appetising of prospects, does it?" Alex said.

Mr Coulter's face acquired an unhealthy pinkish hue. "They're not Christian, and it is an undisputed truth that they are lesser men than we are, incapable of anything but the most menial of tasks."

"They're just like us!" Alex exploded. "The only difference is one of colour."

"They're slaves. Mrs Graham, chattel property – no more, no less." Mr Coulter wagged an admonishing finger. "Never meddle, my dear. A slave owner does as he pleases with his property."

"Do you think it's right?" Alex challenged Don Benito next morning. "Does your God allow for people to be treated differently because of the colour of their skin?"

"They are heathen," Don Benito tried, making her snort. "And they hold on to their wild ways even when offered to join the church." He sighed and looked away. "But no, *hija*, I don't believe God judges people on the colour of their skins. Unfortunately, not everyone within the Church agrees with me."

Alex twisted her hands together, caught sight of her wedding ring and ran a finger over the dark blue stone.

"And him, will someone be treating my husband like we saw those men treat the slave yesterday?"

Don Benito placed her hand in the crook of his arm, patting it fondly.

"Of course not, he's not a slave, is he? And also, he's a Christian."

Alex found that a very doubtful comfort.

On New Year's Eve Alex excused herself from the table and went out into the small yard. Almost a year since she'd seen Matthew last, that early morning when he kissed her and rode off to watch the spectacle of Montrose's re-interment. She closed her eyes and pretended that he stood behind her, his arms round her waist, his thighs pressing against her skirts. And he would turn her to face him and kiss her, slowly, and she would... She broke off, moaning quietly.

"I swear God, that if I arrive to find him dead I'll never forgive You. Never, You hear?" She shook her fist against the sky and stood up straight. She took a deep breath, closed her eyes and placed one hand just below her ribcage. He still lives, thudded her heart, he lives and he waits. In the pit of her stomach she felt the flutter that assured her that he did – not as strong now as it had been, but still a steady, drumming beat.

Before rejoining the supper party she faced the north – or what she thought was the north – and raised an imaginary flute into the air.

"*Skål, Pappa,*" she whispered, sending herself whizzing through time to place a kiss on her father's cheek. As always he was there in his cold and dark garden; he raised his glass in silent salute and for the briefest of second's their mental eyes held and met.

"*Skål, lilla hjärtat,*" she heard him say, before he went back into the light that spilled from the kitchen door.

Somehow the fact that it was now 1662 made Alex regain some of her normal buoyancy, and she became a determined nagger, pestering Captain Miles about details of their imminent departure.

"So, we're done, right?" She stood on deck and patted the new mast, tilting her head back to squint up its height.

"Almost," Captain Miles said. "It will be some weeks yet, aye?"

"How many?" Alex wanted precise answers; departure then from gate x, arrival then at terminal three.

"We'll leave the second week of February."

Don Benito was as eager as Alex to be on his way, happy

to be leaving this constricting little island.

"I'm somewhat conspicuous," he explained to Alex, indicating his clothes. "And it doesn't help that most we meet consider me a spy, here to wrest some agricultural secret from them." He raised his elegant brows into a haughty demeanour. "And that is despite the fact that it was the English who stole the secret of the sugar cane from us, not the other way around."

"But you have been riding around a lot," Alex pointed out.

"*En nombre de Dios, hija,*" he smiled sadly.

She could imagine; broken men, torn from family and home and with no possibility of ever making it back. Men that she occasionally caught a glimpse of, stick thin and weaving with exhaustion as they were herded from one endless cane field to the other. Not like Matthew, she comforted herself, no of course not like him. But she didn't quite believe herself.

Mrs Gordon just shrugged when Alex shared her concerns with her. The master was strong and healthy to begin with, and no matter how badly treated there was plenty of life in him, no? Alex threw her a black look; not exactly what she needed to hear, was it? She produced her pouch and counted and recounted the shrunken pile of coins.

"It will be enough, no?" Mrs Gordon sounded worried. Alex hoped so. The captain had told her he had a buyer for the pearl and had offered to handle the whole transaction for her.

"It will be tight, but we still have those other bits of jewellery as well."

Mrs Gordon nodded and went back to her mending. Alex tied the pouch back where she usually kept it, beneath her petticoats, and resumed her sewing. She shouldn't have bought all that material, she berated herself, but what was she to do? Nine months living in the two skirts she had was beginning to tell, and she couldn't very well show up tattered. Now one skirt was mended and patched, and the other had been torn apart, the cloth turned and measured to make Matthew a new pair of breeches. Still, the russet of the new skirt made her smile and even Mrs Gordon admitted that the stitching was very well done.

"I've made him a shirt," Alex blurted.

"Aye, I know, and the dark serge is for a new coat, no?"

Alex smiled happily. Making clothes for him made it so much more certain that he was there, waiting for her.

"I found these very nice buttons," she said, spilling a set of pewter buttons into the palm of her hand. "They were a bit expensive, but I thought they would please him."

Mrs Gordon chuckled and shook her head. "He won't notice, lass; they never do."

She had a point there, Alex conceded, before going back to doing sums in her head.

"How much do you think it will cost?" Alex asked Captain Miles after supper.

"Cost?" The captain sounded very confused.

"To buy the indenture."

Captain Miles sucked at his pipe for a long time. "At least as much as the passage."

Alex gripped at the pouch through her skirts and left the room for the silent garden.

There was not enough; three times she had counted it, and every time her conclusion was the same. Even augmented with the money for the pearl there was simply not enough to both buy Matthew free and take them home. She leaned her head against her hands and cried.

"*Qué pasa?*" Don Benito sat down beside her.

Alex held out the pouch. "It's too light, there's not enough. How could I be so careless!" She pinched at her new skirt with irritation. "Now what do I do?" she asked Don Benito, but how was he supposed to answer that? She stood up and paced the little yard, her brow wrinkled with concentration. "I'm going for a walk," she announced and moved towards the gate. "Just down to the harbour."

"Now? Alone?" Don Benito shook his head. "It's too dangerous, *hija*."

"I have to, it will help me think." She threw him a pleading look.

Don Benito rolled his eyes and sighed. "Just there and back."

"Absolutely," she assured him, hurrying upstairs to find her shawl.

Don Benito tucked her hand into the crook of his arm and set off. She was quiet, no doubt lost in thoughts of her own, and he didn't mind, enjoying this silent companionship. He had written a letter to Louise during the day and was still weighing whether he should send it to her or not. It was the first time since he had been separated from her that he had put words to his feelings, and he had been surprised at how much he had to say, how effortlessly the quill had flown across the paper.

"Fifteen days," Alex said, her eyes on the *Regina Anne* that was riding the swell.

"Yes," Don Benito replied, feeling a shadow cross over him. He scratched his chest, wondering where he'd be a year from now. Alive, he hoped, even if sometimes he had doubts. Alex gave his arm a squeeze.

"You can still go the other way. No one will ever know."

"We've discussed this repeatedly," he said, "and the answer is still the same; no, I cannot." They stood in silence and stared out across the sea, a heaving darkness under a slightly less dark sky.

Both of them turned at the loud sounds from behind them. A large man staggered out from the dirt road behind the customs house. The man's breath was a noisy, painful thing, and when he moved a length of chain moved with him, scraping over the stony ground. It was too far away to see him properly, but the whites of his eyes stood out in his dark face and even in the weak light of the half-moon it was obvious to Don Benito that he was hurt – badly hurt.

Two other men appeared from the road, one with a cudgel in his hand. They laughed, said something in a casual tone to the two men sauntering behind them, and the man in chains backed towards the water's edge.

"Alex... *hija*, no." Don Benito eyed them nervously, one hand on Alex' shoulder. The slave uttered a guttural sound, and tried to move away. One foot stomped down hard on the dragging chain, and the abrupt jerk threw the fugitive off balance. He went down on his knees and they set upon him, cudgel whistling through the air.

"Stop!" Alex yelled. "For God's sake stop!" She took hold of the sleeve of the man closest and pulled.

"This is none of your concern ma'am," the man said, "and I would that you remove elsewhere lest this be too distressing for you to watch."

"Alex," Don Benito was at her side. "Come, we must leave."

The interrupted man bowed his agreement and went back to his business, pummelling the nearly unconscious man.

"You're going to kill him!" Alex pulled free from Don Benito's grip and kicked the man, sending him to land sprawled across his victim.

"Alex!" Don Benito attempted to drag her backwards, but she shook him off.

The man got back on his feet and turned towards Alex, bared teeth glinting in the weak light.

"You, ma'am, are acting most inappropriately."

"So are you," Alex retorted. "You're beating a man who's already down and out."

"He's a fugitive slave. To be more precise, he's my slave – mine to do as I wish with." He nodded in the direction of his men, and the whimpering hulk was pushed off the edge to land in the water.

"He'll drown!" Alex looked as if she was about to plunge in after him, but the man took a firm hold of her arm.

"Yes. Because I want him to. He's useless anyway, a firebrand and a constant source of unrest."

"Take your hands off me," Alex said.

The man just laughed.

Alex whipped round, slammed her body into him, grabbed at his arm and heaved him to land on his back, all air knocked out of him. She crouched, hands aloft and Don Benito gaped at this avenging angel.

"Get her," one of the other men said.

"Please," Don Benito said, "we're leaving, dear sirs. Let me just..." He made a grab for Alex, but she leaned out of reach, eyes never leaving the slave owner who had regained his feet and was circling her.

"It's the foreigner," one of the men voiced, pointing at Don Benito who shrank away.

"Ah, yes," the planter said, "and this must be the one of the female passengers." He lunged, Alex sidestepped, he lunged again and her hand connected hard enough with his arm to make him exclaim. Don Benito gawked; never had he seen a woman fight like this, and neither, apparently, had the planter.

"No!" the planter barked when one of his men threw himself at Alex. "I'll handle her myself."

"You wish," Alex spat.

The slave owner laughed. "Oh, I most certainly will, and once I'm done with you ..." Once again he flew like a sack of beans through the night, landing with a loud "ouff" on the ground. Don Benito was torn between admiration and irritation; this woman had no sense of self-preservation whatsoever. He swallowed, eyes on the three other men now converging upon them.

Alex moved from side to side, but was clearly hampered by her skirts. Don Benito wasn't sure quite what to do. He was a man of God, and for all that he carried a sword he'd never handled one in his life. Three men; one woman. Steel grated against steel, a blade glinted in the weak light and Don Benito did the only thing he could, he threw himself forward. *Dios mio!* It burnt into his side, and he sank to his knees, curling himself around the pain.

The men retreated, one of them cursing under his breath.

The planter rose to stand, spitting recriminations at Alex. She remained crouched, all of her muscles quivering after the last few minutes of unfamiliar activity. Some skills once learnt never leave you, she reflected, throwing a look at where Don Benito was writhing, strange breathless sounds leaking through his clamped lips.

"On your head be it," the planter said viciously and melted away into the night.

She rushed to the edge in a futile attempt to find the poor slave in the dark, scummy water and then turned back to Don Benito who was still prostrate on the ground, breath hissing in and out. Alex initial reaction was one of irritation.

"You stupid man," she said, crossly, bending down to help him to his feet. "I could have handled them by myself." He gasped when she touched his side and she pulled back her hand. It was sticky and warm, and even if she couldn't see in the dark she knew her palm was red – with his blood.

"You're hurt!" She tried to see his face, leaning in as close as she could. In his laboured exhalations she could make out the smoked fish they'd had for dinner. "Can you walk?"

Don Benito shook his head. "Don't leave me," he wheezed. "Don't leave me to die alone."

"You won't die," she reassured him, "but unless I get help, you will." She used her shawl as a makeshift bandage, gave him a pat on the cheek and ran like the wind up the dark street.

With combined efforts Captain Miles and Mr Coulter got Don Benito back to the house. Once he was in bed Mrs Gordon took over, cutting away both shirt and the hair shirt underneath. Captain Miles made huge eyes at this last garment, but Mrs Gordon snapped at him to stop gawking and make himself useful instead. There was water to boil and linen to tear, and while he was at it mayhap he could find some brandy as well.

"He's going to die," Alex whispered to Mrs Gordon.

There was a strange sound coming from Don Benito's chest, like the gurgling noise a snorkel makes if it's slightly under water and you try to breathe through it.

"Aye." Mrs Gordon tried to stop the air from leaking in and out through the open wound.

"My fault," Alex said.

"That we can worry about later. Now we need to help him as well as we can." Mrs Gordon had by now gotten a bandage in place, but the air still whistled through the hole with every breath he took.

"Alex?" Don Benito's head was full of pain and fear, and he fumbled for her hand. She fell to her knees on the floor and took his hand, pressing it against her chest.

"I'm so sorry," she whispered. "Oh, God… *Perdóname, Don Benito.*"

It doesn't matter, he wanted to say, but it did, and the pain that shot through him at every breath made it difficult to talk. He was going to die! *No, no quiero morir*, I am too young to die… Louise… He closed his eyes, concentrated on breathing.

"Will you deliver the gifts to Sir William?" His voice was a thread in the dark. To his relief, she didn't attempt to smile and tell him not to be silly – both of them knew he was dying, a slow agonised drowning. Instead she nodded and squeezed his hand.

"I want to be buried in my hair shirt," he went on, waving weakly in the direction of the garment. He tried to raise his free hand to her face, but let it drop, heavy like lead beside him. Stupid, stupid woman, this was all her fault. And yet… he smiled at her, coughed. *Ay Jesús!* How that hurt.

"In my small coffer…" He breathed. "… yours. Use it to free your man." He inhaled greedily, wanting desperately to live, not die like this. "Louise…" He licked his lips. " … write."

"I will," Alex assured him. "I'll write to Louise, and to

your brother." Don Benito nodded in gratitude. She would send his letter as well.

"The coffer..." he said, air wheezing through his open chest. She brought it over and opened it, lifting out a heavy pouch in dark red velvet.

"I can't take this!"

Don Benito smiled. It wasn't really his to give, it belonged to the mission of spreading God's writ among the natives of Virginia, but those poor heathen wouldn't miss his presence.

"It's mine," he lied, "and I give it to you, *hija*. For Matthew..." His throat clogged and he swallowed in panic until a tendril of oxygen found its way down to his lungs. "... the man God gave you." She was crying, tears streaking her face and he wanted to hand her his handkerchief but he couldn't even lift his arm.

He breathed again and again. His heart thundered in his chest, his vision was slipping, and he was so terribly cold. Not like this, he moaned, not now.

"*No fue tu culpa*," he whispered to the bent head by his side. "You did what you thought was right." She sobbed, clutching his hand hard. He fell back like a gutted fish, exhausted with the effort of saying all that. He coughed, eyes snapping open when his mouth filled with blood. He was bleeding! Dear Lord, he was wounded! He spat, he choked and swallowed, struggling to sit, mouth wide open as he sucked and sucked air into his lungs.

"Alex?" He couldn't see, oh God, this was it, and why were there no angels, no rays of heavenly light to make his passing easier? I die in sin! I will never stand before Our Lord, not me, not a fornicating priest.

"Shh," Alex' hand smoothed his hair, she kissed his cheek, eased him back against the pillows. So warm, all of her was warm and soft. Louise... I love you, Louise.

"I'm scared." He mumbled a prayer, but he couldn't recall the words, not getting beyond a jumbled *Please God, please, please God, I have tried to be good*. No last rites, no absolution, he was destined for hell. *Santa María, ayúdame.* He thrashed, flailed, and there was Alex, her hands gripping his, her voice whispering that it was alright, it would be alright, and God would understand, of course he would. Don Benito wasn't all that sure.

"*No quiero ... ay, no quiero. Perdóname Dios.*" He panicked; no air, so much pain. Alex pressed him back against the pillows.

"*Estoy aquí,*" she whispered. "I'll be here." She began to sing in Spanish, and he relaxed when he heard the sound of his mother tongue, imagining himself back in his Seville, *la ciudad más hermosa del mundo.* All through the night she sang, and Don Benito floated in and out of consciousness, his hand held in hers.

He was still alive when the sun rose, turning his blurring eyes towards the ray that struck through the small window to pattern the floor and throw a halo of light round Alex' head. *Un ángel...sí, un ángel.* Don Benito squeezed her hand and died.

# CHAPTER 16

On the day of his son's second birthday, Matthew woke up weeping after a far too vivid dream of permanent loss. He lay for a long time staring at the crumbling clay of the damp wall only inches from his nose, trying to collect his thoughts.

He pulled the threadbare blanket tighter round his shoulders and closed his eyes. It was Sunday, and not even here were they expected to work on the day of rest – not now, in late January. During planting and harvesting it was different, but during these slow months of winter Jones had no wish to leave his own bed on a Sunday. Strangely, these days were the most difficult to live through, far too many hours when his mind lay open to the whispered temptation of drowning in memories only to find himself rudely recalled to a reality he wouldn't wish on a dog.

Matthew sighed and got to his feet. Elijah was already up, probably hanging around the cook house in the hope of wheedling an extra helping of breakfast from the grim Mrs Humphries. Once so rotund, Elijah had shrunk to something resembling a pole with a head, long stringy arms ending in extended, narrow fingers with constantly torn or bleeding nails.

Over the last few months Elijah had become Jones' favourite victim, his sniffling begging making the overseer smile cruelly when he ordered Elijah to one heavy task after the other. Always Matthew and Elijah, but where Matthew had learnt to hold his tongue, Elijah would sometimes weep, falling to his knees and pleading that he might be released from this.

Matthew had just finished his breakfast when Jones appeared in the door of the cook house, his ginger hair standing messily around his head.

"Elijah?"

Matthew looked around and hitched a shoulder.

Jones cursed loudly; no one had ever escaped from Suffolk Rose under his care, he growled, and he wasn't about to have that snivelling wreck of a man be the first one.

"Get the dogs!" he snapped to his eternal shadow, Sykes.

"You think he has run?" The thought was so ludicrous that Matthew almost laughed. Deep inside stirred a sense of admiration at this reckless act. Why had he not tried to? Then he looked at himself, inadequately covered in rags, grimy shins protruding from his breeches and sighed. He didn't stand a chance... No, he was doing the right thing, waiting for her to come and find him. Besides, there were the dogs, huge black and tan creatures that were set free at night to roam the estate. He could hear them baying now, a deep sound that vibrated through the air. Poor daft bastard, he wouldn't get far.

Elijah was dragged back shrieking, clapped over the head until he collapsed and locked into one of the storage sheds. Jones stalked over to the big house to confer with Fairfax, and just after noon he walked back and in his hand he held a coiled flogging whip.

"There, now!" he snarled at the men and indicated the main yard with its stout, weathered post. The silence around the whipping post was absolute. Grey shapes shuffled into line and stood in the cold wind waiting. Elijah was led out, his pale skin breaking out in goose pimples, and was tied into place, hands high above his head.

"This man is a thief," Jones began. "He has attempted to steal himself away from Mr Fairfax, thereby depriving him of years of service for which Mr Fairfax has paid dearly." He sauntered up and down the line, the whip displayed prominently. "Mr Fairfax has no tolerance with thieves, Mr Fairfax dislikes when his property ..." Jones emphasised the word and glanced in the direction of Matthew, who dropped his eyes to the ground. " ... I repeat, his property, absconds." He scratched his nose and looked at the silent, assembled men for a long time. "A thief we hang – or maim – but Mr Fairfax has agreed to be lenient. He will be flogged; one hundred lashes." A collective gasp went up from the men and Elijah's legs buckled under him.

"Sweetest Lord," Matthew whispered to Davy. "One hundred lashes – it would be kinder to kill him outright."

"Aye" Davy groaned, "but this way he brings the lesson home to all of us."

Jones handed the whip to Sykes. He nodded that the sentence be carried out.

It took five lashes before Elijah began to cry out, ten more before he began to scream, and then he screamed and screamed for the coming thirty lashes or so. A further thirty and he barely whimpered, hanging so heavily in his arms that the shoulders seemed on the point of permanently popping out of their sockets.

"For the love of God, please stop! You'll kill him!" Matthew said, sickened to the point of vomiting by this spectacle.

Jones lifted his hand to stay the flogging. "One hundred lashes, are you willing to take the last twenty-five in his place?"

A shiver flew through Matthew. Twenty-five lashes for something he hadn't done, and he knew exactly what it would feel like, how much it would hurt. Fear pooled in his gut and leaked downward, making his knees weaken. He looked at Elijah and the blood running down his back to drip to the dust below his feet. The back was laid open from shoulder blades to waist. Twenty-five more lashes would kill him. Matthew raised his chin and met Jones' eyes.

"Aye," he said, hearing a murmur behind him.

Jones nodded his agreement to the exchange. He bowed and waved his hand towards the post.

"At your convenience, sir."

Matthew pulled off his shirt and used all his willpower to walk straight and tall the few yards that separated him from where Sykes was busy dragging Elijah out of the way.

He gripped the ring with his hands, shaking his head when they came with rope, and waited. He waited a long time, and finally snuck a look over his shoulder.

Jones met his eyes and smiled. "I'll be wielding the whip myself. Gentleman to gentleman, like."

Matthew had been flogged before, in gaol. But never like this, never with each stroke delivered at maximum strength, with long, unbearable pauses between them. After seven lashes he gasped. At the tenth lash he bit through his lip, and he leaned his forehead hard against the smooth wood and tried to stop himself from crying out when the leaded tip tore into his tender skin fifteen more times.

His knees were shaking by the time Jones was done and he'd held on so tightly to the ring he was certain his knuckles would burst. But somehow he straightened up and unclenched his clawed fingers from the ring, he even managed to turn and walk back to where he'd thrown his shirt, but if someone hadn't given it to him he would have fallen. He tried to smile a thank you and walked off, every step an act of faith.

She must be some kind of angel, he thought hazily when Kate appeared out of nowhere to slip a hand under his elbow. To his surprise she was crying, and he tried to comfort her.

"I'll be alright, aye? I'm not dead." But he was glad for her support, because his legs were beginning to tremble, and he doubted he'd have been able to walk for all that much longer on his own.

"No," she agreed, wiping her free hand under her nose. "Not this time you're not."

"Not this time," he echoed. There could be no more times; he had to conserve what strength remained to him.

Kate helped him to the laundry shed and washed his back, making him hiss as she poured hot water over the open gashes. His whole back throbbed, shards of pain that crawled up and down from his waist to his shoulders. The waistband of his breeches was dark with blood, but at least

Kate found him a shawl that she tenderly wrapped around him, assuring him he would soon be glad of the warmth. And then she slipped away, returning a few moments later with something hot and steaming, a rich soup of some sort that she spoon fed him, there in the dark of the shed.

"So you work up here now," Matthew said, nodding in the direction of the big house.

"Yes." She avoided his eyes as she gave him a brief summary of events. Jones had come up to her in early December and ordered her to follow him and when she'd asked why he had slapped her – not hard – and told her it wasn't her place to ask. Since then Kate spent her nights in his bed and her days in the kitchen.

Sounding belligerent, she told him that the benefits far outweighed the disadvantages. She was warm and reasonably clean, she ate well and Jones was unimaginative but not cruel in bed.

"In fact, I think he genuinely likes me." For an instant she met Matthew's eyes, before dropping them to her lap.

"We all survive as we can, no?" he smiled, reaching out to pat her face. She pressed his hand to her cheek, but he retook it.

"Nay, Kate, it was wrong. I'm a married man and soon my wife will come for me."

Kate stretched to smooth at his hair, fingers lingering on his skin.

"And what if she doesn't?"

Matthew squared his shoulders. "Then I die." And it was true, no?

He stood, thanked her yet again for her help and limped off towards his sleeping quarters. Halfway there he turned, and she was still standing where he'd left her. She raised her arm in a wave, he gave her a slight bow.

Davy and Duncan had dragged Elijah to lie in the shed, and had even managed to wash the blood off him. Matthew's eyes stung with tears as he took in the extent of the damage. Sykes had done a very precise job, sinking the lead

127

to tear even stripes out of the long back, and in some places they could see all the way to the bone.

"Dearest Lord," Duncan blubbered. "Oh, God, be merciful on him, aye? Take him softly, in his sleep." But God wasn't listening, and Elijah woke and wept with pain, begging for someone to please kill him.

Matthew lay supine on his belly, sunk into fevered dreams for two days. On the third day he was kicked out of bed and told to get to work. He staggered to his feet, and Jones had him working in the curing barn all day. When the supper bell rang Jones just shook his head and pointed at the remaining bales.

"Those, Graham." His eyes taunted Matthew, the large hand running up and down the length of his riding crop. It was completely dark by the time Matthew made it back to his straw pallet and succumbed again to dreams; Alex, and her blue eyes glowed with promise, Kate and her hair was so soft, so soft. When he woke none of them were there, no one placed a hand on his brow, and for the first time Matthew began to doubt that she would come. Still he struggled on, driven by the certainty that somehow he had to survive, a deep red glow burning in the pit of his stomach.

He mended this time as well, but it came at a price, and for weeks he shuffled, any sudden movement breaking up the healing gashes on his back. He no longer washed, all he did was work and eat, tossed by restless, horrifying dreams through his nights – dreams in which Alex looked at him and laughed at the pitiful remnant of a man he had become.

Elijah tottered back, a silent wreck that moved like a ghost through the days, barely eating, never talking. What little flesh remained to him melted away, and Jones ordered him to rest, he had no use for a weakling. Elijah cackled wildly when he said that, a demented light in his eyes.

He took to following Jones around, an obsequious smile on his face that had nothing to do with the ice in his eyes, and it was with wry amusement that Matthew noted just how disconcerted Jones was by Elijah's constant presence. The large man would detour whenever he caught sight of Elijah, and more often than not it was Sykes who did the task assignments while Jones stayed well away from the yard.

One morning Matthew was shaken awake by Davy and hurried after him to the whipping post. There was a shocked silence from the men who were standing in a loose circle around it. Matthew shouldered his way through them. Elijah had hanged himself from the ring and at his feet lay the dogs, sliced open from throat to groin.

# CHAPTER 17

"It was my fault," Alex repeated for the nth time since they had returned from the funeral. "If only I hadn't meddled…"

But she'd been obliged to, still angry with herself for not having interceded when she saw the other man being whipped. She grimaced; it hadn't helped, had it? The poor slave had died anyway, dragged to his death by the length of chain.

"It happened," Mrs Gordon, said. "It wasn't your hand that wielded the blade, no?"

"No, but it might just as well have been. Poor Don Benito, to die so far away from home and family."

"He would have died far away anyway, and surely to die in a bed with your hand held by a friend is a somewhat easier going than to be flayed alive by heathen Indians." Mrs Gordon had some very wild preconceived notions about Indians, Alex sighed before reverting to her original moping. Things weren't helped by the fact that he'd left her well over fifteen pounds. Even Mrs Gordon had looked impressed when Alex poured out gold sovereigns and silver shillings.

"He was well buried," Mrs Gordon said, "and he even got to lie in that horrible hair shirt." She patted the bench beside her and with a little grunt Alex sat down, glad of the shade.

"I couldn't even find him a catholic priest."

"It was opulent enough as it was, no?" Mrs Gordon shrugged. "Close to papist in trappings and rituals, I'd reckon."

"It was definitely not Presbyterian," Alex nodded.

"Absolutely not," Mrs Gordon said. "Anyway, I don't think it much matters, the important thing is that God has welcomed him home. Well; assuming God makes an exception now and then for a papist."

"Assuming God exists," Alex muttered in an undertone. At present she wasn't too sure.

"What?" Mrs Gordon leaned towards her.

"Nothing."

Mrs Gordon gave her a long look before bustling off to find them something to drink.

They were leaving tomorrow, and despite her grief over Don Benito, Alex' heart lifted at the thought. In a month she'd be with Matthew. She crossed her fingers just in case.

"Here," Mrs Gordon extended a wooden cup and sat down beside her. "I'll miss this house," she said, studying their surroundings. It was a pleasant little place, the solid house enhanced by the extended porch that ensured shade throughout the day and the neat little garden.

Alex gave her a sly look. "I'm sure you'd be most welcome to stay." She laughed at the expression on Mrs Gordon's face. "As the new Mrs Coulter, of course."

"Hmph." A nice enough man, Mr Coulter, Mrs Gordon told Alex, but to marry him would be to live forever in the shadow of his defunct wife. "He can't let her go, or mayhap he simply doesn't want to."

"What about you? Have you let your husband go?"

Mrs Gordon turned to face her. "My Robbie is always here," she smiled, patting herself somewhere in the region of her heart. "But I no longer have him in my bed."

"Never?"

Mrs Gordon laughed and shook her head. "Well, aye, there are times when he visits, no? But it's when I invite him in. When it gets too lonely."

"And your girls?" Alex asked hesitantly. Mrs Gordon rarely spoke of her dead family, and it was only by adding up the odd bit here and there that Alex had pieced together the sad story of how Mrs Gordon had lost her entire family in less than a year. Smallpox, an accidental drowning, and then the girl who'd been ill for years had died last, coughing her lungs out.

"My lasses go with me always, and not a day passes when I don't think of them." Her eyes flashed in the direction of Alex. "It isn't right, a mother shouldn't have to bury all her bairns."

Alex gave Mrs Gordon a hug.

No sooner had they left the protective barrier of Barbados, than Alex felt the first waves of nausea begin to climb her back. By noon she was lying in her berth, her stomach hurting after hours spent voiding her guts, and for three days she remained in her cabin, swearing she would never, ever set foot on a boat again. Except that she would have to; how else to go home?

It was a relief to make it out on deck – until she bumped into a man she for a fleeting instant thought was Luke. With a squeak she recoiled, falling against Mrs Gordon who luckily was stout enough to handle it. The stranger gave her a wary look, muttered an apology, and hurried off towards the galley.

"Who's that?" Now that Alex had recovered from her initial surprise she saw that the resemblance wasn't that strong. Luke had hair the colour of a fox pelt, a deep burnished red, while this individual had lighter hair. Also, the eyes were not quite as green, and in stature this lanky person had very little in common with either Luke or Matthew.

"The new cook, on account of Mr Davies choosing to remain on Barbados with one of Captain Miles' little brood." Mrs Gordon clucked with amusement as she explained that it hadn't been only Nell who had made herself available on the earlier crossing. "But this Anne she held herself to the one man, and when they knew she was with child, well, they chose to remain on land. I suggested Mr Davies should talk to Mr Coulter, and Anne would make him a good maid."

"You thought it was yon Luke, no?" Mrs Gordon said later, interrupting Alex in her intense study of the cook who was leaning over the railings, smoking a pipe.

Alex nodded, her hands clenching. "I hate him for what he's done to us. I spend far too much time thinking about how to make him pay."

"Och, aye?" Mrs Gordon sounded very relaxed. "Is it not enough to saw off his balls with a wee knife and feed them to him?"

"No, ground glass would be better, or tincture of monk's hood, or spitting him on a red hot sword. Anything to make him die in agony."

Mrs Gordon paled. "Well; you have been thinking, no?"

"You hang for murder," she added after a couple of seconds of silence.

"I know, and you don't need to worry. I'll never do something like that." Alex turned her wedding ring repeatedly round her finger, lost in thought.

"You worry that the master might."

"If it were me, three things would have kept me alive; Matthew, Mark and the warped wish to avenge myself on Luke." Alex exhaled loudly. "What will that kind of hate have done to Matthew?" She didn't say anything more, she just lost herself in the twisting motion of her ring.

Once she had gotten over her instinctive dislike of the man, Alex found the cook to be an entertaining if somewhat mournful companion. His name was Ignatius, he told her, sighing loudly.

"My father and his brothers were all aitch names, so me and my siblings all begin with an I. Isobel, Isaiah, Isaac, Immaculata…"

"What?"

"She's a nun," he said with a twinkle in his eyes.

"Luckily, given that name…" Alex said, receiving an amused smile in return. "Did your mother really call you Ignatius?"

"No. My family calls me Iggy, and my sister is Im."

"Well thank heavens for small mercies, no?" Alex said. "Look at it from the bright side, it will be easier for your children; James, Jenny, Jane, Janet."

"All taken," he said, rolling his eyes before disappearing down into his galley.

Mrs Gordon wasn't too happy about the fact that the new cook was Catholic, on account of it soon being lent and everyone knew the Catholics went a bit overboard during those forty days leading up to Easter.

"Fish once or twice a week, aye," she confided to Alex, "but every day no." In the event, Iggy seemed possessed of a roomy conscience when it came to religion and food, and won Mrs Gordon's heart permanently when he baked her a marrow pie – on a Friday.

In comparison with the Atlantic crossing, the following month was an agreeable cruise, with steady winds blowing them northwards at a sedate pace. No storms, no days of absolute stillness, and with every passing day Alex felt the anxiety in her grow.

Her dreams were tossing nightmares that had her landing on the cabin floor, disoriented and full of fear. Mrs Gordon soothed and hugged, she sat with Alex' head pillowed in her lap and sang her to sleep, rocking from side to side. But most of all she smiled and repeated time and time again that of course Matthew Graham was still alive. How could he be otherwise when his wife was coming for him?

# CHAPTER 18

"Jamestown." Captain Miles pointed in the direction of the small collection of houses and Alex smothered an incredulous laugh. This the main port of entry to Virginia? Captain Miles gave her a brief history; years of starvation, savages that one day swept out of the woods and killed or carried off more than a third of the little colony, stubborn men that clung to the dream of carving themselves a new home here, far from their English roots.

"They came here, gentlemen with house servants, and found that there was no one but them to till the ground or cut down the forest. It came as a shock, aye? Some refused, but threatened with not eating if they didn't work, they resigned themselves and put those soft lilywhite hands of theirs to good use." Captain Miles studied his own callused hands and smiled at Alex. "In return they claimed large tracts of land, and now their children live the life of gentlemen while the work is done by lesser men – like your husband."

"He isn't a lesser man!" Alex bristled.

Captain Miles assured her that he was certain that Mr Graham must be a most impressive man, but surely in his present circumstances... Alex huffed and went back to studying the shore.

Men were gravitating towards the landing stage, there were cheers that carried across the water. Captain Miles mumbled an apology to Alex and hastened off to see to the unloading of his cargo. Of the original sixty odd women, fifteen had been sold as bond servants, three had died on the crossing, some had slipped away on Barbados, and on deck now stood only thirty-eight, complemented by five red haired girls from the Scottish settlement on Barbados that in Alex' opinion all looked as if they had jaundice – or worms, maybe even both.

The women hung over the railings, waved and bantered with the gathered men, for all the world as if they were here for a daytrip no more. There was a stampede to be first off the ship, but Alex chose to hang back, descending into the last of the longboats.

Alex had not expected such curiosity, and adjusted her straw hat to hide her face. The men who congregated round the landed women studied her hungrily, but with Mrs Gordon as a scowling watchdog on one side, and Smith on her other, Alex made it through the press of men to stand some distance away.

Captain Miles was already on shore, and with a carrying voice took over the proceedings, clearing a space for the women to stand, one by one. Age, religion and status was repeated time and time again.

"Mary, twenty-two, Church of England, unwed." Or "Agnes, thirty-one, Presbyterian, widow." Some men made as if to fondle the goods but were beaten back by Captain Miles' crew. The ten remaining bond servants were disposed of, and one after another Alex saw the girls being led away, with flashes of uncertainty and fear crossing their faces.

Captain Miles had explained that female bondservants were a commodity in this heat infested place and that therefore they would fare better than their male counterparts. Whoopee; not much of a dream scenario, and at Alex' continued questioning the captain had admitted that several of the girls would in all probability end up pregnant, victims of sexual abuse or, in some cases, of genuine affection.

Alex saw one pretty girl – Jenny, twenty, papist, unwed – fall in step behind a man old enough to be her father and shuddered at how the man ogled the girl. Jenny would be warming her new master's bed that very same evening, of that Alex was sure.

"How terrible," Alex said to Mrs Gordon. "Imagine being bonded to someone like that." With her head she indicated a large man who was standing to the side, flicking casually at his boots with a riding crop.

"A bond servant has a term of service, aye? And Captain Miles says how the lasses are generally treated well enough to survive. Once they do, they can choose their own lives. But these ..." Mrs Gordon waved her hand in the direction of the women who were now being led forward. "... these will have sold their lives for the passage. Once you're wed, there is no getting away from the man."

"So you think they have it worse?"

Mrs Gordon raised her brows and scanned the crowd of waiting men.

"These are poor men, no? They work their plots by themselves – you can see that."

Alex followed her eyes. Yes, weathered men in worn clothes; some stood barefoot, and all had a light in their eyes as they studied the women.

"They'll buy themselves a wife," Mrs Gordon went on, "and she will toil beside him. And it's a harsh life, no? Much harsher than being a milkmaid on one of the large plantations."

"But at least they're still free," Alex tried, receiving an irritated headshake in return.

"Free? A wife isn't free. She belongs to her man."

"I don't, I'm free. I don't belong to Matthew." But she did; legally at least, however much it irked her to admit it.

Having seen his human cargo disposed of, Captain Miles strode over to join Alex and Mrs Gordon. He had offered to escort them to a boarding house on the outskirts of the town, assuring them that it was clean and had a very competent cook.

"So, did you make a profit?" Alex asked, making the captain frown.

"No, this has been a loss making trip, aye? Unless I get a good price for the cane spirit, that is."

"Rum," Alex said, "call it rum. And I told you, didn't I? It's a commodity in the making – trust me."

"It smells like the devil," he sighed. "Looks like tar

water and the taste is not much better, is it? Still," he shrugged, "I spoke to one of the innkeepers, and he seemed interested enough."

"Well, that's good, no?" Alex said. Her eyes were darting this way and that, taking in the little settlement. Not that small, actually, with quite a few shops and businesses ranged along the main thoroughfare. "It's bigger than I thought it would be."

"Much bigger than it was," the captain said, "and thriving. A lot of money in tobacco." His arm flew out to steady Mrs Gordon who'd slipped on a patch of mud.

"Not enough to pave the streets," Mrs Gordon muttered, fussing with her cap and collar. She brightened when Captain Miles steered them down a narrow lane, making for a house from which emanated the promising scent of baking bread. "I hope they have butter," Mrs Gordon said.

"I hope they have a hipbath," Alex said, making Mrs Gordon laugh.

Already on her first day in Jamestown, Alex found the registry, but to her frustration it was closed, the chief registrar being busy with his spring planting. A yawning doorman told her to come back Monday two weeks, and refused to allow her inside to flip through the archives herself.

"Please?"

"No," the doorman said, "I will not have you bring disarray to the order within."

"I can't afford to wait two weeks!" she said, her heart tumbling inside her. The man shrugged and closed the door in her face. Alex kicked at it: so close and still too far away, and with every day she could feel how his beat grew weaker, a continuous slowing that had her sitting up at bed, pleading with him to stay alive, please God stay alive.

Mrs Gordon tried to distract her, assuring her that the good Lord would not have led them all the way here only to have her find him dead.

"How do you know?" Alex sniffed, "He hasn't been all that much help this past year, has He?"

"I know, aye? And so do you." Mrs Gordon took hold of Alex' hand and stared into her eyes, refusing to let go until Alex nodded in agreement.

Three days after arriving, Mrs Gordon had a thriving business up and running. Mrs Adams, their landlady, had clapped her hands together at hearing Mrs Gordon was a midwife and had made a massive PR effort, resulting in Mrs Gordon being called away at all hours, delivering one child after the other. Business was further helped along by the elderly apothecary who took one look at Mrs Gordon and grinned like a jack-o-lanterns, exposing a crooked but relatively complete set of teeth.

"One could think they've all been bottling it up until you arrived," Alex teased, serving Mrs Gordon a steaming omelette.

Mrs Gordon gave her a tired look. "It's March, no?"

"March?"

Eliza the cook laughed at Alex' incomprehension. "Babies come in batches, Miss Alex – in March and in September."

A statement which, if anything, made Alex even more confused. She turned to Mrs Gordon who sighed and explained that a lot of babies were made in June and in December.

"In June because all the young lasses go a bit out of their head when the grass is green and sweet and in December because there is not much else to do, no? Don't tell me," she went on with a decided edge to her voice. "It's different in Sweden."

"I wouldn't think so," Alex replied huffily.

"Why don't they pay you in money?" Alex asked as Mrs Gordon lugged a stone jar of honey up the stairs.

"Because they don't have any."

"Are they all poor?"

"Nay," Mrs Gordon said, "but the few coins they have

they need for their taxes. Everything else they barter for."
She eyed Alex for a moment. "Why don't you do that? Take
all this and barter it." She waved her hand at the smoked
hams, the honey jars, the odd candles and a couple of soft
woollen shawls.

"For what?"

Mrs Gordon considered that. "Well, not for yarn," she
said, still unimpressed by Alex' knitting. "But for linen and
embroidery thread. You're good at that, no? You could sew
and sell – like the wee smocks you did for Mark, or the
shifts you've sewn for yourself with that rose pattern around
the neckline."

"I'm not sure ..."

"It helps to keep busy, lass," Mrs Gordon said.

Every morning Alex loaded her basket with an
assortment of items and worked her way round town,
returning with linen and cambric, thread and yards of pale
yellow or green ribbons. In the afternoons she sewed, often
outdoor under the huge sycamore that decorated the furthest
corner of the lot the boarding house stood in, sometimes
indoor in her room.

"This is right bonny," Mrs Gordon said, studying the
first completed baby smock. She inspected the work carefully,
her beady eyes ensuring that Alex hadn't cheated on the
hems.

"Mrs Gordon! I know what I'm doing, okay?"

"Okay, okay," Mrs Gordon muttered back, making Alex
stifle a giggle at this very modern expression.

Ten days after being deposited on the landing stage, Alex
was back, this time to take farewell of Captain Miles. He
promised to ensure her letters would be delivered to
Hillview and swept her into a tentative embrace.

"Be careful, and when you find him, be sure to let your
husband know he is a right fortunate man. Such a wife as he
has is a rare treasure indeed."

"Do you think I will? Find him, I mean."

Captain Miles made a helpless gesture. "That I don't know. But I'll pray, aye?" He turned to hug a surprised Mrs Gordon. "Take care of our lass," he admonished, receiving a glowering look in return. "You need to be down every day," he told Alex, one foot already in the longboat. "If you want passage home, you must catch each coming ship and negotiate with the captain before someone else books the berths." He smiled slightly. "I'll be back next year, but by then you'll be long gone, aye?"

"I sincerely hope so," Alex said.

"Aye well, so do I." He bowed and nimbly stepped aboard.

The day the registry opened, Alex was first in line, her hands tight fists in her skirts. What if he had died already on the crossing? And how was she to find him anyway? The chief registrar listened to her garbled explanation and promised to help, leading the way down dusty shelves as he read his way down indecipherable labels.

"Ah," he said, "the *Henriette Marie*, you say?"

Alex nodded, wanting to yank the leather satchel from his hands and page her way through the papers inside. He limped over to a carrel illuminated by the light from a small window, and sat down, indicating she should pull up a stool and join him. Very slowly he turned each page, not, Alex realised, out of a sadistic desire to keep her on tenterhooks, but because he had to peer his way through each document, his eyes almost crossing with the effort.

"Matthew Graham?" he said after a while. Alex nodded, feeling her insides moving slowly up from her belly to crowd her throat. He frowned as he read his way through for the second time. "Ah... the Suffolk Rose."

"That's not good?" Alex could not keep the fear out of her voice.

"I..." he stammered, "no...well..." But he smiled and tapped at the deed which sold Matthew to a Mr Fairfax for seven years. Alex tensed at the name; this was the bastard who'd made big business out of abducting innocent men.

"We have no notation that he is dead either."

Alex' shoulders dropped half a foot. "Would you always have that?" she said, and to her immense embarrassment her eyes filled with tears.

"No, but sooner or later we are informed." He patted her hand and courteously looked away while she wiped her eyes and regained some composure.

"Is it far?" she asked as he led her back to the door. "To Suffolk Rose."

"Three hours by foot, and there is a road all the way there." He gave her a concerned look. "You should not go out there by yourself."

"I have no choice, do I?"

As she made to step outside he put a restraining hand on her sleeve.

"What will you do if he says no?"

Alex blinked. The thought had never struck her.

"No?" she asked dumbly.

"He may not want to part with him."

"But why not?"

"Well...he, umm, Mr Fairfax, well..."

"I know," Alex said, "a man with the morals of a snake."

The registrar mumbled something about Mr Fairfax being a prominent member of the colony, and such allegations had best be voiced in very selective company. But he wiped at his rheumy eyes and told her she was right, Mr Fairfax was neither a kindly nor a good man.

"And so he may refuse," he said, making a helpless gesture.

"If he says no, I'll crush him." She straightened up to her full height. "He won't; after all, I'm willing to pay a premium price."

On the way back to the boarding house she didn't know whether to dance with joy or crawl with fear. The look on the old man's face as he'd said Suffolk Rose had the hairs on her body standing in premonition. Energy drained out of her so fast she just had to stop, hurrying over to stand in the shade of a tree. She placed her hand just below her sternum and took several deep breaths, closing her eyes as she steadied her thundering pulse.

"I'm here," she whispered, "I'm here, Matthew."

"What is it you're painting?" Magnus leaned over Isaac's shoulder.

"I don't know," the six year old artist said, "I think it's a hill."

Magnus looked at the mass of greens and browns and purples and picked it up to stand it on the easel before taking a step back.

"Yes, I think you're right. It's a hillside, no?"

Isaac slid down from the stool and dug around among the half squeezed tubes of paint until he found a vivid pink, squeezing out a small blob on his miniature palette.

"You think?" Magnus said doubtfully. He rather liked the overall muted impression of the picture in front of him. Isaac ignored him, picked up a brush and added a couple of dots before stepping back.

Magnus looked from the painting to him in amazement.

"How did you know?" The pink spots had brought everything together, and Magnus found himself thinking that if he sniffed long enough he would actually smell the scent of sun warmed heather and briar roses. Isaac flushed at his Offa's praise, and put all the caps back on his paint tubes.

Magnus sucked in his lower lip and regarded his grandson with a slight frown. His eyes slid back to the little painting. The hillside was eerily alive – shit, he could swear he saw the heather move, and what was that, a rabbit darting off? Impossible. A single drop of sweat slid down his spine. Magnus blinked and shook his head. The little canvas settled down into a still life, and Magnus decided he had imagined what he'd just seen. Oversensitive, that was what he was, so scared of finding in Isaac's painting anything that whiffed of magic. Yet another look at the depicted hillside, and he almost laughed: smudges of brown and green, no more no less, right?

Isaac had finished with his tubes and was now tidying the table.

"He's such an adult when it comes to this," Diane had said the other week, standing with Magnus to watch Isaac clear his workspace. Yes, he was; when he was painting Isaac became someone very different from the boy he normally was, turning inward with such concentration that he didn't hear unless you stood in front of him. Now, however, their junior Monet was hungry, and he skipped all the way down the stairs with his hand in Magnus', wheedling that he be allowed at least two hours Playstation instead of the daily maximum of one.

Fridays were Magnus' and Isaac's special days, and had been since the day Alex went missing. Originally because John felt Magnus needed the boy so as not to succumb to grief, and then it had become convenient during the months when John and Diane went through a tentative courtship. Since the twins it was mostly for Isaac's sake, a whole day of uninterrupted access to one of his adults. These days always followed a pattern; Magnus picked Isaac up from school, they went shopping together, and then returned home, one to cook, the other to paint.

"Offa?" Isaac curled up beside Magnus on the sofa.

"Hmm?" Magnus tugged his hand through the short, dark hair of his grandson.

"Why don't we ever go to the churchyard?"

The question threw Magnus completely, and he closed his book and sat up straighter.

"Why would we do that?"

"Stuart goes there all the time," Isaac said. "He goes with his Mum and they put flowers on his granddad's grave."

"But I'm still here, no? So why would you want to go to the graveyard?"

Isaac blew out of his nose so heavily it made him sound like an aggravated rhinoceros.

"But Mama isn't, is she?"

Magnus sighed. How the hell was he supposed to explain this? He looked down at Isaac, wondering yet again where those delicate features came from. In some he saw Mercedes, but there was nothing of either himself or of Alex in the face turned up to meet his eyes.

"Your mother doesn't have a grave," Magnus said, deciding there was no way out of this but to tell the truth. "We don't really know where she is."

Isaac frowned at him. "But Diane says she's gone and won't be coming back."

Magnus nodded. "And she's right. It's just that we don't really know what happened the day she ..."

"Died," Isaac supplied.

"Went missing," Magnus corrected. Isaac eyed him for a couple of minutes, clearly confused.

"But if she's missing, well then she can come back."

"Oh, shit..." This wasn't his decision to take. "Wait here," Magnus said and went over to call John.

John was as uncomfortable as Magnus, studying his son seriously. Finally he opted for an abbreviated version of the truth.

"Alex – Mama – went out for a drive one day and she never came back. We found the car, we even found her phone but we never found her. There was an awful thunderstorm that night and the police think that maybe she was hit by lightning and you know, poof."

"Poof," Magnus nodded in agreement.

"Poof?" Isaac blinked. "Like zapped into a puddle?"

"More or less," John said. "So you see, as there was nothing left of her there was nothing we could bury."

Isaac digested this for some time. Finally he shrugged.

"Can I have some ice cream?"

# CHAPTER 20

Mrs Gordon promised to wait for her in the kitchen, no matter how long it took, and gave her an encouraging pat on the back.

"Close, aye?"

Alex was so nervous she stumbled over her feet as she followed the house maid down the hallway to the master's office. Please let him be alright, she prayed, please let me not have come too late. She was too jittery to sit, and instead walked back and forth across the room, taking in its impressive but somewhat heavy furnishing. Everything was in dark wood; the desk, the chair behind it, the intricately carved chest, the panelling. The floor was laid in a herringbone pattern and stained almost black, and to the side stood a large table, covered in a deep red Turkish carpet.

"Mrs Graham, I believe. What can I do for you?" The man who entered the room looked irritated, his face still heavy with sleep. He settled an impressive wig on his shaved head and strolled over to lean against his desk.

"I wish to buy my husband's indenture from you," she said.

Fairfax looked at her with increased interest. "Your husband?"

"Mr Matthew Graham."

Fairfax hitched his shoulder. "Mr Graham? I have no idea if he's here. My overseer handles the indentures, not me." His mouth came together into a little pout, conveying just how superior he was to the men presently slaving themselves to death on his land. Bastard.

"You bought his indenture late last May," she said, "and as far as I can make out he's still with you."

"He is?" Fairfax was scrutinising her, eyes travelling over her breasts, her face, back to her tits. It was all Alex could do to remain standing still, unnerved by how he was eating her with his eyes. "He might be dead," Fairfax added with a yawn, "they die quite rapidly at times. The heat, I assume."

Helped along by the fact that you probably don't feed them all that much. Alex threw a look out the window at where half a dozen men shuffled by, shrunk shapes in faded, ragged clothes. She gulped. What if he'd died? Starved to death and all because she'd been delayed? No; she took a calming breath, pressed a hand to her stomach.

"But you'd know if he was dead, right?" she said, and she hated it that she was pleading.

"I would? Not likely." He smiled at her – or rather leered – and a pink tongue darted out to wet his plump lips. He indicated that she should sit, and sat down as well, regarding her in silence for a long time.

"Assuming that Graham is indeed working for me why would I want to sell him? He's well broken in by now."

Alex had to stop herself from spitting in his face. Broken in? This was a man they were talking about – her man – not some beast of burden. He was back to gawking at her chest, small dark eyes gleaming with interest. He dropped his gaze to her waist, did a quick up and down the contours of her legs and smiled. Alex shifted on her seat. Fairfax grinned, clearly delighted by her discomfiture. Ignore him, concentrate on the matter at hand.

"He was abducted," she said, "deceitfully sold into indenture. He's an innocent man who has never been convicted in any court and by rights he shouldn't even be here." Once again he smiled, that overlarge tongue coming out to lick his lips. "I've heard the most amazing rumours …" She continued, working hard to remain unperturbed by his staring. "… of a planned venture whereby planters here actively participate in the abduction and subsequent indenture of free men." She attempted a light laugh, raised her eyes in his direction. "But surely that's something no God fearing man would ever do. At least that's what I told Captain Miles before coming here today." That struck home;

the smile was wiped away, replaced by an expression Alex could at best describe as a frightened scowl.

"Miles? Here?" he said, smoothing his features back into blandness.

"I travelled over on his ship," Alex said.

"Hmm." He cracked his knuckles, pursed his mouth together and regarded her for a long time. Finally he shook his head. "Terrible, how terrible this must be for you – and your husband." As if he cared, but Alex nodded all the same.

Fairfax strolled over to the door and opened it wide, barking for someone to find Jones. He yelled some more and a maid appeared with lemonade and heavy cut glass goblets, serving them before she curtsied her way out of the room.

Fairfax sat down, fussed with the tails of his coat to ensure they fell just so, and went back to studying her, a speculative look in his eyes. He conversed about the weather and the strenuous climate, inquiring as to how she liked Jamestown. Was she perhaps planning on settling? No, she told him, perturbed by his continued inspection, she had a son to return to, a boy of two. He nodded that he understood, and drained his glass just as Jones came through the door.

"Ah, Jones!" Fairfax clapped his hands together at the sight of his overseer, a large, heavyset man with huge hands. He carried a short whip, swatting it every now and then against his boots, and Alex recognised him as the man she'd seen at the harbour the day she arrived. "Tell me Jones, is Mr Graham still with us?"

Jones looked nonplussed. "Mr Graham?"

"Matthew Graham," Fairfax clarified.

Jones pulled at his lip. "Yes, he's out on the new fields."

"Ah." Fairfax nodded, swivelling to face Alex. "It would seem you may be in luck, Mrs Graham; your husband is still alive and healthy." Jones coughed, an amused expression flashing over his face. Oh God; she choked on a rush of saliva. He's alive, she told herself, however badly used he's still alive.

She managed to give Fairfax a grateful smile. "May I see him?"

Jones shook his head. "He's a day's ride away. They'll be back in a week."

A week! Anything could happen in a week. Alex' stomach contracted at the thought of being this close and then...

"Maybe I could ride out to him?"

"No," Fairfax replied in a tone that brooked no discussion. "Too dangerous, and I would not want to see you harmed."

Almost fifteen months since she had seen him last and now one more week seemed unbearable. Alex knotted her hands into her skirts and concentrated on blinking back the tears that welled in her eyes. He was alive and that was all that mattered. One more week she could wait, of course she could.

Fairfax dismissed Jones. "Make sure Mr Graham is here next Friday," he said, receiving a surly nod in return. "Good news," he smiled, pudgy fingers toying with the perfumed curls of his wig.

"Very," Alex said.

"And now all that remains is the little matter of the price." Fairfax poured her some more lemonade before sitting back in his chair.

"I will of course compensate you for your purchase price," Alex hastened to tell him.

"Of course you will, Mrs Graham, but I don't think that will be enough." He leered at her, displaying yellowing teeth. Bastard; he was going to charge her an overprice. Alex squared her shoulders. Even if she had to pay twice the amount he'd paid, she had the money to do so – just. Fairfax rose, moved over to his desk.

"So, shall we draw up a contract?" The quill rasped on the thick paper and he blotted the ink before handing her the document to read. "You can read, my dear?"

She nodded, her eyes flying over the scrawled words to find the price. Twenty pounds, the same as he had paid for Matthew, and Alex felt a flush of shame at having so misjudged this man.

"We will sign it afterwards," Fairfax suggested.

Afterwards? Something plummeted inside of her at the look on his face.

He tapped the deed with his finger and grinned. "This is the official price. The real price includes an element of... service." He positively beamed when she began to protest, already half out of her chair. "I hold his life in my hand," he reminded her, "and you, my dear, is the price I set on it." He undid his brocade coat and sat back expectantly.

For an instant she considered blurting that she knew, that she would expose him for what he was to the community, but in the same moment she realised that she couldn't; not if she wanted Matthew returned to her alive.

"Please ...I'll pay you more, I'll ..."

"Oh no, Mrs Graham; I have no need for more money. I do, however, have other urges." He crooked a finger to beckon her over. "It's up to you, my dear," he added when she remained where she was, incapable of taking even one step in his direction. With a sigh he stood up, retrieved the document and made as if to tear it up.

"Wait!" Alex swallowed and swallowed. "I'll do it." She forced her legs to move towards him.

"I daresay it won't take that long," he said as he pushed her down on the desk, hands already shoving the skirts out of the way.

An eternal half hour later, Fairfax buttoned up his breeches, smirked at Alex and left the room, whistling. Alex got to her feet and began to order her clothes. She was shaking from head to foot, crying as she pulled at her garments, yanked at her lacings. Despicable man! She was sore everywhere, and in her mouth lingered the rancid taste of him. She wiped at her lips, dragging the back of her hand back and forth. Oh God! All of her smelled of him, and between her legs...

Folded on her skirts lay the contract, now duly signed, and she tucked it inside her bodice, thinking fiercely that of course it was worth the price. She was nauseous with shame at what had been done to her, and in her head rang a little voice that wondered what Matthew would think of it all.

Mrs Gordon looked at Alex, looked again, and her face set in an impressive scowl.

"What did he do to you?"

"Not now," Alex said. Mrs Gordon muttered but didn't push, hurrying after Alex up the lane.

The afternoon was beginning to shift into dusk and they both walked briskly, none of them wanting to be this far out of town when it grew dark. Halfway back Alex began to cry, long heaving sobs, and Mrs Gordon stopped and hugged her.

"I found him," Alex snivelled, "he's alive, and come next week I can come and get him. Look," she said, digging into her bodice, "look, I even have a contract!" She threw the document onto the dirt road and cried even harder.

Mrs Gordon bent down to retrieve the deed and tucked it into her own bodice. She pulled Alex close and shushed her, stroking her tenderly over her head. Alex cried and cried, she clung to Mrs Gordon who stood like a rock, whispering that it would be alright, and that she'd keep her lassie safe, no matter what.

"So, what did yon worm of a man do to you?" Mrs Gordon asked, once Alex' sobs had subsided.

Alex rubbed her sleeve hard over her swollen face.

"He did what he wanted to do. He set the price and I had no choice but to pay. Which he knew, slime ball that he is." She absentmindedly used her nail to remove a blot of wax from her skirts. "We'd best get moving, the light's going fast."

"Matthew will never forgive me," Alex said once they resumed walking. Mrs Gordon rolled her eyes in an exasperated gesture.

"You had no choice, lass."

"I know that, and you know that, but to Matthew it will never be that clear cut. One part of him will always think I should have refused."

"Aye, and then he would be dead and none of us would

need to worry about his opinion," Mrs Gordon muttered.

Alex smiled weakly.

"Are you planning on telling him?" Mrs Gordon asked.

"I don't know. Should I?"

Mrs Gordon did yet another eye roll. "Of course not! Not unless you absolutely have to."

"But that would be dishonest."

"All truths don't need to be told lass. Trust me, aye? He doesn't need to know ."

Once they got home Mrs Gordon insisted that Alex take a bath and then she tucked her into bed, wrapping the quilts tight around her.

"There is one thing we must do," Mrs Gordon said, frowning down at her knitting.

"What?" Alex asked through a yawn.

"We must make sure there is no child."

Alex' eyes flew open in consternation. A child! With that disgusting toad of a man?

"When did you last bleed?"

Alex counted back the days and relaxed against the pillows. "Four weeks ago."

Mrs Gordon just nodded and went back to her knitting. "No major risk then; we'll wait for some days, and if nothing happens we will help it along. I have what I need, I think, and if not that sweet Mr Parson will find it for me."

"Mr Parson?"

"The apothecary; and a right little treasure trove his store is."

Despite everything Alex smiled; no more than three weeks here and already Mrs Gordon had herself an admirer. What was it with this woman? Did she perhaps use some sort of secret perfume?

Eight days later Alex set out for Mr Fairfax' plantation, and in her pouch she carried the price of twenty pounds, and at her breast lay the signed contract. This was going to create a huge dent in their finances, but she didn't care – not today.

She had washed her hair, put on clean linen and was quivering all over at the thought of seeing Matthew again. As she approached the plantation she began to tremble for another reason; let Fairfax not be here, let her not have to see that satisfied smirk again.

It was a huge relief to hear that Mr Fairfax was indisposed and have the whole transaction handled in silence by his overseer. She hoped the toad would die of this indisposition, or have his member rot and fall off – leave him incapacitated forever. She shuddered; at least she wasn't pregnant, so thank heavens for small mercies.

"Well then," Jones got to his feet after having counted the money for the third time. "Let's go and find him."

He led her out into the yard and told her to wait by the barns.

"I can come with you."

Jones shook his head. He had his instructions and they were very simple; she was to wait here while he found her man.

She watched him stride away and stood and held herself together, wondering why it felt as if she was about to disintegrate into atoms now, when he was so close. I'm afraid, she admitted, I'm so afraid of what he has become.

# CHAPTER 21

"Graham!"

Matthew turned towards the voice. Obey, he reminded himself, always obey. After the flogging he had become pathetically docile, a beast that went wherever he was pointed, and now he shuffled towards Jones hoping that it wouldn't be too much additional work, because he was too tired, too hungry, and some days all he wanted was to lie down and never rise again.

He no longer allowed himself to hope, never looked in the direction of the road, and every now and then he asked God to take him soon, not leave him to die piece by piece in this unbearable existence. And yet... there were still moments when his head rang with her laughter, when she danced before his eyes, and in her blue, blue gaze he could see just how much she loved him. These fragmented images filled him with quiet joy, a conviction that he had to live through at least one more day, a week, a month.

Matthew came to a silent stop in front of Jones. His foot throbbed and he threw a look at the soiled bandage that he'd wrapped around it in an attempt to protect the gash where a hoe had sunk into it, just below his ankle.

Jones flicked his riding crop against his buck hide breeches, once, twice, thrice the leather cracked, and every time Matthew had to force himself not to flinch.

"You have a visitor," Jones informed him.

Matthew kept his eyes on the ground. He'd seen Jones play this particular game far too many times to fall for it, and he wasn't about to give anyone the pleasure of seeing first hope, then disappointment, wash across his face.

"Your new owner," Jones clarified and lifted his whip in the direction of the curing barns. A new owner? Apprehension rushed through him and he raised his face to look in the direction Jones was pointing.

Had he been alone he might have tried to call her name or even broken into a run. Now all he could do was stand absolutely still as the ground under him seemed to sway and fold, praying silently to the good Lord that she not be a mirage, please God, not that.

"Go on!" Jones barked, unfreezing him. "Get yourself over to her, now. I have instructions to see you off the property immediately." At Matthew's continued immobility he raised his hand in a threatening gesture and Matthew, to his shame, cringed and began to move.

He was acutely aware of how he must look through her eyes; dressed in rags, dirty and unkempt, his hair and heavy beard crawling with lice. And that was only on the outside, the damage to his inside was far, far worse.

He stumbled towards her. He must seem a scarecrow, stick thin limbs protruding from what little was left of his breeches and shirt. He tried to lengthen his stride, swayed like a reed and almost fell. His knees buckled, he had to stop, take a breath, take two.

He looked at her from under the fringe of matted hair, and she was just as he remembered her, all the way from the unruly curls escaping constraints of cap and braid to the way she smiled, arms held out. She had come! His Alex was here, her eyes uncommonly dark and brimming with tears.

He lifted his face, stretched his uncooperative lips into a smile. He heard her loud intake of breath, and here she came, the lace cap fluttering to the ground as she ran towards him. She crashed into him, and only her quick reactions saved them both from tumbling to the ground. His Alex; so warm, so strong and full of life. Her arms wrapped themselves around him, she said his name, she wept and laughed. Matthew closed his eyes, stuck his nose in her hair and inhaled.

After that initial embrace they didn't touch on their way back to town. It was a long walk, and Matthew's foot screeched in protest, causing him to limp. And yet he plodded on, wanting very much to take her hand. But he didn't, far too conscious of his griminess, his torn fingernails and heavily callused hands.

As they walked towards the boarding house, Matthew became aware of all the eyes; eyes that regarded him with revulsion, her with pity. She must have felt them too, because suddenly her arm was slipped through his and they walked arm in arm through the town.

"I've ordered a bath," Alex said, "I thought that maybe…" She went a dusky pink. "… maybe you'd like me to wash you like I used to do?"

A lifetime ago, in a world where he was whole. Matthew studied himself in silence. He was caked with dirt, from his bare feet to his crown. God knew what he would find once he started to wash the protective layers of dust off him.

"But maybe you'd prefer to be alone?"

He heard the uncertainty in her voice and wasn't sure how to reply. He didn't want her to see him this way, but she would sooner or later anyway. In her eyes he saw her need to touch him, to let her hands rediscover him, and it made all of him crawl, an involuntary shudder rippling through his body.

"Fine," she said with a brittle smile. "I'll leave you alone then, right?"

His shoulders slumped with relief and with a strangled sound she left the room.

He regained some sense of self with each sluicing, watching with abstracted interest how his body reappeared. Horribly thin, full of welts and unhealed scars, but still, to some extent, him. He stepped out of the dirty water and inspected himself in the shaving mirror. The eyes of a damaged man in a ravaged face stared back at him and he took a shocked step back. It would help to shave, he told himself, and lifted a shaking razor to his face.

The beard came off in narrow swathes, baring skin that was startlingly white in comparison with the rest of him. He fingered his features, trying to reconnect with himself, looking for something of the old Matthew in the stark face that looked back at him. A death's head, he thought, the bones plainly visible under the tautened skin.

She recoiled at the sight of him. He'd shaved his head as well, and the shirt she'd left folded for him hung flapping round his frame. He smiled ruefully at her reaction and ran a hand over his bare skull.

"I had to," he said, and those were the first words he said to her. Even his voice was somehow different, he reflected, as dark as always but cracked. Alex nodded and moved closer, inching towards him as if she feared he might turn and bolt, like an unbroken horse.

He closed his eyes at the look in her face. I don't want your pity, damn you! Still, he stood quiet under her hands, so conscious of her proximity it physically hurt. When she unlaced his shirt to trace light fingers across his chest he flinched, unused to being touched by someone wishing him well. Her hands went on with their inspection, and his cock sprung to active and urgent life, hard beneath the hem of his shirt. He was too weak, his vision blurred, but he didn't care. He was alive, he was safe, and he hoped that he'd gotten rid of any wee creatures, because he was going to, oh dear Lord was he going to! Her fingers found him, closed round him and he jerked at the warmth of her grip.

"Nay," he gasped. "Undress. Let me look at you."

For a long time her eyes held his. She backed away a few steps, undid buttons and lacings, and stepped out of one garment after the other, standing finally only in her shift.

"That too." His gaze never left her as she did as he said. She raised her arms to her head, drew out her pins, and his breath hitched when her hair tumbled down to frame her face in waves of browns and bronze and here and there a dash of deep, deep red. His hand moved of its own accord, fingers finding a long strand of curling hair, tugging at it until she stood close enough for him to feel the warmth of her naked body against his own.

"Merciful Christ," he groaned. "I won't be gentle with

you, Alex. I don't think I can." In reply she stood on her toes and kissed him.

Fortunately the bed was only a few feet away. Whatever strength he had left in him had collected in his cock, and he stumbled and swayed, supported by her. There; his wife, arms held out to him, her thighs wide and welcoming, her secret places bared to him, pink and velvety folds of flesh like petals on a rose. His wife, his Alex. He couldn't breathe. He gripped the bedpost for support and stared down at her. Her hand on his thigh, her fingers finding his, tugging ever so gently and he let go of the post to kneel clumsily on the bed.

She made as if to pull his shirt off, but he shook his head, motioning for her to lie back down. His balls hurt, his cock twitched. Blood pounded through his head, heat pooled in his loins and he fell forward. She gasped when he pressed his weight against her.

A fumble, a positioning of hips and legs that no longer fit together quite as naturally as they used to do, but he didn't care. Ah, at last! His cock inside of her. His Alex. Again, again, and he was vaguely aware that mayhap he was being too rough, that perhaps he should not pound himself quite so hard against her, but he couldn't stop himself. She'd come for him – almost too late, but she'd come. Alex, his Alex. He drove himself into her, she twisted below him, and with a sound somewhere between a sob and a howl he came.

"We'll miss supper," Alex commented a couple of hours later. Her hair was a tangled mess, her skin was rosy in patches, and she smiled lazily at him, one hand drifting up to stroke his cheek. He just shrugged, bent his head to nuzzle her neck. After that first urgent coupling he had curled to shake with dry sobs by her side and then he had slept, his head pillowed on her chest. He had woken and needed her, and there she had been, a solid, reassuring presence beside him. But this time he had taken his time with her, and now she lay sprawled under him, his cock shrinking slowly back to size inside of her.

"Matthew, you need to eat." Alex shoved at him.

"Aye," he said disinterestedly, busy rediscovering her breasts. It was all a dream; her here with him. He bent his head to her nipple and smiled at her responding "oh." Kate never liked it when...Kate! He sat up so quickly it made his head spin. Alex scooted up to kneel beside him.

"What?" she said. "Is it your foot?"

He looked from her to his bandaged foot and back again.

"What?" She cradled his face with her hands. "Matthew, what is it?"

He covered her hands with his and disengaged himself from her hold. He should tell her – no, he must tell her – and he inhaled in preparation of doing so but at the last moment his nerve failed him and he just shook his head.

"I don't know. Mayhap I just need my supper."

Alex narrowed her eyes and under her scrutiny he felt himself flush. But she didn't ask.

Matthew was somewhat overwhelmed by Mrs Gordon. If she was shocked by his reduced state, she hid it well, busying herself instead with the practicalities surrounding his present state of health. He answered her barrage of questions, sat down to allow her to inspect his foot, and smiled when she told Eliza she'd be doing the cooking for Mr Graham – after all, she knew what he liked.

Mrs Gordon plied him with sweetened wine that went directly to his head, she served him stew and bread and watched him like a hawk to ensure he ate it all. When she ordered him to bed, he just nodded. A bed; he was to sleep in a bed with clean, soft linen. He leaned heavily against Alex as she helped him out of the kitchen and up the stairs. He fell into the bed, was kissed and patted. He yawned, turned on his side, and ...

"He wouldn't have lived much longer," Mrs Gordon commented when Alex came back down.

"No," Alex said, emotionally exhausted after this very long day. Eliza set down a slice of spice cake before her and Alex gave her a grateful smile. Just what she needed; a sugar rush. Mrs Gordon sat down beside her and gave her a hug.

"You did well lass, you found him and saved him."

Alex leaned into her. "I would never have done it without you."

"Aye, you would," Mrs Gordon replied. "Of course you would. You Swedish lasses are mightily stubborn, no?"

In the early morning he began to talk to her nape, and over the following hour he told her everything, from the moment he woke on the ship to the day when he crawled at Jones' feet and admitted that aye, he was a slave. He told her of never ending days under a burning sun, of nights spent shivering in the cold and of week after week of monotonous, endless toil. He described how ill he'd been and how he'd almost died, but how it had been her, the dream of her that kept him alive. He told her every detail of this long, long year – but he never mentioned Kate.

And then it was her turn and she spoke of her travels and the storms, of Don Benito and of the night when she'd seen Magnus in the sea. She told him everything – well almost. She didn't tell him about Fairfax.

It wasn't until Monday that they had any reason to leave the boarding house. Matthew winced at the unfamiliarity of shoes, and spent much time adjusting the buckles to minimise the pressure on his healing foot. He was finally satisfied and raised his eyes to stare in astonishment at his wife.

"You won't go out in that," he informed her once he had finished his detailed inventory.

Alex gave him an exasperated look. "What? Don't you think I look nice?"

Matthew smiled at her understatement. "Aye you do. But for my eyes, not for all." He reached across and tugged at a curl. "My wife. My bonny, bonny wife,but this is only for me to see, aye?" He traced his finger over her exposed bosom. "So I'll just wait while you change." He leaned back against the wall, arms crossed over his chest; they were going nowhere until she was appropriately dressed. Alex glared, but he just shook his head and with a sigh she twisted to undo her lacings.

"Other men would flaunt their wives," she grumbled as they hastened down the dusty road some time later. She stopped to adjust her cap, tucking in a stray lock or two of hair.

"I'm not other men, and you're being looked at enough as it is."

"I am?" She sounded quite pleased, and tightened her grip on his arm.

"You know you are." He frowned as yet another man threw his wife an appreciative look, and adjusted his dark breeches. He snuck a look at himself, still surprised to find himself in stockings and shoes, a dark coat and a clean linen shirt. He stretched, preened even, and beside him Alex laughed.

"Eye candy," she murmured and pinched his buttock hard enough to make him wince.

The bored official duly registered the signed deed conferring the ownership of Matthew Graham on Alexandra Graham, prepared a copy of the deed, signed it and with a malicious smile handed it to Alex, not to Matthew.

"Six years remaining, ma'am."

"No, my husband is a free man as of this minute."

The official snickered as he shook his head. "Not while he remains in Virginia. Here he's registered as an indentured." He tilted his head. "You can of course free him, but that requires the Governor's signature." For a moment the veil of boredom lifted from his eyes and he peered at Matthew.

"What did you do?"

"Nothing," Matthew said icily.

"Ah well, they all say that," the official snorted.

"In this case it's the truth," Alex said. The official hitched his shoulders, indicating that he didn't care, one way or the other, and turned his attention to the next person in line.

"We'll leave as soon as we can," Alex said, not liking the mask of anger on Matthew's face. "After all, we have to hurry home to Mark." She thought of something and dug into her petticoat pocket, extracting a folded and refolded piece of paper.

"It's from Simon."

At first he just held the letter, turning it over several times before he unfolded it, long fingers smoothing out the creases. She knew the letter by heart, but she stood on tiptoe beside Matthew to read it once again, her heart heavy with homesickness.

It was a letter pungent with their old life. It told of summer days at Hillview, of their son running wild across the water meadows. It described the long, long days of harvest, how the hayloft filled with sweet, new hay, and the pantries with preserves.

Simon wrote of Mark, of how Joan had given him a kitten of his own. He described a happy little boy, eyes the same light hazel of his sire, hair that fell in unruly curls. ... *but Joan says she dare not cut them, for she lives in fear of her eyes should Alex come back and find her beloved lamb shorn..."*

"Too right," Alex muttered. She heard Matthew inhale and knew he was reading the long post scriptum. *...It may interest you to know that we have had fancy visitors here at Hillview. Master Luke Graham no less, coming to assert his rights of guardianship over both estate and heir. Let it suffice to say he rode away most disgruntled, protesting that it wasn't right that he, the uncle, should have no say in the raising of Hillview's heir.*

"We can still acquire passage on one of the first boats back, and maybe we can be at Hillview for the harvest."

"Mayhap." Matthew folded the letter together and tucked it inside his shirt, offered Alex his arm and set off towards the boarding house.

# CHAPTER 22

"What's the matter with him?" Alex asked Mrs Gordon next morning, holding Matthew's unresponsive hand. Mrs Gordon shook her head and sat back, gnawing at her lip.

"He's wasted, no?" she said, drawing a finger down Matthew's shirtfront. "These last few days have mayhap taken too much out of him." She raised an eyebrow at Alex and smiled.

"Not my doing, I hope." She just couldn't help herself. She had to, and so did he, and she hadn't even considered that maybe he was too weak. "So what should I do?"

Mrs Gordon shrugged. "He needs food and sleep, lass. The rest will take care of itself, aye?" Alex wasn't quite as convinced, describing the last few nights of disrupted sleep, with Matthew flailing beside her.

"That he has to sort on his own, " Mrs Gordon said, cupping the sleeping man's cheek.

Alex sat beside Matthew all morning, her attention focused on the spare shirt she was making for him. He needed an extra pair of breeches as well, and everyday stockings. That made her smile and she bent over to rifle through her work basket, producing a pair of very nice stockings, the first she'd ever finished to Mrs Gordon's exacting standards.

"What are those?" Matthew asked from the bed. He studied the grey stockings hanging from her hand.

"I made them for you," she said, coming to sit by him. "They took me ages and ages, because Mrs Gordon is quite the pain in the arse at times, so she kept on tearing them up."

He laughed. "Pain in the arse, aye? I haven't heard anyone say that for well over a year." He blinked, wiped at his eyes.

"What is it?" Alex stroked his bare skull, his cheek.

Compared to when she first saw him, he was looking far better, the grey tinge to his skin replaced by a somewhat more normal tone, but still his eyes looked sunken in his face, and even if he'd washed himself as well as he could,there were streaks of encrusted dirt here and there.

"I thought…"He cleared his throat. "I sometimes thought…"

"… that I wouldn't come," she finished for him.

He nodded, eyes a golden green.

"And I…" She lifted his hand to her face and kissed his palm. "… I thought I might be too late. But I came, and you were still alive."

"Aye, but I am that glad you didn't leave it much longer." He tightened his hold on her hand, and she widened her fingers to braid them tight, tight round his. It made her relax inside, to feel their fingers intertwined like that.

"Do you recall how I told you, when we first met, that the light in me had grown so much dimmer whilst in gaol?"

Alex nodded that she did.

"It near went out this time," he said, "some days it guttered on the brink of extinction."

"I know," she breathed. "I dreamt of you, saw you lying in a small room surrounded by other men and I knew you were crying inside. And I so wanted you to know that I was on my way, and that I would never, ever give up."

"My wife," he whispered, "my Alexandra Ruth." A long bony finger came up to touch her cheek, follow the shape of her brows, his thick, dark lashes lowered over eyes that shimmered wetly.

Alex coughed a couple of times to rid her windpipe of the congested tears stuck halfway down.

"Right," she said, "you need to rest and I have to get back to my sewing. And then, in some hours I'll bring you something strengthening to eat, with lots and lots of eggs in it, and after that I think Mr Graham is going to have a bath – a long, very hot bath with his wife in attendance."

Matthew's long mouth curved into a smile.

"I don't need the eggs," he murmured, already drifting off.

"Oh yes, you do," she said, patting him fondly over his crotch. "You need dozens and dozens. You have a wanton wife to take care of."

He opened one eye and nailed it into her. "I can handle that."

"I have no doubts whatsoever, but we'll go with the eggs, just in case."

"Just in case," he agreed and fell abruptly asleep, his hand gripping her skirts.

No wonder he had insisted on keeping his shirt on, hiding his naked body from view. So thin, his bones standing in clear outline against his skin. Long ropes of muscle and tendons, but so wasted, so shrunk from the man she'd last seen naked back at Hillview.

"What kind of an animal did this to you?" Her fingers traced welts across his back and down his sides, deep grooves from where the pulling straps had dug themselves into his skin.

Matthew twisted, trying to see his back. "Is it that bad?"

"Bad!" She wrapped her arms around him and leaned her head between his shoulder blades. "My beautiful man," she said, rubbing her cheek hard against him.

"Not so beautiful now."

"Oh yes," she replied. "Very, very beautiful. Get in," she said, indicating the hip bath. She picked up soap and a linen towel and scrubbed all of him until he was a glowing pink. He looked at the scummy water with astonishment.

"It's as dirty as on Friday!"

"Men! You don't really know how to wash." She towelled him dry and re-bandaged his foot before pointing him back to bed.

"Not to sleep," he said, making a grab for her. She squealed when he pressed himself close to her.

"Of course to sleep, you're a very weak man. I have to be careful so that I don't wear you out."

"Wear me out?" He'd eaten a huge helping of eggs with cheese and bread, followed by a slice of pie drenched in creamy, heavy custard. "I'll show you, aye?"

"We must go and see the Governor," Alex told Matthew some weeks later, looking him up and down. His hair was still unbecomingly short, and even if he ate like a horse there was a lingering gauntness to him. "Or maybe we wait, you know, until you're a bit more recovered."

Matthew just nodded and went back to studying the papers he was holding in his hands.

"What's that?" She leaned over his shoulder. "Oh. It's not particularly good, I can't get his hair right…" She extended her finger to trace the soft cheeks of her baby boy.

Alex sighed; more than a year since she'd last seen Mark, and by the time they got back he'd have lived more months without her than with her. Sometimes she had horrible nightmares in which she knelt to hug him and he just cried, his arms stretched out to Joan. All the more horrible because that was probably what would happen; he'd hide behind Joan or Simon and stare at these his reappeared parents in confusion.

"Will he love us, do you think?" she asked Matthew. He tucked back the papers where he'd found them, in the battered book of sonnets she'd lugged all across the world.

"We love him, no? I'm sure that will be enough." He stood, moved over to the small window that faced, ironically, towards the east. "I'll never forgive Luke for this, for taking me away from my son, forcing you to leave him to go after me." He kicked at Alex' workbasket, sending it skidding over the floor. "He has destroyed my life, he's taken and stolen so much from me and I should have put a stop to him. This time I will. Somehow I will."

"How? Will you kill him and then be dragged off to hang? Because let me tell you something, Mr Graham, I haven't spent a year chasing you across the globe to see you end up spinning at the end of a rope."

"I'll find another way." He drove his fist through the wicker of the chair and gazed down at the resulting bloodied knuckles. "I will be revenged on him."

Alex put a hand on his back and waited until he turned to face her. "I want my Matthew, not a man bent on vengeance. I don't want our son to grow up surrounded by the corroding hatred of this family feud."

His eyes flashed with anger. "Will you have me forgive him?"

"No, but maybe forget him."

Matthew laughed sarcastically. "And are you fool enough to think he will let me forget?"

Alex bowed her head; he was right, Luke would never stop, not until his brother was destroyed.

He nodded in silent agreement, grabbed his coat and left the room.

Alex went over to the small window to watch him stride away. Healing rapidly on the outside, but on the inside... At times she suspected he forced himself to play the part of reunited husband, when all he really wanted to do was wallow in anger and hate – alone.

There were barriers between them, whole months of terrible experiences that he didn't seem capable of sharing with her beyond the short factual description he had given her that first morning, and the few attempts she had made to have him speak to her about it had been violently rebuffed.

Give him time, she admonished herself, leave him be for now. To her surprise she found she was crying and rubbed at her eyes. He was safe, no? Alive and whole, and the rest of him would knit itself back into place with time – of course it would.


"Graham!"

To his intense humiliation, Matthew halted, a kneejerk reaction to a voice he'd obeyed for almost a year. Jones sauntered over to him, took his time looking him up and down.

"Well, well, quite the gentleman."

"A gentleman? I think not. But a free man, aye that I am. But then I always was."

"Free?" Jones snickered. "Not as I hear it. You're owned by your wife now." His light eyes glinted, the small mouth opened as if to say something but then closed.

"Get out of my way," Matthew said, "get out before I do you bodily harm."

"Oh I wouldn't do that if I were you, Graham. An indentured to raise his hand to a free man? No Graham, that would be very unwise. It might lead to you being hanged." The small, piercing eyes swam very close to Matthew's. "But please try, give me the pleasure of beating you to a bloody pulp." Jones straightened up, standing a scant inch or so taller than Matthew's six feet and two.

"One day..." Matthew began.

"One day? I think not. One day you'll be dead, Graham, and I, well I'll receive a nice, fat purse in compensation."

He shouldn't have said that.

"Who? Who'll pay you to see me dead?"

When Jones didn't reply, Matthew's fingers closed like a pincer around a fold of skin along Jones' neck, twisting until the overseer was kneeling in the dust, gasping with pain.

"My wife taught me this, it hurts, no?" Matthew twisted some more. "So who?"

"Your brother," Jones gargled. "Fairfax had a letter some weeks back." He squealed when Matthew's fingers sank even deeper into his neck. Matthew released him, and Jones sat down heavily in the dirt. Someone laughed, and to Matthew's consternation he saw that they'd collected a small, avid audience.

"You'll pay," Jones assured Matthew, hands rubbing at his reddened neck.

"So will you, and I have a bigger debt to collect than you do." With that Matthew walked off.

For some minutes Matthew was buoyed by his confrontation with Jones, energy buzzing through his system. He strode through the little settlement, shaking his head yet again at the idiocy of situating a town here, in this swamp infested corner of the earth. Barely a half mile from the town centre the original forest encroached, ground squelching wetly underneath. It was only April and already the heat at midday was uncomfortable, and he could only imagine how it would be to live here in summer, the sun steaming dampness off the ground.

He made his way down to the harbour, as yet empty of any larger ships. A breeze danced across the water and he undid his coat, sitting down on a crude bench to stare in the direction of the east. Over the waters lay his home and there his son was waiting.

Sometimes it struck him that they didn't know: Mark might be dead, carried away by illness or drowned in the millpond. Like his grandfather before him, Matthew grimaced, recalling the day when his Da, Malcolm Graham, had been pulled dead from the water. Not an accident, he mused, no, someone had pushed his unsuspecting father to fall into the cold winter waters of the pond. Margaret or Luke, it had to be one or the other. Luke, of course it was Luke, and Matthew sat with black anger simmering inside of him, wondering how on earth a man as warped as Luke could be his brother. Mayhap he was a changeling.

He was deep in thought when a hand clapped him on the shoulder and he turned to find a familiar face smiling down at him.

"James! You're still alive!"

James laughed and sat down beside him. "You mustn't sound so surprised."

Matthew studied him. Much thinner, arms and legs like brittle twigs, but yet with something of a paunch. He took in the tired face, the sunken eyes and the strange, yellowed skin.

"You've got jaundice."

James shrugged. "I don't rightly know. But as I can't do

170

a day's work without toppling over, I'm sent here to town to earn my living best I can."

"They set you free?"

James smiled crookedly. "Nay. They but threw me out. Why waste good food on a dying man."

"How do you live?" Matthew asked with concern.

"I do this and that. I can read and write, so I've been doing a bit of scribing. And I sleep where I can find some cover." He patted at the small bundle on his back. "A blanket."

Matthew got to his feet and took his friend by his arm. "You'll come with me. We'll find you board."

"We?" James smiled, "so she came then?"

"Aye," Matthew said with pride. "She did."

"I saw you earlier," James said as they walked side by side in the direction of the boarding house. He shook his head at Matthew. "Best be careful lad, Jones is not a man you want as your enemy."

"Not my choice."

"Still; best no go about unarmed – not after today. He won't forgive the humiliation of being forced to his knees."

Whatever doubts Alex had about clasping this ragged, sorry spectacle of a man to her bosom she didn't show them, curtseying in deference to his age. Mrs Gordon took one look at James and called for a bath, promising the man that unless he scrubbed himself clean enough for her satisfaction she'd do it herself – with lye.

"I haven't washed in a year," he protested.

"Aye, I can see that. And smell it." Mrs Gordon handed him a clean shirt and two worn linen towels before leading him off in the direction of the kitchen.

"Where will he sleep?" Alex asked, "I don't think Mrs Gordon will want him in her room." And she definitely didn't want him in theirs.

Matthew laughed and assured her it was all taken care of, James would sleep in the stables.

"Is he very ill?" In her opinion the shrunken man looked

as if he was about to expire at any moment.

"He's dying," Matthew replied, "and he knows it."

Washed and dressed in a clean shirt, James sat with them to eat, but he ate little, and finally Mrs Gordon stood up and disappeared, returning in some moments from the kitchen with a frothing mug. Alex sniffed; spices, hot wine, and very much honey beaten together with eggs. James smiled his thanks.

"I have a problem with the solids."

Alex gave him a narrow look; no wonder he looked so frail if he couldn't eat properly. James gave her a weak smile and sat back, visibly wincing when his emaciated shoulder blades settled against the wall. He looked out at the dark night with disgust.

"It's April, time for long evenings of soft light, for the smell of new leaves on the trees..." He sounded so homesick Alex reached across and patted his hand.

"Maybe one day you'll go back."

James smiled, his eyes misting over. "Perhaps. But I think not."

# CHAPTER 23

The bed creaked when Matthew got out and moved over to the window. One of the shutters screeched against the windowsill, and with an irritated sound Alex sat up. Matthew was standing by the opened window, arms braced against the frame. She padded across the floor and put a hand on his shoulder. The effect was spectacular. Matthew whirled, snarling like a cornered dog. She gasped, raised her arms to shield herself from the blow she expected to come flying her way. Instead Matthew cursed and flung himself towards the door, and a few moments later she heard him in the yard below. His shirt was a blob of white in all the dark, a blob that moved with speed away from her.

"Shit." Alex sat down on the bed. Far too often she woke up alone, him long gone, and if anything his confrontation with Jones had made it worse, with Matthew coiled in constant anger, an anger that had him tossing restlessly through most of the nights. After those first wonderful days the darkness in him tainted their sex life as well, Matthew being too careful, always holding back. Whenever she came too close, whenever her caresses became too intimate, he shied away, retreating into the safety of the mechanics of sex rather than the magic of making love.

He reminded her of a wild fern; one long brush along its fronds and it curled itself up tight around its inner core, a whispered *Noli me Tangere* – don't touch me – echoing in the wind. But this was her man, goddamn it, not some piece of greenery! Worse of all was when he retreated to lie for hours on their bed, rejecting her company as he stared unblinkingly at the wooden ceiling above. It unnerved her, this absolute stillness that left her standing very alone on the outside. She sighed and slid down to lie on her back, eyes locked on the door.

When she next woke it was daylight and he was back, busy shaving.

"Today," he said.

"Today?" Alex had no idea what he was on about, and anyway, shouldn't they first discuss last night?

"The Governor; I want us to see him today." He wiped his face clean. "I won't be an un-free man anymore and after that run-in with Jones I want to do this as soon as possible." A month and more since she bought him free, he reminded her.

Alex resigned herself and inspected her meagre wardrobe. "The russet, it's the best I have."

"As long as you're decent," he warned, and with a quick kiss hurried off to find some breakfast.

"He might not be there," Alex pointed out when they set off. Her linen shift was already sticking to her skin and she found herself longing for air conditioning – or at least a good deodorant.

"He is. I saw him ride in right early."

"Ah." She yawned. Always so tired lately, her body surprisingly heavy. It must be the heat in combination with a humidity that made her hair go Shirley Temple in the extreme, spontaneously transforming into a mass of fashionable ringlets. Not that anyone saw them; Matthew Graham's wife always wore her hair neatly coiled and capped.

"What did you do all night?" she asked him.

"I walked." He pressed her hand tight under his arm. "I'm sorry, lass," he muttered, and she could hear that was all he intended to say about last night – at least for now.

Sir William was bored. He fluffed at his shoulder length hair, still mostly its original dark brown, eyed the line outside his office with irritation, and swept inside to settle behind his desk, quill in hand to convey the impression of a very busy man that must not be importuned more than necessary.

His mind wandered back to his mulberry trees and silk worms, congratulating himself yet again on having succeeded in multiplying them so well. He groaned inwardly at having to be here instead of at home on Green Spring, and in particular now, in May, when his fields were a promising, beckoning green.

An adjustment to his tasselled sash, and with a wave of his hand he indicated to his secretary to let the first supplicant in. Hopefully he could conclude business in time to ride the few miles out to his home before dark.

He suppressed a sigh as he listened to the concocted little story of the couple in front of him. The wife was pleasing to the eye, if excessively modest with an unfashionably high neckline to her linen shift, and he noticed with mild interest that it was she who was doing most of the talking, her husband standing silent beside her. Not out of choice, he decided, but because at present he had no legal status. He considered their situation; she was wed to him and therefore she and all her worldly goods were his to dispose of as he saw fit. At the same time, she now owned his indenture, having exposed herself to a daunting sea crossing to find him and buy him free. So now he was both owned and owner… He stopped listening, sinking into this interesting little conundrum until he realised she'd fallen silent and was expecting him to say something.

"Have you got any proof of his supposed innocence?"

"How am I supposed to get that?" she said. "In general courts only issue documents on convicted people, or people who have at least stood some trial. My husband has not been accused, nor yet been on trial, so how could I furnish you with this document you request?"

He shrugged. He let his eyes wander over them again. The man was a Scot, he heard that in his speech.

"Are you Presbyterian?" he asked, a slight interest sparking in his brain. The man nodded that he was. "A Covenanter? " Sir William inflected his voice with disgust.

Matthew Graham straightened up to his full height,

ignoring the restraining touch of his wife's hand.

"I am."

"A soldier?" Sir William leaned forward, eyes boring into the uncommonly tall man.

"For a while," Graham said. "Four years, aye?"

"How old are you?"

Graham looked somewhat surprised. "Thirty-two."

Sir William sat back; this Graham would have been fifteen at Naseby, twenty-one before that accursed Cromwell won the north. But only eleven when he himself left England to hold Virginia for the crown – after far too many months spent in Scotland fighting for the King.

"On what side did you fight?"

This was a rather needless question, Sir William recognised, watching the tall Scot square his shoulders. But one never knew, did one, and men had been known to change sides – in some cases more than once.

"I was for the Commonwealth," Matthew Graham said, and Sir William frowned at the pride in his voice.

Sir William eyed him with dislike; he had no patience with these extreme religious fanatics, although he had to concede that the couple in front of him looked no threat to law and order, for all that the man admitted to being of Puritan beliefs. The King was restored, he reminded himself and the kingdom was healed. No more rifts, no more conflicts that tore the country apart. Still... He'd loved the old king, and in the younger man's eyes he saw a mild satisfaction at having been on the side that won the armed conflict. It galled him, spurring him to a pettiness not generally in his nature.

"You wish to free him?"

Mrs Graham nodded, presenting a freshly inked deed, rolled together to preserve it from creasing. He read the document through and shook his head.

"No; I have no proof that this man isn't a dangerous criminal, and I fear that he's a potential dissenter. I'll see you back in two months, and then we'll see."

The green flare in Graham's eyes had him sitting back, and he twisted away to look at the wife instead. Blue ice made him recoil.

She curtsied and raised herself back up. "Until then, Sir William. And I will of course wait until that occasion to turn over some effects I have been requested to ensure reach you personally."

He stuttered in indignation. "Are you carrying dispatches for me?"

She gave him yet another cold look. "Am I? Not that I know off. I have gifts to give you, at my convenience." She placed her hand on her husband's arm and swept out of the room, leaving Sir William slack mouthed.

"That went really well," Alex said. Matthew was stone under her hand, walking so fast she had to break out into an undignified trot to keep up. "Matthew! Please..." When he didn't slow, she let him go, stumbling before she regained her footing.

In front of her Matthew's back was moving away and she came to a stop, not quite knowing what to do. Her pouch was heavy with the carefully wrapped objects that she had been entrusted in getting to Sir William, and for an instant she considered throwing the three items into the river. But she didn't, because for some reason handling them – and in particular the larger of the rectangular objects – sent shivers up her spine.

It was all Matthew's fault; she had suggested that she should first give the Governor the packages, and then, once she'd established herself as a once removed trusted emissary from the English court, request he sign the deed. Which she was certain he would have done, not even bothering to read it properly. But Matthew had been adamant; he wanted the Governor to sign the deed based on his own story, not because he was distracted by other things. And now he was off to sulk, or throw himself on their bed and refuse to talk to her while the rage that simmered inside of him cooled down to manageable levels.

She decided not to return to the boarding house, but set off in the direction of the Apothecary. She was sure she'd find Mrs Gordon there, generously dispensing advice in between her elegant flirting with the helpless proprietor, Mr Parson, a tall, thin man with an impressive mane of white hair. His shop was crowded with flasks and jars, with bunches of drying herbs, honeycombs and strange things she preferred not to look too closely at, all of it suffused by a rather pleasing scent of beeswax and cloves.

"Mrs Graham! Come for a spot of tea?" Mr Parson beamed down at her from his ladder and she smiled back. One reason she appreciated Mr Parson was that not only did he sell tea, he also liked tea, having developed an addiction to the beverage during several years spent in Lisbon. Having discovered an avid tea drinker in Alex, he always offered her a cup when she came by. It was horribly expensive, but every now and then she would allow herself the luxury of a two ounce bag, hoarding it for herself.

Mrs Gordon bustled out from the back regions and assured Mr Parson she was quite capable of taking care of his wee shop while he went and had a cup of tea, and in less than five minutes Alex was seated on a small stool in the open kitchen door, sipping with pleasure at the hot liquid in her cup. Mr Parson tsk:ed at her summary of the events of the morning but did not seem unduly concerned.

"In this case it doesn't really matter. As you're his wife, and you hold his indenture, well then his indenture belongs to himself." Alex found that somewhat confusing, and Mr Parson explained it again. Anything a wife owned belonged to her husband. In this particular instance she could see a benefit in that, but for the rest…

"And what if a rich girl marries a nasty character who only takes her for her money?"

Mr Parson chewed his lip. "A girl will marry where her father chooses her to. The father has an obligation to ensure the future husband is a man of good character. He will surely intercede if his daughter is treated badly."

"And what happens when the father dies? Or her brother or whoever has been responsible for arranging the marriage?"

Mr Parson didn't reply; instead he offered Alex some more tea.

It took some time for Matthew to catch on to the fact that Alex was no longer following him. A quick look up the street ascertained she was nowhere in sight, and he was ashamed for taking out on her what was really his own fault. But to have that pompous man deny him something that should never have been taken from him in the first place made him want to gag. He considered retracing his steps to find her, but after some moments of indecision chose to keep on walking, making for the waterfront where he sat down in the shade, discarding his coat to allow the weak breeze to cool him.

He knew his silences worried her, and sometimes he sensed how excluded she felt, but he couldn't let her in, not when all he wanted to do in those dark moments was to hurt someone. He turned his angered thoughts on Luke; this was all his fault. Thinking of Luke only served to incense him further, fuming at fate that had chosen to let this twisted evil creature live instead of having him carried away in a childhood fever.

Red haired and green eyed, Luke had been a bonny, high-spirited lad, a lad so much younger than him that he was more of a nuisance than a brother. And when he'd returned from the war, Luke had tagged after him, admiration shining out of his eyes for this stranger who was his brother and had killed men, several men, in the heat of battle. Somewhere there the relationship between the brothers shifted from one of mutual affection to one of distance.

A year later their rigid father had thrown Luke out for fornicating with Margaret, ignoring Luke's pleas that he be allowed to marry her, for he loved her, loved her, you hear? If only Da had agreed to that, Matthew sighed. Instead, fifteen year old Margaret was left at Hillview pining for the man she had always loved but was convinced would never come back. So she turned to him, to Matthew, and he was flattered by the attention of this beautiful lass – no, woman. He had lain with women before, of course he had, but never had he been touched the way she touched him, never felt himself burn with want, and three years after Luke had left he wed Margaret.

And then Luke came back, coincidentally the day they buried Da. After that it all went wrong; his wife taking Luke to bed in their room, laughing at him when he came upon them. And the child; his son, wee Ian that Margaret told him was Luke's. Except that he wasn't, as he found out many years later.

He sighed and used a stick to trace a capital L in the dust before him. Years in gaol because of Luke – convicted of a crime he'd never committed. A child stolen from him, impossible to reclaim, another child lost to the cruel beating Luke had submitted Alex to. He should have killed him when he had the chance – no one would ever have known. Instead he had sliced off Luke's nose, and for that Luke had done this to him. So much hatred, a vicious yellow bile that tainted both their lives. Now it was too late; there was no way back, no possibility to repair all those destroyed bridges.

He produced the half written letter to Simon from inside his shirt and reread what he'd written so far. He laughed darkly at the task he was lumbering his brother-in-law with; to investigate how Malcolm Graham had died in late 1653, nigh on nine years ago. Well, if anyone could do such it would be his legally trained friend, and behind Simon's cannon ball exterior and joviality there ticked a mind of extreme sharpness. He wasn't sure what he wanted to achieve by his request; a possibility to have Luke convicted of murder? But what if it was Margaret who'd pushed Malcolm to die?

He heard the flapping sound first and raised his eyes from his letter to see in front of him a ship. The crew was busy taking in the sails, anchors were lowered with dull splashes, and the deck was full of men. He gawked; how had it sailed up so close without him noticing? Boats were setting out in the direction of the ship, and with a sinking feeling he realised he recognised this particular vessel.

Matthew stuck the letter into his coat pocket and retreated further into the shade, an unwilling spectator to the events unfolding in front of him. His eyes stuck on the men being lowered into the boats, pale blobs for faces. He was only yards from the landing stage and he stared at the newcomers. Had he looked like that, filthy, with a pervading stink of vomit and a pallor that indicated weeks out of the sun? He wanted to back away but felt obliged to watch this to the bitter end, remaining rooted to the spot as the sad little caravan stumbled towards the auction block on landless, weakened legs.

"Brings back memories, doesn't it?" Jones said, materialising out of nowhere by his side. When Matthew moved away, Jones followed. "Once a slave, always a slave." He brought his riding crop down hard against the leather of his boots, laughing when Matthew flinched at the sound.

"Once a glob of shit, always a glob of shit," Matthew said. Jones raised his crop. "Go on," Matthew taunted. "Go on and use that on me and see what happens."

The whip came down, Matthew sidestepped, and Jones almost overbalanced with the momentum of his movement, but regained his balance with the grace of a huge cat, wheeling so fast Matthew had no possibility of evading the crop. It slashed him across the ear, and with a growl Matthew pounced.

A fist connected with his chin, he grunted, hit back, and then it was all a whirlwind of kicks and punches. Too big, too strong; Jones was sneering, big hands clenched into fists the size of hams. The saner part of Matthew's brain begged with him to break and run, flee, and he actually started to turn when a kick sent him sprawling to the ground.

Merciful Lord! He bit his tongue with the force of the impact, his mouth flooding with the taste of his blood. Up; get up. Matthew shook his head in an effort to clear his mind, a movement flashed to his right and he rolled, Jones' foot missing his head by an inch no more. He was on his feet, levering himself upright when the next kick drove into his flank. Ah! Like a punctured pig's bladder he collapsed to the ground, leeching on to the foot. Jones cursed, tried to tug himself free. Matthew pulled with all his might, and like an uprooted tree Jones toppled towards him. Matthew rolled again, narrowly evading having Jones land on him.

Matthew groaned, heaving himself up on all fours. Jones cursed and spat, sat up and threw himself at Matthew, squashing him flat. No air. Matthew coughed, tried to dislodge this unbearable weight from across his back.

Water; they were by the shoreline, and a huge, meaty hand came down on Matthew's nape, dragging him towards the water. Matthew dug his hands in, his toes, his knees, heaving himself backwards. Jones grunted, sank his fingers into Matthew's neck and lifted him towards the pebbled shore. Matthew bit him, gained a second or so of respite and retreated from the water. Jones said something, his fingers were back, punishing digits that sank into tendons and nerves. An inch, yet another inch, grass became sand, sand became pebbles and here was the water. Jones forced his head under the surface.

In desperation Matthew bucked, his elbow connected with something and the hold on his neck relaxed sufficiently for him to tear himself free. He crawled on all fours and there was the hand again, pulling him back towards the water, while all around men catcalled and cheered. I'm going to die, Matthew managed to think. His head was yet again submerged. He struggled like a fiend, found purchase against the bottom with his hands, succeeded in pushing himself high enough to gasp some air before going down again.

When Alex came out of Mr Parson's shop, she met a

stream of people hurrying off towards the river and fell in step, curious about the general air of festivity. She stopped when she saw the ship, the men. Her eyes flew over the crowd, searching for Matthew, and her heart did an odd little manoeuvre when she saw the knot of men, a tight huddle of loud voices and cheers that was oblivious to the on-going auction.

She shouldered her way through, using feet and elbows when she needed to. Just as she made it to the front the noise died away, and when she broke through the last line of men she saw why. Matthew and Jones were down by the water, Matthew's limbs flopping weakly while Jones was holding his head under water. Alex didn't stop to think.

"Murder! He's murdering my husband!" She launched herself on Jones, grabbed the big man by his hair and pulled – hard. Jones swore and swatted at her, but by doing so he relinquished his hold on Matthew, and to Alex relief she saw her husband's head reappear, mouth wide open as he gulped down air. She tightened her hold and dragged Jones' backwards, him howling like a stuck pig. Her grip on his hair slipped, and with an angry exclamation Jones pushed Alex away, turning back to his intended victim.

"Fifty witnesses," Alex called, "and I swear, Dominic Jones, that I'll see you hang if you as much as lay a finger on my husband again." She planted herself in front of him, all of her tensing. If he tried anything she'd send him flying – she hoped, gulping at the size of him. Jones came to a stop and swept eyes over the by now very silent spectators. He hesitated, looked over to where Matthew was on hands and knees, retching. His hands twitched, they curled themselves into threatening fists, and then the harbourmaster was there as well, coming to stand between Matthew and Jones.

"Go," he said to Jones.

"Get out of my way," Jones growled. "He started it, and now he must pay the price. An indenture to raise his hands to a free man!"

183

"He didn't start it, you did," the harbourmaster said. "And I'll add my voice to Mrs Graham's if need be." A murmur of assent rose from among the men, quite a few shuffled on their feet and two came forward to help Matthew stand. With a colourful curse and one last look at Matthew, Jones stalked off.

"Stay away from him," the harbourmaster said. "Jones is a dangerous man."

Matthew nodded, dragging a shaking hand over his wet face. He inhaled, held his breath and exhaled, repeating the procedure a couple of times before taking the few steps that separated him from Alex. She didn't say anything – she couldn't – she just raised her hand to his cheek, his mouth.

"I'm alright," he said, "truly, Alex, I'm fine, aye?" He led her to where he had left his coat, lying on a makeshift bench. "We won't be trying for a passage with her," he said, spitting in the direction of the *Henriette Marie*.

"Of course not," Alex said. "Although we could perhaps sneak aboard and set her on fire." That coaxed a small smile from Matthew.

"He was going to kill you." Her hands knotted themselves into the fabric of her skirts and she couldn't quite remember what to do to relax the tension in them.

"But he didn't," Matthew said. He worked her fingers loose from her skirts one by one.

"No, he didn't." She stepped up close enough to rest her forehead against him, drew in his scent, so reassuringly warm and alive. Matthew held her to him, long fingers tracing soothing patterns up and down her back. "He'll try again."

"Aye – and all at the behest of my beloved brother." He leaned back to see her face. "You bought me free in the nick of time. Had you but been a few weeks later, I would have been dead, Jones would have been richer, and Luke would have been whooping for joy."

"Oh." Alex snuck her hand into his and they walked back not saying anything much until they turned into the small lane leading to the boarding house, where Alex drew him to a stop.

"Here," she said, digging into her pouch to produce the copy of the contract with Fairfax.

Matthew looked at her in confusion.

Alex squirmed; she didn't really like saying this. "I'm your wife, no?"

He half smiled and raised an eyebrow to assure her that she was.

"Anything I own is therefore per definition yours – even I am yours." She grimaced, he waited, clearly amused. "So, if I hold your indenture and I'm your wife well then it follows that the person who really owns your indenture is yourself. No matter what the Governor says or does, you're free." She waited as he worked that one through and it made her glad to see the light it kindled in his eyes. "I wonder what all this makes me," she grumbled as they turned into the yard. "A cow?"

Matthew hooked a finger in the waistband of her skirt, drawing her towards him.

"You're mine, aye. My wife – no cow." He squeezed her buttock and jerked his head in the direction of the house. "Bed. Now."

Alex laughed, tried to wiggle free from his arms and hands.

"Forget it; I'm starving. You'll have to wait until after dinner."

Matthew took a firm hold of her and propelled her towards the stairs. "Nay, you'll wait with dinner."

He definitely tried, and for some instants it was almost like it used to be between them, sparks flying hot from finger to skin; almost, but not quite, and then the stranger was back, a man who made courteous, distanced love to her. It made her want to kick him in his balls.

# CHAPTER 24

Next morning Alex only had to glance at Matthew to see his elation had faded back into his customary simmering resentment. He was sitting at the little desk, brows pulled into one dark line, busy with his letter. Alex sighed; one of the first casualties to these black moods was early morning sex, mainly because he was out of bed and dressed long before she woke up. She stretched, rolled in his direction. He pretended not to notice she was awake, his quill scratching over the paper.

"Hi," she tried, receiving a grunt in reply. She patted the bed beside her, half sat up. "Come here," she purred, her breasts clearly visible. Matthew sat back and stretched out his long legs, crossing them at the ankles.

"I'm already dressed, no?"

She hunched together for an instant before straightening her spine.

"Fine." She rolled out of bed, dressing with angered haste. She detoured around his chair on the way to the door. "This will never work, we'll never find our way back to how we used to be if you continue closing me out." He extended his hand to her, but she shook her head. "Too late, Mr Graham. I'm already dressed, see?" He flinched as she threw his words back at him and it made her glad. Bastard!

"It isn't only my responsibility. I try and try, I laugh and play happy families, I try to show you that I love you just as much now as before, even if the man I now share my bed with is very different from the man I once met on a moor. It hasn't exactly been a piece of cake for me either, you know."

"It wasn't you sold like a beast," he snapped. "You didn't spend months living like a slave."

"No, I just spent month after month imagining what you might be living, dying inside at the thought that someone was abusing you, starving you." She sent him a dark look, grabbed at her hat and left.

Matthew saw her emerge into the alley, adjust the straw bonnet and set off towards the town. He should go after her, but what could he possibly say? He watched her drop out of sight, sealed his letter to Simon and went down to breakfast, pleasantly surprised to find James there.

"Did you quarrel?" James asked. "She looked right upset, wee Alex."

Matthew shrugged. "I don't rightly know," he said, salting his eggs. "She says I close her out, and aye, I do. I can't burden her with the rage that gnaws at my insides, and in my darker moments I fear that I might take it out on her." He sighed and concentrated on his food until the plate was wiped clean.

"It used to be I would love her in the mornings," he mumbled, keeping his eyes on the table. "Even the first few days back with her I did. But now I wake long before her, and my cock is stiff and hard but it is more rage than love. So instead I rise and dress." He drew his mug of beer towards him and drank. "It hurts her, aye? She likes it when we start the day together – and so do I."

"And today?"

Matthew squirmed. "She wanted me, and I told her I was already dressed."

"Ah," James nodded, digging into his pouch for his pipe. "You have to explain, and you must do it soon."

Matthew drank some more. He already knew that; he just didn't know how.

Alex was still buzzing with rejection when she reached the Governor's rooms. Announcing that she had objects from the king to deliver, she was admitted to the dining room where Sir William sat very lonely at the end of a long table. Still in morning attire, with a plum silk dressing gown over a linen nightshirt, Sir William stared balefully at her.

"What incompetent fool let you in? And unannounced at that!"

"Sir William," she curtsied, ignoring his little outburst.

"Two months," he said, attempting a dismissive wave of his hand.

"I decided I wouldn't allow myself to be as petty as you are." She dug into her pouch and retrieved two small, wrapped objects. "These were entrusted me by Don Ángel Benito Muñoz de Hojeda upon his death in Barbados, and I promised to fulfil his charge and deliver them to you, with compliments from the king."

"A book," Sir William said, hefting the larger of the objects, and the look of pleasure on his face was so spontaneous that Alex smiled, despite the fact that she was still mad as hell. He put down the parcel unopened. "May I offer you some breakfast?"

She eyed the heaped eggs and felt her stomach somersault, a swift wave of nausea flowing up towards her mouth. She couldn't be! Not so soon…

"An orange, perhaps?" Sir William suggested, scratching at his impressive beak of a nose. "I've grown it myself, out at my plantation."

Alex made adequate complimentary noises, doubting the Governor had done much more than oversee the planting. From the look of his hands he wasn't much into manual labour.

"Why don't you open it?" she asked, indicating the book.

"The longer I wait, the more of a surprise it will be. It will keep a few hours more."

Alex nodded, slicing her orange into edible sections. "And the other?"

Sir William weighed it in his hand. "A ring," he guessed, "or perhaps a medallion."

He opened it and showed her an excellent miniature of a man with saturnine features and a lot of long hair; the king, obviously. Around the central image was depicted an oak, and she wondered if that was an attempt to relay the impression that Charles the Second was as stout and long lived as an oak. Sir William laughed at her.

"It's the Royal Oak, the tree in which he hid whilst hunted like an animal by the Commonwealth troops."

Another huge hole in her history education, Alex concluded. The miniature was mounted and Sir William pinned it on his dressing gown to show it off.

"Very nice," she murmured, hiding a smile.

"Yes," the Governor said, "a small reminder, I think, of where my loyalties must lie."

"Thank you for the orange," Alex said once she had finished it and got to her feet. "I hope it's a good book."

Sir William called her back before she reached the door. "The deed, I will sign it now, if you have it with you."

"I do." Alex dug into her pouch, heat flying up her neck, her cheeks and all the way to her ears when her fingers grazed the third package, the one she had chosen not to hand over. She shivered inside just from touching it. She handed the deed to Sir William who unrolled it and signed it before giving it back.

"I was not at my best yesterday," he muttered, avoiding her eyes.

"No, you're much nicer today." She placed a hand on his. "We all have our bad days, right?"

If he was taken aback by her forwardness, he didn't show it.

"Yes, I dare say we all do." He smiled, dark eyes crinkling together.

Once she was back outside, Alex half ran in the direction of Mrs Adams'. She had no idea what had made her unwrap the third package on her way into town, and she had taken but the quickest peek before shoving it deeper into her pouch. Now the package called to her, an insistent whisper that she pull it out and look at it, look closely and drown.

Oh God; sweat broke out along her spine. A painting; one of Mercedes' magic time portals, blue and green swirls leading towards a vertiginous midst of brilliant white. And all the time it had been lying among Don Benito's things, talk about a coincidence! If one was given to fanciful thoughts one could almost imagine the painting was doing its best to find her. Alex laughed shakily. That was totally ridiculous, she told herself, but she had to stop and take a couple of steadying breaths.

She hefted her pouch. It should burn – no, it must burn – and yet ... well, maybe she shouldn't. Matthew would insist it be destroyed the moment he clapped eyes on it, and that insight made Alex come to a halt, turn and set off towards the Apothecary, hoping to find Mrs Gordon there.

She was. Alex blinked and broke out in a huge smile. Mr Parson and Mrs Gordon stood face to face in the little shop, holding hands. Alex watched tall, distinguished Mr Parson creak down to kiss Mrs Gordon on her brow. She turned her back, counted to one hundred and then barged in, catching the courting couple in a heated kiss.

"I need your help." Alex grinned at the mottled red that stood bright against the white of Mrs Gordon's collar. "You can kiss her a bit more later," she said to a peony pink Mr Parson, tugging Mrs Gordon in the direction of the kitchen. "Look at you," Alex said to Mrs Gordon. "Quite the guy magnet you are."

"Och, aye? And what is a guy magnet?" Mrs Gordon patted her starched collar back into place.

"A woman who has men drooling."

"Not all men," Mrs Gordon said primly.

"No, just Captain Miles, Mr Coulter on Barbados and now Mr Parson."

"Mr Coulter was a bereaved widower and Captain Miles is a married man."

"They still fancied you, and you know that." Alex smiled at the expression that flashed across Mrs Gordon's face. "I want you to keep something for me," she went on, digging into her pouch.

In her haste she threw the package at the table but

missed, causing it to teeter on the edge before falling to the floor. The soft cloth around it snagged on the wooden table top, thereby allowing the painting to land uncovered on the floor. Alex squeaked and took an instinctive step back.

"It's not a snake," Mrs Gordon said, bending over stiffly to study the small oblong painting.

Alex looked at her in surprise. "You don't feel it?"

Mrs Gordon shook her head. "Feel what?"

"Hmm," Alex gnawed her lip. "Don Benito gave it to me," she lied, "my mother painted it."

Mrs Gordon picked up the lightweight square and placed it on the table, eyeing it with interest.

"Your mother? Did he know her?"

No of course he didn't, Alex felt like saying, my mother hasn't been born yet– hang on a minute; yes she had, Mercedes had been born ages ago, in medieval Seville. And she'd been here – in this time – leaving paintings behind her, and all of this was so confusing it made Alex want to retreat to bed and sleep for a week. Alternatively throw up.

"No, but he must have found it in Seville, that was her home town."

"She wasn't very good, was she?" Mrs Gordon said, making Alex choke on a bubble of laughter. If only she knew! "What is this? A wee sea? A portion of a river?"

"I don't know, and maybe it isn't good, but it was my mother's, and I'd like you to keep it for me."

"Why?"

Alex sighed. "Matthew doesn't like it."

Matthew didn't even know it existed, but the moment he did, he'd cleave it in two with an axe, and that was something Alex couldn't allow to happen. She had no idea why, the rational part of her mind was telling her that the right thing to do was to destroy it, but her instincts were telling her not to. Mrs Gordon's black eyes darted from the picture to Alex, but finally she agreed.

"We have to wrap it up, cover it completely," Alex said.

Ignoring Mrs Gordon's surprised expression she

approached the painting with her eyes squished shut, wrapping it up by feel alone. At Alex' insistence, Mrs Gordon found yet another length of cloth and by the time Alex was done a neatly tied parcel rested on the table, the seductive whispers from the canvas muffled into an indistinctive hum. Alex relaxed.

"Explain," Mrs Gordon said, her peppercorn eyes indicating none of them were going anywhere until Alex had told her the truth.

"I can't, you won't believe me."

Mrs Gordon shoved the parcel in the direction of Alex. "If you won't tell me, then I won't keep it. I can see you think it dangerous."

Well, she had a point there, Alex conceded, wondering how on earth to begin.

"You can start at the beginning," Mrs Gordon suggested. "You can start by explaining why a lass would wander around in long, blue breeches and her hair cropped short, like the first time I saw you."

Alex gave Mrs Gordon a long, considering look, squared her shoulders and took a deep breath. Here goes.

"Jeans, they're called jeans, the long pants, and where I come from everybody wears them, both men and women."

Mrs Gordon didn't say a word. Not once did she interrupt or exclaim her disbelief. She just sat and listened, her face a perfect blank. Alex talked and talked, unnerved by her silence.

"The painting is a door back, I think," she concluded, looking at the wrapped object with fear.

Mrs Gordon poked at the painting. "You think you might need one?"

"No! Of course not! But I just ... well, you know, sometimes I miss her, my mother."

"Was she a witch?"

"Mercedes?" Alex laughed hoarsely. "Well, yes, I suppose she was." She shivered, arms tight around herself. "But I'm not."

Mrs Gordon's face wreathed itself into a huge smile. "You? Of course not! You can't even knit properly."

At this point in time Mr Parson stuck his nose in through the door to tell Mrs Gordon there was a baby on its way and would she please hurry as the future father had just fainted on his shop floor. Mrs Gordon swept the packed painting into her midwifery bundle, winked at Alex and hurried after him.

Alex chose not to return to her room; instead she wandered down to sit on the landing stage, paddling her bare feet in the muddy water of the James. It had been a relief to tell Mrs Gordon, but her suspicion regarding the back door rankled, especially as it had struck a bit too close to home.

These last few weeks she'd found herself thinking far too often about that lost life; a life of comfort and security, a life where she had her father and a son. Here she also had a son, and she had thought herself to have a man, but the Matthew who had been returned to her was fundamentally changed and she didn't know how to help him heal. She followed the wheeling flight of a couple of terns and sighed.

# CHAPTER 25

"Here," Alex dropped the signed deed in front of Matthew, lobbed her pouch into a corner and threw herself on the bed. She yawned, thinking that maybe she should take a long afternoon nap. Undress, get out of these itching stays and let her body relax into the coolness of the sheets. Almost six weeks since she last bled… she considered telling him, but decided it was far too soon. She peeked from under her arm as he unrolled the deed and read it, his throat working. Her heart went out to him, but she remained where she was, waiting for him to do or say something. Instead he got to his feet and left the room without a word.

Matthew got back late and after looking for Alex in their room went over to where James was sitting outside the stable door.

"Have you seen Alex?" he asked. James shook his head; apart from a brief glimpse of her at dinner he hadn't.

"Is she not down by the tree?" he said, pointing in the direction of the sycamore. "I seem to recall she spends her afternoons there, sewing."

Matthew strained his eyes in the indicated direction. Dusk was falling, and why would she choose to remain out there without any light to work by? His eyes caught on something pale, a flutter of cloth, and he strode towards it.

She had been weeping. When she heard him approach she started and ducked her head to hide her face, but he gripped her by the chin, forcing her to meet his eyes.

"Why?" he asked, tracing the tear tracks. She tried to twist out of his hold, but he wouldn't let her. "Why?"

"Because I don't know how to help." She stood up, turning away from him to stare at the tangle of undergrowth that bordered the little meadow. Alex brushed at her skirts, flicking a light green caterpillar into the grass.

"The first few days it was like it always used to be, but then with every day you've grown more and more distant, excluding me. And I don't understand; why won't you talk to me? Allow me to try to help you?" Alex retreated further under the tree, her face hidden in shadow. Matthew came after and took her hand, twisting his fingers into hers. He stood in silence braiding and re-braiding his fingers with hers, trying to find words to explain.

"Those first days ... well, I was dazed, aye? I thought I might be dreaming, that you'd soon fade away and I'd be dead. And then, as the days passed and I knew myself safe again, I was taken over by rage. It's still uppermost in me; an all-consuming rage at the people who did this to me, and it leaves me less human, more beast." He looked away, tightening his hold on her hand. "The rage is like a barrier; I wake in the night and my cock throbs not with love but with anger, and I won't ... I can't because I fear what I might do to you. So I stumble out of bed and I ..."

He'd sit and watch her, rubbing himself until he jerked in painful release. Nothing of love or pleasure, just a burning urge to take her, force her to submit as he had been forced by others. And so he retreated from passion to the technicalities of love making, he didn't dare to let himself go lest he be overwhelmed by all that black inside of him and God alone knew what he might do then.

"I don't understand," Alex said.

Well, no, how could she? Matthew sighed and tried again, attempting to describe just how scared he was of losing control, because once unleashed, how was he to hold back on all that rage and desperation?

"But..." Alex gnawed her lip, flexing her fingers against his hold on her hand. "Is this how it's going to be? Will you always shut me out? Never trust yourself in bed with me again?"

"I don't know," he replied, and the expression in her eyes made him look away.

"I don't think you would," she said.

"What?"

"Hurt me. I don't think you can."

"Then you have greater faith in me than I do," he said. "I just can't risk it."

He fell silent, his fingers braiding themselves around hers. Around them the elongated afternoon shadows were morphing into early evening darkness, a blackbird flashed by, a small butterfly soared upwards towards the purple sky. Beside him, she was holding her breath, a sure sign that she was making an effort not to weep. Matthew shifted on his feet and tried to think of something to say.

Alex peeked at him from under her lashes. He kept his eyes fixed on something unseen, his jaw clenching and unclenching rhythmically. He shrugged, gave her a lopsided smile and tugged at her hand, his eyes a deep brilliant green in the fading light – green with glints of gold.

"Coming?"

She snatched her hand back, shaking her head.

"Alex..."

"Go," she said, "go on, hurry off to have your supper so that you can hurry up to bed and pretend you're asleep when I get there."

"I don't ..."

"Yes you do! And every time you do, it tears me apart, you hear?" He flinched, tried to take her hand. "No! Leave me alone, just go." She backed away from him.

"I don't mean to," he said. "Of course I don't want to hurt you. But I ..."

"Coward!"

"Coward? For not wishing to harm you?" His hands closed on her arms, pressing her back against the trunk.

"I said, no? I don't think you would."

"And I told you; I'm not willing to take the risk." He was getting angry, she could see it in how his mouth pressed together, the soft curve of his bottom lip thinning out into a straight line.

"But I am!" She glared at him, struggled against his hold. "I didn't travel the world for this... this ... gelded stranger." Oh God, oh God; her heart wrung itself into the shape of a banana at the look of absolute hurt that flashed across his face.

"What?" His fingers dug into her arms and she hated herself for doing this to him, for taunting him, but somehow she had to breach the goddamn wall he was constructing around his inner core, and the only way she could think of doing that was to spur him into anger. Alex gulped; it frightened her, but she saw no other option. She ignored the way his hands were sinking into her flesh, leaned back provocatively against the tree and looked him up and down.

"You know what I mean, Matthew Graham. You've lost your balls, haven't you?" He paled at her insulting tone and she cried inside. She took a long shaky breath. "Let me know when you find them again. Until then, let's put this whole charade on ice, okay?"

She wrenched herself free and made as if to go to the house. Three steps and she was thrown on her back, all air knocked out of her. She fought him, she shoved and clawed at him, she twisted her legs closed, egging him on, very much on purpose.

His breathing was ragged, and in his eyes the golden flecks had vanished, replaced by something far, far colder. He kissed her, furiously, hungrily, and she bit him, attempting to slap his face. He undid her lacings, ignoring her attempts to escape, and she was flat on her back, her shift open to her waist to reveal her breasts to the falling dusk.

"Let me go!" She didn't want to do this anymore. He scared her, he was hurting her, his hands and mouth punishing her. But it was too late, Matthew spread her legs apart, ploughed himself inside. He pinned her down with his weight, he came and he went, her wrists held in a painful grip above her head. She pitched and struggled, yelling at him to stop, let her go. He grunted, he pushed, he drove himself harder and harder inside, and she was being battered by this uncaring stranger, a human *perpetuum mobile* that sent thrust after jarring thrust into her.

He pulled out and sat back, and she took the opportunity to get away, crawling on all fours. Snot clogged her nose, she was hiccupping with tears. His hand closed around her ankle, dragging her back towards him. Alex kicked at him, at this animal that was treating her like this. Ah! She whimpered when he took her from behind, hard hands holding her hips immobile. He groaned and panted, uttered strings of unintelligible sounds, and all the while he came and went, deaf to her protests. She was being ravaged by her own husband – no, not by him, but by the accumulated rage that lived in him.

"Oh, Jesus," she groaned when he flipped her over. She swiped at him, he slapped her and then he was inside of her again, and all of her shrieked at the ungentle treatment.

"Matthew, please! No, honey, please..." She raised her hands to his face in supplication. He froze at her touch.

"Alex?" He stared down at her, eyes black in the fading light. "My Alex?"

She tightened her arms around him, telling him she loved him, that she would always love him, no matter what. A huge shudder rippled through him, the cheeks of his buttocks clenched spasmodically and he collapsed on top of her.

Matthew felt her heaving below him. He knew he was too heavy, but there was no energy in him, not even to shift to one side. His mouth lay wet against her neck, and he kissed her there, where her pulse leapt erratically against her skin.

"I can't move," he croaked. Lord, what had he done to her?

"Then don't," she replied just as hoarsely. Her arms came up around him again, fingers drifting over his cropped hair. He buried his nose in her curls, wanted to stay like this forever.

"I think there's a stone under my behind," she said after

a while. "And I don't really want another bruise." Matthew groaned; he suspected he'd marked her with more than the odd bruise or two.

He rolled off and he couldn't meet her eyes, so ashamed of what he'd done to her. The shift was torn, her skirts were thrown high, baring her indecently. His hands shook as he pulled down first her petticoats and then her skirt. Clumsily he covered her breasts, used his thumb to wipe away her tears and rested his forehead against hers, repeating an agonised 'forgive me' over and over again. She shushed him and told him that of course she forgave him. When he made as if to stand to go inside she gripped his hand and coaxed him back down on the grass.

"No, let's stay here a little while longer. It's still quite warm."

He smiled at that, and patted at his chest. With the back of his hand he located her heartbeat just below her jaw. In his ears rang his own pulse and he tried to separate one beat from the other, isolate his sound from hers, but they were perfectly blended, two halves making a whole. High above stood a sliver of new moon, and as dusk shifted into night stars winked into existence beside it, one by one.

"You hold my heart, Alex," he whispered. She shifted even closer, one hand sliding into his breeches to cup him, her hand warm and exploring.

"Well, I definitely have a good grip on your balls," she replied, and he broke out in relieved laughter.

Magnus almost fainted when he stepped into the studio. On the easel was a painting of a sea, wild waves of water crashing into each other. In blues and greens, it reminded him of Mercedes' time portals, all those little canvases that he'd burnt almost four years ago.

"What's that?" he asked, attempting to keep his voice neutral.

Over his shoulder, Isaac threw him a look. "It's a pirate ship."

Magnus' back softened, shoulders slumping. Atop the cresting waves Isaac had painted a lopsided thing with bulging sails and a Jolly Roger flag.

"And where is Jack Sparrow?" he asked, tousling Isaac's hair.

"It's not his ship," Isaac leaned forward to add some dashes of white to his waves. "Did my grandmother – Mercedes – paint the sea?" he said, turning to face Magnus.

"Why do you ask?"

Isaac hitched narrow bony shoulders and tilted his head to one side. For an instant it was like seeing Mercedes standing before him, down to the curve of the mouth and the dark lines of the brows, pulled down over eyes the colour of cocoa beans.

"I just think she did," Isaac said. He rubbed a finger over the stained table. "See? So much blue paint. But maybe she painted skies."

Magnus smiled crookedly. The only skies his wife had ever painted had been blood red, patterned with dark smoke from the pyres burning at the painting's centre.

"I'm not sure," he said, "she painted a lot of stuff that was just colours."

Isaac just nodded, apparently satisfied with this reply. He went back to his painted ship and Magnus returned to his kitchen and a strengthening cup of coffee.

"Why did you burn them?" Isaac asked over dinner.

"Hmm?" Magnus served Isaac some more mash.

"The paintings – the ones Mercedes made."

"How do you know we burnt them?" Magnus said.

Isaac speared a meatball with his fork. "Die, vile foe." He giggled and stuffed the meatball into his mouth. "Dad said so," he said through his food.

"He did? And don't talk while you're chewing."

"To Diane," Isaac said once his mouth was empty. "They were talking about all the paintings they burnt."

"Ah." Magnus shoved his plate away.

"So why? Weren't they any good?" Isaac said. Two parallel creases appeared between his brows. "You always say I paint like her, and ..."

"They were very good," Magnus interrupted. "I told you. She had exhibitions, made tons of money." He sighed. "But ... well, once she was gone I didn't feel like keeping them. They reminded me too much of her." They scared the daylights out of him, those squares of twisting colour, but he had no intention of telling Isaac that.

"Sometimes ..." Isaac began. He shut his mouth.

"Sometimes what?"

"I hear her. When I paint, sometimes I hear her – or Mama."

"Oh come on, Isaac! How could you possibly do that?" Magnus attempted a little laugh, rolling his eyes.

"I do," Isaac said, lower lip jutting.

"And what do they say? Brush your teeth, eat your greens?"

Isaac shook his head. "Not like that! I just ... it's like someone singing far, far away."

"The radio," Magnus nodded, "or one of Eva's operas." He hummed a couple of bars from Carmen, making Isaac grin. The boy slid off his chair and came to sit in Magnus' lap, thin arms hugging him hard.

"Yeah; it's the radio," he yawned.

I bloody well hope so, Magnus thought.

For the coming weeks, Magnus hovered round the studio whenever Isaac was there, finding one pretext after the other to walk in on his artist grandson. Either it was a batch of cookies that needed tasting, or did Isaac want hollandaise or plain butter with the asparagus, or had Isaac done his homework.

But no matter how often he came into the studio, no matter how hard he strained his ears, not once did he hear anything resembling song – except for when Eva had on the downstairs radio. He smiled at his grandson, for the day engrossed in depicting a volcanic eruption, all the while talking to the little stick figures that were attempting to flee the oncoming lava. The boy had a vivid imagination, that's all.

# CHAPTER 27

It was most elegantly done Alex conceded as she backed away. The little girl she'd heard crying among the abandoned sheds was gone, vanishing between a gap in the fencing that was too narrow for Alex to squeeze her way through, and now she was trapped – or well on her way to it.

Three men advanced in her direction. She licked her lips. The ferret faced man to her right – Sykes, she thought his name was – would be the easiest to kick to the ground, and then she'd make a dash for it, brave the thick thorny shrubs, and so make her way back to the waterfront.

She pulled at her skirts – discreetly – and lifted herself up and down a couple of times on her feet. Muscles bunched all along her legs, she breathed in through her nose in an effort to calm her racing heart. It had been different down in Barbados; there she hadn't even stopped to think – unfortunately – but here, faced with three would be aggressors, all of them moving purposefully towards her, she couldn't quite find her courage. She punched herself on the thigh; get a grip.

"Ah, the fair Mrs Graham," Jones mocked. When she sidled off towards the right he moved swiftly, blocking her way. Oh God, he was huge – no way would she be able to kick him to the ground on one try. His small eyes travelled Alex up and down a couple of times, lingering on her chest. "Now, now, why in such a hurry? Mr Fairfax was most complimentary of your ... err ... assets," he leered, and behind him Sykes laughed.

"Mr Fairfax is a fucking bastard with no assets whatever," Alex replied, waving her pinkie in the air. "Now get out of my way before my husband sees you."

"Your husband? And what do you think he can do?" Jones shifted closer, his bulk crowding her back against the wall of the closest shed. He threw a look at the deserted area around them. "And he isn't here anyway, is he?" Well, he was right about that.

"He knows where I am," she lied. She sincerely hoped he'd noticed when she darted off in the direction of the old, dilapidated warehouses. She did a quick scan; the third man had retreated to stand in the shade of a tilting building, but out of the corner of her eye she saw Sykes closing in on her other side. She wasn't quite sure what it was they intended to do to her, somehow Jones' expression indicated nothing but an intent to humiliate.

"Even if he did, it would be too late," Sykes said, and in his eyes she saw lust, his lips stretching into a hungry smile.

"You think?" Matthew's voice was like a whiplash, slicing through the heavy, humid air. Jones straightened up, and in a flash Alex realised that this was exactly what Jones wanted to achieve, an enraged Graham defending his wife and what was Jones to do but fight back? Jones' huge hands fisted themselves and a cold, calculating look flew between Sykes and Jones.

"There's one behind you," she warned.

"Ah." Matthew wheeled and drove his elbow into the freckled face of Jones' younger acolyte. Without a sound the man slid to the ground. Matthew advanced, a hand on the hilt of his newly acquired sword and suddenly it was flashing in the sun, the blade poised in the general direction of Sykes who backed away. Two swift steps, a lunge and Sykes breeches were sliced all along the right side. Sykes swore, Matthew danced and there was a gash down Sykes' shirt.

"Matthew!" Alex yelled, and Matthew swivelled, just in time to parry Jones' thrust. The blades scraped against each other, Matthew did something with his wrist and leapt back, sword raised. Jones adjusted his grip, did a few trial swings and smiled. His eyes darted over to Sykes, he jerked his head, and Sykes nodded, gripping a long bladed knife.

Stupid men; they'd forgotten about her, both of them

intent on Matthew. Well, she could at least even the odds somewhat. A surprised Sykes squawked when she felled him to the ground, landing heavily on top of him.

With a yell Jones attacked, moving so fast she couldn't quite make out what he was doing. Matthew retreated, caught his heel on a stone and fell. Alex gasped and rose into a crouch. Swish! Jones' sword flashed in the sun. Matthew rolled, came up on one knee. The next blow he succeeded in parrying, and there, he was back on his feet, but he was limping, and Jones pulled his small mouth into a wide grin.

The sun beat down on them. The two men lunged and retreated, crashed into each other, cursed and retreated again. Alex wasn't sure what to do. Sykes was struggling below her, spewing a constant flow of threats. To rush to Matthew's aid would mean releasing her hold on Sykes, and besides, she wasn't all that sure it would be of any help to Matthew should she choose to join the deadly dance that whirled around her.

A grunt and blood welled on Matthew's forearm. Jones laughed, swung again. A yelp, a shuffle, and Jones was holding his free hand to his side with Matthew forcing him into retreat. Back and forth the fight flowed. Both were tall, both had long reach and obvious expertise in handling their weapon, but where Jones was stronger, Matthew was graceful, darting round Jones like an enervating wasp.

The heat was beginning to tell on Jones. Sweat spread in dark patches on his shirt, his breathing was harsh and strained. Alex threw a worried look at Matthew; he was panting, but apart from the limp he seemed relatively undamaged. Jones changed the grip on his sword and swung it in wide arches around him, for all the world as if it were a scythe.

Matthew blocked and parried, he danced to the right, to the left. One moment there, the other here, and all along Jones' arms gashes appeared, down his side and up his front the shirt was shredded, small stains of blood decorating the coarse linen.

Jones roared like a bull. "Stand still!" He swung wildly,

Matthew hooked the sword and sent it flying, and just like that the point of his blade was resting against Jones' neck. Matthew's whole arm quivered, his hand tightened on the hilt to the point of turning white.

"No," Alex said from where she was sitting on Sykes. "Don't."

"Most unwise," a dry voice agreed, and all of them turned to see the Governor of Virginia standing a few yards away. "Gentlemen," he added in a voice of steel, and indicated they should precede him to his offices.

"I will not have it!" Sir William glared at them, eyes flashing between Matthew and Jones. "Not in my town, not in my colony, you hear?"

"He was defending me," Alex cut in.

"Defending you? We meant you no harm," Jones said.

"No? Is that why you lured her into the abandoned yard?" Matthew said. "Is that why you were hindering her from leaving?"

"I certainly felt threatened," Alex said, turning to face the Governor. "He..." she managed a strangled sob. "He pushed me back against the wall, and..." She ducked her head, made yet another choking sound.

"There, there, my dear," the Governor said, "come and sit down." She turned wide eyes on him, smiled unsteadily.

"My husband came just in time."

"Really!" Sir William turned to glower at Jones, and behind his back Alex shared a quick look with Matthew to assure him she was quite alright.

"Sir William," Jones said, "you know me as a man with a steady head on his shoulder, a man of good standing in this community. Graham's attack was unprovoked, and what was I to do, not defend myself?"

"The lady says differently," Sir William replied.

"The lady?" Jones sneered. "That's Graham's wife, what would she say?"

Sir William looked from Alex to Jones and back again.

"She'd do anything for her husband, "Jones added with a malicious gleam in his eyes. "Anything at all, I'd warrant." He inhaled, seemed on the point of saying something more. Right; time to change the subject.

"This man," Alex said, pointing at Jones, "this gigantic bully of a man is anything but an adornment to your colony, Sir William. Have you any idea how he treats the men under his care? Do you..."

"Alex, shush," Matthew interrupted.

"Shush? How shush? You were abducted, and you tried to tell him, didn't you? You asked him to help you, but did he? No, he didn't, he just laughed at you, and hurt you and ... and..." To her huge irritation Alex began crying – for real.

"Alex," Matthew sighed and handed her a handkerchief. "It's alright, aye?" His eyes bored into her, a silent admonishment not to say anything more.

"He did threaten me," Alex said after some seconds, reverting to the original subject. "If you question the other men without him being present, I'm sure they'll bear me out."

"Oh, I will," the Governor said, "in fact I already have. Young Brown was somewhat voluble about the whole matter, and what he says bears the lady out, Jones. The lady," he repeated, staring Jones down – or up, seeing as he was well over half a foot shorter.

"The lady," Jones mumbled, pale blue eyes studying Alex with dislike. "It's still wrong, that he, Graham, go unpunished. He raised a weapon against me, a free man, and him an indenture."

"Oh, no, Mr Jones," the Governor said. "Mr Graham is as free as you are – I myself signed the deed. Something to keep in mind."

Jones looked as if someone had poured a whole bottle of cod liver oil down his throat, small mouth so pursed it resembled a miniscule prune.

"And you, Mr Graham, you wield the sword like a true

gentleman," Sir William went on, "may I ask where you've learnt the art of fencing?"

Matthew gave a short, surprised laugh. "You know where. On the battlefield, Sir William, and I dare say there's no better school, is there?"

"No," the Governor agreed, and for an instant they shared a look, the only two real soldiers in the room. "I'll have your swords, and should I find either of you duelling again I'll have you flogged and in the pillory, you hear?" With that Sir William bade them all a curt good day, and moments later Alex and Matthew were back on the street.

"Why did you stop me from telling him?" Alex asked as they walked back home. "Serves Jones and Fairfax right if the Governor sticks his nose in their dirty abduction business."

"And you think he doesn't know?"

Alex came to a standstill. "No, I don't think he does."

Matthew raised one dark brow, raised both.

"No," Alex repeated.

"Well if he doesn't, others definitely do, and I have no intention of spending every day here looking over my shoulder to ensure we're not stabbed to drown in our blood. It's quite enough to worry about Jones."

"Oh," Alex gulped.

"You were pretty impressive," she added a while later.

"I was almost too late." He stopped to brush a curl behind her ear. "I don't want you walking out alone."

She took his hand. "Nor should you; it's you he wants to hurt."

"Kill, Alex, kill, not hurt. I'll be careful, aye?"

Now why wasn't that much of a comfort? Alex snuck her arm in under his and held on tight.


"No passage!" Matthew threw his hat to the ground. "Not on this boat and not on the last four we've tried. And I won't have us travelling in the hold."

Alex put a hand on his arm. "It's only June. We'll find passage. The harbourmaster says we have a fair chance on

208

one of the coming ships."

He sighed; they'd been down by the water every day, scanning the horizon for ships, and when they anchored he'd hurried aboard only to be informed that the berths were already booked.

Six ships so far, but according to the harbourmaster boats would be plying the seas well into October. October! Yet another lost year! He snuck Alex a look; she looked somewhat greensick, had done so for some days. It must be the heat, or mayhap she was as consumed by homesickness as he was. She gave his arm a little squeeze.

"It's not as if we're starving, and with your odd jobs and my sewing we're almost paying our way." She rolled her eyes, admitting that it still astounded her that anyone would be willing to pay for her efforts with needle and thread.

"Aye well," he teased, "It's good you can sew, you wouldn't keep us in anything with your knitting."

"Huh," she snorted, making him laugh.

They strolled down the wharves, detouring round carts loaded sky high with bales of tobacco. Matthew made a face and increased their pace. Just the smell of it brought back far too many memories, and when he caught sight of Jones' broad back he gritted his teeth and set off at a half run, dragging Alex behind him.

A quick turn and Matthew came to an abrupt halt. Kate, here! He hadn't seen her since sometime in February, and the last time he'd spoken to her was that January afternoon when she tended to his lacerated back. A wave of gratitude mingled with tenderness rushed through him, and when she raised her hand in greeting, he did the same, his face breaking into a wide smile.

"Kate!" He waved again, hurrying towards her.

"Kate? Who's Kate?" Alex' voice was the equivalent of a bucket of ice cold water. Matthew slowed his pace to a casual stroll, rearranged his features into an expression less effusive than before.

"Why Matthew Graham! I scarcely recognised you."

Kate smiled, dark eyes softening when they met his. He bowed, froze at the sight of her protruding stomach. Sweetest Lord! His eyes flew to meet hers.

"You don't need to worry," Kate laughed. "I'm not going to claim on you for its upkeep. I'm not even going to ask you for a name."

Beside him, Alex inhaled noisily and Matthew closed his eyes, his stomach contracting as if he had the runs. His wife disengaged her hand from his hold and took a step back, eyes glued to Kate's swelling belly.

"Matthew?" Her voice quavered. "Is ... Have you ..." He couldn't meet her eyes. "Oh God." She wheeled and walked away in the general direction of the water.

"Alex!"

She stumbled, her arms flew out, but she regained her balance and when he set off after her she broke into a run. He caught up with her and took her by the arm.

"Don't! Take your double crossing hands off me, you bastard!"

"Alex," he pleaded, but she shook her head.

"Not now, just leave me alone." When he remained standing beside her, she added a please and turned her back on him, staring stubbornly at the water.

With an inarticulate sound she rushed off and he let her go, his heart plunging rapidly towards the ground. The look in her eyes, the absolute shock and disappointment written all across her face...

"I'm sorry," Kate said, appearing at his side. "I had no intention to..."

"Aye you did," he cut her off. "You knew exactly what you were doing."

Kate twisted a bit. "Well, maybe she should know."

"Why?" Matthew said coldly. "Why should she be hurt? You always knew I had a wife, I never promised you anything – I couldn't promise you anything."

"You should know at least," she said, placing a hand on her stomach.

"Know what? That you're with child? That you think it might be mine?" He looked her up and down. "How far along are you?"

"Six, seven months."

"Oh, aye? So you don't know then, do you?"

"No, I don't." She put a hand on his arm. "I'm marrying today, by tonight I'll be Mrs Jones. He thinks it's his."

Matthew extricated himself from her hold. "I wish you the best in your marriage," he said formally and swivelled on his feet to go after his wife. He didn't look back, not once.

He found Alex in their room, throwing her things together.

"What are you doing?"

"I'm moving my stuff out," she said, "I'll be sleeping with Mrs Gordon for some time. Forever, perhaps – I don't feel like sharing a bed with a man who's been unfaithful to me."

He looked away, shamed by the look in her eyes.

"Tell me," she said nastily. "Was she the only one? Or did you find far more comfort than I could imagine, going from one set of arms to the other?"

"You know me better than that," he said and heard himself how weak that sounded given the present facts.

"I do? Apparently not! You see, I thought you'd hold to your marriage vows, that you'd be true. But then, I suppose I'm the fool, huh? Men are simple creatures, ruled by their base instincts and we, their wives, must understand and forgive." She took a step towards him, brandishing a knitting needle. "What would you have done if it had been me?"

He felt himself flush and she nodded.

"I thought so. Hypocrite!" She thrust the needle through a ball of yarn and dropped it on top of her other items. A quick twist and she lifted the bundle.

He stood to block her way.

"Excuse me," she said coldly.

"You're not going anywhere. You'll stay and talk this through."

"I don't want to talk, in fact, I don't very much want to see you either. You disgust me." Her words tore chunks out of him.

He lowered his face to eyeball her. "You'll stay and listen."

"Make me," she hissed, her eyes spewing blue fire.

He clamped a hand on her nape and kissed her, ignoring her muffled protests, her attempts to stamp him on his foot. He kissed her until she opened her mouth to his. They broke apart, chests heaving.

"It won't work," she told him, licking her lips. "Just because you can kiss my breath away, that doesn't mean I'll forgive you."

"Nay, but it helps." He made a grab for her and brought them down on the protesting bed. "Now," he said, pinning her under him. "Will you please listen?"

She fought like a spitting cat, her linen cap falling to the floor and her hair a mass of escaped curls on the pillows. He grunted when she landed a punch on his nose. For an instant he raised his hand to hit her back, but instead he kissed her, holding her captive with his weight, and suddenly she was struggling not to heave him off but to bring him close; as close as he could possibly get.

Skirts were shoved aside, his fingers found the velvety skin on the inside of her thigh, and Alex yanked at his lacings, her hands rough and uncaring when they found his member. That way, hey? He pushed her down and entered her, one forceful movement sheathing his entire length inside of her.

She exhaled, softening below him. Again, all the way in, and she flexed her hips to meet his. He slowed his pace and kissed her. She made urgent sounds, but he was having none of it, taking his time to explore her mouth. Slowly; his cock strained inwards, upwards, his balls pressed against her flesh. Oh, so slowly, and Alex near on yowled, hands clutching at his ears, his hair, breath hot against his cheek as she begged him to finish, to not torture her like this. His cock agreed, roaring that it was near on bursting, and could he please, please get on with it?

He lay in silence afterwards, listening to the sound of their combined heavy breathing. She was lying on her back, staring at the ceiling. Matthew inhaled, licked his lips.

"I was very ill, I was near death and she saved me." He described those weeks in October, his face hidden in her hair. "It was wrong, and I betrayed you doing it. But you see..." He sighed and propped himself up to look at her. "Without her I think I might have died."

"Why didn't you tell me before?" Alex asked, an expression she couldn't quite decipher flying over her face.

"I hoped you would never have to know."

She stroked his head, fingering the bare inch of hair. "And is it yours?"

"I don't know."

"You don't? So she was comforting others as well?" That made Kate sound like a whore, and Matthew gave her a reproving look.

"You have no notion, aye? She did what she had to do to survive." He lay back down, pillowing his head on her chest. "Will you forgive me?"

"Yes." She groped for his hand and placed it on her stomach. "This one is definitely yours, so say hello to your next child."

For a couple of heartbeats he didn't move, didn't even breathe. He spread his fingers over her stomach and closed his eyes; thank you Lord, for this miraculous woman, for the life that grows in her. He shifted downwards and placed his lips in a soft kiss on her belly. My bairn. A daughter, mayhap a son; my bairn.

All that night Alex lay wide-eyed beside him. Twice she turned towards him to shake him awake and tell him about Fairfax, but twice her nerve failed her and she slumped back sleepless against the pillow. By morning she knew she had to tell him, however hurtful to them both, because as long as she didn't there was no honesty between them – not the honesty there should be. Besides, it was probably only a matter of time before dear Dominic Jones let drop the odd, insinuating comment or two.

She didn't know how to start but decided to tell him when they were both out of bed, because she didn't want the images of Fairfax to superimpose themselves on that aspect of their life. So she waited until they were down by the water, sitting in the speckled shade of a small oak.

"I have something to tell you as well." Something in her voice alerted him and he sat up straighter. "He made me," she said, trying to avoid his eyes. "He said that there was an official price and then there was an unofficial service that had to be delivered."

Matthew looked at her blankly, wary incomprehension in his eyes.

"If I didn't let him, he wouldn't guarantee that you'd be alive," she went on, her tongue thickening with every word. She could see when he put two and two together, an expression of absolute disgust flashing across his face. He slumped in front of her, dragging his hands through his short hair.

"No," he said, his eyes never leaving hers. "Oh Lord..."

She had expected him to rage, to perhaps hit at something, and this totally different reaction disconcerted her. She sat beside him, wanting very much to touch him, take his hand. Matthew fiddled with some stones, turning them over and studying them intently. He stood and walked down to the water's edge, sending stone after stone flying to land with a soft plop. The last one he threw to skip across the rippling surface before turning to face her.

"Tell me."

Alex bit her lip and shook her head. "What would it serve?"

Matthew was at her side so swiftly she reared back when he fell to his knees before her.

"I have to know," he said, taking her hands. "I must know, aye? This is not yours to carry alone."

Alex leaned towards him. "It wasn't too bad, I'm okay."

Matthew embraced her and kissed her ear. "You're a bad liar, lass, and I'll have you tell me."

He released her but kept hold of her hands, his thumbs running in caressing circles over her wrists. She hung her head and began to talk. She described slug-like fingers touching her, how he smelled of cloying eau-de-rose, and what he had done to her from the moment he threw her over the desk to the moment he exited the room.

"I was so scared that somehow you'd notice or that I wouldn't bear to have you touch me." She gave a strangled little laugh and met his eyes for the first time since she had begun to tell. "The moment I saw you, I knew that wouldn't be an issue. In rags and barely able to walk, you were still my Matthew and whatever price I'd had to pay was worth it."

"Will it matter?" she asked in a small voice. His continued silence was making her nervous.

Matthew tightened his hold on her hands and drew her close enough that she could rest her head against his chest. They sat like that for a long time, him with his nose in her hair, she with her ear to his heart, listening to how his heartbeat thudded its way into her, how his rhythm merged with hers, multiplying itself through her bloodstream to echo in her head.

"Nay," he finally said, kissing her cheek. "It won't."

"You told him?" Mrs Gordon sat down with a thump. "Why did you do that?"

"I don't know, it felt as if I should." But she probably never would have if it hadn't been for Kate showing up. Something dived inside of her at the look on Mrs Gordon's face.

"What have you done?" Mrs Gordon gave an exasperated shake of her head. "Dear Lord, lass, what have you done? Have you no idea? He's a man, aye? And you have just told him you've been abused by a man he already had reason to hate."

Alex froze inside. "He wouldn't!"

Mrs Gordon huffed. "You think not?" She shook her head. "He will make Fairfax pay and God help us when he does, aye?"

# CHAPTER 28

Alex exclaimed with pleasure when she read the slip of paper presented to her by one of the Governor's doormen. Just the distraction she needed from her constant surveillance of her husband, her fear that the moment her back was turned he'd set off to kill Fairfax.

"Look," she said, waving it at Matthew. "We've been invited to a reception."

Matthew seemed less than thrilled, making Alex sigh. He disapproved of the friendship that had sprung up between her and Sir William and made no secret of it. Well tough; she enjoyed Sir William's company, and if anything the incident with Jones down at the waterfront had intensified the relationship, with Alex a regular guest whenever the Governor was in town.

On the evening of the reception they walked arm in arm towards the Assembly House. Alex had overruled Matthew's objections and was wearing a borrowed deep blue bodice with a rather daring neckline that had both James and Matthew ogling her before they left, one with appreciation, the other with a scowl.

Matthew was in sober black, with dark silk stockings and blindingly white linen at cuff and neck of the long, well cut coat – all of it courtesy of Mr Parson. Alex threw Matthew an irritated glance. She was looking forward to this evening and had no intention of seeing it ruined due to him being a possessive jerk. He met her eyes, his mouth curving into the slightest of smiles.

"You look lovely," he said, drawing her to a stop to kiss her hand. They walked the remaining yards hand in hand.

Alex almost died when the first person she came face to face with after having queued her way down the receiving line was Fairfax. In an embroidered coat, greens and reds on pale yellow silk, with a green sash around his waist and matching silk ribbons at the knees of his breeches, he looked quite the courtier, bowing over her hand.

Her initial reaction was to slap him, or pull out one of her hairpins and stab it through his piggy eye, but she managed to retain some composure, her eyes fleeing to Matthew for support. A muddy green eye captured hers – an eye that spoke of the intent to murder, here, now, should she ask it of him. I'm okay, she assured him silently, but his eyes flitted to her clenched fists, and one large hand came down to envelop hers. That was enough. His touch, his reassuring presence made her capable of breathing again.

When Sir William popped up by Alex' side, Matthew retreated to stand by the wall. Most of the guests were men, most of them as soberly dressed as himself. Only Fairfax stuck out in his gaudy coat, reminding Matthew of a giant blowfly – and just as nasty to boot. He frowned and stretched, sauntered over as if by chance to stand only a yard or so from Fairfax, close enough that he could pick up the overpowering smell – no, stench – of rosewater. Fairfax threw him a look over his shoulder and paled, taking a few steps further into the throng. Matthew just smiled and followed.

Once again Fairfax gave him a look and with a strained laugh excused himself from the man he was talking to, moving away. Matthew strolled after. This vermin of a man had trespassed where no man was allowed, and Matthew spent an enjoyable hour hounding Fairfax round the room, laughing silently as the fat, bewigged and increasingly nervous man attempted to evade him. Ah no, Fairfax; nowhere to run, not here. When Fairfax turned his way, Matthew smiled, displaying all his teeth. Fairfax shivered visibly and shuffled away.

Matthew nodded his thanks to one of the footmen and drained the offered cup in one swallow. The sweetened wine was going to his head, and he retreated to stand in a corner, considering just what he was going to do to Fairfax once he got him alone. One agreeable alternative after the other presented itself, all of them ending with a squealing, begging Fairfax. Oh aye; he caught Fairfax' eyes and ostentatiously cracked his knuckles.

"Matthew!" Alex said, appearing by his side.

"Hmm?" He relaxed his hands, tore his eyes away from Fairfax.

"I want to go home," Alex whispered, slipping her hand into his. "I'm not feeling well."

"No?" Matthew kissed her on her rosy cheek. "You look radiant."

She flushed, but insisted that she wanted them to leave. "It's him, I don't like seeing him."

No; nor did he. After bidding their host a hasty goodbye, they were soon making their way through the silent darkened town.

Alex woke with a start in the predawn darkness and without checking she knew that Matthew's side of their bed was empty. She also knew immediately where he'd gone, and she nearly fell down the stairs in her haste to go after him. Why, oh why had she told him, she gulped, why hadn't she listened to Mrs Gordon's advice?

"James!" she shook him hard. "Please James, I need your help."

James scrunched his eyes together in protest, but sat up, listening to Alex somewhat garbled tale.

"So you think he's gone to kill him?" he asked, tightening his breeches round his narrow frame.

"Yes," Alex hiccupped. "And then they'll hang him and I will die."

"I'm sure it won't come to that," James answered.

Alex insisted that James should ride the mule and walked, no ran, at his side, one hand on the saddle to hold her steady. The three hour walk was covered in slightly more than half the time, and by the time Fairfax' plantation rose out of the shadows before them, the eastern sky was shifting into lighter hues of grey, dashed with pink.

There were flickering lights in the window of Fairfax' office, the main door stood ajar and they walked on silent feet down the passage way, halting before the entrance to the study. Alex stepped inside and fell back, hard enough to crash into James.

"Oh God! What have you done, you stupid man?"

Fairfax was sitting in his chair, head lolling to reveal he was – or had been – somewhat remiss about washing his neck. The sumptuous coat he'd been wearing earlier in the evening hung on the back of his chair, and the wide gathered sleeves of his French linen shirt had been pushed back, a quill on the floor under his open hand. Ink spattered the front of his breeches, and round the dirk buried in his chest there bloomed a stain of blood.

"He was sitting like this when I came," Matthew said, appearing from the relative darkness of a corner. "And look, you can see he's been dead for quite a while." He spat to the side. "I wish it had been me, it should have been me plunging the steel into him, making him squeal in terror and pain. But it wasn't, aye?"

Now that he pointed it out, Alex could see that he was right. The blood looked dry as did the ink, and when Alex touched the hanging hand it was an icy cold.

"And," Matthew added, "that isn't my dirk." No, because his still hung from his belt, although Alex was doubtful as to how much that would help.

"We have to get out of here," she said. "We have to leave before someone comes."

"Too late for that, I'm afraid," Jones interrupted, blocking the doorway. "Well, well, Graham. Now what have you done? At any rate you'll hang for this. I dare say it will smite your brother hard." He smirked, his fingers coming together in a money rubbing gesture.

"I haven't touched him!" Matthew flared. Two constables pushed their way into the room, eyeing Matthew with suspicion.

"No? And then why are you here at this ungodly hour?" the elder of them said, letting his eyes travel over Matthew, Fairfax and Alex.

"I had business to conduct with him," Matthew said.

Jones laughed loudly. "Of course you did; business relating to Fairfax and your wife."

Matthew's face went a dark red. "What business I had with Fairfax is none of your concern," he said through gritted teeth.

"Now it is," the elder constable said, "but maybe you should save it for the trial."

Matthew backed away from them and in his eyes Alex could see a flash of panic at the thought of ending up yet again fettered and incarcerated.

"Oh for God's sake, you incompetent morons!" Alex exploded. "That man's been dead for hours. Since well before midnight! Anyone with half a brain can see that." She saw a shadow cross over Jones' face and narrowed her eyes at him. "You did it!"

The elder constable gave her an irritated look. "Jones is − or was − a trusted employee. He has worked for Mr Fairfax for over ten years. And even allowing for the fact that we are but simpleminded fools, your husband seems a far more likely candidate." He walked over to where Fairfax was sitting and touched the bluish skin. "You are right in that he has been dead for a long time, but that in itself does not preclude your husband from killing him, does it?"

"He wasn't here! He was with me, in bed."

The younger officer gave a mild snort. "My pardon ma'am, but you would say that."

Alex stepped between Matthew and the officers, heaving herself up to balance on the balls of her feet.

"He didn't do it. You're just looking for the easy way out. I'm telling you he did, Jones did, and I can bet why as well." She half crouched, ready to spring, and before her the officers halted, throwing her wary looks. Smart move; she'd kick their teeth out before she'd let them get close to her Matthew.

"Oh really?" Jones drawled. "And why would that be?"

Alex gave him a cold look, hands busy bunching her skirts out of the way.

"Let's bring your wife in, shall we?" She knew she'd hit bull's eye from the way Jones' mouth tightened, but before she could capitalise on that the younger constable lunged. Alex whirled, a kick sending the young man staggering back.

"Alex!" Matthew said. "What are you doing?"

"I can't…" She began to cry. "I can't let them take you away for something you haven't done. Not again, Matthew."

"But you can't kick an innocent man like that!" Matthew sounded scandalised. "He was just doing his duty."

"I'm sorry, I didn't mean to hurt him, but I just can't."

The constable straightened up and studied her with grudging respect. "Where did you learn that?"

"In Sweden," Alex replied, mentally apologising to the Japanese while deciding this was not the time to give him a breakdown of Budo history. She was still standing poised in front of Matthew, but his hand was on her waist, trying to move her out of the way.

She shook her head. "They're not taking you. Not unless they kill me first."

James had been watching the proceedings in silence. There was no way Matthew would save himself from this, the constables had already made their minds up, and wee Alex' impassioned defence had not helped, rather the reverse. He threw a thoughtful look in the direction of Jones. He'd seen it too, the flashing expression of guilt when Alex had confronted him, but to insist he'd done it would not help. In this part of the world Jones was a known quantity while Matthew Graham was but flotsam, an inconsequential nuisance. No, there was but one thing to do, however much it made his bowels cramp. He straightened his back and stepped into the centre of the room.

"I did it, I killed yon fat bastard." James spat in the direction of the dead man, feeling a blinding surge of rage.

He fervently wished he had killed him, in revenge of the life he'd stolen from Matthew and hundreds like him, and he was glad the fat maggot was dead. "For years, aye? For decades he's been stealing innocent men off the street to work them to their death." He narrowed his eye at the elder constable; a hastily averted face. "And you knew. You heard too many men protest their innocence and yet you did nothing." He spat again, sinking his eyes into Matthew to warn him to shut up. "So, now he's dead. And I hope he burns in hell."

"You?" Jones couldn't keep the ridicule out of his voice. "You couldn't kill a fly – look at you, a walking bag of bones."

"Oh, aye I can. And I have. I did it, I took the dirk and ran it through his heart." Once again he glanced in the direction of Alex and Matthew, willing both of them to remain silent. He could see Alex was about to protest, but Matthew's hand closed around her arm and she subsided, eyes never leaving James.

"You can't seriously believe this preposterous tale," Jones blustered as the constables moved over to tie James' hands together. "Not only the accusations he levied at poor, dead Mr Fairfax, which are of course nothing but fancies, Mr Fairfax being a most Christian and upright character, but also all this nonsense about him killing Mr Fairfax." He waved a hand to indicate Fairfax' bulk and turned to stab a finger at Matthew. "He did it! I swear he did!"

"That's not what you said when you came to fetch us," the elder constable said, "then you told us you'd found your employer dead and had no idea who the perpetrator was." He frowned at his own comment. "Strange, isn't it? To kill, slip away unnoticed and then return to the scene of his crime."

"And now you get it," Alex muttered. She seemed on the point of saying something more, but Matthew's hand twisted into her arm and she snapped her mouth shut.

James sighed theatrically. "I have confessed, no? So why

are we still here?" He threw his head in Jones' direction. "He's just out to grind his own axe, aye? On account of him not knowing if the bairn in his wife's belly is his or Matthew's." James smiled maliciously at the look on Jones' face and raised a brow to the constables. "See? A jealous man."

Jones broke out in one last voluble protest. How could the constable think this teetering wreck of a man would have the strength to overcome a florid man like Fairfax? Did they perchance think that Fairfax had sat still, perhaps even using his own digits to indicate where to run the knife in? The constables gave him irritated looks; one dead man, one self-confessed killer – why make matters any more complicated? Besides, as the elder pointed out, unless Jones had actually seen Graham kill Fairfax there was no proof, was there? He cut any further discussions short with an angry gesture, bowed in the direction of Alex and led James outside.

Matthew dragged Alex from the room in their wake. Only once they were outside did his hold relax. James was boosted onto a horse, and when the company of three rode off, Matthew raised his hand in a silent salute. Alex wanted to cry. Matthew took her by the hand, grabbed the mule's reins with his free hand and began the long walk home.

Now that Matthew's death by hanging was no longer imminent, Alex found herself prey to a varied assortment of emotions, foremost amongst them anger.

"How could you do this to me?" she said, trying to disengage her hand from his. "What in the world possessed you go there in the middle of the night?"

"I had to, I had to somehow make him pay. But I wasn't planning on killing him."

Alex gave an incredulous snort. "No, just some GBH, right?" At his puzzled expression she sighed. "Grave bodily harm; GBH."

"Aye, that fits."

"Sometimes you're incredibly stupid; what do you think Fairfax would have done had you assaulted him? Never told anyone? He'd have had you dragged from our bed in revenge, either by the constables or by Jones and his likes, and they would have left you more dead than alive." She saw that he had never considered that, and exhaled loudly through her nose. "Vengeance is mine saith the Lord, remember?"

They walked without speaking, stopping now and then to rest by the verge. Alex sat back against a slender sapling, having first ensured there were no snakes in the vicinity.

"If I hadn't woken up, it would have been you, not James on the constable's horse. And no matter how innocent, they would have tried you and found you guilty." He nodded his grudging agreement. "And now James will die instead."

"Aye," Matthew groaned, "he has condemned himself for me."

# CHAPTER 29

"Somehow we have to find a way to prove that Jones did it," Alex said, tagging after Matthew on their way to the temporary jail. In her basket she carried food, stone bottles of beer, candles and a few sheets of paper as well as a clean shirt and the worn Bible Matthew had fetched from James' little bundle.

Matthew didn't reply; this had been the constant theme in everything she'd said since they got back, and he had to quell an urge to turn on her and yell that there was no proof. In fact, it might not be Jones at all, even if both Alex and he were convinced it was. He was battling huge coils of guilt that twisted in a writhing heap inside of him. If only he hadn't gone, or if at least James and Alex hadn't come. But if they hadn't, it would be him sitting under lock and key, watching as the gibbet was constructed outside his window. That was the worst of it; the sense of acute relief at having avoided death by the noose. He had no illusions whatsoever about James' fate – the court would condemn him to hang.

"I want to see him as well," Alex said, but the guard shook his head.

"He has requested that only Mr Graham be allowed in."

"Why would he do that?" she grumbled to Matthew, handing over her basket.

"He's my friend, and it's my life he's saving."

Matthew followed the guard to the makeshift cell. Once he was inside, the door swung shut, leaving him blinking at the sudden disappearance of light.

"James?"

"Over here," came the reply, and Matthew dropped to sit beside him in the straw.

"How are you?"

James shrugged; he hadn't been mistreated, and the

guards had brought him water and bread. The bedding was as comfortable as any he had had lately, and he'd even been given a blanket.

"That's good then," Matthew said.

"Aye, that's good." James explored the basked and smiled with evident pleasure at the candles and the paper. "Will you carry my letters back with you? I wish to write to my wife and my son."

Matthew nodded and cleared his throat. "Why are you doing this? Why are you throwing your life away?"

"Throwing my life away? Don't you want to live?" James leaned forward. "Don't you?"

"Aye," Matthew admitted weakly. "I do."

"Well then," James said, "then I'm not throwing it away, I'm giving it that you may live."

Matthew moaned, crushed by shame, and hid his face in his hands. James patted him on the head.

"I'm an old man and I'm dying anyway. You know that and so do I. It's no great matter."

"But you'll hang," Matthew said, "you'll die branded a murderer."

James uncorked the beer bottle and drank before handing it to Matthew.

"You and I both know I'm not a murderer, and so does the good Lord. And as for the hanging…" He swallowed, he swallowed again, and even in the weak light Matthew could see how his face paled, how a hand came up to rub at the scraggly neck. Guilt burnt like red hot coals down Matthew's gullet and landed to hiss recriminations in his gut.

James shook himself, gave Matthew a small smile. "Every day I die, lad. Look at me, you can see me wasting away, no?" James pinched at his thin arms. "He was right about that, yon Jones; I couldn't have run a dirk through that fat man, not unless he held himself very still and had the patience of an angel." He drank some more and pushed the cork back into the bottle. "It's right painful, aye? Do you know the story of the Spartan boy, the lad who hid a fox cub under his cloak?"

Matthew nodded that he did.

"Well, I have a fox cub eating at me all the time, eating through my innards in slow, agonising bites. The Spartan laddie he didn't cry out, he just fell down dead when the fox bit into his heart. I fear that I won't be that brave, that instead I'll cry and scream like a lassie." James clapped a surprisingly strong hand on Matthew's shoulder. " 'Tis better to die quickly. I'm dying already, lad, I've just chosen the way to do it."

Matthew came out of the jail feeling relieved, the guilt shrinking to more manageable proportions. James had explained several times that the constables would never have looked further than the man already there, present at the scene.

"Except that I wasn't, not when he died," Matthew had said.

"Nay, the only one there at the time was Jones, no?" James had replied.

Matthew seethed inside, his hands clenching into fists.

"No, Matthew, you must not; you must promise me that you won't."

Matthew attempted to twist away from those brown eyes, his mind swimming with the urge to revenge himself on Jones for everything.

"You mustn't," James had repeated urgently. "You'll never win against him here. He's the establishment, you're but a disgruntled former slave."

Matthew had promised, seeing James sink together with relief.

Now he stood in the uncomfortable heat and regarded his wife, sitting on the bench where he had left her. Her wide brimmed hat hid most of her face from view, one rebellious strand of hair having escaped to shimmer in the sunlight.

"You look like a demure maiden," Matthew said, sitting down beside her.

Alex made an irritated noise and returned her work to her pouch. "Appearances can deceive."

Halfway home she hurried over to stand in the shade of some trees, complaining loudly about this infernal heat.

"This is nothing, you wait until August, then you can talk about heat." He stood relaxed beside her, his eyes studying the few people who had dared the humid midday heat of this Sunday late in June. "The guards were talking about you."

"Me? Why?"

"On account of what you did earlier today."

"Earlier? Oh, you mean when I sent the constable flying." She hitched her shoulders. "I didn't hurt him, you know I can do far worse."

"It isn't seemly."

She stuck her tongue out at him. "See if I care."

"Alex," Matthew sighed, "they could have put you in the pillory." He nodded at the look on her face. "Aye, you don't want to experience that, do you?"

"What was I supposed to do? Have them drag you away?"

"I don't need you to fight for me," he said stiffly. He softened his tone at her hurt look. "You're my wife; it is I that should do the defending."

"This is a tough world," she said, "and I must be able to defend myself and mine." He agreed but extracted a promise that she would do no more fighting until the child was born before asking her how she retained her skills.

She shrugged. "I practice." Twice a week at minimum, she told him.

After a couple of minutes in the shade they resumed their walk, Matthew with his hands clasped behind his back and a severe look on his face. He looked haggard – no wonder, given that he hadn't slept all night, and on top of that he was probably wallowing in a quagmire of recriminations. Her eyes drifted to his neck, her hand strayed to her throat.

"Is he scared?" Alex asked.

"Nay. He seemed… at peace." He gave her a brief summary of the conversation he'd had with James.

"Not my choice of euthanasia," Alex said, vividly imagining the burning sensation as the rope closed around the tender skin of her neck.

"The drop will kill him," Matthew said, "and we'll give him the means to get royally drunk beforehand."

She just nodded, sick to her stomach; Poor James to die in front of so many people and not one to hold his hand.

A shout behind them startled them, and they turned to see the stout figure of the harbourmaster waving something at them.

"A letter," he smiled, handing it over. "And I have berths for you."

Alex whooped.

"The ship sails in three days," the harbourmaster added, looking from one to the other expectantly. The joy dissipated as fast as it had come, leaving in its wake an echoing hollowness.

"Three days? Is there not a possibility for it to wait a week?" Matthew sounded pleading.

The harbourmaster shook his head. "No, it sails on time. It's already taking aboard cargo."

Matthew took both Alex' hands in his. "I can't let him die alone."

"I know," Alex replied, working hard to contain the roaring, angry voice inside of her. His fault – all of it his fault!

"I appreciate your kindness," Matthew said to the harbourmaster. "But we can't leave on such short notice. We have a dying friend."

The harbourmaster nodded. "I heard: not that Fairfax is a great loss to mankind, if I may say so." He gave Alex an encouraging smile. "There'll be more ships, ma'am." With that he was off, no doubt to find new buyers for the precious berths.

Alex leaned her head against Matthew's chest and wept.

Home! Had he not gone out to Suffolk Rose, obliging her and James to come after, they'd be on their way home. He rested his cheek against her head.

"I'm so sorry, lass, I'm so very, very sorry."

Finally she wiped her eyes. "At least we have a letter to read," she said, "but let's read it back in our room. Let's save it for later tonight."

What she really wanted to do was to yank the letter out of his hands and tear it open to read it now, immediately. Her eyes hung on the thick paper square as he nodded and tucked it inside his shirt. Matthew put the back of his hand against her face.

"You can go with this ship," he said, sounding as if he'd choked on something unpalatable. "I can buy you passage and come after on a later boat."

Leave him? She met his eyes and shook her head.

"No way; I'm not leaving you. With your luck you'd probably find yourself on a boat bound for Greenland or something."

"Sounds like a wonderful place," he said, with a smile in his voice.

"It isn't, it's a misnomer, or an indication of the Vikings having a very peculiar sense of humour. It's covered with ice. And polar bears."

In an effort to distract them both, she launched into a detailed description of Eskimos and igloos and how in the future men would explore the barren wastes of snow. Sometimes she missed the diversity of her previous life, she told him, the availability of information about so many different things.

"Mmm," Matthew said. "But why would anyone living here need to know about yon Eskimos?"

She looked away and sighed; in this time and age it was always about the here and now, a slow plodding pace that sometimes drove her crazy.

"Do you think of it often?" Matthew sounded belligerent, surprising Alex into turning towards him.

"Think about what?"

"About your other life," Matthew clarified, his eyes scanning her face.

"Not really, every now and then yes, but not so much about my life as such, as about my people."

"We are your people," he corrected harshly. "Mark and I, Joan and Simon, even Mrs Gordon."

"Soon to be Mrs Parson," Alex smiled, eliciting a responding glimmer in his eye. She opened her fingers to twist them into his. "They are my people too; Magnus, Isaac and John. They will always be my people."

He grunted, clearly dissatisfied by this reply. They walked in silence for some time, swinging their braided hands between them like infatuated adolescents.

"So you never wish yourself back, then?"

"No, never. They are my people, but you, Matthew Graham, you are my life." She kissed his cheek and tore away to run the last few yards home.

Mrs Adams had long ago resigned herself to her guest's obsession with cleanliness, and had agreed that she might use the laundry shed for her ablutions, thereby eliminating the need to carry pail after pail of water up the stairs. So when Alex rushed by her and asked if she could use the shed, she just nodded, bustling to find towels and soap.

"A taper?" she asked, nodding in the direction of the hearth.

Alex shook her head. "In this heat?"

Mrs Adams gave her a condescending smile. "This isn't hot," she said, echoing Matthew's earlier comment. "Come August, well then you can talk about heat."

"I can't wait," Alex mumbled.

"God willing you will be on your way home by then," Mrs Adams chirped. She was a remarkably cheerful person, Alex reflected, at times borderline enervating.

"I sincerely hope so."

"The harbourmaster said how he'd arranged berths for

you, hasn't he found you then? He ..." Alex slammed the kitchen door hard behind her.

Alex propped the door open to let in some light into the dim interior of the laundry shed and sat down on one of the work benches, kicking at the washboard propped against the trough. Home... and Mark... She tried to picture him in her mind. He would have outgrown all her smocks by now, a small boy, no longer a baby. Someone else was making his clothes, and at this rate it would be Joan, not her, that would be the first to dress him in shirt and breeches. The thought gnawed like a rabid rat at her heart. She was going to return to face a little stranger, a boy whose likes and dislikes she didn't know.

She sighed; of course they owed it to James to be there for him when he died for Matthew. God, he was an idiot at times! If only...But no; how was she to blame him when all he had set out to do was to avenge the harm done to them both? Stupid, stupid man! She bit off a piece of nail and chewed it meditatively. There would be other boats, she decided as she undid her shoes and took off her stockings. For a long time she stared down at her toes, not really seeing them when her eyes misted over with tears. She scrubbed at her face, took several steadying breaths and turned her attention to the business of washing instead.

He had closed the wicker shutters and lit candles, throwing the whole room into a dusky half-light. Alex let out a surprised "oh" when he moved towards her.

"Undress," he said, taking in the way her wet hair hung in heavy ropes down her back. He loved this; to stand and watch as his Alex shed one piece of clothing after the other until she was naked and white before him. Her breasts were already rounding with pregnancy, and above her dark pubic triangle there was an obvious little bulge. He rested his hand against it, his thumb caressing her skin.

"You're beautiful," he whispered, and her skin flushed into pink. He combed his fingers through her wet hair, unravelling one tangle after the other, and she leaned against him, pressing her naked breasts against his shirtfront. His cock was thudding by now, demanding to be let out to swive his wife, but Matthew was in no hurry, he had all day, and he concentrated instead on the intricate whorls of her ear, the line of her neck as it flowed down towards her collar bones, the way she fitted perfectly into him. Minutely he inspected her nipples, the birthmark on her right hip, the dimples just above her buttocks, and she stood breathing heavily under his touch.

He backed her towards the bed, kissing her until he had to break away to gulp air. He eased her down to sit and guided her hands to his breeches, standing stock still when she released his cock from its constraints. Her mouth, Jesus sweet, her wonderful, warm mouth, her tongue, her fingers fluttering over him, caressing his balls. He could barely breathe, drowning in a sea of sensations that centred round what she was doing to him.

"Now." She shifted back and pulled him down on top of her, and he stumbled on his breeches and fell awkwardly, hearing the rope frame groan and squeak.

"Now," he agreed and his cock was like a homing pigeon, burying itself in her. He filled her, he cupped her buttocks and held her so close he could feel her womb. He rode her, he drove her before him, he came and he went, and it built and it built and still he held back, because she had to know she was his, had to feel in every tingling nerve that he was in her, on her, possessing her. Only when he felt her begin to buck and saw her eyes glaze as she lost herself to him did he let himself go, uttering a deep guttural sound of animal release.

# CHAPTER 30

They read the letter in bed by the light of the headboard candle. They were all well, it began by assuring them, but wee Mark had been sick with the measles over his birthday and had then succumbed to a nasty ear infection that had them all up for several nights running. In the end, Simon wrote, his eardrum had burst, and a large quantity of pus had leaked out.

"He's deaf!" Alex sat up in consternation.

"Nay, that isn't what it says. It says his eardrum burst – no great matter is it?"

"It hurts like hell," she said, "and we should have been there, with him."

"Aye well; he had Joan and Simon there, no?"

"Hmph!" Alex said, but nodded for him to go on reading.

Simon went on to describe what had been planted and on what fields, how the cabbage patch in the kitchen garden had been ravaged by rabbits, and how Gavin had narrowly escaped with his life intact after an incident involving bees, an irate Rosie and the new bull.

"New bull?" Matthew frowned down at the paper. "What happened to Atlas?"

"Roast beef?" Alex said, which Matthew didn't find at all amusing.

The letter ended with a very apologetic paragraph, where Simon began by explaining that he had not felt himself to have any choice, and that he was sure Matthew would agree that was the case. After all, what was he to do when Margaret showed up with wee Ian in tow, weeping that she had nowhere else to go?

"What? She's at Hillview? Bloody hell! " Alex slammed her hand into the bedpost and ended up sucking her knuckles, eyes narrowed into blue slits. Simon went on to say that of course Margaret wasn't staying at the big house, but was back in her little cottage. By the way, he added, Ian was a copy of his father, as was that little rascal, Mark.

"What does he mean? That it's obvious they're brothers, not cousins?" Alex looked as if she'd been fed a handful of worms.

"Half-brothers," Matthew said.

"Huh; last time I saw him, Ian was all you – just like Mark."

Matthew folded the letter together in silence. He shared Alex' dislike of having Margaret back at Hillview, but deep inside it thrilled him that both his sons were there.

"Why is she there?" Alex settled down to rest her head on his shoulder. "Do you think Luke's thrown her out?"

Matthew had no idea, and nor did he care. Margaret and Luke deserved each other, and he hoped they would tear as big chunks out of each other as they had torn out of him. But he pitied the lad, and said as much.

"Yes," Alex said, "poor kid. Not a good role model in sight."

"Role model?"

"Someone to emulate," Alex explained.

"Simon is there," Matthew said. "Surely any lad could use him as an example."

Alex hid her face and laughed. "How many boys would want to use Simon as an example? Mostly he looks like a meatball on legs, and he sits a horse like an egg on a hot skillet, sliding this way and that."

"You shouldn't judge on looks alone," Matthew said, trying to sound reproving. But he grinned all the same.

"I don't, but small boys definitely do. They want heroes, dashing men with cloaks and swords – not a brainy small town lawyer."

She turned on her back, caressing her belly. He covered her hand with his, following her movements up and down.

"Has it quickened yet?" he said, feeling a twinge of jealousy that only she should be allowed to experience that moment in time when the wean sprang from possibility to certainty.

"No, not yet. Do you think it's a boy this time as well?"

"Nay, this time it's a lass. A lass as wild and magnificent as her mother. A lass who will follow her man to the ends of the world and beyond, no matter what it costs her." He smiled down at her. "And if this isn't a lass, then the next one will surely be, or the one after that, or the next…"

"Five?" she croaked.

Och aye; at least five. He wanted many bairns with this woman, a line of strong, healthy sons and daughters. He cocked his head, looking at her. Theoretically, they could have a dozen children, but he saw no point in telling her that, given how shocked she seemed at the notion of five. Ah well; she'd get used to the idea successively, with each bairn slipping from between her thighs.

"Do you mind?" he said.

"What? Five ? Let's say it's a bit daunting to a girl who grew up in a time where a woman can decide how many children she wants. In general people opt for two." She turned on her side, uttering a long "mmmm" when, he spooned himself around her. "We'll have as many kids as we make," she said, reaching back to pat him. "Because I definitely don't intend doing without."

"Me neither," he said, "and my wife is most accommodating – dutiful and obedient." He laughed when she slapped him on his thigh, yelped when she pinched him instead.

There were still days when Matthew woke far too early, awash with rage, but after that time with Alex down by the sycamore he had learnt to trust that she'd be able to handle it should he need her to. This morning it was enough to lie and hold her, hearing her steady breathing. Today was the day of James' trial, and he worried; about the trial as such, about Jones being called to the stand and insisting that Matthew Graham had killed Fairfax, not James. What would the court say, faced with the obvious frailty of the defendant?

When Matthew entered the cell later that morning,

James was ashen faced with pain, but he refused the laudanum, drinking an impressive quantity of whisky instead. He hung on to Matthew's arm as they crossed the little square, but once inside the court room he straightened up and walked on his own to his designated place. Neatly dressed, down to borrowed shoes and stockings, James stood throughout the proceedings, leaning heavily on the table before him to keep himself upright.

It was a quick business, thank the Lord, the judge listening with severity to the described crime and nodding at the conclusion drawn by the constable. No innocent man would profess himself a murderer, and James repeated that yes, it was him who had ended the despicable Mr Fairfax' life by driving twelve inches of Toledo steel into his heart. The outcome was given and Matthew barely listened to the sentence, his eyes on his pale and trembling friend.

"You will hang, Mr McLean," the judge said. "A week from now you will hang."

"A week?" James breathed hoarsely. "Why wait a week?"

The judge looked at him with puzzlement.

"If it pleases your honour, I would ask you to hang me as soon as possible. Today, or tomorrow."

"A week," the judge insisted, slamming his gavel down with finality.

"I'll be dead before the week's up," James said to Matthew. "And I'll die here, in this soiled straw without a glimpse of the sky." He strained his face in the direction of the small window covered by a grimy square of oiled skin, and for the first time it seemed he would weep.

"I'm so sorry," Matthew said, "Oh God, that I could help you somehow."

James looked at him for a long time. "Ask Mrs Gordon, mayhap she can help, no?"

Matthew managed a weak smile. "Not Mrs Gordon for much longer. Mr Parson has proposed and been accepted."

James chuckled, broke off with a gasp. He waved Matthew's hand away, took a couple of breaths.

"He's a most fortunate gentleman, be sure to tell him, aye?"

"Oh, he already knows," Matthew said, "and if he doesn't, she'll be sure to inform him herself." Before he left he took down the yellowed skin, allowing in a ray of bright sun that fell like golden rain into the gloom of the little room.

James smiled. "Thank you."

The soon to be Mrs Parson refused to do anything more than what they were already doing.

"I can increase the laudanum so that he sleeps most of the time, but more than that I can't do."

Matthew sighed but nodded his agreement. To poison someone, even if it was by their explicit wish, was to invite unnecessary attention from the authorities.

"Do you think he'll die? Before..."

Mrs Gordon shook her head. "Nay, I think not. There's a very strong flame in that man, and it won't allow him to relinquish life easily. I pray for him, aye? Every day I pray that God have mercy on him and take him home."

"Aye," Matthew said, "so do I. But it would seem our Lord has other matters on His mind."

"The Lord does as well as He can, I reckon," Mrs Gordon shrugged.

On the penultimate day of his life, James asked that Alex be allowed in to see him together with her husband. James lay wheezing in the straw when she entered the small space, and even in his exhausted state he registered the shock that swept her face at the sight of him. A living skeleton, he was, so thin it hurt to lie for long in one posture, his bones protesting at the unpadded pressure of the wooden floorboards. She smiled, a broad, strained smile, and came over to him.

"I brought you a clean shirt," she said. To die in; he hoped she'd taken it in at the sides so that it wouldn't flap like a sail around him come the morrow.

"That is kind of you," James said between shallow

breaths. It was pushing against the diaphragm, this thing in his belly, and every breath was an effort. Strange, how something as natural as breathing should become an endeavour requiring fortitude and concentration. He rested his eyes on Alex. He had wanted to see the lass one more time because she reminded him slightly of his Elizabeth, all those years ago when they first met.

"Would you mind undoing your hair?" he asked.

Alex shook her head but looked at Matthew – as she should, married woman that she was. Matthew gave a nod, and she lifted her cap off her hair and undid it.

"Ah…" James exhaled, beckoning her closer. His hand rose from the floor, fingers spread to comb through the wavy hair. Alex took his hand in hers and guided it through her curls, silent tears coursing down her face.

"Shh, don't cry, lass. Tomorrow I'm released from this prison of pain, and I'll stand humble in front of my maker – humble, but free." James fumbled with his other hand and took hold of his Bible.

"I would ask you a favour, that you carry the Book back home with you and that you give it to my wife." He stopped for breath, closing his eyes as he re-oxygenated his blood. "Tell her that I love her. That even as I lie here, so far from home, it is her I see as I draw my last breaths." He fingered her hair. So soft, like a live pelt, just as Elizabeth's had been. Now his wife's hair was grey but still as soft, and he slipped away, drifting into a half dream where the lass presently at his side was in fact his beloved woman. "Tell her she was everything a wife should be and more," he whispered, and warm tears slid from under his shut lids.

"Will you be coming tomorrow?" he asked as Alex stood to leave.

"Do you want me to?"

"Aye I do. And I would like it if you smiled at me."

Alex nodded, gave him a watery smile and hurried from the room.

Matthew moved over to sit in the spot Alex had vacated

and pillowed James' head on his lap.

"Will I tell you then? Will I tell you of Scotland?"

James sighed in agreement and Matthew began to talk; of moors that stretched endless under pale summer nights, of hills that shifted in browns and deepest pinks. He spoke of gorse and heather, of lapwings and hawks. He described the rocky backbone of their country, the silence and the cool, clear nights. He whispered to James of the bluebells in the forest and the glitter of frost on the rowan trees, of how water sprang fresh and cold from the hillside, and how in winter the sky hung bejewelled with stars, seemingly so low one could stretch out a hand to touch them.

He talked until James was fast asleep, his breath rapid and shallow, and still Matthew stayed with his friend, recounting the wonders of their homeland so that James would die on the morrow with the memory of the land of his birth fresh on his mind.

In the blackest hour of the night James woke in panic, and Matthew held him and plied him with whisky until he subsided again. At dawn James woke again, clearheaded despite the whisky and the pain, and he stood shakily as Matthew helped him dress for one final time. There were no words between them, there was no need, and when the guards came to get their prisoner they found him calm and surprisingly strong, an almost eager shine to his eyes.

The gallows had been built at one end of the small square, and before it thronged people, far more than Matthew had expected. He scanned the crowd to look for Alex, finding her straight in front, her face a startling white. Beside her stood Mrs Gordon and Mr Parson, and Alex met Matthew's eyes, assuring him that he could stay as close to James as he needed to be, she would be fine. James grasped Matthew's hand one last time.

"Go with God, lad."

James walked on his own up to the noose and stood still as the rope was tightened into place. He swallowed and swallowed, gulped down air, wonderful air. Any moment now and he'd be dead. James felt a wave of panic rush through him and he looked desperately for something, for someone to ease his way. That was when Alex stepped forward, took off her straw hat and shook out her hair, smiling so hard he feared her face would break. James smiled back, his eyes locked on her.

A faint breeze lifted her hair to float. Someone was droning to his left – the reverend, no less – one of the guards adjusted the noose, shoved him to stand in the right place. Alex raised two fingers to her mouth and blew him a kiss. A drum roll. Another drum roll. Yet another blinding smile from Alex. A third drum roll. He fell, gasped. His eyes flew over the crowd, found her again. His Elizabeth; no, Alex Graham. Elizabeth... My Elizabeth... My.

# CHAPTER 31

Mrs Gordon came to an abrupt stop, her whole face scrunching together until it resembled a wrinkled winter apple.

"Him again," she said.

"Him?" Alex asked, adjusting the heavy basket on her arm.

"Him." Mrs Gordon jerked her head in the direction of a man, standing on the opposite side of the street. When Alex looked at him, he backed away into the shadows before walking away. She had but a glimpse of a heavy set man, bearded and with a distinctive limp.

"Who's he?"

"I have no inkling; but this is the third time I spy him on our heels, and I don't like it, aye?"

Well, no; nor did Alex, and over the coming few days she kept her eyes peeled, confirming that Mrs Gordon was right. This unknown man seemed to pop up wherever she went, limping out of sight the moment he realised she'd seen him.

"A man? Following you?" Matthew frowned. "And why have you not told me before?"

"Well, I didn't know, did I?" she replied, smiling down at the finished smock. This one was not for sale, this one was for her baby. "Mrs Gordon says he came with the ship that berthed last week." She threw him a cautious look; ships – or rather the lack of berths on them – were at present a sensitive subject. "There's bound to be a few more," she said, "the harbourmaster said, how the stragglers and the ships that do double trips come in now, late in August or September." She made a face; she'd be the size of a whale before they got on board, and the idea of braving the Atlantic in late autumn held little, if any, appeal.

"So; this man," Matthew said, clearly not that concerned

with ships at present. Alex leaned back against the tree under which she was sitting.

"He sort of skulks around. From what little I've seen of him, he's on the fat side with dark hair and a beard."

"Hmm," Matthew said. For some time he sat in silence, looking pensive. Then he shrugged and stood up gracefully. "Home?"

Since some weeks they lived with Mr Parson as did Mrs Gordon, and Matthew had overruled Mr Parson's insistence that they not pay, they were after all friends of the family. Instead, the two men had compromised on a rate substantially lower than what they'd paid at Mrs Adams, and in return Matthew chopped wood, did repairs and had offered to build new shelving for the store. Alex was in two minds about their new accommodations. She recognised the need to be careful with their money – berths could come very dear as they approached this time of the year as a consequence of supply and demand – but she missed the general bustle at Mrs Adams, and she definitely missed the laundry shed.

"Four years and more you've been in my life," Matthew said, interrupting her thoughts. "And tomorrow you'll be thirty."

Alex mock shuddered; in this day and age more than halfway to her grave.

"Do I look horribly old?" she asked coyly, knowing for a fact that she didn't. Being pregnant suited her, putting pink tones into her skin that made her look rosy and warm. Matthew chuckled and stooped, pretending to inspect her.

"Nay, not entirely decrepit," he said, ducking as she attempted to whack him over his head. He dug into his pouch and brought out something, opening her hand to place it in her palm.

"Happy Birthday."

She closed her fist around it; another little wooden carving, like all her birthday gifts from him had been. When she opened her hand she felt herself heating into a vivid red.

"I can't show this to anyone!"

Matthew slipped an arm around her waist. "Nay, I think it best not."

She stared down at herself, legs wide, back somewhat arched, and her head slung back in abandon.

"You have a very dirty mind," she reprimanded him. She twisted the dark piece of wood over and over. "How do you do it? How can you produce something so small and fragile and with such exquisite detail?" He grew with her praise and kissed her on her cheek, assuring her that in this specific case it was a matter of inspiration.

They took the long turn home, strolling along the periphery of the little town. As they came round the corner of the Assembly House they almost barged into Jones.

"Shit," Alex said in an undertone, noting that Jones was as flustered by this impromptu meeting as she was. The large man was carrying an overflowing leather satchel, rolled deeds sticking out all over the place. He was accompanied by the chief registrar, and whatever conversation the two men might be having died away at the sight of the Grahams. A curt nod from Jones, a slight inclination of the head from Matthew, and they were off, with Alex more or less dragging Matthew along.

"Alex..." Matthew brought them both to a stop. "I won't do anything foolish."

"No, but he might."

"You think? I get the impression he's been avoiding me of late." He threw a black look in the direction of Jones, still in discussion with the registrar. "I wonder why."

"Maybe Sir William managed to warn him off, you know, when he reminded Jones you were a free man too."

"Maybe," Matthew said, but he didn't sound convinced. Alex threw a look over her shoulder at where Jones was still standing in discussion with the registrar.

"You don't think ..." she broke off, shaking her head.

"Think what?"

"Well, the man. Do you think it might be him, Jones, that has hired him somehow?"

"To do what? Spy on you?" Matthew shook his head. "Whatever for?" But she could see the thought made him nervous. Welcome to the club, mister; that makes two of us.

They detoured by the cemetery, standing for a moment before James' stone. Matthew hadn't stinted when it came to burying his friend, and on the smooth surface was engraved not only his name but the name of his wife. No birth date, as Matthew didn't know it.

"What will you write on my stone?" she asked him, repressing a cold tremor down her spine. He frowned down at her. "My birth date," she said, "you can't exactly put 1976, can you?"

"1632, that's in line with your age, no?"

"Yes, but it doesn't tell the truth, does it?"

His quick reply made her realise that this was something he had spent time thinking about, and it made her feel ill at ease. For reassurance she smoothed her hand over her rounding stomach. Life was growing in her, strong vibrant life that turned and wheeled inside of her. And she was only thirty and had many, many years before her with Matthew at her side. She slipped her hand into his.

"Do you know how old Mrs Gordon is?"

Matthew wrinkled his brow in thought. "Fifty-five?"

Alex gave him an admiring gaze. "Almost. She's soon fifty-two." And looked at least a decade older... Alex had struggled hard to keep the astonishment out of her face when Mrs Gordon told her. "And she's been married twenty years, had both husband and children die away from her..." Alex let her voice trail off. "How can she still be so generally cheery? If it were me, I'd be permanently depressed."

"I dare say she's had those moments too, no?"

"She was seventeen when she married," Alex went on, "that seems awfully young."

"My Mam was eighteen when I was born," Matthew said, smiling down at her.

"Still very young. I hope any daughter of ours will be older."

"They will wed as I see fit," he said with a shrug. "A lass of eighteen is well capable of being both wife and mother."

"Hmm." She threw him a look that she intended as forbidding, but it only made him grin.

Two days later Matthew came into the kitchen with Mr Parson at his heels.

"Very odd," Mr Parson said, "we've been through all the inns and boarding houses, and nowhere have we as much as caught a whiff of this man you say has been following you."

"So maybe we've just been imagining it, right?" Alex said, even if she knew that wasn't the case.

"Hmph!" Mrs Gordon said. "I saw what I saw, aye? That man is up to no good, mark my words."

"And the harbourmaster recalls him disembarking," Matthew said, "a silent man who flitted off before the clerks could get his name."

"He could be staying at one of the plantations," Mr Parson said.

"Yeah; like the Suffolk Rose," Alex muttered. But why? A chill rushed through her. "Maybe I'm right; maybe Jones had hired him to, well, finish you off," she said, staring at Matthew.

"Me?" Matthew shook his head. "It's you he's been following."

Alex was sufficiently concerned to raise the issue the next time she met Sir William. He brought his eyebrows together in a worried frown.

"Following you? An unknown rogue?"

"That's what it seems like," Alex said.

"And what does your husband say about all this?"

"That I should stay at home and not walk anywhere alone." Alex grimaced; she'd sneaked out this afternoon and Matthew would be anything but pleased, even if it was only a quarter mile walk from Mr Parson's shop to the Governor's offices.

Sir William laughed and wagged an admonishing finger

at her. "You should do as he tells you," he said, "although I am most delighted to see you here." With that he stood, and a minute or so later Alex was out on the street, being escorted back home by the governor himself.

Halfway there they met Matthew and Alex was rather irritated by how the two men began to talk over her head, for all the world as if she was a disobedient child.

"No, no," Sir William said, "I am in total agreement with you, Mr Graham. And you've not found him?"

"Nowhere," Matthew sighed, "and I've looked."

"Well, mayhap he's gone, no? It would seem neither lady has seen him these last few days."

"Mayhap," Matthew agreed. He bowed, took Alex by the hand and led her home. He marched her up the stairs, more or less jostled her into their room, and closed the door with a bang. Boy, he was angry, eyes a very light green as he shouted at her to do as he said, and what had she been thinking off, to walk off like that?.

"What is it you don't understand?" she said. "I'm perfectly capable of taking care of myself, okay? And I won't – I repeat, won't – stay stuck in here all day. It drives me crazy!"

"You'll do as I say." Matthew looked at her and exhaled. "It worries me, lass. What if he aims to snatch you off the street, abduct you like?"

"Me?" Alex laughed. "Why on earth would anyone want to kidnap me?" But she promised she'd do as he said and never leave the house alone.

"I'd like to come with you," Alex said to Mrs Gordon one day. "You know, when you deliver a baby." Anything to alleviate these hours of boredom, cooped up in the house.

"Why?"

Alex patted her stomach. "I guess I'd like to know a bit more. After all, it's something I'll be doing a bit of myself." At times it scared her; anything could go wrong! So she had decided that she needed to know as much as possible, in an attempt to educate away her fears.

"You had an easy time of it with Mark," Mrs Gordon said, "and you're wide enough around the hips. You'll have easy deliveries, I think." She tilted her head to one side, black, bright eyes studying Alex. "But you can come if you wish; mind you, it will be at night. It almost always is."

Alex shrugged. "I'll cope."

A week or so later, Mrs Gordon knocked on their door well after nightfall and told Alex to hurry, there was a man waiting to take them at speed to attend a birth. Alex dropped a quick kiss on Matthew's shoulder, tied her apron into place and joined Mrs Gordon outside the door. The man on the horse nodded at them and pointed at the mare on a leading rein.

"We must make haste," he said, dismounting to boost Mrs Gordon to sit behind Alex. Halfway there Alex realised where they were going.

"This is the road to Suffolk Rose!" she said to Mrs Gordon.

"There are women there as well, no?"

They were led directly into the big house, and Alex noted with surprise that they were making for the master's bedroom – as far as she knew Fairfax hadn't left a wife. She peeked into the office on their way, shivering as she remembered last time she was here, with Fairfax very dead in his chair.

"Bloody hell!" Alex came to a halt upon entering the bedchamber. Lying in the huge, ornate bed was Kate, a Kate who was writhing with a contraction but otherwise seemed to be in the best of health.

"What are you doing here?" Kate snapped, as disconcerted as Alex was.

"She's here to help me," Mrs Gordon said and dispatched the maid to find water, clean linen, oil and a soft, woollen blanket.

"There," Kate pointed to a corner. "You'll find the blanket there. I knitted it myself."

Mrs Gordon wasn't listening, hands on Kate's distended belly. "Hmm," she said, prodding the pelvic area. "Hmm," she muttered again when her hands moved further up.

"What?" Kate struggled up to sit.

"Twins."

"Twins?" Kate squeaked, and squeaked even more when Mrs Parson proceeded to wipe her between her legs, all the while muttering comments to Alex.

"You didn't know?" Alex asked Kate, who shook her head, eyes panicking as her womb hardened into a contraction.

"Oh God," Kate said weakly, slumping back against the pillows. Alex had by now done her arithmetic and grinned.

"Not Matthew's."

"We don't know that," Kate said.

"Not his," Alex repeated, "these were conceived in December."

"Later than that," Mrs Gordon corrected, "twins are generally never carried full term." She raised a brow at Kate. "Where's the father to be?"

"I don't know, I think…" she broke off, mouth pinched shut, eyes bugging out with a new contraction.

"You can't fight it," Mrs Gordon admonished as the contraction faded away. "You must work with it."

"Easy for you to say," Kate muttered, dark eyes flashing.

"So, where is Jones?" Mrs Gordon repeated some time later.

"I think he's hiding in the stables," Kate said.

"Send someone to find him," Mrs Gordon instructed Alex, "this will be over right quickly."

Jones looked as shocked as it was possible for him to look, blinking down at the two bundles.

"Two?"

"Apparently, and definitely not Matthew's." Far too ugly for that, Alex decided, thinking the two little boys unfortunately looked very much like their father. She retreated a step or two, uncomfortable with being in the same room as him. The bastard didn't deserve one jot of happiness, not after what he'd done to Matthew, not after what had happened to poor James.

"Twins…" Jones extended a finger, grazing the ginger fuzz that stood from the head of the closest.

"Healthy lads," Mrs Gordon said, "but you'd best get a wet nurse." The exultant father nodded, mumbled a "well done" to Kate and hurried from the room.

In the bed Kate had sunk back into the pillows, purple hollows round her eyes. Mrs Gordon was still busy with the last of the babies, cooing as she swaddled it. Alex cleared the room, bundling wet and bloodied linen in a corner, shaking pillows and smoothing clean sheets into place. In the weak candle light the room was peaceful, the soft snuffling sound of new born babies the only thing that broke the silence. A hasty look out the window confirmed dawn was still some hours off, all in all a quick and easy birthing. Mrs Gordon muttered something about finding some honey and hurried out of the room, leaving Alex and Kate alone.

"I killed him." Kate seemed fast asleep.

Alex sat up straight.

"He tried to force me, saying that Jones wouldn't mind, that he'd been sharing me occasionally before." Kate made a disgusted face, one hand picking at the coverlet. "So I picked up his dirk and killed him." She laughed, opening her eyes to look at Alex. "It surprised him, he sat and looked from me to the knife a couple of times and then he just slumped back and died."

"Does Jones know?"

Kate nodded.

"And still he tried to blame it on Matthew?"

Another nod.

Alex knotted her hands. "And if James hadn't been there to take the blame, would you have let him hang?"

Two brown eyes met hers. "We all do what we have to do," Kate said. "To survive, I mean."

If Mrs Gordon hadn't returned at that moment, Alex would have punched Kate. Now she just turned on her heel and walked out of the room, swamped by a desire to leave this damned house. Immediately.

Halfway home it began to rain. Alex shivered and cursed, wiping her face free of all this water that was making it even more difficult to find her way.

"Stupid," she remonstrated with herself. "This was a really stupid thing to do."

Too right; it was pitch black and with the rain the dirt road converted into a mud slide. Here and there she lost sight of it, and for a couple of minutes of absolute panic she lumbered round among the trees, sure she was forever lost before she realised the road was only feet away. Well; at least the weather had the benefit of keeping any potential rogues at home, and with this reassuring thought foremost in her mind Alex made it all the way back to Jamestown, staggering in muddy and wet just before dawn.

She was almost at the Apothecary when something was thrown over her head. She tried to scream, but the cloth muffled her sounds, and so she fought instead, kicking out wildly at her unknown attacker. There was a satisfied snicker behind her, she drew in breath to cry out again, but a clap to her head sent her to her knees. Yet another clap and Alex was no longer sure where she was. She was dragged off, whoever it was who was pulling her grunting with the effort. Once more she tried to free herself. The responding blow knocked her out.

# CHAPTER 32

"Where's Alex?" Matthew pounced on Mrs Gordon the moment she came through the door. It was well after sunrise, and for the last few hours he'd been keeping an eye on the road, his heart tumbling at the sight of Mrs Gordon returning with only the groom as her company.

"Alex? Is she not here? She left on her own, several hours ago."

"Alone?" Matthew said. "Why?"

"I don't rightly know; she had a tiff with Kate Jones, and then she just stormed out, aye?"

"And you didn't stop her?"

"Well, I didn't think she'd gone much further than the kitchen. It was dark outside, no?" Mrs Gordon twisted her hands hard together. "What might have happened to her?"

"I don't know," Matthew said, "but I aim to find out."

The Governor of Virginia looked most displeased. "A woman, abducted; I will not have it, you hear?" He frowned at the constables, at the table, kicked with irritation at one of the chairs. "Either she was taken there, by someone at the plantation, or somewhere close to here," he continued, "there's nothing but wilderness in between." He pulled at his lip, did a little turn, clapping Matthew supportively on the back as passed him.

"He took her here," Matthew said. He held up her shoe. He had problems speaking and found it near impossible to stand still listening to the governor when what he should be doing was to scour the surrounding area for his wife.

The governor frowned. "Is it that man, you think?"

"Who else?" Matthew shrugged. But why? Who would want to ... He froze. Luke. Aye, that was it. This all smelled of Luke, a failsafe sent off to ensure Matthew never made it home, no matter if Alex found him in time. A huge wave of relief rose through him; Alex wasn't harmed, she was but bait in a trap meant for him.

"The ship," he asked, "the boat he came with, where was it from?"

"From London, as I recall it," the harbourmaster said.

Matthew nodded. "It's me, I'm the one he wants."

"You? So you know this man?"

"Nay; but I'd warrant he's been sent here by my brother – to kill me." He swallowed. What had this man done to his Alex? She's just the lure, he comforted himself, worthless unless she's kept alive.

Sir William had not for nothing been an officer in the army. In a matter of minutes he had a strategy devised whereby he called in every single child in Jamestown and promised whoever came back with news as to where a stranger was holding a woman prisoner a huge reward.

Eyes widened at the size of the pouch Sir William hefted into the air, and off they went, barefoot and silent, to scurry like rats through the little town.

"Bairns?" Matthew was not convinced.

"Send in men and it'll scare him – or warn him. Send in maids and lads, and he'll at most think it a childish game. Besides," Sir William said, "who do you think knows every single nook and hideaway in this our little settlement?"

It was well after noon when a wee laddie, no more than six, darted into the room. He was muddy up to his waist, the shirt had a tear down the side, but his eyes were bright and there was a huge grin on his face.

"I found him," he said, "he's on the other side of the harbour, in one of them old sheds." His grin faded away. The laddie twisted at his shirt. "She screamed."

Matthew's guts tightened into impossible knots. Please don't do anything daft, lass, don't try to fight him, not now that you're heavy with child.

"I swear," Matthew said, "if he's harmed her, I'll ..." He wheeled, rushed for the door.

"No!" The governor was fast for his age, his hand closing on Matthew's coat. "We do this intelligently. We must do nothing that risks Alexandra's life."

She'd woken to the sound of gulls, and after a few moments she'd grasped she was lying in mulch, the ground close to her eyes swarming with little bugs and ants. With a yelp she'd sat up, and the man had loomed over her, telling her to shut up, or else ... He'd set the knife to her neck and dragged it lightly over her skin. Alex had scooted away from him and nodded.

Now she was sitting with her back against what remained of a wall, trying to stop her teeth from chattering. Jesus, she was cold, her clothes were far from dry after last night's downpour and sitting in the damp of a swamp wasn't exactly making things better. The man had so far been sitting a yard or so away, but he had begun to fidget and Alex drew her legs up in preparation. The moment he stood to piss she'd be off.

"And now what?" she said.

"Hold your tongue," he growled. Idiot. Very scary idiot, she shuddered, a hand coming up to rub at the shallow cut on the side of her neck. She sneezed. Her throat hurt and she wondered if she might have a fever, given the chills she was having. Her head ... a tentative hand to the bump ensured it was none too bad – his blow hadn't broken the skin.

Just as she'd expected, a few minutes later he got to his feet and limped over to a nearby bramble. She took off. The ground was soft and squelchy, in a matter of seconds her skirts were soaked, and she was nowhere as fast as she'd thought she'd be, made ungainly and clumsy by her swelling belly. A hand closed on her sleeve, she pulled free. He grabbed her again.

"Next time you try such I'll knife you," he gasped as he dragged her back towards the little hut.

"Take your hands off me!" She dug her heels in, raised her free hand and with a grunt brought the blade of her hand down over his nose. He shrieked, blood gushing. Unfortunately, he didn't let her go, and the way his eyes disappeared into his face, two miniature pebbles of undisguised dislike glaring at her, made Alex worry she might have overreached.

"Once I've killed your man, I'll take my time over you," he said, squashing her flat to the ground. She couldn't breathe. There was mulch in her mouth, in her nose, and she screamed. A yank on her hair, something smelly shoved into her mouth, rope burnt into her wrists and she was being hoisted into the air, arms impossibly stretched, only her toes reaching the ground.

"Or maybe I should start with you," he said, "the brother won't mind, will he? As long as you both end up dead, as long as none of you return to discredit his name."

Luke? Oh my God, Luke had sent this... this... torpedo all the way from England? The man pulled his knife, lips thinning into a smile. She didn't want to do this anymore; she wanted to go home. He walked around her, and Alex couldn't see him, only hear him. Her bladder contracted. It made him sniff and laugh.

"Not so cocky now, hey? Maybe I should slice off an ear or something and include it with my little note to you husband. Would he like that, do you think?" Something sharp prodded at her back. "That should convince him to come right quickly, and then ..." The man cackled, his hot exhalations far too close to her ear. "...well then I kill him, and you can watch."

Out of the corner of her eye she saw the knife. She shrank away, he laughed again. A long, jagged tear on the sleeve of her bodice. It hurt; like being caught in barbed wire. He stood in front of her, his swollen nose so close she went cross-eyed.

The dagger tapped at the tip of her nose. Oh God; he was going to slice it off. But he didn't. He walked round her. She turned her head to try to see him. Like a jack-in-the-box he popped up before her and the knife drew a long gash along her forearm.

Alex screamed and screamed, but the gag muffled any

sound she made to a weak whimper. How long had this gone on? An hour? Two? The sun was well to the west, her arm was a mess of shallow cuts, sleeve and shift slashed to shreds. The man giggled and dug the point of his knife yet again into her arm. Blood trickled down into her armpit. He wiped the blood off with his finger and smeared it over her face.

Jesus! Here he came again. She tried to knee him, but there was nothing to take purchase against, and with a sneer he slapped her leg away. He tore her shift open and touched her breasts. She tried to pull away, her skin puckering when his dirty fingers grazed it. He laughed, set the knife to her right breast. A swift movement and a thin line of red appeared, blood welling like sweet water pearls along the gash. It itched more than hurt – until he set his finger to it and rubbed, hard. She screamed again, choking in the gag.

She sneezed. Her nose was beginning to clog. Concentrate, Alex; don't cry, for God's sake don't cry. Breathe in slowly, open your mouth as wide as you can and pull in what air you can through the rag. Like Darth Vader; a sound that reminded her of a malfunctioning vacuum cleaner, but at least she had air in her lungs. She sneezed again. She slumped into the rope, not caring how it hurt her arms, her wrists. So tired...

Sir William tied back his hair and gestured for Matthew to circle to the back of the dilapidated structure before them. Step by careful step Matthew moved through the undergrowth, flinching at every sound he made. A quick look over his shoulder showed him Sir William and his men were approaching the shed just as cautiously, and to his far right he could make out the round shape of the harbourmaster flitting silently over the marshy ground.

Too slow; this was taking far too much time! What if ... no; Matthew forced the horrifying images of his wife lying dead to the back of his mind. He crouched and crawled, slid like a serpent along the ground, and after what seemed a lifetime the hut rose before him, a grey ruin of a building.

The back wall was gone, and there, hanging from the roof beam was Alex. For a horrifying instant Matthew thought she might be dead but then she sneezed and a man appeared by her side. Alex shrank together in her ropes and Matthew wanted to weep at the sight of her. A blade glinted and Alex' eyes flew open, a sound like that of a drowning kitten in a sack escaping from her gag.

Matthew roared. Like a bear he charged, low to the ground and with his dirk in his hand. The man jumped, grabbed hold of Alex and pressed his knife to her neck.

"I kill her," he screamed. "One step closer and I kill her."

Matthew slid to a stop. The man laughed. A shot went off and with a surprised 'eh' the man slid to his knees, knife falling from his hand. Matthew sprinted the last few yards that separated him from Alex and from what remained of the front door came Sir William, pistol still in hand.

"How unfortunate," he muttered, using a toe to nudge at the dead man. "Now we'll never know the truth behind this, will we?"

Matthew didn't care; he was glad the bastard was dead, but what had he done to his wife? He stood holding her while Sir William cut the rope, and with a little whooshing sound Alex collapsed into his arms.

"It's not too bad, aye?" Mrs Gordon looked up from where she was bandaging Alex' arm. "He's cut her a couple of times – it'll heal right quickly."

A couple of times? The arm was patterned with cuts, shallow for the most of it, but here and there deep enough for Mrs Gordon to put in a few stitches. She frowned and sat back. "No, I fear the damage done to her by yon ruffian is no great matter, but a whole day in this damp heat in wet clothes ..." She shook her head.

"I'm okay," Alex croaked. "I'll be fine. I just ..." She moaned and closed her eyes.

For well over a week, Matthew didn't leave their little

room. Occasionally Alex woke, smiling in weak recognition when she saw him before she sinking back into heavy, feverish sleep.

When Mrs Gordon offered to sit beside Alex so that he could take a little turn or mayhap rest, he refused. He had to be here, with her. He changed sheets and shifts, helped her to pee and watched with concern as the fever rose and fell, rose again and fell but slightly.

On the eighth day Mrs Gordon examined Alex thoroughly and sat back.

"It'll be alright," she said in a voice weak with relief. "You see? The phlegm she coughs up has thinned and her fever is much lower – still high, but lower." Matthew wanted to cry. Instead he picked up Alex' hand and placed his thumb against her wrist. Not her normal beat; a fast, strong pulse that pumped her blood round in an effort to combat the invading disease.

"Will it have harmed the bairn?"

Mrs Gordon shook her head. "Nay, the wean will be alright."

Alex lay for a long time blinking up at the ceiling. She turned her head. Matthew was dozing in the chair. When she called his name he jumped, fell to his knees and hid his face against the blankets.

"Matthew?" Alex licked her lips. She was terribly hungry and very thirsty. She patted his head. Why was he crying? Had something happened? She blinked, trying to recall where she was. Slowly it came back to her. In Virginia… Kate had twins, and the bitch would have let Matthew hang to save her own neck. A jolt of red hot anger coursed through her. The man … the knife … Her hand rested on her stomach for an instant; a soft kick, a gentle prodding inside of her.

"Matthew," she murmured, yawned and fell asleep.

It was early October by the time she was sufficiently recovered to be up and about, and by then it was too late.

No more ships, not this year, the harbourmaster said. Alex was washed with relief – and despair. She stood for some time staring out across the waters, her cloak pulled tight around her shoulders.

"He'll keep, lass," Matthew said, draping an arm round her. Alex sighed. By the time they got home Mark would be well beyond three, and all his life he'd lived without them. No doubt safe and cosseted, but by other people, not by her.

For a couple of days she moped, but when Mrs Gordon's wedding day dawned grey and rainy she was back to her normal self, bustling about as she helped Mrs Gordon get dressed. In black, of course – why change the habits of a lifetime – but with a pretty shawl around her shoulders and a brand new lace cap.

The ceremony was a quick affair, the party was not, and it was well after midnight before Alex could undo her stays. From below came music and song, and Alex suspected the new Mrs Parson intended on partying for quite some hours more. Where she got her energy from was an open question, but whatever it was Mrs Parson was imbibing, she wasn't sharing it with Alex, who sank down to sit on the bed.

"God, I'm tired," she said.

"Oh aye?" Matthew was standing in only his shirt, a foot or so from the bed. Well, okay; not that tired. The look in his eyes made her toes curl, and with a little smile he pulled off his shirt.

He was back to being the man he used to be – almost. His back was disfigured by a crisscross of scars, his hair was still too short and there were days when his eyes would darken with memories of humiliation and pain.

But right now his eyes glittered in the candle light, and when he jerked his head she stood up to go to him. He enveloped her, a slow dance with her pressed tight against his chest. His lips on her ear, her neck, his fingers flowing down her spine. He was so gentle it made her skin prickle, his fingertips incensing her until she was certain she would die unless he did something else and did it quick.

They made it to the bed, lips locked tight, hands braided together. She made harsh, guttural sounds when first his fingers, then his tongue found their way to her cleft. Oh yes! There, there! He kissed her, rose up to kiss her mouth, and she tasted herself on his tongue, on his lips. Now; she wanted him now, and she raised her hips and arched her back in a wordless imploration that he please, please, please... It made him laugh, and he took his time about it, bracing himself on his arms to keep his weight off their growing child. She barely registered when he came, so lost in herself that all she could think of was how everything that was alive in her came together into one point of burning, searing want.

"We must do this again," she murmured afterwards, biting his shoulder. "Soon."

"Aye, very soon. But you must let me rest a while first."

"And I'm the one who's supposed to be recuperating," she grumbled, making him promise that he'd have her eating her words. Soon. Once he had regained his strength.

On one of her walks around town Alex saw Kate Jones. Both of them came to a halt, Kate mumbled a 'good day' and rushed off, while behind her Alex spat in the gutter, took an even firmer grip of Mr Parson's arm and hurried home to tell Matthew what Kate had told her about how Fairfax died.

"Kate?" Matthew laughed. "Nay," he said, "she couldn't. And she was pregnant at the time."

"Well, that's what she said, and as far as I know being pregnant doesn't leave you incapacitated," Alex said, not at all liking how he immediately sprang to her defence.

Matthew shook his head. "She only said it to protect her husband. And besides, she's left-handed."

"Oh, and how would you know?" Alex snorted, before remembering that in all probability he did know. He looked away, a deep flush staining his cheeks.

"I just do, aye? The dirk was driven in by someone

right-handed – and very strong. It was sunk to the hilt and Fairfax would have struggled, wouldn't he?" His mouth quirked. "Quite elegant; she admits to murdering Fairfax for a reason she expects you to be sympathetic with, and yet she knows that once you tell me I'll know it's a lie." Well; that little oblique reference to the intimacy between him and Kate didn't exactly improve Alex' mood.

"She admitted to being willing to let you hang," Alex said. "But I suppose if you spend enough time thinking about it, you'll be sure to come up with an exonerating circumstance for that as well." He attempted to put an arm around her but she backed away. "Don't; not just now."

Matthew sighed and let her go. Alex stamped her way up the stairs hard enough to have Mrs Parson stick her head out of the kitchen and wonder why someone had brought a horse indoors.

"So what do you think happened?" Mrs Parson asked Matthew, pouring them both a healthy tot of whisky despite it being not yet noon. "It's cold, aye?" she muttered at his surprised expression, exaggerating a shiver.

"I reckon Kate is telling the truth – partly. I can well see Fairfax doing to her what he did to Alex." He grimaced in disgust. "In Kate's case he would see it as his right, no? A bonny lass working off her bond, well, she has no protection." Mrs Parson nodded; too many of the lasses she delivered were unwed, she told him, the bairns the unwelcome effect of equally unwelcome lovers. Like wee Jenny, the lass must have gotten pregnant the night she came off the boat, and every time Mrs Parson saw her the lass was weeping, terrified of her master.

"Mmm," Matthew said, not all that interested in the fate of this unknown Jenny. "Anyway," he said, "in this case the bonded lass did have some protection." Jones; a man who liked the lass, enjoyed having her in his bed and was not at all willing to share – not this time. So he warned Fairfax off, and Fairfax might have laughed and hitched his shoulders, allowing his prowling eye to rest elsewhere. On my wife, Matthew thought, tightening his grip on the pewter cup.

"It happened," Mrs Parson said, jerking him back to the present. "It happened and it didn't harm her greatly, but it saved your life."

Matthew unwillingly agreed.

"And then?" Mrs Parson prompted.

Matthew drummed his fingers on the table, deep in thought.

"He tried again, mayhap he requested only her hands or her mouth, but somehow he forced himself upon her. And she told Jones."

Fairfax returning home from the Governor's reception, carefully hanging up his resplendent coat before sitting down to do some work. The door opens and there stands Jones. Fairfax realising too late that he has seriously overstepped, promising Jones money, property, anything really. Except that Jones already is a partner, and what can Fairfax give him that he doesn't already have? Fairfax attempting an act of desperate bravado, sitting down to draft a document and sign it, only to turn and see the knife. See it and feel it, the signed document fluttering to the ground as the steel strikes home.

"But there was no document there," Matthew said. A quill, a blotch of ink, but no paper, nothing on which the quill could have been used. "I wonder..." he said, a smile spreading across his face.

"You'll not do anything," Mrs Parson said.

Of course not, Matthew assured her, still smiling. He wouldn't have to.

# CHAPTER 33

"Why are you spending so much time with the registry clerk?" Alex asked Matthew one day.

"Am I? Ah, you mean John. Nay, it is just that we have a lot in common, and he gives me the odd scribing to do."

"And you tell me I'm a bad liar," Alex said, shaking her head. Her brows pulled into a slight frown; something was afoot, and it didn't exactly require the sharpest brain on earth to come to the conclusion that this might all lead back to Suffolk Rose. Especially once she asked Mrs Parson, receiving a study of insincere blankness in return. So one afternoon Alex slipped out of the house and made her way to the Governor's office, hoping Sir William would be there.

Sir William was delighted to see her, but admonished her for being out on her own and with only a shawl against the cold.

"You've lived here too long," Alex grinned. "Remember England? Cold foggy autumns, even colder winters?"

"Pray don't remind me," Sir William shuddered. "It is enough just to think of it to bring on the gout."

"You have gout?" Alex glanced down at his calves, elegantly presented in silk stockings. No, they seemed in excellent shape. Sir William assured her that he didn't – at least not yet.

"But I will soon be fifty-eight, the grave is beginning to beckon."

Alex laughed. In comparison with most people he was remarkably well-preserved, and they were soon in a long discussion about the effects of a varied diet on longevity and health. Given the subject, Alex managed quite subtly to move on to the issues of inheritance, inquiring as to what was needed for a will to be considered legal.

"Why, that it be signed of course," Sir William said, "and that it be witnessed."

"And must the witness know how to read?"

Sir William raised a brow. "It would be difficult to witness a deed without being able to read it."

"Stranger things have happened," Alex said, making a money rubbing motion.

"What exactly is it you're after, my dear?" Sir William asked, his intelligent eyes boring into her.

"I was simply wondering…" Alex let her voice tail off on purpose. "I found it strange, you see," she added, confusing Sir William even more.

"Found what strange?"

Alex frowned and stirred her tea. Yet another budding tea fanatic, Sir William, although she suspected this was more dictated by fashion than any genuine appreciation of the beverage as such.

"When Mrs Jones was delivered, she was installed in the master bedroom of Suffolk Rose, for all the world the lady of the house, and I thought it strange that Mr Fairfax should have left his property to his overseer. But then, that may just be me – what do I know, maybe Fairfax had no family."

In response Sir William blew at his tea, long nose visibly twitching as he thought this through.

"Mr Fairfax had a nephew," Sir William said.

"Ah. Well, maybe he didn't like him, right?" She sipped at her tea but shook her head at the sugared plums. "Quite a motive for murder," she said after a lengthy silence.

"Fairfax was murdered by that Scotsman, James McLean," the Governor said rather stiffly.

"No he wasn't, and neither was he killed by Matthew. My husband may be a lot of things, but he isn't stupid, and to first kill a man, succeed in escaping unseen and then return to the scene of the crime several hours later…" Alex made a derisive sound. She set down her teacup, and stood, indicating that it was getting dark and that she had to get home. "We'll never know."

"No, my dear, I suppose we won't." Sir William smoothed

down his sash and collar, for all the world as if he were brushing this distasteful subject off him. "I'll have someone see you home," Sir William said, gallantly kissing her hand.

"That's not necessary."

"I think it best." He placed a hand on Alex' sleeve. "You will not pursue this matter, my dear." There was a finality in his tone that made her nod.

Matthew stood waiting for her, thanking the footman but assuring him that he was capable of seeing his wife home.

"How did you know where I was?"

He was upset, she could feel it in the way he held her arm, steering her in front of him rather than holding her to him.

"What were you doing there?" he asked, ignoring her question. "And you know I don't like it, that you walk out alone. Not after that ..." He broke off, shaking his head.

Alex drew the shawl closer around her, a tremor rippling up her spine to make her nape prickle.

"He's dead," she said, angry with him for reminding him of something she worked hard to forget.

"Very," he assured her, changing his hold to circle her shoulders instead. "So why did you go to see him?"

"You have your secrets and I have mine," she said, refusing to say another word until they were back in their room.

"Uhhh," Alex grunted, sighing with relief as she stepped out of her stays. She stretched her back in all directions, hearing the soft pops as bones and muscles shifted. "Almost two months to go," she groaned, patting her bulk. Matthew laughed and handed her the bed jacket.

"I'll make you a wee gamble, I bet you the babe comes before the New Year."

"That's at least two weeks too early." She wouldn't mind if he was right; she felt like a giant blimp. She adjusted the knitted soft cream jacket so that it covered as much of her as possible and sat down in the single chair.

"I went to see him to ask about inheritance," she said, assessing Matthew's reactions. "I found it strange that Jones should be living in the main house."

Matthew gave her a flicker of a smile. "And what did he say?"

"That I should leave this matter alone. And I will. But I'll have you promise that you will as well."

Matthew sat down on the floor beside her and rested his head against her leg.

"It's already set in motion, so aye, I can promise that I will do no more."

He explained how he and his new best friend had found reason to review the registered wills of the last six months, Matthew insisting that he had seen an error in one of them, but being adequately vague about where or when. And so they had found the will by which Fairfax bequeathed everything to Mr Jones.

"I merely pointed out that wasn't it quite the coincidence that it should be signed the same day Mr Fairfax died," Matthew said. "John was wetting himself with excitement, going on and on about Mr Fairfax' nephew back in England."

"So now what happens?" Alex asked.

Matthew made a disinterested sound. "Mr Jones will find himself having to respond to a lot of questions – in particular as Sykes stands as witness and he doesn't know how to read. And somewhere along the line they might also choose to question his wife." He sighed. "They won't, I think, reopen the inquest regarding Fairfax' death – it would reflect badly on them all – but they may make it difficult for Jones to remain here. He'll live under a permanent cloud of suspicion once the gossip begins."

"The gossip?"

Matthew laughed softly. "John has a very bad head for beer. He will be blathering about this in every inn he visits. And it will stick; gossip always does." He smiled with satisfaction.

"That's why he's backed off from you," Alex nodded.

"Hmm?"

"Well it's obvious, no? Since Fairfax died, Jones has kept well away from you – you said so as well."

"And?"

"He doesn't need Luke's money anymore, does he? All he wants is to be as discreet as possible, do nothing to attract attention to himself while he works his way unobtrusively into the salons of his new peers, with as few questions as possible asked as to how he came into his property." She wet her lips. "He isn't going to like it, being talked about, and he'll know exactly whom to blame for all the rumours."

Matthew grinned. "Aye; John."

A week later, Matthew came home in a foul mood.

"Someone warned him," Matthew spat, slamming the door closed as he entered their room. "In any case Mr Jones has seen fit to leave."

"Leave? Now? How?" Alex was having a bad day. Her bladder was being used as some kind of punch ball, Mrs Parson had taken one look at the baby cardigan she was knitting and torn up half of it, telling her that you knitted one row, purled the other, aye? On top of it all, she was into a major chocolate craving. Matthew glared at the driving rain and took a couple of deep breaths.

"He's sold Suffolk Rose. John came rushing to find me as soon as the deed came in."

All Alex could feel was relief. The further Jones was from Matthew the better, and to some extent there was an element of achieved revenge in forcing him to leave Virginia, setting off to recreate himself somewhere else with wife and children. Not that she doubted he'd manage very well – Jones was like a huge cat, landing always safely on his feet.

"And has he already left?"

Matthew shrugged; he didn't know. "At least it will be costly; the few boats presently plying the coast will charge him dearly." He pulled at his lip. "Maryland, that would be the closest, aye?"

In the event he hadn't left. Not until three days later did Mr Jones and his household embark and by then the gossip had begun to spread, further fuelled by this very strange behaviour. To uproot your family and carry them off in the middle of the winter – surely no man with a clean conscience would risk that? People speculated loudly; Fairfax had no doubt been killed by his overseer, some said, while others insisted they heard the nephew was coming out to claim his uncle's estate, and this was Jones fleeing with as much of his ill-gotten gains as he could.

The whole town came out to watch Jones leave, a Jones who rode ramrod straight by the cart that contained his goods and family, ignoring the whispered abuse, the low rustles of laughter and the open finger pointing. At one point an egg flew through the air, landing squarely between Jones' shoulder blades, but he didn't even twitch, keeping his eyes straight ahead.

"Pretty impressive," Alex said in an undertone to Mrs Parson.

Just as her husband, Kate sat silent and straight on the slow ride through town, her shoulders stiff, her chin raised. It struck Alex that this move might be very much to Kate's liking, a new start in a place where people wouldn't know she was a bonded servant. Kate had dressed up; in dark silks and a heavy woollen cloak she was quite the lady, smiling sweetly at her husband when he helped her off the cart. Her hair hung in golden curls, loose about her shoulders, and when her eyes scanned the crowd they rested a bit too long on Matthew, a slow smile spreading as she lifted her hand. Matthew raised his hand in response, his head inclined in a slight bow. He inhaled loudly when Alex ground her heel into his foot and gave her an aggravated look. Alex just smiled, as sweetly as Kate had just done.

The last longboat, carrying the worldly goods of the Jones', capsized halfway between the shore and the sloop, with the three rowers coming up to clutch at the overturned keel. From the sloop there came muted exclamations of anger, and even at this distance Alex could see Jones' large frame, his fist extended towards the sky. Beside her she heard Mr Parson chuckle, and then Mrs Parson began to laugh as well.

"What?" Alex had difficulties in seeing anything amusing in the present ongoing drama. Those three poor men! They might drown, or freeze to death or be attacked by an alligator – although this latest alternative did seem somewhat unlikely. Then she noticed that all around people were laughing, and when she studied the longboat it was apparent all three men could swim, they were towing the longboat with them back to shore. "Oh, my God! They did it on purpose."

"You should be careful of what you say," Matthew said. "This was an unfortunate accident, aye?"

"Accident my arse," Alex muttered.

Sir William leaned forward with interest, listening as Alex retold the events.

"… and once they made it back to shore they were dragged off to warm themselves. I think mainly on the inside," Alex said, describing the generous servings of brandy the three men had been plied with.

"Unsalvageable," Sir William said, "with all that silt nigh on impossible to locate."

"Who cares?" Alex said. Sir William gave a short bark of laughter and refilled her sherry glass, overruling her protests.

"It's just what you need, my dear, you are looking somewhat pale, if I may say so."

"That's because every time I try to sleep this one decides it's time to exercise." She mock punched at her belly and then sat back against the cushion that Sir William had politely pushed into place.

Sir William looked at her, twirling his glass. "Mr Fairfax

was not an adornment to this colony and the way he and his overseer treated his indentures reflects badly on all of us."

Alex was somewhat taken aback by the abrupt change of subject, but didn't show it, instead she sipped at the sherry. Well; kudos to him for raising the issue, but after what Matthew had told her earlier she was so disappointed with Sir William that she'd considered not showing at this prearranged little tête-a-tête.

"You knew, Sir William. You did, the constables did, the men in the registry did, your fellow planters did, and all of you chose to turn a blind eye." She succeeded in sounding very severe, making the governor squirm.

"Not all of us are like Fairfax was."

Huh; Fairfax might have been a snake, but the men around him had been lowly, spineless worms – and the biggest profiteer of them all was sitting in front of her.

"I think you found it easier to turn a blind eye when you knew the men were mostly Scots and thereby in all probability Covenanters. Dissenters, as you called my husband. Had they been Church of England, you would have reacted, right?"

Sir William had the grace to look ashamed. "They must be stopped," he muttered. "The Puritans and the Quakers with all their far flung notions of all men's equal value. Representative government, pah!"

Alex set down her glass. "In the end it is their view of the world that will prevail," she said, "in a hundred years or so, most men living here will subscribe to the view that in the face of God all men are equal and must be given a say in how they are governed."

Sir William gave her a condescending little smile. "I must disagree with you, my dear."

"That, of course, is your prerogative." She stood up, bracing back against her hands, and looked down at the seated governor.

"I hear you bought Suffolk Rose. At a bargain price,

including all indentured servants on the rolls. What did you do? Blackmail Jones?"

A business transaction, Sir William explained with his beet red face averted, an opportunity that he couldn't leave unexploited, and the colony was better off now that Jones was gone, did she not agree?

Alex raised her brows. "I hope you treat your workers as men, not dogs," she said, making her way to the door. She swept him a curtsey and left. She doubted she'd see him again – in fact, she didn't very much want to.

# CHAPTER 34

"Not on New Year's Eve!" Alex shook her head, placing both hands on her distended belly. "You stay in there until tomorrow, I have things to do, places to see, okay?"

The little person inside did not seem to care and Alex watched as her stomach shaped itself into a pyramid, stone hard under her hands.

"Fine," she grumbled, once the contraction had passed. "But I do intend to take a bath first."

The house was empty and Matthew had placed the hipbath close to the kitchen hearth, promising he would help her once he was back from his clandestine service. Ten severe Presbyterians in one room, Alex sighed, how fun could that be? Mrs Parson had agreed to go to church with her husband, although she confided to Alex that in her opinion the Anglican Church was far too popish, with too much attention to ritual and too little on content.

"Hmm," Alex had replied, not daring to voice an opinion one way or the other.

By the time Matthew got back, Alex was clean but stark naked, having retreated back to their room as the contractions increased in intensity.

"Oh, good," she panted when she saw Matthew. "I think the baby's on its way." He made as if to turn and run for Mrs Parson but she stopped him.

"No, stay here with me and hold my hand. She'll be back in time anyway."

It was obvious Matthew was rather frightened, eyes flying every other minute to the door as if he hoped Mrs Parson would materialise there. But he was also clearly entranced, and when Alex had him sit spread legged behind her in bed, his hands settled on her stomach, two pools of reassuring warmth on her skin.

"You almost fall asleep," he said to her, jiggling his

shoulder under her.

"Yes," she replied drowsily. "It's all so... peaceful." Not during the contractions, it wasn't, with her breathing like a train engine under duress, but as soon as they faded away she relaxed against him, taking huge, gulping breaths of air. "I'm glad you're here," she whispered, letting one hand drift up to stroke his cheek.

Half an hour later it was all far more intense. Alex insisted on getting up, walking round the room and bracing herself hard against Matthew with each contraction.

"They're getting very close," she gasped, laughing at the look of sheer panic in Matthew's eyes. Once again he made as if to leave her, to run for help, but she hung on to him, shaking her head. "Water, there's boiled water in the kitchen. And towels or something. But don't leave me, not now." He promised he wouldn't, and dashed down, returning to find her leaning against the window, her legs shaking.

"What are they doing?" she moaned. "Celebrating Christmas, New Year and Easter and everything else rolled into one?" Shit; what if things went wrong? If the umbilical cord got stuck or something?

Matthew jumped when the waters broke, cascading down her legs. Alex felt a jolt as the head screwed itself even further down the birthing channel, and now the contractions grew from the small of her back and forward, strong, long and terrifying. She remained where she was, refusing to let go of that new mainstay in her life, the windowsill.

"But you can't stay there," Matthew tried.

"Watch me," she said, groaning as yet another and another and another contraction swept through her. She felt an increased weight between her thighs and her knees wobbled like mad.

"Help me! The bed."

Matthew almost carried her there.

"Nnnnngh!" she exclaimed through gritted teeth. She panted heavily. "Can you see something?" She definitely couldn't, there was a huge belly in the way.

Matthew peeked between her legs. "Aye, oh God, Alex, it's huge, aye?"

"Tell me about it," she hissed back, and then began to laugh – for like five seconds. "Right," she said after hyperventilating through yet another contraction. "Next time I push. You just be there, catch it or something."

Matthew felt totally useless; he sat between his wife's legs, hands on her splayed thighs and talked soothingly to her, watching as the miracle of his child's birth unfolded before his eyes. The head, pushing out and slipping back in. And then the head was out and the shoulders – oh Lord, how were they to come out? Having seen both calves and foals into the world, Matthew placed his hands on that wee body and twisted, and suddenly his arms were full of warm life. His wife was laughing and crying, and all of him was bloodied and wet, but in his arms lay that perfect little creature, his child, and its eyes were open, deep dark wells of knowledge and calm. Matthew cradled it to his chest and wept.

Matthew greeted Mrs Parson with a huge grin. Alex was already nursing the wean, the umbilical cord neatly cut.

"And the afterbirth?"

Matthew made a face. He had near on died of fright when that blob of dark red had expulsed itself from inside of Alex.

"She says it's whole."

Aye, Mrs Parson nodded after inspecting it. "So what is it?" she asked

"What is what?"

"Lad or lass," Mrs Parson elucidated.

"Ah." Matthew couldn't stop himself from smiling. "A wee lassie."

"Let me see her," Mrs Parson said, "Make sure she's fine, aye?" She was, squishing up her face in protest at the cold air that touched her skin. Mrs Parson cooed at her and wrapped her up, giving her back to Alex. "Wee you said?"

Mrs Parson said. "Nine pounds at least, I'd reckon. You make big, bonny weans you and your wife."

"Tell me about it," Alex muttered, shifting in the bed.

"And her name?" Mrs Parson said.

"Matthew won the bet, so he gets to name her," Alex yawned.

Mrs Parson laughed. "Our Matthew will name all his bairns, lass. That's the kind of man he is. I'm right, no?" she said, turning to face Matthew.

"Aye," he said with a little smile. "The naming is mine to do."

"Hey," Alex protested, "I might have some ideas as well, you know."

"I do the naming, lass. That's the way it is."

"But …"

"No buts." He placed a finger on his daughter's nose. "Rachel," he said, "after my Mam."

"Rachel?" Alex drew her nose over the soft fuzzy crown and smiled up at him. "Rachel."

"Right," Mrs Parson interrupted, "I have work to do here, and I'll not have you in here while I examine your wife's privates." She shooed Matthew in the direction of the door. "Find some food," she suggested, "and Alex could do with some beer as well."


Much later Matthew woke when Alex ran her fingers through his hair, making him turn towards her, Rachel held in his arms.

"You look good together," Alex said, tucking a loose corner of the wean's shawl tighter. She rubbed her hands together briskly, muttering something about it being bloody cold out in the yard.

"The yard?" Matthew sat up. "What were you doing in the yard?" He frowned at her; and in only shift and shawl as well. What was she thinking of, and she a recently delivered mother?

"It's New Year's Eve," Alex said. "I had to toast Magnus."

"Ah." He nodded, deciding there was no purpose to remonstrating.

Rachel began fidgeting, face shifting from its previous pink to a more irritated red, and Alex sat down against the pillows, undoing her shift. The wee body relaxed as soon as Rachel found the teat, and for some minutes the only sounds were the soft noises of a feeding child. When she shifted the wean to the other side Matthew slid over to rest his head on her lap. For the first time since the January day he'd set off for Edinburgh, almost two years ago, he felt content, even safe.

"I love you," he said.

Alex' hand rested on the back of his head. "I know, even if you only tell me once a year."

He laughed, muffling the sound against her. "You don't say it too often either."

"No, only about twenty times every time we make love," Alex snorted, slapping him playfully.

"That doesn't count, aye? You're wild with it then, you'd say anything to make me do as you want." He could feel her thighs shift under him and burrowed even closer, drawing in her scent. She still smelled like she used to; a lingering fragrance of winter apples, of green wood, but now overlaid with the heavy sweetness of milk and the warm, irony smell of womanhood. Alex stroked his bristled cheek and traced the shape of his ear.

"I love you, Matthew Graham. And I think I did from the day you promised you wouldn't leave me alone on the moor."

"Aye well; I knew you for a weak and defenceless woman from the first moment I saw you," he said with attempted seriousness, protesting loudly when she pinched his ear.

# CHAPTER 35

The first ship that sailed into Jamestown bore the proud name of *Regina Anne*, and Alex didn't know whether to cry or laugh when Captain Miles strode onto the small wooden wharf. If he was surprised by her enthusiastic welcome he didn't show it, and at her question told her that of course they had berths with him, she and her husband both. And Mrs Gordon as well, he added quickly.

"Well…" Alex glanced at him. "I don't think she'll be coming along." Captain Miles looked crestfallen but perked up when his cargo came ashore.

"No women?" Alex said, quite pleased that he should have stopped with such business.

"No," Captain Miles replied before hastily turning away.

Not quite the truth, as Alex gleaned from her conversations with the crew, and mainly with Smith. Instead, the captain had planned things better this time, offloading a shipment of wide-eyed girls in Barbados, filling his hold with barrel after barrel of cane liquor and setting off for Jamestown as soon as the weather permitted. Here the captain hoped to sell off some of his cargo, fill the space with tobacco and arrive back in England before anyone else with these two very marketable commodities.

"Made quite the profit last year," Smith confided, tapping his nose.

"Ah," Alex nodded, before moving over to introduce the captain to Matthew.

Captain Miles shook hands with Matthew, gawking at him. It made Matthew frown, and Captain Miles muttered an apology.

"Safe and sound, aye?" the captain said.

"Now," Matthew said, "not a year ago."

"No, I imagine not; you have a remarkable wife, Mr Graham, somewhat opinionated and stubborn to a fault, but loyal – most loyal."

"Stubborn? Me?" Alex raised her brows, took in identical expressions of amusement on both their faces.

"Biblical almost," Matthew agreed, "comes with the name, I reckon – Alexandra Ruth, my Ruth, companion through life and death." His eyes softened into a mossy green and Alex felt her face turn a deep pink. But inside she clutched his words to her heart and disco danced with joy.

By late March the *Regina Anne* was ready to go, and Alex and Matthew spent their last evening in Virginia with the Parsons, a long evening of reminiscences as Alex and Mrs Parson relived out loud these last two years. Slowly their voices drifted to a stop, and Alex leaned forward to clutch Mrs Parson's hand.

"I'm going to miss you, " she said.

"And I you, lass."

Alex nodded; come tomorrow they would no longer be together and how on earth was she going to survive that? She converted a sob into a coughing fit and with that as a pretext escaped to the little kitchen.

For a long time she stood staring through the small window at the darkened back yard, crying in silence. An arm came round her waist, a voice on the verge of breaking told her to shush, aye, it was not like her lass to weep, was it?

"I ..." Alex gulped. "Oh God; I'm not sure how I'm going to cope."

"You'll do fine, lass," Mrs Parson said, smoothing back her hair.

Alex shook her head. "You don't understand. It feels... well, it feels as if I'm leaving my mother." She wiped at her eyes, her nose, she pressed the heels of her hands to her eyes but it didn't help; tears kept on flowing down her cheeks.

"You're a daughter of my heart, Alex Graham." Mrs Parson stood on her toes and kissed Alex on the brow. "My lass, aye? And wherever you are, I'll be there with you."

That only made Alex cry all the harder, hiding her face against Mrs Parson's shoulder.

"I really, really hate this," she said after a while, dabbing at her swollen eyes.

"It's life, " Mrs Parson replied with a faint smile. "And we both know that you must go with him, no?" She gave Alex a little shake. "It's the price you pay for loving, that it tears at you to say farewell. But the love remains; no matter how far apart we'll still love each other." And that was no comfort whatsoever, at least not now.

Next morning Alex was dumbstruck, incapable of doing anything more but hug Mrs Parson.

"I..." she began, but couldn't continue.

"I know," Mrs Parson replied, eyes shiny with unshed tears. "I know, lass." She disengaged herself from Alex' clinging hands, pressed her lips to Alex' brow and stepped away. "Go with God, Alex Graham."

"And you," Alex managed to say before her voice broke. One more hug, a whispered 'I love you' and Alex stepped into the longboat to join Matthew who sat waiting, Rachel in his arms.

Once on deck, she moved over to stand by the railing, trailed by Matthew.

"I'll never see her again," she said, looking towards the point where Mrs Parson was already dwindling into an anonymous dark dot.

"Probably not," he agreed, sounding very sad.

Captain Miles popped up beside them and patted Alex on her shoulder.

"Look to the east, lass; towards your home and your son." He turned her so that her back was towards the receding Jamestown and pointed at the river estuary. "First the river, then the bay and then the sea... and on the other side lies Scotland."

Alex gave him a grateful smile. Thinking of Mark did help. She felt Matthew's arm come round her shoulder and stood silent with her eyes on the heavy eastern cloudbanks, dark and full of rain. Below her the tidal waters of the James swirled brown with silt, behind her the overwhelming greenery of Virginia was quickly dropping out of sight, and before her, flat like a modern day skating rink and as grey in colour, lay the waters of the Chesapeake.

"Happy Birthday," she said to Matthew, receiving a surprised look in return. "It's the last of March, no? You're thirty-three today, and according to my father that is one of the best ages of man. Three, thirty-three and sixty-six – the magical years in a man's life... Don't ask me why," she added, seeing the leaping questions in his eyes. "I suppose it has to do with perfect childhood, perfect manhood and wise old age."

Matthew snorted with amusement. "And have you planned a celebration?" His hand slid down to caress her backside.

"Forget it, the berths are the size of rabbit hutches, and on top of that I get seasick. Very seasick." Already the swells were getting to her. "But I think I have a gift – of a sort," she said, meeting his eyes. Not a gift she really wanted to give him, not so soon, but Mrs Parson had agreed with her own diagnosis, muttering something about the consequences of not being able to keep their hands off each other.

"Are you sure?" Matthew asked when she took his hand and placed it on her stomach.

"It's very early days yet, but yes, I think I am." She smiled at him before pressing her face into his shirt to hide the confused emotions this made her feel.

"It's too soon," Matthew said, but his tone and the way his arms tightened around her stood in clear contradiction to his words. Between them Rachel squirmed and whimpered, a protest that soon grew into an indignant holler, making them let each other go.

After spending most of the initial days in their cabin, Alex finally made it out on deck; unsteady and pale, but determined not to spend any more time indoors.

"Perfect combination," she muttered to herself, clinging to the railings. "Seasick and pregnant. Whoopee." She turned in irritation towards Matthew. "How can I be seasick? Look, the sea's perfectly flat." More or less; now that she actually looked, the whole horizon was heaving, tilting this way and that. "Oh shit," Alex groaned.

Matthew gave her a worried look and hefted Rachel higher on his shoulder. "Should you go back inside?"

Alex shook her head and adjusted the heavy cloak closer round her shoulders. "It stinks in there. And it's much better to be outdoors, plus once I get my sea legs it will all pass anyway."

"Sea legs?" Captain Miles appeared by their side. "You'll never get sea legs, Mrs Graham." He peered at her. "Feeling better? You look less green today, if I may say so, more of a normal pink."

"Why thank you; let's just hope we don't run into any bloody storms."

Captain Miles laughed and shook his head. "You don't like the sea, do you, Mrs Graham? Not one whit of sailor in you."

"Well thank heavens being a sea captain isn't top on my career list," Alex said, turning her back on him.

"But you, Mr Graham, you're a born sailor," Captain Miles went on, sounding very amused.

"Aye," Matthew said in a rather more cautious tone. "It would seem the sea agrees with me."

"It would seem the sea agrees with me," Alex mouthed to herself, sticking her tongue out. She straightened up. "I'm taking a walk, and you, Mr Sailor, keep an eye on the baby, alright?"

Alex nearly fell over one long, extended leg and righted herself to glare in the direction of its owner only to find herself face to face with yet another acquaintance.

"Iggy! How nice to see you again!" She extended her arms to give him a hug, but let them drop at the warning look in his eyes. Turning, she found Matthew looming over her, his eyes glued to poor Iggy with undisguised dislike. Matthew gripped Alex by her arm and propelled her forward towards the bow.

"What are you doing? Iggy is a friend, okay?"

"You will not greet other men with such familiarity, and…" Matthew inhaled a couple of times. "Don't you see it?"

Alex looked in the direction of Iggy; redheaded and light-eyed. Of course Matthew had been reminded of Luke, just as she'd been the first time she met him.

"Not anymore," she said, "but I definitely did the first time I saw him."

Matthew threw Iggy yet another ice cold look. "I wish it were Luke," he said through gritted teeth. "Then I would just lift the bastard into the air and throw him into the sea." He unslung Rachel's carrying shawl and handed her to Alex. "Take her, I just can't. I must…" and with that he hurried over to the opposite side of the ship.

Alex watched him go, saw him stop to steady himself, and knew he was swimming in a sea of anger and pain and that there was nothing she could do but wait for him to come back to her. Even from across the deck she could see how his hands fisted and she wondered what particular part of his own personal hell he was reliving. Months at the beck and call of Jones, months in which his dignity was shredded off him to leave nothing but a silent, obedient slave. Humanity is a thin veneer, Alex reflected, a protective coat that is so easily ripped from us and so very difficult to patch back up. In Matthew's case he had lost the capacity to forgive; as long as he lived one part of his soul would be given over to nurturing the hatred he felt for his brother, and that, in Alex' opinion, was by far the severest damage done to him.

It was an uneventful journey, one day following upon the previous one with no change in scenery or weather. With every league closer to home Matthew's restlessness grew. He glared at the empty sails, scanning the horizon for anything indicating that soon there would be winds to hasten their way, and then dropped back down to sit beside Alex on the deck. Early May, more than a month at sea, and when asked, Captain Miles shrugged and said it would be two, perhaps three weeks before they moored in Edinburgh.

"The planting will all be done by now," Matthew said, "and the lambing as well." Alex patted his hand as well as she could with a nursing wean at her breast.

"You'll be back for the harvest. And you've done your share of planting haven't you?" She went a bright pink, making him smile. He lifted Rachel out of her arms.

"She's asleep," he said unnecessarily, eyes lingering on Alex' chest.

"Yeah, food tends to have that effect on her." She met his eyes, and in his loins warmth surged, a coursing heat that rushed through his veins, pooled in his balls and rose like molten iron through his cock. "Maybe we should all take a nap," she suggested, getting to her feet.

Matthew's eyes didn't leave her face. She blushed again, delicious waves of pink rising up her neck and all the way to her ears. Her pupils dilated and he knew it was because of him and the wordless promise that all of him was giving her. He let her precede him to their cabin, stifling a smile at the way she was walking, a new-born foal on ice.

He took her on the floor, she on hands and knees and he rising behind her, his hands holding her still. In one of the berths Rachel slept peacefully, and on the floor he just had to… again, and now Alex was naked and so was he, and it was almost as it had been that first time except that here they lay in a cramped space that enclosed them in dark wood, and the only sky they could see was the glimpse of grey through the small porthole cut into the door, not the miles of empty blue of a summer sky in Scotland. Not that he cared; he was lost to the world, aware only of his warm and wonderful wife.

"He's a sweet boy, isn't he?" Eva said, waving at Isaac.

"Not sweet enough to like it that you're waving at him in front of his mates," Magnus said, grinning at how his grandson chose to ignore them, detouring as if by chance in the direction of the football pitch.

"Oh." Eva dropped her hand, looking somewhat flustered. "I didn't know."

"No big deal," Magnus shrugged and settled himself on the bonnet to wait. "Hi," he said once Isaac had joined them. "Your Dad called. He'll be picking you up before dinner."

Isaac nodded eagerly. "We're going to see Spiderman 3."

"Spider who?" Eva asked.

"Action hero," Magnus said.

"Ah," Eva nodded, looking none the wiser.

Isaac disappeared upstairs the moment they got back from school, mumbling something about painting the sea, and needing more blues and greens. Eva followed him to the studio and came back down a bit later, nodding when Magnus offered her a cup of coffee.

"He just grabs a brush and throws himself into it," she said in an impressed voice. "I was up there for what? Fifteen minutes? And already there's a sea on the canvas. That boy is going to be world famous some day."

"He would prefer to be a football player, he doesn't even like to talk about his painting."

"Not all that strange, is it?" Eva said.

John looked flustered when he appeared just before four.

"This early?" Magnus said. "He hasn't even had his cake yet."

John sat down on a chair and poured himself some coffee. "I just had to get away. This client of mine is driving me nuts." He shook his head at the cake. "No thanks, I have to be a bit careful," he said, patting himself on his very flat stomach.

Eva smirked and Magnus huffed, serving himself a huge slice.

"Isaac?" Magnus raised his voice, "Come on down, son. There's cake." There was no reply and Magnus shrugged. "Suit yourself."

John regaled them with a series of anecdotes starring his new client, making both Eva and Magnus laugh when John swore that next time that excruciating barnacle of a man requested another change in his security setup he'd cram the system code down his throat.

"Where is that boy?" John said, looking at his watch.

"Probably immersed in his little sea," Eva smiled, "or otherwise he's arranging his paint tubes again."

John broke off a piece of cake. "We have to go," he said through his half full mouth, and Magnus nodded and got to his feet.

"Isaac?" Magnus stood by the stairs. "Isaac, come on down. If you don't hurry there won't be any cake left because your Dad will eat it all."

"I haven't even had a whole slice," John protested.

"Isaac?" Magnus frowned, taking the stairs two treads at a time with John at his heels.

Isaac was sitting on the floor, and in his lap was a small picture. John threw himself across the room towards his son.

"Isaac? What are you doing?"

Isaac just stared through him before lowering his eyes to the wooden frame he held between his hands. He smiled dreamily at it; a small painting in blues and green, all of it swirling together towards a point of extreme depth and light in its centre.

"*Herre Gud,*" Magnus gasped, "where on earth ..."

"I thought we'd burnt them all," John said, attempting to prise Isaac's fingers off the frame. His arms shook, his hands trembled and he sat back, his face the colour of boiled cod. "Oh God," he moaned. "I just can't be near it."

"Let me," Magnus said, extending his hands to grab at the painting. Isaac wrenched himself free and flew to his feet, backing away with the picture held to his chest.

"Isaac, come here," John said, "come here and give Offa the picture."

"I can see her," Isaac said, his brown eyes huge. "I see her, in there." He peeked at the painting again.

"Who?" Magnus said, "Who do you see?"

"Mama," Isaac said.

"Oh, Jesus," John whispered, and extended his hand to Isaac. "Give me the painting, Isaac, we have to destroy it."

Isaac shook his head and moved so that the large table stood between him and the two men. He put the painting down.

"It's beautiful," he said, tracing a whirl of blue with a small finger. When Magnus came too close, Isaac retreated below the table, clambering over the old-fashioned trestle legs.

"Isaac," John's voice begged, "just get away from it, don't look at it son."

Magnus was beginning to panic, a cold sweat breaking out along his spine as he remembered a long gone afternoon when he'd seen a man fade away in front of his eyes in this very room – and all on account of a whispering, magic painting. He kneeled and began crawling towards the boy.

It was too late. Bright light poured from the painting, noise rose in waves around them, and Magnus was incapable of moving, the floor heaving like a sea serpent's back below him. Behind him John was screaming, for Isaac, for Magnus to do something. Isaac leaned into the painting, a wide smile on his face as his hand reached for an object or person unseen.

"No!" Magnus's fingers closed around Isaac's ankle. For an instant he held his grandson suspended, halfway here, halfway in the funnel or roaring, painful light, and then with a tug Isaac was pulled free, sucked shrieking into nothingness.

"No! Isaac!! Noooooo!" John keened, high pitched sounds that tore at Magnus, carried through the open window and had Eva rushing up the stairs.

"What happened?" she panted, rushing over to where Magnus was still kneeling. "My God, Magnus, where is Isaac?"

"He's gone!" Magnus set his shoulders to the table and upended it, sending paints, brushes and jars of turpentine to crash against the floor. "You hear? He's gone! A seven year old boy! I should have set fire to the whole fucking room!" He cursed and kicked, and the little painting sailed in an arc across the room to land by Eva's feet. She bent to pick it up.

"...*I have heard the mermaids singing...*" she quoted, collapsing to sit on her knees.

"Don't touch it!" Magnus said, throwing himself towards her. "Don't even look at it. Oh God; Isaac!" He picked up the canvas and ripped it apart, strong fingers tearing at the fibres. He fell forward until his forehead hit the floor, hid himself in his arms and wept.

* * *

Isaac screamed when he was sucked into the painting. He no longer wanted this and he tried to claw himself free from this funnel of light. Everything narrowed, his body stretched, and he was torn from where he was to skydive to somewhere else. He fell... And it hurt and he was scared, and all around him time roared, a constant sound of voices and clamour.

He landed with a dull thud. Something in his leg snapped. Isaac lay on his back and slowly the whirling stopped, the ground below him became solid and he could breathe again. He began to open his eyes, hoping that he would be back in Offa's house, but his nose told him he was outdoors. He could hear birds and creaking branches, the soft flutter of leaves, and when he allowed himself to look he knew he was very far away from home.

He was lying on his back in a heap of last year's leaves, and above him he saw the huge spreading branches of old trees with the sky a clear pale blue beyond. He tried to sit up, but his leg hurt and he lay back down. To his shame he could smell he had peed himself and the damp cloth stuck uncomfortably to his crotch.

"Mama?" he called. He'd seen her, there in the picture, so she should be here. "Mama?" he repeated, receiving nothing but a gust of wind in reply. Isaac Lind rolled onto his side and cried.

A hand on his back made him start and he tried to move away, only to whimper when his broken leg was jolted by his movements.

"Shush, laddie," a voice said, "shush." Isaac turned to face a very round man with mild blue eyes and scraggly, reddish hair.

"Who are you?"

The man laughed, studying him with interest. "I'm Simon Melville, and you are?"

"Isaac. Isaac Lind."

Simon swallowed back on a surprised exclamation. His eyes flew over this Isaac, taking in a small lad with surprisingly short hair and strange clothes.

"Lind you said?"

The lad nodded.

"And where did you come from?"

"I don't know," Isaac stammered, his eyes filling with tears. "I just fell through the painting. I saw my Mama and I fell."

"The painting? You fell through a painting?" Simon couldn't keep the disbelief out of his voice.

Isaac nodded in confirmation, holding up his hands in an approximation of the painting's size.

"And would your Mama be an Alexandra Lind?" Simon asked, ensuring his voice remained casual. In his chest his heart raced, a painful pressure building from halfway up his windpipe and all the way to his mouth.

"Yes," Isaac said, and Simon smiled at the hope that shone through the dark eyes. "Is she here?"

"Nay," Simon shook his head. "But she's coming. Soon, we hope." He wrinkled his nose at the smell emanating from the boy. "You've pissed yourself."

"I know, I'm sorry."

"Not to worry," Simon said and swept the laddie into his arms, "it happens, no?"

# CHAPTER 37

The *Regina Anne* arrived in Edinburgh on the twenty-seventh day of May, and had he been able to, Matthew would have gathered his family in his arms and leapt ashore instead of having to wait while the ship was moored and the gangway dropped into place. As it was, he was first off anyway, exhaling loudly when he had the solidness of his homeland below his feet. More than two years away... He turned to help Alex and hugged her hard.

"We're back."

She just nodded, bending to place a hand on the ground.

"A word," Captain Miles said to Matthew, snagging his sleeve. Matthew threw him an irritated look; he was in a hurry to be off, had his head full of things he needed to arrange. Transport to Edinburgh, room, horse, deliver James' letter and Bible to his wife, mayhap drop in on Minister Crombie, and then set off for home. "Go canny," the captain said, nodding in the direction of the further end of the wharves. Matthew followed his eyes and saw someone duck out of sight.

"Me?" he asked with some surprise.

"Well, it's definitely not me, and the moment you jumped off the gangway he popped up, gawking at you." Captain Miles threw a look at Alex, busy making her farewells. "Your brother seems a most tenacious man."

"Aye," Matthew said, all exuberance draining out of him. Any further discussions were cut short by Alex, who embraced Captain Miles before kissing him on the cheek.

"Don't forget," she said, and the captain promised that he wouldn't, he'd personally deliver Alex' letter to Mrs Parson next time he came by Jamestown.

For most of the slow ride from Leith to Edinburgh Matthew was mute. At first Alex assumed this was due to an overload of emotion, but his continued silence woke an uneasiness inside of her.

He paid the drover, unloaded family and belongings from the cart and set off up the hill, telling Alex they were making for Minister Crombie's home.

"We're staying with him?" Not that Alex minded; she liked the minister in question, a gaunt man who was sensible and kind, tempering a strong faith with a general acceptance of mankind's multiple weaknesses.

"If he'll have us," Matthew replied over his shoulder. His eyes darted all over the place, and he was walking at a pace that had Alex running, a very exhausting exercise through Edinburgh's steep, narrow closes.

"What's the matter?" she puffed, wrinkling her nose at the odour that wafted their way from the Nor Loch.

"Nothing."

"Matthew!" She stopped halfway up a close. He exhaled and set down his burdens before turning to face her.

"It might be unsafe for us here, and as yet I have no arms, no horse."

"Oh, hell; why can't Luke Graham just fall into a vat of boiling syrup and die?" Alex scowled at the cobblestones, the dirty gutters, the enclosing walls. "It's him, isn't it? Again!"

"I don't know, and it may all be fancies." Briefly he explained about the man in the harbour, taking her hand to hurry her along while he spoke. "Once we're out on the moors it'll be alright," he finished. "I doubt city rats will be comfortable out there, in the open."

Minister Crombie was delighted to see them, assured them they could stay with him and went on to say it was an open secret that Luke Graham had men watching for the potential return of his brother.

"Oh," Alex gulped. The tall man of God threw her a worried look, swept his bony hands down his long, dark coat.

"For what purpose, I don't know, but I doubt it is to

welcome you home. Ah well; you're safe here, and by tomorrow you'll be gone."

"Yeah; all alone on the road to Cumnock with a band of paid assassins on our tails," Alex muttered, fingering the spiderweb of faint scars on her left arm.

"Tonight; we leave tonight," Matthew said. "Can you help me find a horse?"

"What? Now?" Minister Crombie looked out at the overcast afternoon, bushy eyebrows pulled low over his eyes. "Mayhap, but it might come dear."

They returned a few hours later, Matthew with a sword on his belt and a dagger for Alex as well as a musket. Yes, he assured Alex, he'd delivered the letter to James' wife, had told her as much as he could of what had befallen her husband, and had with relief turned the weeping woman over into Minister Crombie's capable care while he went to buy them a horse.

With them came yet another minister and Alex did a discreet eye roll before arranging her features in a pleasant smile. Sandy Peden was not her favourite among Matthew's boon companions, not by a far stretch, but she could see how animated Matthew was to be walking with this his friend and preacher, and so she held her tongue.

Sandy was a relatively new acquaintance for Alex, having become a recurrent guest at Hillview only during the last few months before Matthew's abduction, but Sandy and Matthew went years back, even if Simon – who wasn't too enchanted by this very impassioned minister – had confided to Alex that he couldn't recall them being more than casual companions in their youth.

"Minister Peden," Alex said, curtseying to the minister.

"Alexandra," he replied with a slight nod. A nondescript man of medium height with a shock of fine, mousy hair, his saving grace were his eyes. Large and luminous, two grey pools fringed with the longest and fairest lashes Alex had ever seen, they studied her with amused respect. "An admirable rescue," he said, nodding in the direction of Matthew.

"Purely for egoistical reasons," Alex replied, and Sandy burst into laughter.

"Aye well, men like Matthew Graham don't grow on trees."

"No they don't; one in a million, I'd think." She smiled at her husband and excused herself to do something about her hollering child.

Matthew followed her out of the room with his eyes, thinking that women like her were quite rare on the ground as well. With a private smile he re-joined the heated discussion between the ministers, and over the coming half hour Sandy and Minister Crombie took turns in filling him in as to what had happened in his homeland during his absence.

"Evicted from my living, no less," Sandy blustered. "Thrown out of my own kirk as have most of our fellow Presbyterian brethren, and then what do we have but a religious war in the making? Again, I might add."

"Now, now," Minister Crombie said. "We don't know that, dear Sandy, do we? And it might behove you to at times curb that tongue of yours, mayhap even scrape your foot and bow symbolically in the direction of the powers that be."

"Hmph!" Sandy said and left the room.

"That bad?" Matthew asked.

"No, not yet," Minister Crombie said. "But it's getting difficult. The king – or at least his parliament – intends to push us all into Episcopalian rites, and the first to go are of course us, the ministers who refuse to kowtow to his Anglican beliefs and the Book of Common Prayer."

"But he promised not to!"

"A king does as he pleases," Minister Crombie said. "Ah well, it need not concern you, at least not yet." He leaned forward and patted Matthew on the leg. "I am that glad to see you back home, I've prayed, aye? For you and your remarkable wife." He opened his mouth to say something more but there was a commotion at the door, and they got to their feet, Matthew's hand dropping to his sword.

"Ha!" Sandy Peden said, manhandling a young man into the room. He held him in a choking grip, ignoring the guttural sounds that signalled the man had problems breathing. "I found him sneaking about outside." Sandy released his prisoner to fall face first to the floor.

"Ah, did you now?" Matthew pulled his knife and advanced on the man who squealed and tried to crawl away. It didn't avail him much and once Matthew had explained just what he was going to do to him should he choose not to speak, the unfortunate man told them everything, words spilling like a garbled waterfall from his mouth. Matthew released his hold on the greasy hair and stood up.

"If I leave now they won't know, and if you can keep this rascal under lock and key until tomorrow or the day after they'll never catch us."

"No," Minister Crombie agreed, looking rather green around the mouth – no doubt due to the ruffian's admission that their task was not only to kill Matthew, but also his wife so as to ensure there remained no witnesses alive.

"I'll ride with you," Sandy said, "and so will my brother." Matthew nodded his curt thanks, and in less than an hour he had a small company assembled, consisting of himself, Alex, Sandy and his rather impressive brother, and John Brown, a most devout neighbour from down Cumnock way.

"I wish I could come with you," Minister Crombie sighed, "but with my piles, well..."

"Oh," Matthew said, not wanting to know. He helped Alex up on the horse, swung himself up behind her and nodded a farewell to Minister Crombie.

"God speed," the minister said in a hushed voice, "and don't cross the Clyde at Lanark – they're bound to ride in that direction – well, unless I convince the constables to collar the wretches first."

"More than one lookout," Alex said through chattering

teeth several hours later. It was sometime between midnight and dawn, and the light from a waning moon silvered the moors, throwing everything into different shades of grey through black. It was cold, her calves cramped after nearly two hours hidden behind the thicket, but right now she was very grateful Matthew had insisted they spread out and hide, leaving decoys in place round the fire.

"Mmm," Matthew agreed from where he was sitting beside her, eyes never leaving the five men who were slinking down the hillside towards the little campfire and the blanketed humps around it. "Fools," he breathed into her ear. "Look at them, like sheep to the slaughter, no?"

Alex suppressed an urge to burst out in loud, nervous laughter. Sheep? Very well armed sheep – even from here and in the dark she could make out the odd glint on an uncovered blade.

"Stay here," Matthew said, and then he was gone, leaving Alex to keep her eyes peeled on the path, just in case there should be more than five.

A shape moved swiftly down the slope. Matthew, she realised after squinting for a while, and at his back was John Brown – or a shape she assumed to be John, it was impossible to make out. Someone sent a stone bouncing, there was a hissed curse and everything froze. The five ambushers shrank to crouch, Matthew and John disappeared into the shadow of a crag. One of the horses nickered, but down by the fire the shapes remained immobile – well, they would, given that they consisted mostly of twigs and stones. Alex swallowed, threw a look up the path. No one there.

They were almost at the campsite by now, five shadows that communicated with hand movements no more. And behind them came Matthew and John, moving as stealthily as foxes. A rustle and Alex bit back on an exclamation. Something was coming up the path, but once it got closer Alex relaxed. Things moving on four legs weren't her major concern at present. She returned her attention to the dell. Any moment now ...

It was unfortunate that just as the trap was closing, Rachel should wake from sleep, crying loudly. The would be attackers whirled in the direction of the sound, saw Matthew and John Brown advancing on them and threw themselves in a concerted effort against them. From their hiding places came the Peden brothers, rushing to join the fight, and Alex couldn't stand it, to sit here crouched while only yards away her husband and their friends were fighting a far too even battle against the bastards who wanted them dead, so she placed a screaming Rachel under a bush and launched herself into the melee.

"Get away!" Matthew barked. "Stay away, Alex!"

"In your dreams," she shouted back. But she kept to the fringe of things, not wanting to get in the way of all those blades. Still, every now and then one of the combatants would stumble into range and it was with a certain satisfaction that she felt her foot connect with someone's nether parts, a howl indicating that specific person wouldn't be moving very much any time soon.

Matthew was everywhere, and it was his sword that brought the fight to an end, the apparent leader shrieking for mercy as the blade dug into his uncovered neck. There was a moment when Alex thought Matthew was going to slice his throat wide open and kill him then and there, but to her relief Sandy popped up by Matthew's side, and whatever it was he said was enough to make Matthew lower the blade and spit the ruffian in the face. And then it was all over, the five men hogtied and dragged forward so that their faces could be studied in the light of the fire, now kicked into life by Matthew.

Rachel was still sobbing, the odd half-hearted wail escaping from her between her energetic pulling at the breast.

"Bad timing," Alex told her, "what was I to do? Nurse you and let your father fight it out on his own?"

"I wasn't alone, Alex," Matthew said with a smile in his voice.

"No, but I helped, no?"

"Helped? You've left the man maimed for life," Sandy put in. "Not that he will live for all that much longer."

"What? You're going to kill them?"

"Of course not. That would be a grievous sin, a permanent taint on our souls. No, we will ride back with them to Edinburgh, and there turn them over into the tender care of the constables." Sandy looked the men over with a certain disdain. "They'll hang, as they should, ruffians that they are." He turned back to Alex, a wrinkle appearing on his brow that had her sighing inside.

In difference to Minister Crombie, Sandy Peden had made it his own little mission in life to ensure the foreign Mrs Graham was properly instructed in all aspects of the Presbyterian faith, lecturing her for hours on the Bible, the relative importance of men and women, the qualities of a good wife, and she could see yet another speech coming on. She looked to Matthew for support, but her husband was busy inspecting knots, rearranging bedding, seeing to his new horse – anything in fact that made it impossible for her to catch his eyes. Sandy was already at it, his beautiful voice berating her for the unwomanly behaviour she'd just displayed. Alex pretended to listen, her eyes on her nursing child.

She glanced over to where her husband was still busy with Ham. She could make out no more than the general shape of him, but that was enough to tell her he was stiff with tension, and to Sandy's evident surprise she stood, handed him the by now sleeping Rachel and walked over to join Matthew.

"I don't think Ham has any stones left in his hooves to dislodge," she said, kissing him on the nape.

"No." Matthew continued smoothing his hands up and down the horse's legs.

"Stupid name for a horse," she added in an effort to distract him.

"You think? It would have been worse if he was a pig,

no?" He tweaked at her hair. "We could have been dead."

"But we're not, right?"

"No, we're not," Matthew said, "but no thanks to my twisted, evil brother. He wishes us both dead, Alex, both!"

"He won't try again," Sandy said, having come over to join them.

"He won't? How so?" Matthew said.

"There are ways to rein in a maddened beast; you start by talking to its master."

"What? Matthew should go to the king?" Alex held out her arms to receive Rachel back.

"Hmm, no that would not be wise, I think. Leave it with me, aye? It is I, is it not, that has the gift of the word – not that I seem to entrance all audiences." Sandy winked at Alex and sauntered off to talk to his brother.

# CHAPTER 38

Two uneventful nights, and just before noon of the penultimate day of May, Matthew turned Ham up the last stretch towards Hillview. Clouds chased each other across a sky blue in patches and a gusty wind tore at cloaks and hoods, lifting Ham's mane to float like an elongated set of medusa curls around the powerful neck. A very good horse, not quite as impressive as Samson, but with strong cruppers and clean legs and a good head, with those flat, dished cheekbones that spoke of Arab ancestry.

Matthew smiled wryly; he was only thinking of the horse to distract himself from the snakes that presently inhabited his stomach. Would it have changed? Two and a half years since he'd last seen his home on a cold January morning, and with every step the horse took down the road, Matthew felt his heart pick up pace, a weakening sensation in elbow creases and knees.

"Are you okay?" Alex asked.

"I'm afraid it may have changed."

Alex blew out loudly through her nose. "Of course it will – superficially. Just as it had when you came back from those years in prison." She adjusted the shawl that held Rachel to her chest and reached back to pat Matthew on the leg. "The heart of it doesn't change. The fields, the hill, the way the stream meanders across the meadow – all of that remains as it always was. It's the earth as such that calls to you, the place where you've lived as a child, where your family has lived for generations. And no matter how changed, it's still the place where you belong, forever rooted there." She sighed and gave a shaky laugh. "Not like me, hey? I have no roots, no place on earth eternally labelled 'home'. A proverbial rolling stone, that's me. Even in my old time – or should I say my future time – that's the way it was."

"You belong here too," Matthew said, spreading his hand over her stomach, "you belong with me." He disliked it when she spoke of that old life of hers, even as tangentially as she had just done. It made him too aware of how random their meeting was, a fickle misalignment in time and two people who should never have met ended up eye to eye.

He widened his fingers, pretending he could curl them round the wee stranger in her womb, keep it safe and cosseted. He chuckled; the bairn lay well protected under the steady beat of her heart. He pressed his hand harder into her belly, swept by a primitive pride in his own virility; his woman, his child. She pushed back against him. It made him blood fizz, how his wife softened at his touch, and he bent his head to nibble at her ear, laughing at how all of her shivered in response.

"Tonight, in our bed, aye?"

"Maybe," she said with a little shrug. He bit harder and she squealed, promising him that of course tonight in their bed.

"What do I say to him?" Alex asked Matthew a bit later. "Come here, come to Mama? What if he doesn't want to?" She shifted, clearly nervous. "I keep on seeing him hiding behind Joan's legs, staring at us from a safe distance."

"You'll say the right thing; you're his mother."

"You think?"

"Of course you will, lass." His son; no longer a wean, but a laddie. He couldn't visualise this unknown little being, seeing instead the babe he had left behind, all dimples and folds of baby fat with light hazel eyes. Alex feared Mark might not recognise her. He feared he might not recognise his son.

Matthew held in Ham just before they crested the last little hill and dropped off.

"I must piss."

Alex fussed with her hair, smoothing it back before replacing cap and hat, and in Matthew's eyes she was very beautiful, sitting the horse with their daughter clasped to her chest. He took the reins and walked the last few steps, and there before him lay Hillview, spread out in the summer greenery. The barn, the weathered stable, henhouse, dovecot and privy − still all there, solid and permanent. His eyes flew over the buildings, noting that they stood strong and well maintained. Two horses in the meadow, the glittering line of water where the stream cut its way behind kitchen garden and storage sheds. Alex inhaled, and he twisted his head to look at her.

"Home," she said.

"Aye; home." He turned his eyes to the main house, nestled back against the hill − grey stone, dark slate roof and two chimneys. Home. He dashed a hand over his eyes and drew in a lungful of Hillview air − finer air than anywhere else on earth. Exclamations of delight floated up from below, Matthew took a firm grip on the reins and began the last walk downhill, towards his home, his family and son.

She should have been scanning the waiting faces, but the one thing that caught Alex' eyes as Matthew led Ham down the slope was so incongruous she nearly fell off the horse. It couldn't be! She looked again at the solitary garment hanging to dry and suppressed a desire to knuckle her eyes. Light blue, long legged and with a copper zipper up the front; jeans... here! She was mesmerised by them, her head swivelling, but then she was being helped off the horse, Rachel was swept from her by Matthew, and she was surrounded by arms, by people welcoming her home. There was Joan, still as thin as a rail, her grey eyes shiny with tears, her hair covered by an overlarge cap, and here came Simon, weeping openly as he squished her to his chest.

Alex was propelled in the direction of the house and she had no doubts what to do or say. She sank down onto her knees and held out her arms.

"Mark," she said, fighting the urge to cry. "My beautiful

Mark! Look at you, such a big, strong boy." Her son hung back, but at a gentle shove from Simon moved towards her. So solid, so real, and with that scent so uniquely his own still clinging to his hair... She had to force herself to let him go before she crushed him, feeling the little body stiffen in her hold. She sat back on her heels and took his hands. "I've missed you so much and I've tried to imagine what you would look like. And I was right; you look just like your father."

She hid a smile at how Mark stretched when she said that. Clearly the boy had been told a lot about his father, at least to judge from how he was staring at Matthew. It was almost risible; her son and her husband stared at each other out of the exact same eyes, identical smiles appeared on their faces. Talk about dominant genes, she grinned.

"Son," Matthew said, hunching down to Mark's level. "Come here, aye?" He opened his arms and Mark threw himself into them, bursting into tears.

"Alex," Joan's voice had an urgent edge to it and Alex tore herself away from watching son and father. "There's someone else you must see." Joan took Alex by the hand and lead her into the house.

"Someone else?" Alex bunched up her skirts to follow Joan up the staircase, a vague premonition in her gut. The jeans!

"Simon found him," Joan said, "two weeks come Sunday. He was all alone in the woods, crying."

"Who?"

"Here," Joan said, opening the door that stood ajar at the end of the landing.

"I can't believe it!" Alex clasped her hands together and looked at Matthew as if he could somehow sort this mess. He gave a helpless shrug.

"I mean, Isaac! Here!" Alex resumed her restless pacing up and down their bedroom. "How Matthew? How the fucking hell can he be here?"

Matthew winced at her language, but she didn't care. She was being torn into atoms by this. Two sons, two boys who had lost their mother, and both of them reunited with her on the same day.

"Joan said how the laddie says he fell through a wee painting." Matthew looked ill just saying it.

Alex groaned, tugged at her hair. Bloody impossible! And fuck you, Mercedes, for painting these damn time portals. Matthew made a grab for her as she walked by and pulled her down to sit on the bed, one arm keeping her still.

"It'll be fine, we'll make it fine."

Alex relaxed against him. "He actually recognised me, but that's because he's seen so many pictures of me."

Isaac had sat up with a little shriek when Alex entered the room.

"And all he's heard is that I'm gone, so when he saw me he supposed that meant that he was gone as well, and he didn't want to die." Alex mouth stretched into a brief smile. "I still suspect he thinks he's dead, and he isn't that impressed by heaven so far. But it is, isn't it," she went on, resting her head against Matthew. "This is a slice of heaven, right?"

He had opened the small window wide on the warm evening and the room was full of the heady scents of early summer, a rich top note to the underlying familiar smells of stone, wood and linen.

"Aye, it is." He slid off the bed to kneel before her, took her hand and raised it to kiss her palm. "Thank you; I wouldn't be here if it hadn't been for you."

She didn't know what to say, not quite able to meet the naked look in his eyes. Her hand cupped his cheek for an instant.

"I did it mostly for me," she whispered.

"For us, for him," he whispered back, nodding in the direction of their son.

"No." She wound her arms round his neck, pulled him close enough to kiss him. "I did it for me; I'd have died without you." The smile that spread over his face made little fireworks explode throughout her body.

She shifted her gaze to the trundle bed where Mark was fast asleep, thrown on his back. Not once during the day had he let go of his father, and Matthew had agreed to let him sleep with them this once, overruling Joan's objections.

"He knew you," Alex said, "he didn't know me." It hurt; not as much as she had feared it would, but still it knifed her to see the way Mark automatically turned to Joan, not to her.

"Nay, he didn't know me," Matthew answered with a slight twist to his lips. "He's just a wee laddie come face to face with his hero. Like you said; small lads dream of tall men that have lived through adventures. I fear Simon has been telling him a wee bit too much about me."

Rachel fed and tucked into her basket, Alex turned towards her husband.

"I'm just going to check on Isaac, I'll be right back."

"Aye, or I'll come and find you."

She stuck her tongue out and darted off.

The door to the nursery squeaked when she eased it open. In the bed her son from the future was sleeping all alone now that Mark was in with them. He had been crying, the lashes sticky with wet saltiness, and she caressed his cheek softly, not wanting to wake him. He sighed in his sleep and tried to turn over, his brow pulling together in a frown when his splinted leg protested.

She looked down at the sleeping boy, fingers hovering millimetres from his skin. How old was he? Alex counted years in her head and concluded he was seven, going on eight, slight where Mark was sturdy, with a pretty, almost feminine face, saved by two straight, dark brows. His hair was cut short, bristling like hedgehog spines across his scalp, and in his sleep his mouth had fallen open, a trail of wet trickling out of the corner of his mouth.

She sharpened her gaze, scanning his features for any resemblance to his biological father. It was there, alright, in everything from the shape of his brows and mouth to the nose. But mostly he reminded her of Don Benito – and perhaps of Mercedes. There was nothing of herself in the sleeping child; not in colouring or in features. Alex brushed her lips against his brow, tucked the quilt closer round him and returned to her room and her waiting man.

Next day Alex succeeded in getting Isaac tell her what had happened. At first he refused to talk about it, but bit by bit Alex got it out of him, listening to his description of how he'd fallen and fallen before landing with a thump. He looked very pale as he recounted this and Alex suspected it hadn't been quite that simple but chose not to push.

"Explain a bit more about the painting," she said instead.

"I like being in Mercedes' studio," Isaac said. "Offa says I can paint as much as I like there."

"You paint? Wow! Can you draw as well?"

Isaac made a depreciating gesture. "I like colours."

He'd been digging through the cupboards for a new tube of green paint and right at the back he'd found the little painting, stuck between the shelf and the wall. He'd tugged it loose, attracted by the brightness of the colours and how it – he threw her a worried look – well, how it sang, sort of.

"And I could see you," he said in a surprised voice. "I saw you there, at the end of the tunnel."

Alex chewed at the inside of her cheek. So it was true; Mercedes' swirling pictures were backdoors into other times. It made her feel faint, cold sweat breaking out all over her body. Her mother a witch, some sort of repetitive time traveller... She banged a mental door on these thoughts and concentrated on her son instead. Among her belongings still rested the little picture destined for Sir William and maybe he could go back the same way he came – if he wanted to.

"Would you like to go back?" she said. Congratulations, Alex Graham; first prize for the most stupid question ever.

Isaac gave her an astounded look. Go back? Did she think he could? Yes, oh yes, he so wanted to go back, he missed Daddy and Diane and Offa and even the twins.

"The twins?"

"My baby sisters," Isaac said, "Olivia and Alice."

"Ah," Alex said, inundated by a wave of jealousy. "Diane's twins?" With her John? Well, okay; not her John, not anymore, but still ...

Isaac just nodded, looking rather irritated at this interruption to his litany of how much he hated it here.

"Hate it here?"

Isaac waved his hand at his surroundings. No TV, no computer, and look at the bed... The window was small, and someone had taken his jeans and put him in a long white dress and everyone smelled.

"Even you, although not as much as the others." He went on to tell her that he hated the food – breakfast was alright, he supposed – but dinner was awful and why were there never any tomatoes?

"And I haven't brushed my teeth once," he finished, sneaking her a look.

"Hmm, well, we can't have that, can we?" Alex sniffed at her sleeve. As far as she could make out she didn't smell – she was wearing a clean shift. "Have you been stuck up here all the time?" she asked, intercepting a longing glance towards the window.

Isaac nodded unhappily. "She – Aunt Joan – says I mustn't move."

"You can still sit outside, and I'm sure Samuel can make you some crutches or something. The problem is going to be to find you some clothes." The jeans lay folded on a chair, but firstly they wouldn't fit over the bandaged leg, and secondly Alex had no intention of letting him wear them. "You'll just have to sit around in your shirt I suppose."

"But..." Isaac blushed. "I... I don't have any underwear on!"

Alex laughed. "Welcome to the club, mister. And let me let you in on a secret – no one does."

Matthew carried Isaac outside and helped him sit on a stool by the kitchen door, his left leg extended awkwardly in front of him. Isaac regarded him curiously; this was the man his mother was married to, and that made him some kind of relation to him as well. Matthew's long mouth curled upwards.

"Will you be alright then?"

Isaac nodded. Grownups were more or less the same everywhere, and he could see that Matthew was in a hurry to be off.

"Your mother will be down shortly, and if your wee brother comes asking for me, tell him I'm with the horses, aye?"

"Brother?" Isaac blinked in bewilderment.

"Mark," Matthew clarified and strode off.

Isaac sat looking after him, tasting this new word – brother. He didn't like it; not at all did he like it, and when Mark did rush by he pretended to sleep, studying Mama's new son from under his lashes.

All that morning Isaac sat on his stool, resting his back against the warm stone of the wall behind him. He saw Matthew walk this way and that with Mark a scampering shadow at his heels, and just watching them together made his insides clench with longing for Dad. He sighed; if only he hadn't... His eyes filled with tears and he sobbed, feeling excluded from this strange existence that went on around him. He didn't want to stay here, and he threw an angry look at his leg. Once he could walk he'd run away, it couldn't be that far to Edinburgh, and at least he'd be home, in a city he knew. And he would wear his jeans, not this stupid, flapping shirt. He heard steps behind him and wiped his face, using the wide sleeve as a handkerchief.

Alex had been standing in the shade for some time watching

him, this tangible reminder of a life she'd made such huge efforts to forget as much as possible. Her heart went out to him when she realised he was crying, a small boy in an oversized shirt that hid his face in the sleeve when she approached him.

"Hi," Alex said, sitting down on the grass beside him. She swung Rachel into her lap and undid her lacings. Isaac stared at her uncovered breast.

"Is that how she eats?"

Alex nodded, cupping her daughter's head. "Until she's about one or so. She gets the odd biscuit mashed with milk as well, or carrots."

"Did I?" Isaac looked disgusted at the thought.

No, she thought, you didn't, because I couldn't bear the weight of you in my arms, and just the thought of having you at my breast filled me with panic.

"You didn't like it," Alex lied, and saw how he sagged in relief.

"Diane says it ruins your figure," Isaac said.

"Well she would," Alex muttered. "She doesn't have much of one to begin with, more or less flat like an ironing board." She shifted Rachel to the other side and smiled up at her son. "You like Diane?"

Very much, he said, describing with enthusiasm how much time they would spend together on WoW.

"WoW?"

"World of Warcraft," Isaac said. For a couple of minutes he actually looked happy, his eyes bright as he explained everything about this game to her. Not that she understood all that much, but she did manage to look very captivated.

Alex handed a replete Rachel to Isaac.

"Here, you hold her for me. I'll go and find us something to drink, okay?" He just nodded, his arms tight around the baby.

When Alex came back carrying a jug of cold milk and a piece of pie to go with it, Isaac was singing to Rachel, in Swedish.

"Who taught you that?"

"Offa," he grinned, "but he says I mustn't tell people what it is about."

"No better not, and he shouldn't be teaching you stuff like that, you're only seven. Anyway, your sister seems to like it."

Isaac stiffened. "My sister?"

Alex nodded, her mouth full with pie. Isaac shook his head and shoved Rachel off his lap to land on the grass.

"She's not my sister! My sisters are Olivia and Alice, and they're pretty girls, not fat like this one. And they don't smell, either."

Alex lifted Rachel up, glaring at Isaac. "She's not fat! And she's a baby. You could've hurt her." She stood to tower over him, a still shrieking Rachel in her arms. "Obviously you haven't been taught manners, have you?" She stalked off, leaving Isaac to sit alone.

# CHAPTER 39

For two days Alex hovered at a distance from Isaac, minimising their communication to what was absolutely necessary, no more. He should apologise for what he did, she told herself, he could have hurt Rachel. And yet; he wasn't much more than a baby himself, a little boy lost in space. She sighed and turned to her other son who was tugging at her skirts.

"Yes?" she prompted when Mark remained standing silent, an expression of deep concentration on his face.

"Isaac cries at night," he blurted, and before Alex could say anything he was flying out the door.

"You've been a wee bit harsh with him these last few days," Joan said, coming over to sit beside Alex at the kitchen table. She handed Alex a bowl of early peas and they sat in companionable silence shelling them.

"He shouldn't have pushed Rachel off his lap." Alex tried to sound stern, find some anger inside her. In reality what she felt was guilt; for not missing him all that much during the intervening years, for knowing that should she be given the choice between this time and that, she would always choose to stay here, with Matthew and their children.

"Nay," Joan agreed, "but he's a small lad, very far from home. Not only far in place, but also in time."

Alex gave her an admiring look; Joan sounded quite relaxed, and yet she'd gone the colour of a dirty sheet when Alex came clean a couple of nights ago, admitting that yes, she'd dropped through time as well – just like Isaac.

"It doesn't scare you anymore?" she asked.

"Scare me?" Joan laughed. "It does my head in." She bit into a discarded pod, looked at Alex for a long time. "Poor lad; so unhappy here."

Alex squirmed. Joan was right; she'd been far too harsh on poor Isaac.

"Do you know where he is?" she asked, getting to her feet.

"Out, I reckon. He's been avoiding the house lately."

Alex found Isaac down by the stream, staring longingly at the pool. Struck by inspiration she ran back to the house and returned with towels and soap, dropping to her knees beside him.

"Right, you're taking a bath. Mind you, the water's bloody cold this early in June, but you really must wash before your ears grow fuzzy with mould."

Isaac's hands flew up to his ears.

"Kidding," Alex said, "but you do stink, you know." He didn't; he smelled of small boy, sun warmed hair and a slight salty tang that she hoped was sweat, not tears.

"So do you," Isaac retorted.

Alex grinned and shed her skirts. "That's why I'm going bathing with you."

From the way Isaac looked at her, he'd never seen a naked woman before and he went a dusky pink when she stripped him, undid his bandage and studied his leg.

"I'll carry you out in the deep end, and then you can test if you can move it. You can swim, right?"

"Of course I can!"

She picked him up and walked into the water.

"Shit, shit, shit," she exclaimed through gritted teeth, making Isaac giggle. He squealed when the cold water hit his skin and held on hard to Alex as she towed him into the deep end.

"So, can you use your leg?" she asked, letting go of him. He paddled, a bit clumsily at first, but was soon moving gracefully through the water, laughing in loud peels when she chased him with the soap.

Afterwards he sat close beside her in the sun, still butt naked, and Alex gave him a quick hug.

"I love you, and even if I've been gone from you for very many years I've never forgotten you."

Isaac looked away. "That's what Offa's always said, that you were still peeking down at me."

Alex rested back against her arms, raising her face to the sun. "I miss Magnus a lot, is he alright?"

Isaac shrugged; Offa was big and strong, made the best chocolate cakes in the world and talked and talked about plants.

"Just as always, then," Alex laughed.

"Eva says he must exercise more, but Offa doesn't want to."

"Eva?"

"Offa likes her," Isaac said offhandedly. "He kisses her a lot. Diane says its yucky, two old people going on like that."

Now why didn't that surprise her? Alex bit back on a caustic remark, hating that it was Diane and not her that was the one with access to Magnus.

"And Diane," she asked, pulling on her skirts. "Is she okay?"

Isaac gave her a guarded look and nodded.

"And do you miss her?"

"Yes," he said in a whisper.

"It's alright," Alex told him. "I'm glad that you do. That means that she's been good to you, right?"

Isaac swallowed back a sob. "I ... she ... she always wakes me up for school, and then ..." He wiped at his eyes. "We watch scary movies together, only Diane and me, when the twins are asleep and Dad's still at work, and ..."

"Shh," Alex said, pulling him close. He reared back, and Alex dropped her arms. Isaac sat with his back to her, digging his fingers into the sandy ground. Shit; this was much more difficult than she'd expected it to be.

Alex finished dressing before re-splinting his leg.

"It's healing very well, but from now on you're ordered to swim at least once a day, okay? It will help the muscles, I think." She helped him into his clothes and handed him his crutches, matching her pace to his as they walked back to the house. "Once your leg is healed I'll see what we can do. Maybe there's some way to get you back."

Wild hope flared in Isaac's eyes, hope that died away as quickly as it had come.

"How?"

"I don't know, but maybe I can think of something ." She stopped him as they came in full view of the house. "First you have to get well. Then we'll see."

"How can you tell him that?" Matthew looked at Alex with a disapproving groove between his brows. "You can't get him back, can you?"

Alex squirmed inside. He wasn't going to like this, but there was no way out of it now.

"I think I can."

"Oh aye? How?"

They were sitting on the bare head of the hill that gave their home its name, and below them were spread the buildings, the meadows and the closest barley fields. They had walked up hand in hand through the woods, stopping often to kiss as Matthew insisted that this was one tree they had not kissed under before. It was the first time since they had gotten back home that they were alone, the children left in Joan's competent hands.

"I found another painting," Alex said, and went on to tell him about the package that she was supposed to deliver to Sir William and how she had opened it, driven by an unexplained impulse. "I considered burning it," she finished.

"Why didn't you?" Matthew's voice was very distanced.

"I don't know," Alex replied, pulling at the grass. "I... God, this sounds silly, I just felt I shouldn't."

He nailed her with eyes that glinted a dangerous green. "Why?"

She just shrugged, and he got to his feet.

"Did you think you might need it?"

"No!" she protested, but deep inside a little voice cackled in objection. She gripped his hand and tugged until he sat back down. "I honestly don't know why I didn't burn it. But I swear I never planned on trying to leap back into my own time."

He studied her in silence, looking anything but

convinced. "And will you burn it if I ask you to?"

"Gladly. But not before I've tried to get Isaac back through it. He doesn't belong here, his heart belongs there."

Matthew frowned – no, scowled – and shook his head. "He's but a lad. We should keep him here with us, not send him flying through time. I don't like it, those wee paintings are full of witchcraft. Ungodly, they are... And what if he ends up somewhere else entirely?"

Alex swallowed at the thought. "I said we have to try. And I have no idea how this works, or even if it works, but I'll need you very close, okay?"

Matthew bit his lip, eyes gone very dark. Finally he wrapped his arms around her.

"Aye, I'll be very close."

She reclined against him, sitting between his legs. He relaxed his hold, letting his hands travel down to rest on the slight bulge of the new child.

"Are you sorry? That you're with child again?"

"I think it's too soon. Rachel will barely be weaned when the next one comes and that isn't exactly a pleasing notion. My tits will be like the udder of a cow if I'm not careful." His hands came up to cup her breasts, squeezing them with appreciation. "But no," she breathed. "I'm not sorry for the child as such. How can I be?" But she made a mental note to build up a sizeable supply of Queen Anne's Lace seeds and all the other herbs Mrs Parson had told her about, because she had no intention of becoming pregnant quite as quickly next time round.

"I like it when you're like this, when you grow round because of me."

"One could almost think you'd prefer me to be permanently pregnant."

"It suits you. You're never as beautiful as when you carry my bairn in your womb."

"It makes me look like a giant peach." She glanced down at herself and made a little face; everything swelled – her tits, her belly, even her feet.

"More like a pear, no? Somewhat heavy round your bottom." He wiggled a hand in under her, gave her posterior a little squeeze.

"Matthew!" She batted at him.

"Well I like pears, aye? Much, much more than peaches."

"Huh," she said, but was pleased all the same.

# CHAPTER 40

"And so..." Simon spread his hands in a helpless gesture. "He's untouchable."

Matthew grunted, reading his way through the documents compiled by Simon. Rich and well connected, his brother had over the last few years reaped success after success. It stuck in Matthew's craw to find out just how good a life Luke Graham was enjoying. Horses, jewels, part ownerships in various businesses – including a shipping company that traded exclusively with the Colonies – decorated for his valour by the king, a constant member of the court that circled round Charles the Second. A true wit, an educated man and an impressive chess player, Matthew read, snorting with irritation.

"There must be something I can do! Can't I press charges for unlawful abduction? For setting paid assassins on my wife and myself?"

"With what proof, Matthew?"

Matthew cursed, loudly and creatively. "It's not right."

The would be murderers had been turned over to the authorities, but to a man they'd refused to name their employer, insisting they didn't know him – and in all probability they were telling the truth.

"Nay," Simon sighed. "But whoever gave you the notion that life is fair?" He looked over to where Alex and Joan were hanging laundry, smiling when he heard his wife laugh out loud. "Forget him."

"I can't."

"I told you," Alex said later that evening when Matthew complained to her about the sheer injustice of it all, that his brother should get off scot free. "But it doesn't really matter, does it? After all, you're back, safe and sound, and that in itself is probably enough to have Luke yowling like a cat with his balls in a mousetrap."

Matthew laughed out loud at her simile. "You think?"

"Mmhh." She brushed at his hair. "Simon's right. Pretend he doesn't exist and concentrate on your own life, okay?"

"It's just ..." He fisted his hands, clenching them hard enough to have his knuckles protest.

"I know, of course I know. But don't give him the satisfaction of tainting your whole existence. He isn't worth it." She snuggled closer, a heavy warmth against his chest. "God, I'm tired," she mumbled, "and I swear, if Rachel doesn't sleep through the night I'll hang her out the window." She yawned, eyes blinking heavily. "Did you see Isaac and Mark today?"

"Aye," Matthew smiled, "more enthusiasm than skill."

"Well it's not easy, kites are tricky to build – and fly."

"I noticed," he teased, "your design was somewhat top heavy."

"Let's see you do better, mister kite-expert. Anyway," she added through yet another yawn, "my point was that they were playing together."

Over the coming weeks, Isaac grew into Hillview. He woke at dawn when the household began to rise, and now that he could move around he was first down to the breakfast table, downing porridge and ham and bread in impressive quantities. After that he'd limp down to the hen house to do his daily chore – feeding the hens and collecting their eggs – and most of the morning would fly by as he was told to do this or that.

He was useful here, and Matthew would at times praise him gruffly. Like when he managed to save some of the piglets from their farrow-mad mother by using the crutch to whack the sow repeatedly over the snout until someone else could come and save the little piggies.

Still, no matter how well he was conforming to his new reality there wasn't a day when he didn't long for home. Most nights he fell asleep staring at the wall as he forced himself to remember their faces: Daddy, Offa, Diane and the twins. Sometimes it all got too much, and he would struggle up into the woods and hide himself away and cry, hoping that soon he'd wake up and find all this a dream.

On one of those afternoons he was interrupted by the appearance of a boy he hadn't seen before, and Isaac sat up, scooting back until he had his back to a trunk. The boy was roughly his age, perhaps a bit more, and his dark chestnut hair hung almost down to his shoulders. Hair surprisingly like Matthew's and Mark's, as were his eyes, a light hazel that regarded Isaac with frank curiosity.

"Who are you?" The boy hunched down some yards away, studying the crutch.

"Isaac."

"Ah, the foundling." The boy laughed at Isaac's surprised expression. "We all know what happens down at the big house. And now the master is back we're all that much more curious." He sat down. "I'm Ian," he said, and it was obvious he assumed this would mean something to Isaac. "Ian Graham, nephew to the master."

"I've never seen you there," Isaac said.

Ian looked away. "Nay, we don't go there much."

"We?" Isaac saw a whole troop of Ian lookalikes headed by an obvious twin brother to Matthew.

"My Mam and I. We live up there – in the wee cottage." He pointed up the slope.

"Why there?" Isaac said, making out a small, dilapidated house. "Why not down in the big house?"

Ian mumbled something about not knowing why.

"Are you family then?" Ian asked, turning inquisitive eyes on Isaac.

"Yes." Isaac didn't want to say much more than that, but Ian pestered him with questions until Isaac told him he was Alex' son, here for a long overdue visit and that he had broken his leg falling off a horse.

"It must have been a huge horse."

Isaac nodded and they both fell silent. A high voice called for Ian and he stood.

"Mam; mayhap I'll see you again."

"Sure," Isaac smiled. Ian grinned back and then he was gone, melting into the woods.

It became the highlight of Isaac's day, these meetings with Ian. Every afternoon he'd duck out of sight behind the privy and make his way up to the millpond where Ian would be waiting. A boy, almost like him, and they fished and told each other stories, lying flat on their backs to stare up at the revolving skies. And then one day Matthew walked into the clearing, and Ian flew to his feet, took one look at his uncle and fled.

"Ian?" Isaac called after him. No reply, just the crashing of someone rushing through the undergrowth. Isaac frowned up at Matthew, not at all understanding why Ian had been so scared.

Matthew shrugged, eyes locked in the general direction of Ian's hasty departure.

"There's bad blood between his father and me, very bad blood."

Isaac moved closer to Matthew. "He looks just like you."

"Aye – and like Mark." For some reason Matthew's brows pulled together into a frown.

"You've seen them?" Alex sat back.

Matthew muttered something about having been round to all his tenants.

"So you've spoken to them."

"With her, not with the lad. And it was only very briefly."

"Really?"

"Well, I had to, no? It would've been impolite not to thank her for her financial help."

"Oh, of course. Alternatively one could consider it the least she could do, given that it was her lowlife husband who had you abducted in the first place."

"Alex," he sighed.

She moved over to sit in his lap, arms hard around his neck.

"I don't want you to see her. Or him." Especially not Margaret, not beautiful, willowy Margaret with her black, black hair and light blue eyes. She sneaked a look down herself. Definitely not willowy, and if she was going to be quite honest she never had been. Not fat either, just a bit more round all over. But she hated it that Margaret and she were so alike, alike enough to compare.

"You're much prettier," Matthew said. Alex threw him an irritated look; was she that transparent? Apparently yes, at least to judge from his grin.

"Yeah right; any man with a modicum of self-preservation would say that with his pregnant wife in his lap," Alex snorted.

Matthew bit her ear until she squealed. "Are you calling me a liar?"

"That or potentially blind," she said through gusts of laughter as he tickled her. He kissed her, a long, promising kiss.

"I'm no liar," he said, once he allowed her up to breathe, "and there's nothing wrong with my eyesight."

She kissed him back. "Promise? That you won't see either of them?"

"Aye, I promise," he sighed.

Joan was reticent when Alex badgered her about Margaret next day, saying shortly that Margaret had come with the lad and asked that she might stay at the cottage again.

"But why? Why on earth would she come here?"

"She knew you weren't here, and I fear she thought you'd never return — at least not him." She used her head to indicate her brother presently crossing the yard with Mark and Isaac at his heels. "They gravitate towards him, no?"

Alex followed her gaze. "Like the three musketeers."

Joan huffed, making Alex smile. Alex had told them the story over the last few summer evenings, and Joan had been captivated, eyes wide as she bombarded Alex with questions about d'Artagnan, Cardinal Richelieu, the unfaithful queen and the wicked, depraved Milady de Winter.

"Is it true?" Joan had asked repeatedly. "Did the French Queen betray her husband with the Duke of Buckingham? Because if she did, well then the present king of France is a bastard, no? And an English bastard to boot!"

"It's a book," Alex had tried, "not necessarily the truth."

"She could have gone somewhere else," Alex said, reverting to the subject of Margaret.

Joan shook her head. "She came home. This is the only home she's ever known." There was a thread of implied criticism in her voice that made Alex shut her mouth before she said anything more. Inside she was fuming; this was her home now, not Margaret's, and she could bloody well get off her arse and leave. Preferably immediately.

It didn't exactly get any better when she found Matthew with Ian a couple of days later. She had tucked a fretting Rachel into her shawl and gone for a long walk, doing a silent high five when the child fell asleep. She was halfway down the slope with the birches when she heard Matthew's voice, coming from behind a thicket to her right. She moved closer and saw him sitting with an unknown boy, so much an older copy of her own Mark that she had to swallow back on an exclamation of surprise.

They were paddling their feet in the little stream, and she couldn't hear what they were talking about, but she could see the way the boy's eyes hung off Matthew, and how her husband placed his arm around the boy. Matthew closed his eyes at the proximity of the boy, and one half of her felt sorry for him, the other was dying with jealousy that he should be here, with Ian, instead of with their son. He had promised her! She retraced her steps and made her way back home.

"Did you have a good day?" she asked later that evening.

Matthew yawned and nodded.

"I missed you in the afternoon, I went looking for you." Take it! she told him mentally, take the opportunity and tell me about you and Ian.

"You did?" Matthew said. "I must have been somewhere else, no?" He patted the bed beside him. "Will you be coming?"

Alex shook her head. "I'll just get myself a mug of milk, I'll be right back." She sat in the dark kitchen until she was certain he was asleep.

# CHAPTER 41

It didn't take Matthew long to work out that something was chafing at his wife, and not that much longer to understand that somehow it was him who had affronted her. She maintained a constant distance, leaping to her feet to hurry off when she saw him making for her, and keeping an impressive bulwark of children around her. If he tried to kiss her, Rachel had to be fed or changed or have her rash seen to. When he took her hand, she disengaged herself and told him she had promised Isaac to go swimming, or Mark to go into the woods. In the evenings she complained about the heaps of mending she had to do, waving him off to bed while assuring him she would be up later, once she had finished this shirt or that smock. He never managed to stay awake until she came up.

Not until he saw a flashing movement as he came down from yet another afternoon with Ian did he put two and two together, and he went in to supper with a sinking feeling in the pit of his stomach.

"Yet another good day?" she asked in a barbed tone, keeping her eyes on her plate.

"Aye."

"Meet anyone in particular?" she asked with enough frost to freeze a horse. Joan and Simon shared a quick look and left them the battlefield.

"You broke your promise to me," she said once they were alone. "And even worse, you didn't tell me you'd seen Ian, even when I gave you the opportunity to."

"He's my son," Matthew said belligerently. "Will you deny me to see him?"

"He isn't your son! He's their son! They've had the raising of him since he was a baby, it's their values and their opinions that form his world and way of thinking, not yours. He's lost to you, he's been lost to you since the day you signed him away. Besides, that isn't the point. The point is that you promised and broke your promise. So how am I to trust you? Maybe you've been seeing her as well on the sly, what would I know?"

His cheeks heated with anger and shame at the insinuation in her words.

"You know I'd never dishonour you." An image of Kate flashed through his head and his skin burnt even hotter.

"Do I? I thought you'd stand by your given word as well." She subsided into silence, shoving her mostly uneaten supper from one side of the plate to the other. He studied her, sighing inwardly. How could she feel threatened by the fact that he saw his son?

"I couldn't help myself. I swear, I had no intention of breaking my word, but seeing Ian leap away from me in fear as he did that afternoon when I came upon the lads up in the wee clearing, well, it tore at me. " He leaned his face into his hands. "He's caught in between; he doesn't understand why he and his mother can't stay here, with his kin. And you're right in that he isn't mine, not like he would be had I had the caring of him. But can't you understand that I take these few moments with him and try to give him something of myself to carry with him?" He kept his eyes on the table. *My Ian; my wee laddie, and they stole him from me, and now, well now it was too late.* A hand stroked his head, rested for a while against his cheek.

"I've lost a son too. Isaac is hers – Diane's – much more than mine."

It was different, he wanted to yell, Isaac had not been wrested from her through lies, had he? No, this unknown Diane had done the right thing by a motherless laddie – but she wouldn't want to hear that.

"Aye, but your Isaac is in hands you trust. I… well I've thrown my son to the wolves."

There was a long silence, he could hear her every breath, how her stays creaked when she shifted in her seat.

"See him as much as you want then." She cleared her

throat. "But if I ever see you loitering around in the woods with her, I swear I'll do you severe bodily harm. For both our sakes, don't break that promise to me, okay?"

Matthew raised his eyes to hers. Finally he nodded, once.

"I'll speak to her only as I must."

They spent most of the evening in the parlour, Matthew playing chess with Simon, Alex conversing with Joan. Every now and then he'd sneak her a look, and every time he did she'd meet his eyes. He suppressed a little smile; reconciliation sex, she'd once told him, was considered to be spectacularly good, and from the way his pregnant wife was eyeing him, he had a memorable night before him. In his breeches his cock twitched and stretched. Alex yawned and excused herself, and once Matthew had check mated Simon he stood as well, bidding Simon and Joan a good night before hastening up the stairs.

She'd lit candles and turned the bed down, and there, right in the centre, she was lying on her back, as naked as the day she was born. He didn't say anything, he just stood looking at her, and her toes curled, her legs widened.

He kissed her ankle, her calf, her knee – both her knees – the inside of her thighs. Her hair; He loved her hair, the way it shifted from plain brown through bronze to deepest copper. He undid the braid, spread out her curls over their pillows. One long curl he used to decorate her breast, smiling at how her nipples hardened when he brushed his fingers over them.

A warm hand snuck into his neckline of his shirt, tugged none too gently at his chest hair.

"Take off your clothes," she said.

"Mmm?" he teased, dropping a series of kisses down her front. She wiggled, laughing when his hair tickled her flank.

"Your clothes," she said, struggling with his belt. Breeches, shirt and stockings landed on the floor. Blood pounded through his head, through his cock. Her fingers danced up the length of him, a hand cupped his balls, and he heard his breathing grow loud and ragged when first her tongue, then her teeth – ever so gently – found the tip of his member. With a groan he fell back, legs splayed, arms thrown out, and let her have her way with him. She nibbled and teased, she kissed and stroked, and his cock thudded and swelled to the point of bursting. She released him and sat up, licking her lips.

"Turn over," he said. She complied, and he took her from behind, his hands cradling her breasts. She pushed against him, bringing him even deeper into her. Ah! Oh aye, there, almost there.

"I love you," she whispered – no panted. "I love you, I love you, I love you."

And I you, my Alex. My woman, my heart.

Isaac was overjoyed the day he was let out of splints, gambolling like a spring fevered calf on the thick green grass under the apple trees. Alex watched him with a half-smile, glad that he was undamaged, sad because now the decision she had been putting off with the excuse of his leg had to be taken.

"Your leg seems okay," Alex said, lowering herself to sit beside Isaac. She winced as she stretched her legs in front of her, wiggling her bare toes. Her whole body was screeching in protest after yet another day's heavy work. For the last week she'd been busy in the kitchen garden from early morning to late evening, harvesting redcurrants and raspberries, peas and radishes and basketfuls of cucumbers for pickling.

"Here." Alex extended a muffin to the boy. He bit into it and smiled at the sudden rush of warm jam that filled his mouth.

"It's not all crap food," Alex muttered, regretting her tone when Isaac blushed.

"I still miss things, like orange juice and hamburgers and fish and chips and how Offa makes chocolate desserts."

"Yeah," Alex said wistfully. "I definitely miss chocolate."

"Nothing else?"

Alex stretched out on the ground and closed her eyes.

"Not food, not really. I miss other things, though." She opened one eye to squint at her son. "Like a washing machine, or toothpaste."

Isaac flopped down to lie beside her. "But you don't really miss us." It was a statement, not a question, and Alex twisted her head to look her son fully in the eyes.

"No, I don't. I think of you often – of you and Magnus mostly. But my life is here, and if I were to be torn away from this I think I would die." Much too serious for such a young boy, she reprimanded herself, but to her surprise Isaac nodded as if he understood.

"It's the other way around for me. I miss them so much it hurts. All the time."

Alex struggled to sit, and drew her legs up beneath her. "I have a painting," she said keeping her eyes on anything but him. "You know, like the one you fell through. I think maybe you can go back through it."

"Now?" Isaac sat up as well, brown eyes hanging off her.

"No, we have to do this properly. You can't just disappear. And I'm very scared, so we'll have to be very careful."

Isaac had gone white around the mouth and Alex studied him with tenderness.

"In a week?" Alex suggested, smoothing his hair off his brow. "But only if you think you can do it." She looked at him for a couple of heartbeats. "I would love for you to stay with me, Isaac. You know that don't you?"

The boy crawled into her arms and nestled in as close as he could. "I don't want to," he whispered. No; she already knew that.

"A week?" Matthew shook his head. "He's a wee lad, and now you've told him he has to wait a week for something he wants but also fears."

"You think he does?"

"Aye. The lad pales every time he talks about it. He's a brave boy to be willing to do it again to get home."

"That or he's desperately unhappy here."

"This is not his place," Matthew said, "and you know that as well as he does, no?" Alex stroked Rachel's head, settled her in the cradle and more or less fell into bed. God she was tired; and all this stuff with Isaac wasn't exactly helping.

"Yes, of course I do."

Matthew was right, Alex concluded, watching an Isaac who grew increasingly nervous with each day. She tried to distract him, keeping him busy with his siblings and a long list of chores, and Isaac nodded and did as he was told, but he wasn't really there, not anymore. There was so much Alex wanted to say to him, now that she'd restricted their remaining time to a few paltry days, but she was tongue-tied around him, incapable of anything but warm hugs. And Isaac hugged her back, his thin arms tight around her expanding waist.

Alex drew pictures of Mark and Rachel, of Matthew and even of herself, using the mirror to help her see, and she tucked them into the pocket of his jeans that he might have something to remember them by once he got back. But most of all she drew Isaac, quick sketches that she hid away so that she would never forget what he looked like again. It was one long, protracted goodbye, and by the end of the week she was emotionally drained, as limp as a wrung dishcloth.

On Isaac's potentially last evening with them, Matthew took him by the hand and led him up to the small graveyard that sat halfway up the hillside. Isaac had never been here before, and he shrank back when he understood this place was full of dead people. Matthew laughed and patted the bench beside him.

"They'll do you no harm." He waited until Isaac was sitting down before he dug into his pouch and produced a small wooden figure. Isaac exclaimed when he saw his mother, sitting with her skirts spread round her and her face split into a wide smile.

"This isn't for you," Matthew said, "this is for Magnus. I want you to give it to him and thank him for the gift of his daughter."

Isaac looked confused but nodded.

"One day she and I will lie here," Matthew went on, pointing at the graves around them. "When you get back to your time mayhap you can find us here." He could see this was too much for the lad to handle and dropped the subject. Instead he produced another little carving.

"This is for you, so that you never forget that you whacked a maddened pig across the snout." It was the sow to the day, down to her small, aggravated eyes and Isaac threw himself into Matthew's arms, crying until he was hoarse.

There was an argument on the morning of Isaac's departure, a hissed, intense discussion between the four adults sitting round the kitchen table.

"It's wrong," Joan said. "No mortal should tamper with things such as these."

"He shouldn't be here to begin with," Alex tried, but Joan set her mouth into a very straight line.

"Two wrongs don't make a right, Alex, and look at the laddie – all stiff and pale with fear. We should keep him here, with us, not send him flying through time!" She turned to Simon who nodded his agreement.

"He could stay with us, with Joan and me," he said, "and besides, how do you know this will work? I still find it difficult to believe, aye? People leaping from one time to another, and all through a wee painting."

"He wants to go back," Alex said, "and I've promised him I'm going to try and help him, okay? End of discussion. And I'm not too thrilled about this either. It scares the daylights out of me, but what can I do? He hates it here, he pines for them, the people he loves." With that she rushed from the room. Matthew made as if to follow, but Joan waved him down.

"No, I'll go, it's me who upset her to begin with." With a brief smile she hurried after Alex.

Simon sighed and settled back against the wall.

"All of this makes my head spin; if I were to leap into the future and find a wife I might be marrying my own descendant."

"Seeing as you don't have any bairns, I don't see how," Matthew said, receiving a hurt look in reply.

"Not for want of trying, aye?"

"No, and I apologise for jesting about it." He placed a hand on Simon's arm. "She isn't too old, you may still have that child."

Simon sighed and rubbed a hand through his hair. "You think? More than seven years married and not once has she missed her courses. And you soon have four bairns."

"Only three that are mine to raise." Matthew swallowed back on a wave of acrid bitterness.

"Aye, but now that you look back on it, don't you think our Lord had some kind of plan? Had you not been deceived by Margaret and Luke, you would not have been given Alex."

Matthew had never thought of it that way, but now he nodded thoughtfully.

"Mayhap; and there isn't a day when I don't thank the Lord for her."

Simon rolled his eyes. "Besotted, the both of you."

They had decided beforehand that they would ride out to the crossroads where Alex had almost been dragged back to her time more than three years ago, Alex commenting in an attempted matter-of-fact voice that reasonably this should be an appropriate spot.

Alex was bitterly regretting not having burnt that stupid little picture the moment she knew it for what it was.

How could she even be considering to send her boy through time with the help of one of Mercedes' magic paintings? Out of the corner of her eye she studied Isaac where he sat behind Matthew, now in his jeans and t-shirt, and in his face she saw a mirror of her own fear but even more a shimmer of joy. He was so eager to get back, no doubt he'd throw himself around Diane's neck in a way he'd never done with her. She caught Matthew's worried eyes on her and smiled bravely, urging the placid roan mare into a trot.

It was early evening once they reached their destination. Matthew scanned the surroundings, stamping at the middle of the crossroad before walking back to where Alex stood immobile, overwhelmed by the memories of that muggy May day when time cracked open at her feet, just here.

"Nothing," he said, and Alex quivered back into normality. She took one big breath, held it for some seconds and turned to her son.

"Right; explain what you did last time."

Isaac hitched his shoulders. "I just looked, and then I saw you."

Alex crouched down beside him. "This may be dangerous, so we have to agree on some ground rules, okay?"

Isaac's tongue darted out to lick his lips, but he nodded all the same.

"You'll look first, and I'll be holding you. Only if you see a place or a person you recognise will I let you go." She clasped her son's head between her hands and stared him into the eyes. "If you don't see anything from your old life you have to say so. We can't risk you falling into some other time." She kept her eyes sunk into his for a long time. "Do you understand?"

He nodded again.

She swept him into her arms and kissed him. "I'm so glad that I got to see you again. You're a beautiful boy, and you have a very proud mother. Remember that, sweetheart." She cleared her throat, looking away as she wiped at her eyes. "And when you get back I want you to do three things for me. One; kiss your Offa from me and tell him to stop teaching you bawdy songs, two; hug John and tell him he's got a fantastic son, three; eat a huge helping of chocolate cake, okay?"

Isaac smiled at this last part and promised he would.

Matthew went to retrieve the wrapped painting. Even through all the layers Alex could hear it, the soft murmuring of a seashell calling you towards the sea, the wailing song of Sirens that twisted itself into your head and whispered to you to come, come closer and look. She breathed through her mouth, suppressing the urge to clap her hands to her ears, leap to her feet and flee.

Matthew brought a coil of rope with him and looped it round the crossroad oak before knotting it around himself and Alex. Isaac made huge eyes but didn't say anything, holding the little package unopened in his hands.

"A hug lad," Matthew said and drew Isaac close. "I'm honoured to have made your acquaintance, Master Lind, and don't forget you carry messages from me as well."

Alex gave him a surprised look, but she didn't say anything, kissing Isaac one last time before nodding in the direction of the parcel.

"Go on. But just so you know, I'm a bit of a coward so I'll probably keep my eyes closed."

Isaac smiled and undid the strings. Alex wrapped her arms around his waist, and Matthew tightened his hold on her shoulders.

She couldn't stop herself from peeking. Blue paint smiled up at her, bright, bright light poured from a little point towards which all the blue tumbled, and in her arms Isaac tensed, leaned back with a little whimper, but then relaxed, hands extended to what to Alex looked like a widening funnel of eye scorching light. So much noise, bloody hell, so much damned noise! Matthew gasped, his voice rose in a loud prayer, and Alex wet her lips, wanting to join in, begging whatever God existed to keep her safe.

"Look! Offa!" Isaac heaved forward, struggling against her arms. "Offa!" He wriggled and twisted, a live eel in Alex' arms. "Offa, I'm coming Offa!"

No matter how she tried, Alex couldn't unclench her hands. She was dragged into the painting with Isaac, and the rope around her waist cut into her, burning her skin, but then it was no longer there and she was free falling and she didn't want this, oh God, she didn't. Matthew! She could feel his hands on her arm, round her waist, hear his voice, how he pleaded with her, with God, and still she couldn't let Isaac go. Magnus; in his garden, mouth falling open in shock, and she knew that he was seeing her and that she had to get back, quickly, before she was forever lost. Small hands struggled with hers.

"Go!" Isaac screamed. "Go back to him, Mama!" He was free, falling towards the ground, yelling that he was safe, and there was the rope, there were Matthew's hands, his arms. Her vision shrank together, the previously so wide funnel of bright light converted into a pinprick. No Magnus, no Isaac, no nauseating sensation of hanging suspended between the here and there, only the reassuring solidity of the ground below her, of Matthew's arms around her. She turned blank eyes on him, blinked, blinked again. Her brain checked out.

By the time Alex came to, she was lying wrapped in her cloak, Matthew's coat a pillow under her head. All of her ached; from the smallest joint of her pinkie toe to the hairs that grew on her crown. She let her face fall to her right and saw Matthew a distance away, feeding a fire into a burning blaze. She knew what he was going to do and was glad that he'd do it without her help. She would never dare to touch that canvas again. Nor did Matthew. Instead he sharpened the end of a branch and speared the picture, carrying it dangling to roast above the fire. Almost like hot dogs on a scout trip, Alex giggled.

The fire caught and pale white smoke uncurled itself from the picture to hang hovering in the air above. Alex closed her eyes and sniffed. Lemon peel and cinnamon, the heavy tang of sun warmed rosemary, and with one last plaintive cry it was gone. Alex shuddered in relief.

Magnus couldn't stop hugging him. Isaac squirmed.

"I'm fine, but if you have some chocolate cake I wouldn't mind a piece."

Magnus laughed and cried at the same time, unable to stop himself from touching Isaac's cheek, his shoulder, his hair.

"We have to call John," he said, but Isaac hung back.

"Can we wait a bit? I…" He looked confused, dark brows forming one single line of concentration. "I want to talk to you first."

Magnus nodded. The poor child must be suffering a major shock at finding himself back in his time, so if he wanted to wait, then so be it. Come to think of it, Magnus was trembling all over as well.

He led the boy into the kitchen and served him milk and cake, watching with amusement as he wolfed it down.

"You didn't like the food?"

Isaac grimaced and shook his head. "It was pretty awful."

"Well, Alex was never much of a cook," Magnus said.

Isaac hitched his shoulder; she did as well as she could, he told Magnus, it wasn't her fault they didn't have tomatoes and pasta, orange juice or ice cream, was it? Isaac sighed, eyes drifting out to the garden.

"Mama…"

"Isaac?" Magnus shook his grandson. "Are you okay?"

Isaac gave him a watery smile and held out his glass for more milk.

Magnus listened in silence to Isaac's long and muddled tale, plying him with cake and milk at regular intervals. Isaac ate and talked, and at the end he dug into his pocket and drew out a little wooden figure.

"It's for you." Isaac dropped the dark wood into Magnus' open palm. "He says thank you for your daughter."

Magnus twisted little Alex round and round. She was still his girl, in the way she laughed and held her head. But the weight of hair at her nape and the unfamiliar clothes made it difficult to recognise her. What was beyond doubt was the love that had gone into the making of the little piece, hours of careful whittling to create this miniature effigy of a woman who sat and laughed at the world.

"He loves her," Magnus said, feeling ridiculous saying this to a child.

Isaac nodded seriously. "And she loves him. She never wants to leave him." He dug into his back pockets and produced several sheets of thick, heavy paper, handing them to Magnus.

He couldn't tear his eyes from the little family spread across the table in front of him; Rachel, Mark, Matthew and Alex. There was a severe looking young woman that Isaac explained was Auntie Joan, and a glittering, beaming man who was Uncle Simon, and then there was Matthew, fast asleep with his daughter held in his arms. The tenderness with which Alex had drawn him mirrored the love that had gone into the little carving, warming Magnus to the bone.

Time and time again his eyes returned to the astoundingly honest self-portrait, his Alex standing more or less naked on the page, and he traced the woman she had become, finding very little of the girl she once used to be.

She was rounded with yet another child, and Magnus felt a flare of irritation with Matthew for not letting her be, surely one child a year was a bit too much. But then his eyes fell once again on the sleeping Matthew and he shook his head in amusement. She wouldn't let him stay away from her.

He went back to his detailed study, and she looked healthy enough, arms and hands strong with manual chores. He laughed at the caustic comment by her shins, explaining that yes, that was hair, a lot of hair, but they hadn't really gotten round to waxing yet.

Magnus fisted his hand round the paper, spent a considerable time smoothing it back out. His Alex; alive and well in another time, just as he'd always hoped. So why didn't it make him feel better, to know that she was loved and loved? If anything, all of this just turned the pain of losing her up yet another notch. He sighed, looked up to find Isaac fast asleep, his head resting on the table. Magnus kissed him and stood to reach the phone. It was time to call John and tell him to come and get his son.

# CHAPTER 43

"Tell me again; why are we doing this?" Alex asked, sitting down on the bench. Matthew grunted with the effort to get the stone in place, snug against the roots of the tree. He stood and wiped the sweat from his brow, studying the little memorial with satisfaction.

"He'll come looking," he said, using his shirt tail to dab at his damp face. "And when he does, he'll find this and know you never forgot him." He smiled down at his wife and trailed his index finger along her jawbone, leaving a smudge of dirt behind.

Alex leaned forward to read the wording. "*Isaac Lind. Never forgotten, always present.*" She sat back and sighed. "... not even born," she muttered.

Matthew stretched. It was peaceful underneath the solitary rowan, the July evening quiet and warm. He studied the ordered lines of stones around him; his family, reaching back across time, most of them dying well before their sixties. He kneeled in front of Da's grave, brushing it clean from debris.

"Has Simon gotten anywhere with his investigations?" she said.

Matthew didn't reply, his fingers lingering over the carved name before coming over to join her at the bench.

"Some, aye." He extended his legs. His bare shins were tanned a deep copper after a summer in the fields, as were his feet. " I told you he died in the mill run, no?"

"Yes, and seeing it was December and he couldn't swim, it seemed an odd place for a spontaneous bath."

He gave her a stern look. "It isn't a matter to jest about."

Alex loosened her linen from her sweaty skin and apologised.

"Samuel recalls how my father received an urgent message that there was a problem at the mill, and swears he set out just after the morning chores, telling Samuel he'd be back before dinner." Matthew stopped and cleared his throat. "I actually saw him, aye? It was the last time I saw him alive, and I called out to him as he crossed the meadow, making him stop and wave before he went on his way. And when he wasn't home for dinner, I went looking." A cold December day, him hunching against the wind as he strode off towards the mill, Mam's worried voice ringing in his ears.

"Simon has spoken to the miller, and he insists he sent no message. The waterwheel was working as it should, and he spent most of that day in the mill as such, unfortunately too busy to look outside. He only noticed something had happened when the wheel clogged." Matthew grimaced. Da had been dragged down and under, the body mauled under the heavy shovels of the wheel before escaping crushed and deformed into the millrace. Poor Da, Matthew shuddered, I hope he was dead by then.

"The ring," he said out loud. "We never found the ring."

"What? It slipped off his finger?" Alex sounded mildly incredulous.

"Nay, he carried it on a chain. It was his mother's. She died in childbirth with his youngest brother and that is what he had of her."

"It must have been torn off him in the water, and then it was swept away, right?"

"Aye, perhaps." He doubted it. Da always kept the ring tucked out of sight, safe under his shirt, and despite the damage done to his body, shirt and breeches had been relatively intact, the neckline of his shirt still laced close. No; the only way it could have come off was in a struggle, a hand closing round the chain and yanking it off. Now that would require quite some strength, he mused. Not Margaret, then, and he was surprised just how relieved that conclusion made him.

"So no luck there," Alex said. She'd produced a stocking from her pocket and was busy mending the worn heel.

Matthew looked away; Simon had been right; too late, too little.

"Nay. But there's one witness that recalls seeing the master arguing loudly with someone, and he swears it was a man, not a woman, on account of the person's height and general size."

"Luke; told you so."

"Not enough, though," Matthew sighed. "Do you really think he would do it?" he asked after a moment of comfortable silence. Alex folded the stocking together in her lap and looked away across the fields.

"Do I think he planned it? No. Do I think he could do it? Yes."

She took off her cap and undid her hair, shaking it free to fall over her shoulders. A bright curl tickled his face. He sneezed, she laughed.

"Simon and Joan are leaving," Matthew said.

"I know, Joan told me. Edinburgh. I don't understand, why can't they just go back to Cumnock?"

"Life doesn't stand still, lass. These years when Simon has been tending to Hillview have been detrimental to his lawyering. Others have established themselves, and now there's not enough work to be had." That too was Luke's fault; Simon's budding practice ruined, and now his best friend and his sister would live too far away for more than two or three visits a year. "I offered him a share, I told him he and Joan were welcome to stay, that Hillview is theirs as well."

"Really? Without asking me?" There was a distinct edge in her voice, making Matthew smile. At times she forgot that some decisions were only his to take. "And what did he say?"

"No. That he wasn't cut out to be a farmer and that he longed to stick his nose back among the heavy tomes of law, to use his brain in drawing up a complex deed."

"He has a point, all farming requires is brawn, no brains. Ouch!" She glared at him, rubbing at where he'd pinched her. "Well okay; some brains then. Anyway, Simon is somewhat lacking in the brawn department." She chuckled, shaking her head. "It still amazes me, that someone can be so ... err ... so round, no?"

"Like an apple," Matthew laughed. "Round, but solid, aye? I can assure you there's a lot of brawn there as well."

All of Hillview swung into harvest mode in late July, and the coming weeks were filled with work, from early dawn to late at night. Matthew yawned his way through supper and stumbled up to bed, falling asleep long before Alex had closed down the house round them. It felt empty now that Joan and Simon were gone, and there were days when Alex hungered for the company of an adult, someone she could properly talk to. Rosie had been replaced by a new girl, Sarah, and the other maid, Janey, was efficient but taciturn, evading Alex' attempts at conversation.

With both Joan and Mrs Parson gone, it fell on Alex to manage the household by herself. She enjoyed it, liked being in charge, no longer nominal mistress of Hillview. In the morning, she'd decide what was to be done during the day, making weekly plans in her head to ensure meals were varied, laundry washed and the house kept aired and clean.

She scurried from kitchen garden to dairy shed, from the pantry to the orchards, and at her instructions the apple trees were picked bare, with most going directly for cider but some kept back for winter apples. It was bloody exhausting, all this work, and every now and then Alex would sneak off into the woods, a stolen hour spent only with herself and her own thoughts.

Had Alex been able to, she would have turned and walked away the day she ran into Margaret. As it was, her apron was filled with mushrooms and she had a bawling Rachel slung across her chest. So instead she knelt, slipped the carrying shawl over her head and jerked her head in the direction of the screaming child.

"Do something, preferably something that makes her shut up."

Margaret held Rachel at arm's length, her eyes darting between Alex and the baby.

"She's hungry," she guessed.

"She's always hungry." Alex tied her apron together and looked around for somewhere to sit.

"You can come in," Margaret offered, indicating her cottage just up the slope. "I won't bite you." Alex followed her into a small but very clean room and sat down on one of two stools, holding out her arms for a Rachel that by now was the colour of a beet.

"Temper, temper," Alex said and bit back on a hiss when Rachel clamped down hard on her breast – probably in revenge.

Margaret sat down opposite, eyes on the feeding child.

"It must be uncomfortable," she said, looking at Alex' swelling belly. There was a longing tone to her voice, hands smoothing over her flat abdomen.

"Tell me about it." Alex half reclined against the wall to allow Rachel easier access to her food.

"Where's Ian?"

Margaret stretched with obvious pride. "Helping with the harvest. Matthew said he could."

"He's a nice boy," Alex said generously. He was, a polite boy that now and then came into her kitchen to eat.

"Aye, he is," Margaret smiled.

"He has quite a hand with his cousin," Alex said, emphasising the last word.

"Aye, he's quite fond of wee Mark. Talks a lot about his cousin." Same emphasis. Margaret stood to find a pitcher of cider and some wooden mugs.

"I'm glad that you let him come down to the big house," she said keeping her back to Alex. "It's lonely for him here, with me."

It had to be lonely for Margaret as well, evening after evening spent in solitude up here. Alex was swept by a most unwelcome wave of compassion, but set her jaw at the idea of inviting Margaret to Hillview. She just couldn't.

"Why are you here?" she asked, not to challenge but to understand. Margaret extended a brimming mug to her and stared off at absolutely nothing for a couple of minutes.

"Luke and I had words." Margaret finally said.

"About your gift," Alex nodded.

"Aye. But I had to, I couldn't not help Matthew." Margaret shook her head, making her black hair glisten and shine where the sun caught it. "On the king's coronation day, no less, and Luke wanted me to wear the large pearl, and I ..." She gulped. " ... well, I had to tell him, aye?"

"It made him very angry," she said after a few moments of silence.

"I can imagine," Alex nodded, having no problems at all envisioning just how angry. Luke was, in her considered opinion, borderline crazy, or at least in dire needs of constant medication – not exactly available in the here and now.

"I don't think you can," Margaret said quietly. She inhaled, exhaled, twisted the fringes of her shawl tight around her fingers. "We made it up, and for some months things were as they used to be. And then ... well, he'd had too much to drink, aye? So the next morning I left, taking Ian with me."

"But you've been here over a year!" Alex shifted Rachel to her other side.

Margaret nodded, sitting down opposite Alex. "More than that." She shrugged. "I had nowhere else to go."

"Oh. But you're not planning on staying, are you?" It came out rather frigid, but Alex couldn't help it; no way did she want Margaret as a permanent resident.

"No," Margaret replied coolly. "Why would I? Once Luke is back from Holland, we'll be going back to London."

"He's in Holland?"

Margaret nodded. "At the request of the king." She smiled, running a hand over the shimmering silk of her shawl. "He gave me this, aye? He had it delivered to me with a letter, begging me to forgive him."

"And you did." Alex said, rolling her eyes

"I did. I couldn't do otherwise."

It was said with such simplicity that Alex leaned forward and clasped Margaret's hand.

"Love is a pain in the arse at times," Alex smiled.

"Oh aye; very much so," Margaret smiled back.

Matthew was not pleased when Alex told him of her run in with Margaret, muttering that he would prefer it if she kept well away from her – he didn't much fancy the idea of his present wife conversing with his former wife.

"Well, at least now we know why she's still here," Alex said. "It's because Luke is off on the continent somewhere – has been for several months." She gnawed her lip. "It irks me; you know, that Luke's so high in favour with the king that he's sent off on missions like that."

Matthew raised his brows. "Would you have me playing the courtier as well?"

"You?" Alex laughed and shook her head. "Somehow I don't quite see you carrying it off."

"Ah, no?" He made a foppish hand movement, smirked and crossed his eyes.

"No; for a start you dress too plainly, and I can't see you prancing around, bowing left right and centre." She finished brushing her hair, braided it and turned on the stool to face him, sprawled as he was on their bed. "But you must remember that Luke has the ear of a king, and kings make very uncomfortable enemies."

"Aye, they do, no?" Matthew pounded his pillow into shape and patted the bed. "I'd best tell her to leave – before he comes for her."

"You can't; she has nowhere else to go – unfortunately." Alex made a face and stood.

"Are you planning on keeping that on?" Matthew asked, looking with obvious interest at her rounded figure.

"What? This?" Alex tugged at her shift and grinned. "No." The linen rustled to the floor behind her.

Some days later, Sandy Peden rode down the lane, looking

most complacent. With a little flourish he handed Matthew a document, chuckling as he explained this was a copy of the letter he'd sent to His Majesty, and being quite a man of the world when he needed to, he'd used one of the royal mistresses as the go between.

"What? You know her? The Castlemaine?" Alex was quite impressed.

"Really, Alexandra! How would a lowly preacher like me know someone like her? But I do know one of her lute players, and so ..."

Matthew had by now finished reading the letter and handed it over to Alex.

My, my; this little epistle dripped of venom as it described just what Luke Graham had done to his brother, starting with that unjust accusation of treason eight years ago and ending with the ambush on the moor.

Alex gave him an admiring look. "Do you think it will work?"

Sandy beamed, displaying teeth that were in serious need of some TLC.

"Oh aye; the king is right fond of family ties – holds them sacred, near on."

Sandy stayed for the better part of a week, monopolising Matthew into long, convoluted discussions about religion in general and the present precarious state of affairs for the Kirk in particular.

"We're back where we started," he said. "Back to how things were before we all signed the Covenant. It is but a matter of time, mark my words, before we're all asked to abjure that holy vow."

"But ... no!" Matthew shook his head. "The king cannot meddle in men's faith! We went to war over that once, will we need to do it yet again?"

"War?" Alex squeaked. "Here?"

Sandy sighed. "No, Alexandra, I think not; there are no lords and earls hastening to the cause, not this time, and so ..."

He spread his hands in a defeated gesture.

Well, thank heavens for that. Alex snuck a look at her husband, sitting like a pillar of salt in his chair.

"And what will you do?" she asked Sandy.

"Me?" The minister stood up, brushing at the dark cloth of his overlong coat. "Why, I will fight it of course. As long as there's breath in my body I will raise my voice in defence of my Kirk, and if I must, then I'll die for it as well."

"Oh." Alex swallowed.

"I'll stand by you," Matthew said. He clasped Sandy's hand in his, and Alex stood and left the room.

Her cloak, her new boots and she was out of the house, making for the moor. Her belly protested, a sharp pain digging into the small of her back as she puffed her way up the slope. For some minutes she stood leaning against the stem of an elm, willing the pain to recede. No great matter; it happened all the time that women had early contractions, and this one had been very short, however painful. A couple of deep breaths and she pressed on, but now at a slower pace. From below came the sound of her name, loud and clear Matthew's voice carried through the crisp October air. He caught up with her just at the edge of the moors, face red with exertion.

"What?" he panted. "Why did you just walk out like that?"

"I'm not too fond of fanatics," she replied.

"Fanatics? Who? Sandy? Me?"

"To hear it yes; all that crap about dying in defence of his faith." She made a face. "Let's just say I don't much fancy being the widow of a bloody martyr, okay?"

"A widow?" He laughed and took her hand. "Nay, lass, you're being fanciful. It will not come to that and I'll not do anything daft, but I will help as I can, aye? And as yet we don't know how things will develop, do we? The king – or rather his accursed Anglican counsellors – may back down."

"You think?" Alex shook her head.

"What ..." He hesitated. "... well, do you know what will happen?"

"I have no idea, okay? All I remember is that Scotland had it pretty rough under the last of the Stuarts."

"The last?" Matthew echoed.

"Not this one," Alex said, giving him an irritated look. "This one will be followed by his brother, and then …" She wrinkled her brow. " … his nieces." She hitched her shoulders; she didn't give a rat's arse as to the fate of the Stuarts, but all this religious stuff, it scared the daylights out of her. Matthew would never compromise on his faith, he'd lost too many years of his life to win the right to proclaim his beliefs.

She had to stop several times on the way down, waving away his concerned suggestion that he carry her.

"It's nothing," she said, giving him a faint smile. Too soon; they were only in early October, and the baby wasn't due in six weeks or so. Once inside she was ordered to bed, and she gladly complied, lying curled on her side while she willed the contractions to stop. Sandy popped his head in somewhere mid-afternoon to bid her farewell, urging her to pray for herself and the bairn. If she'd had the energy she'd have thrown something at him, as it was she yawned. A few hours later Matthew came up with a tray.

"Are you still hurting?" Matthew sat behind her, massaging her tense shoulders.

"Not as much. I guess it's just been a bit too much lately."

"You should have said. You've been working far too hard for a nursing mother with a new babe in the coming."

"It's all mostly done now," Alex yawned, "so I'll just rest up for a couple of days." She leaned back against his hands. "A bath," she said dreamily. "A long, hot bath…"

By the time Matthew came back after arranging for the hip bath to be brought into the kitchen, she was fast asleep, his pillow crushed to her chest. He stood for a long time looking down at her and stooped to rest his cheek against hers. A hand drifted up to caress his head.

"I love you," Alex whispered. "So very, very, much."

And I you, he thought, straightening up, God's gift to me, that's what you are, Alexandra Ruth.

"Are you sure?" Magnus looked back down the road that led to Cumnock.

"Yes," Isaac nodded, hunching deeper into his thick down jacket. This excursion was a little secret between him and Magnus, an innocent Friday outing that would end with a meal back in Edinburgh. "I'm not," he added a bit later, squinting at the landscape around him. "I don't see any trees."

"Probably all cut down ages ago," Magnus muttered. They crossed the Lugar Waters and Isaac brightened.

"Yes, down there, look, just follow that road."

"Road?" Magnus looked at the dirt track.

"Well it's a road if you're on a horse," Isaac said defensively.

Magnus parked and got out, shivering in the gusts of ice cold air. November, and after a couple of minutes he could feel his nose begin to run with the cold.

"Come on then," he said to Isaac, now hanging back against the car. "I'm freezing my balls off."

Isaac giggled. "Me too." He skipped over to take Magnus' hand. They walked in silence up the long inclination, hand in hand.

"Why don't they want me to talk about it?" Isaac asked.

Magnus scratched at his nose with his free hand and hitched his shoulders.

"It scares them. And I suppose they're worried that if you talk about it, you'll remember it, and they would prefer you to forget."

"I don't want to forget and even if I don't talk about it, I still think about it. You know, Mama and Matthew and Mark…" He half sobbed. "Even Rachel. Even if she was only a baby."

Magnus drew them to a stop. "Of course you do. And

now it all seems like a magical adventure, doesn't it?"

Isaac nodded. "Why..." he began, but fell silent.

"Why what?"

"Why mustn't I tell the police?"

Magnus sighed; the police had been a pain in the nether parts, convinced that Isaac had been abducted by his mother – after all, they still had open files on Alexandra Lind.

"Would they believe you, do you think?"

Isaac thought about that for some time. "No."

They crested the hill and when Isaac saw the house, he began to run, his bright red woollen scarf streaming behind him.

"Mama! Matthew! I'm back, it's me, I'm back!" He slowed as he got closer. The windows were dark and uninviting, and the whole place looked deserted, halfway to becoming a ruin.

"They're not here," Isaac wheeled towards Magnus. "It's here, but they're gone!"

"Oh, Jesus ... You already knew that. I've tried to explain it to you, no?"

"But they can't be dead!" Isaac kicked at him. "They can't be! I saw them last summer and they were alive, you hear? My Mama and Matthew, they were here, and they're not dead!"

Magnus regretted having ever agreed to come here. Isaac had wheedled and nagged for weeks, and Magnus had finally caved in, assuming the boy just needed to see that the place he'd experienced existed. Too late Magnus realised that Isaac had been hoping to find it all intact, a small soap bubble of suspended time.

"I thought you'd understood," Magnus said, sitting down on a collapsed stone wall to pull Isaac onto his lap. "I tried to explain that when you were here it was very long ago." Isaac snivelled and rubbed at his bloated face.

"I do understand," he said in a small voice. "Here," he added indicating his head. "But not here." He put a hand on his heart.

Magnus rested his cold cheek against Isaac's head. "No, the heart just won't let go, will it?"

They both stood up, and Magnus took Isaac's hand.

"Be my guide, describe to me how this looked." So Isaac did, and they walked for hours around the empty house and the few remaining outbuildings.

"That's the graveyard," Isaac said, pointing in the direction of a rowan tree. "The tree is to protect the souls."

Magnus followed Isaac up to the small space, now sadly overgrown. Tall, yellowing grasses covered the headstones, many of which had crumbled or fallen flat, quite a few leaning crazily against each other. A rosebush, impossibly ancient, hung over a small stone that still, surprisingly, stood, and there was one, no, two, more that looked relatively whole and undamaged – but old, very old.

Magnus wanted to leave, the hairs on his body sprouting like antennae with disquiet. He wasn't going to look; not try and decipher these old battered stones, and see if perhaps his daughter lay beneath one of them. Isaac had let go of his hand and was hunched down beside the rowan, his fingers extended to trace the words on a small, weathered stone.

"Look," he said, turning to Magnus. "Look Offa, it's for me!" The inscription was barely legible, eroded by wind and water, but still possible to make out. "*Never forgotten, always present,*" Isaac said out loud and hugged his Offa hard. "That's the way it is, isn't it?"

Magnus nodded. "Yes, I carry her with me always."

They were silent all the way back to Edinburgh, and once they were inside Isaac shrugged off his jacket and rushed up the stairs.

"Where are you going?"

"I have to, I have to paint it as it was. Now, before I forget."

Magnus heard the door to the studio slam shut and sank down to sit on the stairs. Not once since he'd come back to them had Isaac painted, refusing to enter the room where he'd found Mercedes' magic picture. He supposed it was a step in the right direction that the boy now wanted to paint, but just in case he climbed the stairs and opened the door.

"We'll keep the door open, okay?" he said.

# CHAPTER 45

Alex had her arms sunk to the elbows in a dough when she heard the horses. A quick glance out of the kitchen window and she cursed, wiping hands clean of the sticky dark rye. He had quite the nerve, did Luke Graham, to come riding down their front lane, looking as if butter wouldn't melt in his mouth. Bastard!

She placed a hand on her stomach and gulped down long breaths of air. This child was a miracle; Rachel was a miracle, because if Luke Graham had had his wishes come true their father would have been dead. Breathe in, breathe out. It hadn't happened; her Matthew was alive and safe, and they had years and years before them – time aplenty to make up for the year and more Luke had stolen from them. God; she wanted to ... To her surprise, Alex found herself gripping the musket. How had that happened? She had no memory of retrieving it from Matthew's study. Carefully she set it down and stepped outside to face this most unwelcome visitor.

He hadn't come alone. Maybe he hadn't dared to, or maybe Luke Graham no longer could do without servants. She stood on the stoop, one hand on her belly, the other on Mark who was hanging on like a leech to her skirts, and watched Luke ride the last few yards down the lane. Weak sun glimmered on his silver nose, and to her huge irritation Alex' just couldn't keep her eyes off it. Vaguely she wondered how it was fixed into place, but the resulting images were a bit too disturbing.

Luke had dressed up, velvet breeches in a mossy green, a short coat of the same colour piped in palest yellow, a froth of lace at cuffs and neck and a most impressive hat, adorned with ostrich feathers. Silk stockings, a heavy cloak and shoes with silver buckles – very dashing, the effect further enhanced by the sword at his side and the pale yellow gloves.

He dismounted and bowed. She stood stiff and silent. Luke did a slow turn, for all the world as if he was coming home – well, okay, to some extent he was – and said something to one of his men before returning his attention to her. Mark shuffled, Luke glanced his way and froze. It almost made her laugh, the way his mouth fell open at the sight of her son. She ruffled Mark's hair, so like Ian's, and finally met his eyes. Green and bright, they locked into hers.

"Sister," Luke said, nodding again in her direction.

"Sir," she replied, distancing herself from any blood ties that might exist between them. She made no move to invite him inside – no way was she ever going to be under the same roof as this creep of a man.

"I have come for my wife," Luke said after a couple of tense moments. She continued to stare at him, and to her grim amusement he scuffed the ground, the pale skin on his neck shifting to a rather unattractive dark red.

"I'm sure you can find your way. You know, up the hill, take a right by the old oak and there you are." With that she retreated inside, slamming the door hard. Her legs gave way and she sank down to sit.

"Mama?" Mark crouched down beside her.

"I'm okay," she said, "It's just ... " she patted herself on the belly. Where was Matthew? The mill; she slumped with relief. Nowhere close to Margaret's cottage.

The miller's lad came rushing up the slope, eyes huge.

"What?" Davy the miller said, sounding exasperated, "What is it lad?"

"..." Andrew replied, pointing down in the direction of the main house. Davy rolled his eyes and winked at Matthew who smiled back. Wee Andrew might be well grown and bonny, but there was not much but wood between those two ears.

"The master's brother," Andrew said between gulps of air, "he's here, aye?"

Without a word Matthew turned on his heel and set off

down the hill – in the direction of Margaret's cottage. Halfway there he came across Ian who was throwing acorns in the stream.

"Your Da," he said curtly, and Ian flew to his feet.

"Here?"

Matthew just nodded, and Ian ran off, with Matthew following much more slowly.

He stood under the trees and watched Ian – his son, goddamn it – rush into Luke's arms. His hands closed into fists, the muscles in his legs bunched, and for a few seconds he wallowed in the pleasing fantasy of dismembering his brother, tearing one limb after the other off him while Luke shrieked and begged for mercy. Sweetest Lord; he shouldn't be here, not this close to a man he would gladly rip to shreds, not caring one whit who saw him do it.

In the clearing Ian was doing a little dance, head tilted back to laugh at Luke. Matthew swayed, his pulse loud in his ears. He took a step in their direction, took another, and there came Margaret, leaping like a doe towards her husband, face alight with joy. He just couldn't watch.

Matthew turned away, steadying himself against the gnarled trunk of an oak. You'll hang, he reminded himself, you'll dangle like a sack of barley from the gibbet; not worth it, man, no, he isn't worth it, and you have a wife and bairns to care for. He heard Luke laugh, a sound that faded away as the little family left the clearing, making no doubt for the cottage. With a groan he straightened up and walked off downhill, wanting to ensure his family was unharmed.

In the yard he found Mark staring with huge eyes at Luke's horse. Not a mare anymore, but still a chestnut, no doubt chosen so that its coat would match the colour of its rider's hair. It was a splendid animal, with long clean lines and not one single mark of white. It rolled its eyes and stamped when Mark got too close and Matthew lifted him out of the way.

"No, son, that's a high-bred horse, aye? You must keep your distance."

Mark nodded and backed into Alex who'd come out of the house.

"You okay?" Alex wondered in a low voice.

"Nay, I should stay away, but I just wanted to make sure you were alright."

"We're fine," Alex said. "I think your hoity-toity brother was sort of pissed because I didn't invite him in." Her face screwed up in distaste. "Rather a cobra than Luke Graham in my house."

Matthew was sorting out all these new words; Hoity-toity? Cobra?

"Venomous snake," Alex explained and then stuck her nose in the air to show him what hoity-toity meant. "They'll be back down any moment," Alex said nervously. "So why don't you go? Take a walk up the hill or something." She was watching his hands, and Matthew followed her eyes; not clenched but so stiff the fingers stood straight out. He nodded and turned to go at the exact moment when Luke and his family appeared from under the trees.

Even then things could mayhap have been avoided if Luke had not chosen to look disdainfully at him and laugh.

"So you made it back, did you? I had hoped you'd find the colonies so much to your liking that you'd never return."

"Luke!" Margaret gasped.

"Matthew... no," Alex moaned, but it was too late, and Matthew was on his brother, punching him, tearing at him, cursing this spawn of Satan, this misfit, this maggot of a man. He took Luke by surprise, throwing him to land on his back with Matthew on top of him, and for some long seconds Matthew was certain that this time he would put an end to him, this time he would kill his brother with his bare hands. He squeezed, Luke's eyes bulged. He did it again, and Luke's mouth opened wide. But then Luke began fighting back, and in his hand appeared a dirk.

"No!" Margaret lunged and grabbed at Luke's knife arm. Alex was on Matthew, her arms around his neck, crying as she pleaded with him to stop, please stop this, and what about the children, for God's sake, Matthew, the boys!

Alex kept hold of him as he got to his feet. He was trembling all over, his right ear was ringing from where Luke had clapped him one, and when he wiped his mouth he noticed he was bleeding. Luke was a mess and the silver nose had been knocked askew, baring his maimed face to the world. Matthew couldn't stop himself from staring. He heard Mark ask of someone what had happened to his uncle's nose, but he didn't catch the reply, all of him focused on his brother.

Luke rose. The dashing courtier was in serious disarray, his fashionable coat torn, the elegant linen shirt flecked with blood and dirt. At least his breeches were whole this time, he thought fuzzily, not like that day four years ago when Alex had hindered him from literally cutting his brother's balls off.

Luke's hands shook when he adjusted the nosepiece back into place. At his back hovered his two grooms, having wrested themselves free from the restraining grips of Samuel and Gavin.

"I'll never forgive you for this," he said to Matthew, cupping his nose. Matthew almost spat in his face; what was he on about? With a heave he shrugged off Alex' restraining hold and tore off his shirt to display his scarred back. There was a collective gasp from the household, Margaret exclaimed and even Luke, bastard that he was, looked stricken.

"Forgive me? Nay brother, you have the shoe on the wrong foot. It is I that won't forgive you. Not for your attempts to murder me and my wife…"

"Luke! No!" Margaret said.

"Ridiculous," Luke blustered. "Unsubstantiated accusations, and …"

"Don't pretend innocence, dear brother," Matthew interrupted. "Had it not been for good friends and quick wits, Alex and I would both have been dead by now."

"I …" Luke began, but Matthew just raised his voice.

"And what about the years you've stolen from me, first with your false accusations that led me to gaol, then by having me sold as a slave." Matthew inhaled, grinding his teeth to force the red veils of anger into submission. "I took a wee bit of your nose. You've damaged me for life, and you stole my son." He heard Alex gasp behind him, but he couldn't stop, not now. He raised his finger and pointed at Ian.

"My son, Luke, mine. And you know it as well as I do. You need but look at him to see it, no? Every line of him shouts to the world that he's mine. Mine!"

Ian shrank back against his devastated mother. If Luke had been red with rage before, he was now a deathly white, eyes the colour of a mountain cat's.

"Ian is my son. But you'll pay for these slurs on my manhood."

"Manhood? You don't have a manhood. You connive and scheme, you backstab and when you can't beget a son of your own you steal mine! And ..."

"How dare you?" Luke interrupted, his voice shrill. He took a step towards Matthew, sword pulled halfway free. Matthew grabbed at what was closest, a pitchfork. Ian made a strangled sound and threw himself towards Luke, blubbering with fear. Both men froze. The sword slid back into the scabbard, the pitchfork was lowered.

"Go," Matthew said, "be gone, Luke Graham."

Luke backed away, shielding his wife and son.

Alex came to stand beside him and they watched in silence while Luke got his family onto his horses and set off up the hill. At the top Luke wheeled his horse, rearing it to kick with its forelegs.

"You should have been dead, brother."

"But I'm not, am I?" Matthew called back.

"Not yet," Luke shouted, brought the horse down and without a backward glance rode off.

"Right," Alex said in a carrying voice. "Show's over, everyone. Sarah, take the children inside, will you? Janey, there are windows to be washed." She stood with hands on her hips, waiting until they all scurried away to resume their tasks. Then she walked off, leaving Matthew to stand half naked in the deserted yard.

It took time for Matthew to collect his thoughts. His body was shaking with tremors and he sank down to sit on the ground, staring at his hands. If Alex and Margaret hadn't intervened, he or Luke would have been dead by now. The shivering increased and Matthew found his shirt and put it back on, fumbling with the lacings.

Where was Alex? He felt abandoned, a wee lad in a yawning plain of nothingness, and he desperately needed his Alex to somehow put the scattered pieces that were him together again, but she had just walked away. He got to his feet, his brain unscrambling itself to give him a clear rerun of the whole incident. And then he knew why she had left him sitting alone in the yard.

Alex was in the kitchen garden, working her way up an empty bed. In all her movements, in the set of her shoulders he could see she was not only upset, but furious. He dropped a hand onto her shoulder and she shrugged it away.

"Alex," he wheedled. "Come here, aye?" She shook her head and sank her wooden spade into the earth. "What has changed? You knew Ian was mine already before, didn't you?"

"But he didn't, and you didn't see the look he gave you." She turned to scowl at him. "And what about Mark? He's too small to understand, but he heard you, didn't he? He heard you say Ian is your son. You're such an idiot!"

"Surely it isn't that bad," Matthew tried, ignoring the insult.

"You think? You just gave away our son's birth right by announcing to the world that you have an older son." She clumsily got off her knees, threw the spade to the ground and strode away.

Matthew sighed and dragged his hands through his hair. She was right: it had been a foolish thing to do, and even if Ian was legally Luke's lad, not his, he had inadvertently opened a window through which Ian, aided and abetted by Luke, could attempt to claim Hillview. His eyes followed Alex as she crossed the water meadow, forded the stream and continued up the farther slope. She dropped out of sight below the trees and he got to his feet to go after her.

He found her by the millpond, sitting on a rock and throwing pebbles into the water. Her cap lay discarded, her hair bared to the world, and at his approach she threw him a look over her shoulder. Blue, blue eyes, regarding him in a way that made him twist inside.

"I'll never let any harm befall Mark," he said.

She sighed and looked away. "I know you won't. The problem is that you won't be around, will you? The issue of inheritance sort of depends on you being dead to begin with."

He smiled crookedly at her matter-of-fact tone. "I'll speak to Simon, but I'm sure there is no legal issue."

Alex plopped yet another stone into the millpond. "Probably not. I suppose that by Luke taking him as his, Ian is no longer your son in the eye of the law. Not unless Luke decides he must renounce the boy. And he'll rage about having had the boy foisted on him, that you disowned him despite knowing he was yours."

"But that's not the way it was," Matthew protested.

"No," Alex sighed, "but who cares about the truth?"

Matthew sank down on his knees beside her.

"I swear to you that Hillview will be safeguarded to our son."

She looked at him for a long time before stroking his cheek, in a gesture far more maternal than wifely.

"I'm sure you'll do your best, but what will you do the day Ian comes to claim his paternity? Will you be able to turn him away, knowing without a doubt that he is as much yours as Mark is?"

"Nay he isn't," Matthew lied stoutly. "Of course he isn't."

"That's not what you said today."

Matthew winced at her tone and tried to take her hand.

"No," Alex shook her head. "I just need to be alone, okay?"

"Will you come down for supper?"

Alex nodded but kept her face averted from his.

It was dark by the time she came down from the hill, no longer angry even if she had no intention of letting him know that just yet. After all, how could she be angry with him for losing his temper when he'd been so cruelly goaded by that toe-wipe he had for a brother? Instead she busied herself with supper, chatted casually with Sarah about tomorrow's tasks and made sure the children were fed and put to bed before joining him in the parlour.

They didn't speak much throughout the evening. The silence grew tangible and Alex was aware of every single breath he took, only feet away from her. Finally she folded together the half-mended shirt, stood and extended her hand to him.

"Bed?"

She almost smiled at how his shoulders dropped with relief at the sound of her voice. Matthew followed her up the stairs, undressed, helped her with her lacings and retreated to bed. Alex took her time, spent an inordinately long time cleaning her teeth and slipped in to lie beside him. He rolled her over on her side, curving his body round hers. For some minutes they lay close and silent, fingers braided hard together, a general sinking together that was restful. Alex drifted off, suspended halfway between sleep and wakefulness.

"Do you think…" Matthew shifted himself even closer. "… is there any possibility do you think?"

"Possibility?" Alex wanted to sleep, not engage in complicated discussions, but she smothered a yawn. "Possibility of what?"

"That we forgive each other."

Alex laughed. And then she wasn't laughing, she was crying, and he had to hold her and shush her until she was able to talk.

"I think you can forgive him," Alex said, "because ultimately you have what you want in life; Hillview and your family." She rolled over with the grace of an overweight elephant to properly see his eyes.

"You; I have you," he corrected her.

"Whatever," she mumbled. "Do you want to? Forgive him, I mean."

Matthew fell over on his back, eyes caught on a fold in the bed hangings.

"I don't know," he replied after a while. "But all this anger, it threatens to drown me."

She propped herself up on an elbow to see his face, visible only as a grey oval in the darkness of the little room.

"Well, don't expect him to be wallowing in self-recriminations, and after today he most certainly won't forgive you – not after you shouted out to the whole world he's incapable of siring children."

"You're most comforting at times," Matthew grumbled.

"I'm just telling you the truth," she said. "Anyway, the king seems to be keeping him busy, and if we're lucky he might send him off on a diplomatic mission to Mongolia or somewhere." She turned back on her side and scooted closer to him. "He'll never disown Ian," she yawned, "not for his own sake, not for Margaret's sake, but because he doesn't want you to have your son back." She was very comforted by her own conclusions, nodding in agreement with herself. "Very warped, your brother is, and if you ask me someone should have bundled him with the kittens and drowned him as a baby."

"Alex!" Matthew sounded horrified.

"Well okay, not as a baby," she amended. "Too bad someone didn't, though, because Luke will be back. I don't know when or how, but one day he'll be back to take this from you."

"He can try, aye?" Matthew said, "try and fail." He placed

his hand on their unborn child, splaying his fingers in a protecting gesture.

The next morning Matthew rose to do his chores and found his yard full of people, all with a sudden errand to the master. For the coming week people milled about, their eyes travelling with interest over Matthew. Conversation would be cut short at his appearance, only to resume as he walked away, and he could hear his workers, his tenants, buzzing with the repeated story of how the Graham brothers nearly killed each other. And had they seen the master's back? Badly flogged, and all because of that miscreant of a brother.

Occasionally, Matthew heard a muttering about the lad, the boy of just nine, and how was it, was he the master's or wasn't he? Wasn't, the majority seemed to agree, for surely a mother would not have cheated her own son out of an inheritance as fine as Hillview. Speculations were swallowed back at the look in Matthew's eyes and the men would hurry back to their work.

"Tough," Alex shrugged when he complained. "That's what you get when you decide to air a reality TV show." She laughed at his incomprehension and went on to explain that there were people who invited the public in to partake of every facet of their lives, from squabbles over breakfast to full blown fights in the marriage bed.

"Why?" Matthew asked. Alex rubbed her fingers together in a money grabbing gesture, making him smile.

"And you watch? Unknown people living their lives?"

"Some do," Alex said. "And you," she said, kissing him on the cheek, "you're Hillview's own first class celebrity."

For well over a fortnight, Alex kept a constant watch over the lane, convinced that any minute Luke would come storming down with a full complement of men at his back. She took to keeping the loaded musket in the kitchen, went nowhere without her dagger and never let her husband out of her sight – unless he was accompanied by others.

At night she'd start awake at any sound, and it was at her insistence that Matthew brought home a dog – an old dog, already grey around the muzzle, but according to Matthew a renowned guard dog that now slept in the yard. It irritated her that he should be so unconcerned, shrugging off her worries with a laconic comment that as far as he knew Luke wasn't a fool, and to plan any kind of full scale attack on Hillview would be the act of a madman, bringing with it the risk of trial, disgrace and potential death. Hmm; maybe he had a point.

Alex relaxed back into normality as the days became weeks. Luke was far away in London, no doubt a heavily occupied man, and with time he'd forget all about Matthew, everyday life reducing his obsessive hatred of his brother to a mere irritation. Besides, on one of his visits Simon told her Luke was now Sir Luke, proud owner of a manor in Oxfordshire, and if so what on earth would he want with Hillview?

Simon had agreed; Luke was a man of the world, entrusted with one more complex mission after the other, expected to remain at all times at his royal master's beck and call. And, he added with a twinkle to his eyes, as he heard it a wee bird had whispered details of Luke's doings into the king's ear, causing wrinkles of displeasure to form on the royal brow, and so Luke was forced to watch his step – at least for a while.

So instead Alex concentrated on preparing for the imminent arrival of their third child, wondering how she was to cope with two children in clouts. At least Rachel was weaned, delighted with her discovery of a world that contained butter and milk, and nice, sticky things like porridge that could be used to decorate one's hair with.

One night early in December Alex got out of bed, wrapped herself in her cloak and stepped out into the yard. The budding football player who lived in her womb was kicking its way into the world and she braced back against her hands, face to the sky. She smiled when she felt Matthew slide his arms around her and leaned against his chest.

"It's coming," he stated needlessly, letting his hands rest on her hardening belly. She just nodded, relaxing into his arms.

"You best come inside," Matthew said a bit later. "I won't have my son born out in the cold."

"Son?" Alex laughed. "And I suppose you've already named him as well."

"Aye, of course, but I won't tell you. You have work to do first."

"Work," Alex muttered, "what a bloody euphemism." She took another breath of cold night air and turned towards the door. "Well, come on then, because if you think I'm doing this alone you've got another think coming, mister."

It was just after midnight and the bedchamber was quiet again. A single candle lit the room, throwing most of it into an agreeable duskiness. On the little stool stood a tray, there was still a whiff of blood and fluids in the air, and Alex closed her eyes, tired to the bone.

"I told you, a lad." Matthew was sitting beside her in bed, the child cradled in his arms.

"It's a fifty-fifty chance. You're just a lucky guesser." Alex sank down, feeling exhausted. A quick birthing, Rosie had commented, quick and easy. Alex wasn't all that sure about the easy part, but it had all been uncomfortably fast.

"The next one will be a lad as well. Here, he needs you."

"The next one?" Alex struggled up to sit, took her newborn son from his besotted father.

"The next one." He rubbed the bald crown of his son, crooning softly. "My wee Jacob," he whispered, "and you so bonny and strong, hmm?"

"Nothing wee about him," Alex protested, "he must be well over ten pounds." She smiled at Matthew and leaned towards him to kiss his cheek.

"Jacob, hey?"

"Aye, Jacob Alexander." He ran a finger down her neck, up again to touch her mouth. "I love you."

"Huh, you're only saying that because you want to get back in my bed – soon."

Matthew laughed and pummelled his pillow into shape.

"I'm already here, no?" He scooted closer to her, hugged wife and child to him. "And I don't plan on sleeping elsewhere," he yawned. A few minutes later he was fast asleep.

"I love you, too," Alex murmured to his sleeping head. One eye opened wide.

"Of course you do. Insatiable, you are."

"Matthew!"

But he was asleep again, a soft, steady snoring emanating from him. Alex placed her son in his cradle and moved over to open the small window. She stood for some moments in the cooling draught, listening to the rustling sounds of the night.

"Thank you," she said to the far away heavens. "For my home and my children, but mostly, dear God, for him." She grinned; the Alex Lind of old would have laughed herself silly, but then what did she know, hey?

"Alex?" Matthew's tousled head rose from the pillows.

"I'm here," she replied. "I'm always here."

For a historical note to this book, please visit my website, www.annabelfrage.com

For more information about the Matthew and Alex books, please visit www.annabelfrage.com

For a peek at book three, *The Prodigal Son*, just turn the page.

The Matthew and Alex story continues in *The Prodigal Son*

## CHAPTER 1

Four shadows rose out of the darkness of the moor, darting from patch to patch of vegetation. Here and there they found cover behind a boulder, now and then they huddled together under a stunted tree, gliding noiselessly due north.

It was too early for birds, so when a sharp whistle cut through the air the leading shadow set off at speed, his companions slinking after him towards a protective outcrop of stone.

"Hush!" Matthew Graham sank down, the three men accompanying him doing the same. He pointed to where a group of six riders were making slow progress on a marshy stretch of ground.

"More soldiers," he said, his voice a low hum.

"And here was I thinking they were but angels of deliverance," the man sitting closest to him said, and despite their situation Matthew smiled. The speaker moved closer to Matthew, his mouth a scant inch from Matthew's ear. "They won't find us."

"You think not?" Matthew tried to sound unconcerned but his eyes were stuck on the approaching group of soldiers, his brain scrambling to find a way out of this neat little corner. Summer dawn was only hours away, and no matter that he and his companions were all cloaked and hooded in dark colours somewhere between brown and grey, they would be visible the moment they stood to run.

"Nay," Minister Peden replied comfortably. "They may look, but they won't see." With a slight nod he indicated the strands of fog that were multiplying over the wetter ground. Days of insistent heat had dried out the moor, resulting in clouds of evaporated water that reverted to fog and mist when night was at its coolest.

"At least the weather is with us," another of the men commented in a low voice.

"God, my friend," Sandy Peden corrected. "God is with us, and this is yet another sign that He hasn't forgotten us." Without another word he moved off and one by one the others followed him, shrouded in the early morning mist.

"That way," Matthew said a bit later. "If you keep to the left of yon stand of trees you'll find a passable path that will lead you to onwards all the way to Kilmarnock."

"Thank you," the tallest of the three men said. "And be sure to convey my gratitude to your wife as well."

"Aye," Sandy grinned. "Please tell Alex how appreciative we are of your hospitality."

"Umm," Matthew said. Alex wasn't quite as enthusiastic about extending help to their Presbyterian brethren as he was, and even if she cooked and packed baskets with food, sent along blankets when she could, he knew she didn't like it, and in particular not now, not since the last few arrests that had dragged at least one of their neighbours before the court to answer to charges of treasonous activities. The man had been flogged publicly.

"Truly," Sandy said, and now there was no laughter in his grey eyes. "Do thank her, Matthew. I know it costs her in fears." With that he was off, taking the lead as the three ministers made for the depths of the moor. Not until they'd dropped out of sight did Matthew set off for home.

"Where have you been?"

Matthew started when his brother-in-law popped up to block his path.

"Out," he said.

"I gather that," Simon Melville said. He frowned, taking in the sword and pistol, the long cloak that was now bundled over an arm. "This is no game."

"Hmm?"

"Never mind." Simon gestured in the direction of the

yard. "You have visitors."

"Visitors? At this hour?"

"Oh, don't worry," Simon said with a certain edge. "They're not soldiers here to drag you off for questioning – not this time. It's your ex-wife, no less."

"Margaret?" Matthew came to a halt. "What might she be doing here?"

"I have no idea; mayhap she's hankering for long morning walks over the foggy moor."

"I'm doing what I must, Simon, you know that."

"What you must? You're helping them break the law! They've been ousted as ministers, they're not allowed to preach or teach, they may not perform any types of rites, and to aid and abet them is to risk the full displeasure of the powers that be."

Matthew just shrugged.

"Oh well," Simon sighed. "You'll do as you please."

"Aye."

"Hmm." Simon threw him a sidelong look. "She brought Ian with her."

"Ian?" Matthew increased his pace.

"She's in the yard. I don't think Alex intends to invite her inside, and even if she did, I doubt Margaret would enter. She insists she'll wait outside until she can talk with you." Simon's face broke out in a wide grin. "I don't think she helped herself by reminding Alex that any decisions are yours to take anyway, so why waste breath telling Alex what she will then have to repeat to you?"

"Nay," Matthew said, smiling faintly. "I reckon Alex didn't like that."

The two women turned towards them when they entered the yard. Of similar height and colouring, with dark well-defined brows, high cheekbones and shapely necks, at a distance they could be taken for sisters. But where Margaret was all willowy grace, Alex was rounder of breasts and hips – assets presently accentuated by her very trim waist. She must have tightened the stays a notch or two before going out to receive their visitors. He studied his wife; silent, arms crossed over her chest and dark blue eyes never leaving Margaret or the half grown lad beside her, Alex looked icily impressive – and displeased. With an inward sigh Matthew went over to greet his guests.

Alex watched Matthew come towards them, long legs striding at such speed Simon was jogging to keep up. She gave her husband a thoughtful look; yet another morning waking to an empty bed, and she had a pretty good idea of what he'd been doing. It was a constant source of contention between them, his insistence that he had to help his brethren, her loud protests that it might come at too high a price. Bloody stubborn man! She gnawed at her lip and frowned.

Having Margaret show up with Ian in tow hadn't exactly improved her mood, nor did the fact that Margaret, as always, looked gorgeous. Not for Margaret practical skirts in brown, no, dear Margaret sported a gown in a vibrant blue that complemented her eyes, her neckline was adorned by Brussels lace and on her head she wore a rakish hat of the same hue as her dress, glistening, black hair falling in arranged ringlets well down her back. Long riding gloves in soft red leather completed the outfit, although on a day as hot as this Alex suspected they were quite uncomfortable to wear.

"Mama?" Mark tugged at her skirts. "Who's that?"

Alex smiled and brushed his hair back from his brow. Nearly six, Mark was normally his father's shadow, but the tension in the air had made him gravitate towards his mother, bringing his two siblings in tow.

"That's your cousin, Ian."

She was convinced Mark had forgotten the events surrounding the last time he'd seen his cousin nearly two years ago, but from the wary look in Ian's eyes she could see that he had not – and nor had any of the adults presently in the yard. Not that she blamed them; two grown men, brothers, fighting with deadly intent until their respective wives managed to step between.

"He's my son," Matthew had said on that occasion, pointing at the then nine year old Ian. "My son, and you know it, Luke Graham."

Alex threw a quick look in the direction of Ian; still a startling copy not only of Matthew but also of Mark – same dark hair highlighted by chestnut strands, same hazel eyes fringed by thick, dark lashes. The resemblance as such was not all that much of an issue given that Luke and Matthew were brothers – or it wouldn't have been if it hadn't been for Matthew's angry outburst. Why have you brought him back, Alex thought, throwing eyebolts at Margaret, why couldn't you stay well away from me and mine?

"I have nowhere else to go." Margaret kept round, imploring eyes on Matthew as she spoke.

Smart move, Alex fumed, because for some inexplicable reason Matthew had a soft spot the size of an elephant when it came to his ex-wife. Totally incomprehensible, given how the woman had behaved – married to the one brother while betraying him with the other.

"And I had to get away, people are dying like flies, and I hope you'll allow me the use of the wee cottage yet again."

What? Alex took a hurried step back. "The plague? You've brought the plague?" Even this far north they'd heard of how London and the villages around it were suffering a virulent outbreak of the Black Death.

"Nay, of course not," Margaret said. "We haven't been in London proper for months. But what with the heat of the summer and the increasing number of deaths I thought it safer to repair even further north. I can't risk my son."

Matthew's eyes strayed to Ian and Alex sighed. She could commiserate to a point with his feelings for the boy that should have been his but no longer was – this due to Margaret's lying insistence that Luke had fathered her child – but his comment almost two years ago could put her children's inheritance at risk, and there were days when she still had problems forgiving him for that.

Alex' eyes fluttered over to Simon Melville who winked

at her. She stuck her tongue out, making Simon grin. A thousand times he'd told her not to worry, that there was no way Ian had a claim to Hillview, not now that he was the recognised son of Luke. Besides, he'd said rather smugly, he'd drafted the documents himself, and so he could assure her there were no loopholes, none at all.

"You may stay," Matthew said, and Alex glowered at him. He should at least discuss it with her first. At times Matthew was a bloody old-fashioned man – to be expected given that this was in fact the seventeenth century and the odd one out was she, born in 1976.

Not that it showed, she reflected, throwing a quick glance down her body. In skirts and bodice, her head neatly capped and a clean apron covering the dark material of her skirts, she was undistinguishable from most of the women of the here and now. All in all a good thing, because to shout to the world that she was from a future time would be the equivalent of tying a noose and placing it around her neck. Witches hang, she swallowed, and no one would listen to her protestations that she'd done nothing to transport herself from modern day Scotland to here, it had all been due to the thunderstorm.

Her eyes flitted to the sky and she almost laughed at herself. No storm brewing, and besides, it had to be a once in a lifetime experience, to live through a thunderstorm so gigantic it caused a rift in time. Once in a lifetime? It should be impossible, and yet here she was, a living, breathing example of the fact that sometimes impossible things happened – as they had done to her seven years ago when time tore apart at her feet.

Alex returned her attention to Margaret who was beaming at Matthew. To Alex' huge irritation Matthew smiled back.

"Thank you." Margaret dismissed the hired grooms who'd escorted them and set off in the direction of the cottage, her son at her heels.

"You'll stay away for the first few weeks," Matthew said. "As a precaution, aye?"

"Aye, a precaution. I see." Margaret paled, looking so frightened Alex felt sorry for her.

"I'll send up Sarah later, you'll need food and such, right?" she said.

Margaret gave her a grateful look and hefted the rather insignificant bundle she was carrying.

"Aye, we left in haste."

"I can imagine." An instant of shared motherhood flew between them.


"That was generous," Simon muttered to Matthew as Alex strode away to arrange for a basket to be taken to the cottage. Matthew nodded. Not that it surprised him, because this wife of his might on occasion blow both hot and cold but was mostly a temperate warm, being in general kind and cheerful. He put out a hand to stop Rachel from whacking Jacob over the head with her wooden doll.

"Nay, Rachel! You mustn't fight with your wee brother. It's unseemly."

"He pushed me."

"He did no such thing," Matthew said, sinking down onto his haunches to give her the full benefit of his stare. "If you hit him then you mustn't be surprised when he hits you back."

Rachel gave her baby brother a sly look. At almost three Rachel was tall and sturdy for her age and topped Jacob by a head. Let him try, her face told Matthew, let him try and I'll send him flying.

"One day he'll be taller and stronger than you, and you won't want him hitting you then." He sincerely hoped his children had grown out of squabbles by the time Jacob overtopped Rachel, but eyed his daughter doubtfully. He adjusted her cap and gave her a gentle shove in the direction of Mark.

"Keep an eye on your sister," he said. Mark's face clouded, and Matthew beckoned him over. "And you won't go near the cottage." Mark looked crestfallen. "You can help me carry up the basket later, but only if you watch Rachel first."

Mark sighed but took Rachel's hand to wander off in the direction of the swing Matthew had made them.

"And you make sure she stays with you, all the time," Matthew called, receiving a despairing look in return that made Matthew smother a smile. Where Rachel got her boundless energy from was an open question, although Matthew insisted he had been a most biddable child – at least until the age of seven – so therefore it had to come from her mother, no?

"For my sins," Alex would sigh every now and then, making Matthew laugh out loud. Even worse, wee Rachel had her brothers firmly in hand and showed a hair-raising creativity when it came to new activities, leaving a wake of destruction behind her.

"Come you," Matthew said to Jacob and swung him up to sit on his arm. "Let's find your Mama." He kissed the hair of his youngest before going off in search of his disgruntled wife.

"I couldn't do otherwise," Matthew said to Alex' back.

"Of course not," she replied, a trifle too coolly to sound sincere. She put a loaf of dark bread into the basket, added eggs, cheese, a flask of beer, half a pie, and as an afterthought a piece of currant cake. Jacob smacked his lips, waving a chubby hand in the direction of the cake.

"After dinner," Alex said. "And only if you eat all your greens."

Matthew made a face. Obliged to act the role model, these days he found himself eating large quantities of uncooked vegetables, his muttered protests along the lines that he was no cow ignored by his wife who insisted it was good for him.

"I can carry the basket," Matthew offered once she'd finished loading it.

"I have no doubts whatsoever on that score, but you're not. Sarah will take it."

"I've promised Mark he can go with me," Matthew said, receiving a long look in return.

"Neither of you will, and both of you will stay well away from them, at least to begin with. Make sure Mark knows that as well."

Matthew frowned at her peremptory tone. "You can't stop me from seeing them. I have to help them settle in."

"You go up there, Matthew Graham, and you'll find yourself sleeping very alone at night, in the hayloft. Your choice." She hefted the heavy basket off the table and went to find Sarah.

Matthew considered chasing her up the stairs for a very serious one on one conversation regarding her duties and roles as a wife, but decided to save it for later. Much later, and possibly in the hayloft...

Halfway through the afternoon, Alex decided to escape the heat by settling herself under the large ash that stood on the further side of the stables. A quick look in the direction of her youngest children showed her they were muddy and happy by the trough, and Mark would be with Matthew somewhere. She reclined against the trunk, produced her work and with a little sigh set to.

"You know you don't need to worry, don't you?" Simon flopped himself down in the shade beside Alex, his light blue eyes intent on her.

"Worry about what?" Alex held up the boy's shirt she was sewing against the light. The hemline was uneven, but she decided it would do. She was sick of sewing and mending, and sometimes she would long for a shopping centre with one shop after the other; GAP, H&M, M&S... she sighed and picked up the next garment in her basket. An impossible dream, given that this was 1665.

"About her; Margaret."

"I know I don't," she said. "But as too Ian ... he eats him with his eyes!"

Simon hemmed in agreement.

"And it must be difficult for him – for Ian. I wonder what they've told him to explain that sorry mess two years ago. It's not as if they can wave a paternity test at him."

Simon sat up, eyes bright with curiosity. Of a need he knew her background, and he was always pestering her for details about life in the future.

"Paternity tests?"

"They take blood from the baby, the mother and the father and then they can see if it all matches." She smiled and beckoned him closer. "They say that on average one child in four is a cuckoo," she confided, grinning at his horrified expression. "I dare say it's more or less the same now."

"No!" Simon shook his head. "You can't think that married women would do something like that!"

"Have sex? Or have sex with someone other than their husband?" She laughed, her sewing forgotten in her lap.

"Hmph!" Simon lay back and stared up at the sky through the rustling leaves of the apple tree. "A man never knows for sure if it's his child or not."

"No, and that's the starting point of all this sorry mess with Ian, isn't it?"

"Did he tell you?" she asked a bit later.

"No," Simon said. "But it doesn't take a genius to work out where he's been."

Alex hugged her knees. "I don't like it, and from being the occasional meal, the odd night's lodging, now it's Matthew guiding them across the moor, helping them find other hideouts." She leaned her cheek against her skirts.

"I'm sure he's careful."

"Of course he is," Alex agreed, mainly to convince herself. She smiled down at Simon and poked him in the gut. "That wasn't very nice of you, to leave poor Joan all alone with your aunt Judith." She'd only met Judith Melville once, a quarrelsome, nosy woman with no similarities whatsoever to Simon. Matthew's sister Joan on the other hand, was one of the sweetest people she knew.

"Joan doesn't mind, I think she even likes the old bat, aye? Anyway, she'll be here tomorrow."

Someone called for the mistress, and Alex got to her feet.

"Now what?"

She slowed her steps halfway across the yard. "Who are they?" she asked Simon.

"Dragoons," he said, frowning. He buttoned up his coat as he walked and brushed his collar into place. By the time they were at the door, Simon Melville was all lawyer, joviality wiped from his face. He expanded his considerable girth, nodded at the officer, and placed a hand at Alex' waist.

"Mistress," the officer said.

"Captain," Alex curtsied.

"We will not importune you for long," the officer continued, jerking his head in the direction of the stables. Alex' heart nosedived at the sight of her man being marched across the yard. He was struggling, his arms held in a tight grip by the two soldiers flanking him.

"What on earth ..." Alex gasped, wheeling to face the officer. Behind her Matthew cursed, his voice loud in anger. Oh God; someone had seen him on the moor last night, and now they'd cart him off and flog him for it.

"We are taking him in for questioning," the officer said.

"Questioning? About what?" She turned, eyes flying until they found Matthew's. He was not only angry, he was afraid, she could see that. Calm down, she tried to tell him telepathically, furrowing her brow in concentration. Okay, so she seriously doubted she was a new Mr Spock, but he did stop struggling, informing the soldiers he wasn't about to run anywhere, so they could unhand him.

"Now, now, Mistress Graham. Surely you've heard. Fugitive preachers abound all around, and to aid them ..." the officer's voice tailed off.

She widened her eyes. "Matthew? When? How?"

"Last night. We had them surrounded, three of them, and out of nowhere appeared a man." He glared in the direction of Matthew. "A capable swordsman at that, leaving one of my men badly wounded."

What? Alex forced herself not to look at Matthew. To wound a soldier... They might hang him! Her throat tightened, and it took considerable effort to turn to the officer and give him a little smile.

"Well, I can assure you it wasn't him," Alex said. "He was snoring his head off in bed, with me."

"And if so a spot of questioning will do no harm, will it?" the officer shrugged, clearly not believing her.

"I'm going with him," Simon said.

The officer raised a brow. "I think not."

"I think aye. I'm his lawyer."

That didn't please the officer, narrow face pinching together into a frown. But he acquiesced, muttering something under his breath. Simon scurried off to see to his horse and Alex moved close enough to touch Matthew's hand, a light graze no more.

"It'll be alright," Matthew said, swinging himself up into the saddle. She heard it in his voice, how he was struggling to sound matter-of-fact. Alex wanted to say something reassuring, but her vocal cords had somehow gone numb, leaving her mute. Instead she stood beside his horse, holding on to his leg. Matthew leaned towards her, eyes lightening into a greyish green.

"I love you," he said in an undertone, and that only increased her anxiety because he rarely said such things to her. Alex managed a wobbly smile and stood on her toes to caress his cheek.

"And I you," she said.

Her husband nodded once and at the officer's command followed him up the lane with Simon in his wake. Not once did he look back, but Alex stood rooted to the ground for as long as she could see him.